ALSO BY

C000077227

A Summer Soun
The Faerie Hounds of York
The Bayou
Obsidian Island

THE FLOS MAGICAE SERIES

The Novels

The Bachelor's Valet
A Novel Arrangement

Supplemental Novellas

The Botanist's Apprentice
Winter's Dawn
The Solstice Cabin

A
THIEF
AND A
GENTLEMAN

Flos Magicae

ARDEN POWELL

A Thief and a Gentleman
Copyright © 2023 by Arden Powell

TABLE OF CONTENTS

A
THIEF
AND A
GENTLEMAN

CHAPTER ONE

IN WHICH A LONG-LOST FRIEND
IS DISCOVERED, AND ALSO ROBBED

Sebastian normally prided himself on his smooth charm and unflappable demeanour, but as he climbed the steps to the little townhouse that was Kitty Delaware's last known residence, he couldn't muster up any expression but annoyance. He could feel a sharp crease sitting between his brows, which only made him more irritated, but trying to mask it was pointless. Kitty knew him too well.

Rapping the bronze lion-headed door-knocker against the wood, he resisted the urge to tap his foot as he waited. Patience was a skill he'd honed to perfection over the years, necessary to his line of work and his

ARDEN POWELL

survival, but after his earlier row with that pompous, good-for-nothing Whistler, he had run clean out of that particular virtue.

The door swung open. Kitty, wearing only a thin silk kimono over her slip but with her hair and eyes already done up, leaned one elbow against the doorframe as she looked him over. She had huge black doe eyes and a glossy bob slicked into perfect waves, baby hairs curling over her forehead and around her ears. Sebastian had never seen her look anything less than a film star, like wherever she was, she'd just stepped out of the silver screen.

"Hello, stranger," she said. "What happened to you?"

"Whistler kicked me out. Can I come in?"

She raised one perfectly arched eyebrow. It was like being judged by a particularly sharp Josephine Baker. "That didn't last long."

"No. He was a horrible bore and I would have walked out within the week regardless."

"It must have been a blow to your pride for him to beat you to the punch like that."

"It would've been, but I nicked his silverware on my way out, so we'll call it even." He gave a pointed look into the flat over her arm. "Have you got coffee on? I've never been up this early in my life. It's terrible."

"You poor thing," she said dryly, but she moved aside to let him enter. "Adam," she called as she shut the door behind him. "We have company. You two entertain each other while I finish getting dressed." She swished past Sebastian to the bedroom, the silk whispering against her skin as she went.

After shedding his coat, scarf, and gloves, Sebastian strolled through the flat with his hands in his pockets, partly as a show of fashionable nonchalance but also as a reminder to himself that this place was off-limits. Which was a shame, really, because it was one of the nicest flats he'd ever seen. Adam had money and he obviously liked to spend it; Kitty was lucky to have bagged such a specimen. And Sebastian might be a bit of a bastard, but he wasn't going to ruin that for her. So, he kept his hands to himself and he offered Adam a smile when he came upon him in the kitchen.

Adam was sat at the breakfast table with a newspaper sprawled across his plate, ignoring his toast in favour of coffee and the entertainment section. He was fair and well-dressed, even in his robe, with light brown hair in a neat side part and thick-framed glasses. He had the kind of easy good looks that made him as tempting a mark for a night of fun as his money made him for a con. Unfortunately, Sebastian actually liked him, and he lived by few rules, but not conning his friends was one of them.

Or at least, not conning them in any serious way.

Besides which, Kitty would skin him alive if he tried anything. Adam was very much, very exclusively hers, and Sebastian was lacking the specific feminine wiles he would have needed to lure Adam away from her. The man was, regrettably, on the straight, if not necessarily the narrow.

"Hello, Sebastian," Adam said cheerfully. "Bad luck with the latest mark, was it?"

"That's unusually pessimistic of you," Sebastian observed.

Adam laughed. "You only ever come to find Kitty when your games aren't going according to plan. To see you before noon is entirely unheard of. Or have you suddenly changed your pattern?"

Sebastian mulishly kicked out a chair and dropped down to sit opposite Adam. "Fine, yes, it was bad luck. I hate when you're right."

Adam hummed and turned to the next page of his paper. "You should listen to me next time when I tell you someone is a bad idea."

"I'd only just met you."

"Well, now you know better. Help yourself to breakfast, by the way. The coffee's still hot."

Sebastian got right back up to beeline for the coffee, pouring himself a cup filled to the brim before taking Adam's invitation at his word and raiding the pantry, coming up with a handful of eggs to scramble on toast. "Want any?"

"Generous of you to offer, but no, thank you."

Sebastian cracked the eggs into the frying pan before popping two slices of bread in the toaster. He'd eaten at Whistler's before leaving, but he had yet to break the habit of hoarding food whenever the opportunity arose. Luckily, Adam didn't seem inclined to comment on it. Maybe Kitty had spoken to him privately, which Sebastian ought to find embarrassing, but instead all he had was a pathetic kind of gratitude he would never allow himself to voice. The toaster popped as the scrambled eggs solidified, and he slathered everything in butter and salt and shovelled it onto a dish before reclaiming his seat to wolf it down. Adam politely hid behind the paper.

"Anything from our friend Inspector Johnson today?" Sebastian asked around a mouthful of toast.

"No, I haven't seen his column in the paper in weeks."

"What a shame. I miss all his inane opinions and misguided theories about the criminal underground."

"You just miss him talking about your exploits and making a fool of himself."

"That too."

"There's a good writeup on the Cheapside Hoard exhibit at the National Gallery, though. It's proving very popular. Look, they've got an illustration of the main display and everything."

Adam offered Sebastian the page, newspaper rustling like an enormous bird rearranging its wings. The Cheapside jewels, so captivating in real life, looked scratchy and crude in pen and ink. They made Sebastian's heart flutter all the same.

"Black and white doesn't do them justice," he said.

"No, I'd imagine not."

Kitty swanned back from the bedroom, now wearing a little dress that was far too flashy for the daytime. "So? What did you do to finally push Whistler over the edge?"

Sebastian scowled around his eggs. "He may have found out about Blackwood."

Adam winced. "Tough luck, chap."

"I take it the ensuing conversation went poorly," Kitty guessed, folding herself elegantly into the remaining kitchen chair.

"Rather." With a disdainful curl of his lip, Sebastian swigged down a bitter mouthful of coffee. "It's alright; he was much too serious for me anyway. All he ever wanted to talk about was stocks or politics, and his idea of a good time was going over his accounts. What's the point of having all that money if you never use it for anything fun? At least you, Adam, you know what you can get out of your wealth."

"Cheers to that," Adam agreed, lifting his coffee mug.

"I don't suppose you're looking for a second partner to spoil," Sebastian asked, without much hope.

"Much as I enjoy your company, I'm afraid Kitty here is already the light of my life, and leaves me wanting for nothing."

"Ugh."

"Also, he doesn't fancy men," Kitty added, just for the sake of sprinkling salt in the wound. "And once your sex appeal's stripped away, you're not left with much to offer."

"My sparkling conversation and penchant for thievery, darling."

"Don't fret about it," Adam said, giving Sebastian a reassuring pat on the arm. "I'm in the habit of spoiling my friends, too. As a matter of fact, I'm heading to The Stag's Head this morning, and you should come with. Whistler's ilk may bore you, but if you can't find someone there to sink your teeth into, there's no hope for you whatsoever."

♦ ♦ ♦

The Stag's Head was a fashionable London club populated entirely by wealthy gentlemen with too much time on their hands and too few hobbies. Sebastian found that crowd dull to a man, but his personal taste could hardly be allowed to figure into it. He needed money, so the wealthy and well-to-do were by necessity his targets. Never mind that they had never struggled for anything in their lives, nor had a single independent thought, nor any evidence of passion. That was unimportant.

If anything, their vapid personalities made them easier marks. Not because they'd never met anyone like Sebastian before, because that wasn't true, but because Sebastian found it easier to tamp down his last scrap of sympathy in the face of their bland, overbearing privilege and fleece them for everything they had. Swimming through a place like The Stag's Head, he might as well have been in a fishbowl, being asked to empathise with the dumb goldfish staring back at him.

Adam excepted, of course.

But, to be perfectly honest, he would never have befriended Adam without Kitty to act as an intermediary, and Kitty wasn't present. The Stag's Head was for gentlemen only, absolutely no women permitted, and those gentlemen needed to hold a membership and be in good standing. Sebastian would have never been allowed to set foot inside without Adam's explicit invitation.

Upon entering the club, the main room was wide and open, dotted with round, dark-stained wood tables around which little groups of men clustered, eating breakfast or reading the paper or engaging in trite gossip. It was a place of understated luxury, every inch of it designed to cater to wealth and class, and Sebastian found it unspeakably boring. Any man with the kind of money to buy a membership to The Stag's Head could be spending it on glitz and glamour and entertainment, but instead, they chose *this*. What a waste.

"I know you're not physically sulking," Adam said, with no regard for Sebastian's pride, "but I can tell you're doing it on the inside. If I point out one or two likely marks, will you cheer up?"

"I'm fine," Sebastian replied automatically. "Anyway," he added in a lower tone, "it's not as if I actually liked Whistler. I'll be much better off without him just as soon as I have a little spending money in my pocket again. I'd rather be alone than have to spend any time with someone like that. So, you can keep your cloying pity to yourself, thank you very much."

"You and Kitty have a plan to get your hands on that spending money, don't you?"

They most certainly did. They were going to steal the most impressive collection of jewels London had ever seen. "One that doesn't rely on hanging off the arm of any of these pampered, overdressed airheads. No offense."

"I'm sure."

If all went well, Sebastian would never have to rely on anyone else ever again. He would be entirely independent, and his finances would be no one's business but his own. On the other hand, if it went badly, he'd be back inside Blackwood faster than he could say his own name, and they wouldn't be so lenient with his sentencing a second time.

A less desperate man might balk at stealing the Cheapside Hoard, but Sebastian was too hungry to play things safe, and Kitty wasn't a man at all.

"Don't worry," he said to Adam. "I'm sure Kitty will want to continue basking in the pleasure of your company regardless."

"Yes, because that's the only worrying thing about your plan," Adam returned with a roll of his eyes. "Come on, let's see who's here. What exactly are you looking for?"

Sebastian had no interest in running another long con on any man as distasteful as James Whistler, or perhaps in running another long con at all. They were exhausting, and when they didn't play out as intended, a complete waste of time.

It was easier for Kitty. A gorgeous young vamp like that had no trouble finding someone to pay her way in the world, and she'd lucked out twice with Adam: a sugar daddy almost her own age, and one happy to give her everything she could think to ask for. Sebastian was no slouch, but he couldn't compete on that level. If he'd been a woman, things might have been different, but he had to work with what he'd been given.

"Anyone present will probably do," Sebastian said carelessly. "Filthy rich, bored with what they've got, and not bright enough to notice I'm using them. Or desperate enough for a little friendly company that they don't care."

"I think I can find someone to fit the bill."

On cue, a blond man of about their age caught Adam's eye from across the room and gave a jaunty wave before heading over.

"This one is off-limits," Adam told Sebastian in an undertone as the blond crossed the room to join them.

"Is he?" Sebastian countered, looking the newcomer up and down. At first glance he seemed to fit Sebastian's requirements to a tee, but perhaps he was unsuitable in some subtler way.

"Spoken for," Adam said apologetically, "and he has too many people in his circle who would see right through you. You'd be run off in no time."

Sebastian sniffed. "I'll take your word for it."

"Hollyhock!" Adam greeted.

A little ping of recognition sounded in Sebastian's head at the name.

"How are you, chap? I haven't seen you here in a while. Sebastian, this is Alphonse Hollyhock. Hollyhock, this is Sebastian…?"

"Just Sebastian," Sebastian replied smoothly, offering the blond his hand.

"Pleased to meet you!" Alphonse said brightly. "Are you new here? I don't remember seeing you around, but then, as Adam says, I haven't been here all that much lately."

"I heard you'd got married," Adam said. "I have to admit, I didn't see that in the cards for you."

"Nor did I!" Alphonse gave them both a sunny smile, and Sebastian inwardly lamented Adam's warning. The man seemed perfect for him. "But marriage is really so much better than I'd expected. I don't know what I was so afraid of. Every man should be so lucky as to get a wife like Aaliyah." Alphonse paused. "Or rather, no, I suppose she's a bit of an acquired taste," he amended. "Maybe not for everyone."

"Did you bring any friends along this morning?" Adam asked.

"No, no, I only dropped in to see how things have been ticking along in my absence. Nothing much has changed, of course. Things rarely do around here, what? I suppose that's the charm of it. To provide a steadfast home away from home when the need arises. Not that I've needed to escape the old homestead in a fair bit. But back before things settled down, it was always nice to know the old Stag's Head would be waiting for me exactly as I left it."

"They did get a new clock for the wall behind the bar," Adam offered.

"Did they? Spiffing. I can never seem to keep my watch running properly. It's good to know there's a reliable clock somewhere about. Speaking of the bar, I ran into my cousin there just a moment ago. You know Morgan, don't you?"

The ping of recognition turned into a full-blown alarm.

"Only in passing," Adam said.

Sebastian knew a Morgan Hollyhock more than passingly. Or, he'd used to, at any rate. Whether it was the same Morgan Hollyhock, he couldn't say.

"Well, you should go have a chat, if you've got a minute. He's been ever so glum lately, and nothing seems to be shaking him out of it, so maybe you can give it a go, what? A spot of distraction for the chap?"

"I will, if you care to introduce us," Sebastian offered, keeping his caution from his tone.

If the name was a coincidence and this cousin was anything like Alphonse, Sebastian might just be in luck. But if the man was the same Morgan Hollyhock Sebastian knew from childhood...

The memory of fresh oranges hit Sebastian like a tangible thing.

He hadn't thought about Morgan in years.

"Will you talk to him?" Alphonse asked eagerly. "Brilliant! Come on, then; I'm sure he's still drowning his sorrows over there, whatever they are."

Alphonse cheerfully led the way to the bar—he seemed to do everything cheerfully, to Sebastian's amusement, though such sunny charm would likely prove tiresome after more than an hour in his company—where his erstwhile cousin sat alone, nursing a drink.

Like Alphonse, Morgan Hollyhock was blond-haired and fair-skinned, though his hair was ashier, and his eyes were grey rather than blue. He leaned against the curved sweep of the bar with a drink in one hand, surveying the rest of the club with something approaching a grimace.

Though it had been over twenty years since Sebastian had laid eyes on the man—the boy, back then—this was indeed the Morgan Hollyhock Sebastian had once known. He looked much improved compared to Sebastian's memories: sturdier, and with better colour in his cheeks. Less sickly. Now, in a reversal of fortunes, it was Sebastian who looked rather worse for wear.

Morgan's suit spoke of money, and he had a good face, handsome and square-jawed. As a boy, he'd been serious but kind, with a secret sense of humour he kept hidden the vast majority of the time. Sebastian had always been so pleased with himself when he succeeded in making the other boy laugh.

Looking at him now, full-grown and healthy but still so serious, Sebastian felt an ache of nostalgia in his chest. He'd tried so hard to separate his adult self from the boy he'd once been, but to reconnect with Morgan—maybe even as a friend, not a mark at all— might not be so bad.

Not that he was particularly keen to introduce Adam to his past. What Adam knew, Kitty would know shortly thereafter, and Sebastian didn't want to get into all that. He didn't owe anyone an explanation as to why he'd turned out as he did. Explaining himself to anyone was exhausting, and ruined his air of mystery.

Still, it couldn't be too difficult to draw Morgan away for a private word and a moment of catch-up.

If Morgan wanted to.

If Morgan even remembered him.

"Any insights?" he murmured to Adam as they approached the bar.

"All I know is that he lives alone in a modest flat in Portman Square, he mostly keeps to himself, and as far as anyone is aware, he's never been engaged."

"That's incredibly neutral."

"He's an incredibly neutral man. No gossip, no scandals, and no sex life to speak of."

"Sounds thrilling."

"Maybe he'll surprise you."

"Maybe he will."

"Hullo, Morgan, old thing," Alphonse announced, going up to his cousin and giving him a friendly clap on the shoulder.

Morgan braced himself against the sudden intrusion on his solitude, his gaze sliding over the three of them before he offered a nod of greeting. He seemed as reserved as Alphonse was outgoing, as given to quiet and melancholy as his cousin was to bright cheer. It was quick work, determining so much about a man from a single impression, but Sebastian made his trade by reading people at a glance, and they rarely surprised him anymore. The only thing was, he couldn't be sure whether he was really reading Morgan cold, or if he was letting childhood memories influence him.

"Making new friends?" Morgan asked, not sounding particularly interested in the answer.

"I always am," Alphonse agreed, either oblivious to Morgan's disinterest or so accustomed that he didn't bother acknowledging it anymore. "I think you've met

Adam Cunningham before, though, what? But here's some new company!"

Sebastian met Morgan's eyes with a smile, expectant, and Morgan—

Gave him nothing.

There was no spark, no recognition in Morgan's gaze, nothing but cool disinterest.

The taste of oranges abruptly soured.

Maybe it was for the best that Morgan didn't remember him. Sebastian had always preferred marks to friends anyway.

To Sebastian, in an undertone, Alphonse said, "Sorry, chap. What did you say your name was, again?"

For a second, Sebastian didn't answer. He could introduce himself properly, jog Morgan's memory, but then what? They would sit around making awkward small talk, asking each other how they'd been, and how were their families; two strangers in all but name, without any personal connection to carry them forward. They'd spent a single summer together when they were ten and twelve. After parting ways, Morgan would have been given some other tutor, with or without a son his own age to keep him company. Sebastian's role in his life would have been replaced within a week. And then, later, when Morgan returned to school, he would have had no shortage of playmates. Small wonder he'd forgotten Sebastian had ever existed.

A fresh start, Sebastian told himself. What he'd always wanted.

"Tom," Sebastian managed, before swallowing the lump in his throat and smoothing out his voice. "Call me Tom. A bit early to be drinking, isn't it?"

"Coffee," Morgan said, lifting his drink with one hand as he accepted Sebastian's shake with the other. "Though I've seen others start earlier than this. I like to think I'm not quite there yet." Setting his drink down, he looked Sebastian over with bored scrutiny. "New to town, or just new to the club?"

Sebastian re-centred himself. Morgan wasn't a friend. He wasn't a mark. He was just some stranger with whom Sebastian needed to make polite conversation until he was able to excuse himself without prompting Adam to accuse him of running away, which would only invite questions Sebastian didn't want to answer.

"Adam here has been showing me around," Sebastian replied, neatly sidestepping the question, "taking me everywhere he says is worth going."

"The Stag's Head is an interesting choice."

"You don't care for your own club?"

"It's worth coming to if you have literally nothing better to do with your time. Certainly nothing I'd show off to my friends."

"That's a shame. He said it was a good place to meet an interesting character or two."

Morgan snorted. "I think he's having one over on you."

Sebastian slid onto the open stool on Morgan's left. "Where do you recommend I go instead?"

After taking a long, considering drink, Morgan said, "You might like Eden."

Sebastian knew about Eden. Every self-respecting hedonist in the city did. The fact that Morgan knew it too made him exponentially more interesting.

"It's a different kind of club than this," Morgan said. "It seems like more your scene."

Sebastian leaned in a little closer, one elbow on the bar. "And what scene is that?" he asked, dropping his voice a notch like he was inviting intimacy, when really, he was inviting Morgan to actually see him. Which was pathetic, but Sebastian was all sorts of pathetic these days. He was coming to terms with it.

Morgan glanced at him sideways, resisting the invitation. "You seem like you appreciate a good party. Something livelier than a gentleman's club."

"And what about you?"

"Me, not so much."

"You've always preferred a quiet night in, haven't you?" Alphonse said, giving Morgan a light jostle from behind.

Sebastian shot Adam an unimpressed look, mostly because he knew Adam would be expecting it of him. Adam merely shrugged and tipped his head towards Morgan, silently encouraging Sebastian to keep at it.

"Eden is a ripping good time, though," Alphonse continued. "I think everyone should go to a party at Eden at least once."

"I do love a good party," Sebastian said. "Drinks, dancing; what's not to like?"

"Oh, he'll talk for hours about what's not to like about parties," Alphonse warned, though his tone remained jovial.

Morgan sighed, studying the interior rings of his coffee cup.

"Go on, then," Sebastian prompted, nudging him. "It sounds like you've got a whole monologue prepared, and I want to hear it." He absolutely didn't; he wanted to get out of there as soon as possible. He felt slightly ill and more than slightly disappointed, mostly in himself, for daring to feel hurt by the lack of recognition. But he was good at pretending otherwise.

"It's all just so terribly vapid, isn't it?" Morgan said with a tired gesture. "Take The Stag's Head, for example. Half of us are over thirty, yet we're still eschewing any sense of responsibility and larking about like schoolboys. Everything about it feels so empty and immature."

"I haven't hit thirty yet," Alphonse pointed out. "Nor has Aaliyah or Adam or…Tom? How old are you?"

"Just under," Sebastian lied automatically.

"There you go. And who's to say we can't be mature while we enjoy a party here and there? Why, look at me! I've only gone and got married, haven't I? How's that for mature? And Percival over there, he's just inherited his father's land, and only last week I heard James Whistler went and got himself a cat, and if that's not a sign of settling down, I don't know what is." Alphonse had the air of a lawyer who had just closed an inarguable defence.

"A cat," Sebastian repeated flatly. "He said he got a *cat*."

Adam glanced at him worriedly.

"I don't know the details of the cat-getting," Alphonse said, "but you could ask him about it next time you see him, if you're curious."

"That's quite alright," Sebastian said icily. "I think you'll find that he didn't keep his cat for very long."

"Oh? That's a shame. We have a cat; she's really such a lovely creature. And awfully clever, too."

"Look," Morgan said, "I agree that we're all adults, complete with the trappings of adulthood, as you say: land and marriage and…" He cut a glance to Sebastian. "Cats, and what have you. But if you put a group like this in Eden, you can't see anything other than a gang of unchaperoned schoolchildren hopped up on drugs and alcohol, running amuck. Which is fine, in itself. I just wish there was evidence that they had any deeper thoughts in their heads, but this seems to be it for them, and there's something so damned tragic about that idea that I simply can't stomach it."

Alphonse looked at him strangely before shaking it off. "Suppose you're right, old chap. You usually are. Though I can't say I understand what's so bad about wanting to enjoy the moment and have a good time. It's one of those carpe diem things, what? Thought that was supposed to be all the rage."

"No, you're right. I'm being a killjoy."

"Why *are* you here?" Sebastian asked, genuine curiosity colouring his tone. "This isn't Eden, but if you find your peers as vapid as you say, why bother coming out at all? It can't be fun being the only person in the room with a solitary thought occupying your head."

"I thought I should get out of the house before I became a full-blown hermit, though I think now that perhaps hermitage is underrated." Morgan gave Sebastian another once-over. "And yourself?"

"Oh, I enjoy vapidity. There's nothing more delicious than a night of style over substance."

"I'll have to take your word for it."

"You mean to tell me you've never let go and indulged for a single night? With your money and your looks, it can't be for a lack of opportunities."

"A lack of interest, then."

"You've never been tempted?"

"I've gone to Eden before, haven't I? I've gone enough times to get the measure of the place. I keep waiting to see whether anything will tempt me, but there's nothing. Maybe I haven't got the appetite for it."

"That's a shame," Sebastian murmured.

Morgan looked at him speculatively, but Sebastian didn't give him time to linger.

"What do you like, then, if not drug-and-alcohol-fuelled parties? Tell me something interesting."

"I'm afraid you're going to find me terribly boring," Morgan replied, not sounding the least concerned at the prospect. "I dabble in art. On an extremely amateur level, you understand."

Amateur art, Sebastian had little use for. Art was only worth stealing if it was famous enough to be resold, and Morgan Hollyhock was decidedly not a famous artist, not even locally. He'd used to fill sketchbooks with botanical studies, Sebastian recalled, sitting in the garden with ink and graphite smudged up the side of his hand.

He soldiered on with his charade, which was making him feel worse by the minute. This entire encounter needed to be put out of its misery. "What kind of art?"

Morgan shrugged. "Just sketches, really. Figure drawing. Something I do for my own amusement; I never intend to show it or anything like that. I'm not good enough, and besides which, I'm not sure I want the attention."

Which meant he was unlikely to whip out a sketchbook and start taking Sebastian through his old work, thank god.

"It's good for a man to have a hobby," Sebastian said neutrally. He himself didn't have hobbies so much as habits he had ruthlessly monetised.

"Hm," said Morgan, with equal neutrality.

Sebastian paused, giving him the chance to continue. He did not. Sebastian was more than ready to escape the conversation and the club at large, but he couldn't resist the compulsion to leave people wanting more. He rose and turned in one fluid movement, his hand landing on Morgan's chest, brushing over the lapels of his suit. "It was nice meeting you," he purred. "If you ever change your mind about Eden, maybe I'll see you around."

"Maybe," Morgan replied, turning to watch Sebastian leave.

Sebastian was pleased to note that Morgan's throat sounded dry despite the coffee. Maybe Morgan wasn't as indifferent to him as he'd put on. But that wasn't quite enough to make Sebastian stay and suffer through another ten minutes of conversation to find out for sure. He remembered enjoying Morgan's company as a boy; he'd thought Morgan had enjoyed his company then, too. Clearly, they'd both changed. Leaving Alphonse to his own devices, Sebastian took Adam by the arm and steered him away from the bar.

"That's a no, then, is it?" Adam asked mildly.

"Would you have stuck around talking to him longer than you had to?"

Adam gave an easy shrug. "I'm not in your situation, though, am I?"

"Do you *want* me to go for him? I didn't expect you to be so willing to deliver your friend up to my tender mercies."

"We're not friends," Adam countered. "We're mild acquaintances, at most. And it's not as if you're actually dangerous. What are you going to do? Leech off him for a few weeks, maybe steal his silverware on your way out? You're hardly intending to ruin the man, and anyway, he already looks miserable. I doubt you could leave him in a much worse state."

"Fair enough. Though honestly, I'd rather hold out for someone less depressing."

"Alright. Shall we see who else is here?"

"Another time. Any minute now, he's going to realise I nicked his pocket watch on my way out, and I'd like to be gone before that happens."

And with that, he swept Adam out of the club and back onto the street, having accomplished next to nothing except for making himself both nostalgic and depressed, and scratching his ever-present pickpocketing itch. Kitty was going to be terribly disappointed in him.

CHAPTER TWO

A BET AND A CONFIDENCE GAME

"I can't tell whether you're upset because he rejected you, or because you can't find anyone to meet your impossibly high standards," Kitty said that evening.

It was after teatime and the three of them were lounging around the sitting room, the radio crackling quietly in the corner. The evenings got dark early as they passed the middle of October, lending themselves to cosy quietude, which rankled Sebastian unfairly. He'd set up camp in Adam's guest room, though he doubted he'd be staying long, regardless of whether he found a decent mark. Domesticity didn't suit him. Kitty and Adam weren't nearly as bad as Whistler, but unless he was going out to parties or running cons, Sebastian didn't know what to do with himself. Sitting still made him irritable. It always had done, even before Blackwood, though after, that irritability came laced with an awful anxiety that made him so restless he needed to pace, digging his nails into his palms like a self-destructive cat trapped in a cage.

"He didn't reject me," Sebastian said haughtily, flipping the pocket watch over his knuckles. "We just didn't click. Adam can back me on this."

"There was no spark," Adam agreed, idly thumbing through a paperback.

"Why didn't you make a spark?" Kitty asked. "You could spark off a brick wall, if you tried hard enough."

"Bored people are boring. He might have money, but he's horribly dull. I couldn't possibly shackle myself to him for any amount of time."

That, and the fact that the longer Sebastian spent around him, the more likely that Morgan would eventually remember who he was, which could only lead to an awkward conversation about why Sebastian had lied about his name, and then, even worse, a conversation about what had happened to him in all those years since they'd parted ways. Sebastian hadn't thought about Morgan in a terribly long time, and he wished he could have continued not thinking about him far into the future. There was simply no point in dwelling on happiness from the distant past. It couldn't be re-created, so, like a pretty but functionally worthless rose, it was best put away in a little box where its thorns couldn't accidentally draw blood.

Sebastian toyed with his stolen pocket watch, flipping it idly between his fingers. It had a good weight to it, the metal etchings worn smooth by years of handling, the gears ticking away at a steady pace. There was a little dent on one side, making it unlikely to fetch more than a few pence if he pawned it, and the initials *R. H.* engraved on the inner lid. Some previous owner: a father or a grandfather, most likely. A common watch hardly worth stealing in the first place. He hadn't known that before lifting it, but even if he had, he couldn't help himself. Pickpocketing was second-nature to him; his hands did it of their own accord.

"I didn't think he was all that bad," Adam said. "He's our age, he's very good looking, and he's interested in art. You have plenty in common."

"Hardly."

"And you haven't stopped playing with his watch since you got your hands on it."

Sebastian pressed the watch firmly against the arm of his chair, just to prove he could stop fidgeting. Adam was right, though; he had been playing with it nonstop since leaving the club, and, furthermore, he hadn't stopped thinking about its owner. The nostalgia he'd felt on first seeing Morgan after so long had immediately turned to hurt, which was now turning to regret. As a rule, he disliked feeling regret, and generally did everything in his power to avoid it. However, he couldn't help but feel he'd made the wrong decision in playing the part of a stranger. The rose was out of its box, and its thorns were uncomfortably prickly.

"Do you think he suspects me of taking it?" Sebastian asked of the watch. "Or do you think he just assumes he lost it somewhere?"

"He blames you, one hundred percent," Adam said. "He doesn't seem careless with his belongings."

"You want him to suspect you," Kitty accused with a playful smile. "You like the idea that he's as preoccupied with thoughts of you as you are with him."

"I'm not preoccupied," Sebastian objected. "But yes, obviously I want him to be thinking about me. I want everyone to be thinking about me all the time."

"Then go find him again. Take him to bed to get him out of your system, at least. You can do that even if he's not suitable for anything else."

"I'll just go back to The Stag's Head, wait for him to turn up, and proposition him right there in the open, shall I?"

"Or you can do something more discrete," Kitty replied, rolling her eyes at his drama. "Find out where he lives and use that pocket watch as an excuse to go see him."

"I'm not sure I care enough to put the effort in."

"Then stop thinking about him," Adam said from behind his book.

"Look," Kitty said. "I can literally give you his address. It was in the paper this morning." Leaving the room, she returned a moment later with Adam's breakfast paper, tossing the classifieds into Sebastian's lap. "You said he was an amateur artist. He puts out ads looking for models. If you want him, there he is, as easy as you could ask for. Whatever you want to do with him after the fact is up to you."

"Hm."

Adam flipped a page. "I'll bet you twenty quid you can't seduce the man," he said, without looking up.

Sebastian stumbled over that for a second before forcing himself back into the role Adam expected.

"Twenty quid," he repeated incredulously. "That's hardly worth getting out of bed for."

Actually, there wasn't much Sebastian wouldn't do for twenty quid, but he didn't need to publicise it.

"It's enough to get you a room in a flophouse for a week or two," Kitty said, "not that you'd need it, seeing as your seduction would end with a place in Hollyhock's flat. Or his bed, rather. What have you got to lose?"

"Other than your pride," Adam added. "I asked around about him some more this afternoon, and Morgan Hollyhock is notoriously reserved. He's hardly interested in socialising; he's never had so much as a whiff of a scandal attached to his name. He's never publicly dated any girls, but he seems too boring for anyone to speculate on whether he's swinging for the other team."

"You want me to seduce a monk," Sebastian said. *A childhood friend*, he didn't say. He wasn't sure which was worse.

"He's right," Kitty confided in Adam. "Hollyhock's maybe too great a challenge. After getting dumped by Whistler, perhaps he's better off easing back into things slowly."

"Fine," Sebastian said, knowing he was playing right into their hands, but helpless to resist the bait. "If that's the way you want to be, then yes, I *will* seduce him. The bet's on."

Taking up the paper, Sebastian scanned the ads until he found Morgan Hollyhock's name in black and white, offering ten shillings an hour to any model willing to sit for him. Portman Square was a nice, upscale neighbourhood not all that far away. Kitty was right: Sebastian had no excuse not to pursue him. Even if Morgan did seem prone to melancholy and possibly as terrible a bore as Whistler had been, it wasn't as if Sebastian had found anyone better. He needed someone to pay his way, and somewhere to stay that wasn't with his friends. He and Kitty had lived in each other's pockets before, and they'd been ready to tear each other's throats out by the end of it. He had no wish to repeat that experience, even though Adam's generous hospitality was begging for him to take advantage.

But something resembling a sense of morality reared its head, for once in Sebastian's life. He had no problem seducing a stranger to use for his own ends, whether there was a bet involved or not. But something bothered him about the idea of trying to seduce Morgan, of all people, especially under a false name and identity. If Morgan knew who he was, that would be different. The problem was in the deception, which was a first, but then, Sebastian have never dealt with this specific scenario before. Evidently, he had a single line he wouldn't cross, and, quite by accident, he had found it. How terribly inconvenient.

So: what to do. He wasn't interested in keeping up this false identity and playing a long, slow game with Morgan in order to win his trust and slide between his bedsheets like a snake. That felt like a darker shade of criminality than Sebastian liked, even if there was no measurable difference between doing it to a stranger as compared to an estranged friend. Luckily, Sebastian had an idea. Morgan Hollyhock was desperate for something interesting to happen to him, and, after the Whistler embarrassment, Sebastian was equally desperate for a change of pace. It might not prove a good idea, but it sat better with him than out and out deception.

"I'll go hunt him down in the morning."

"Excellent," Kitty said. "Because I need you in top form if we're going to pull off our little Cheapside heist, and moping around like a wet blanket is *not* it. Adam says this Morgan Hollyhock is pretty enough, as far as he can tell, so go get laid and come back in better spirits."

Sebastian had taken worse advice, so he went to bed that night intending to do just that. The pocket watch stayed on the bed beside his pillow like a good-luck charm, ushering him to dawn.

◆ ◆ ◆

Eleven the next morning found Sebastian outside Morgan Hollyhock's door. It was still earlier than he liked to do business—he'd always been a nocturnal creature by habit, and then Blackwood had knocked what was left of his natural circadian rhythm all out of sync. Still, he'd made his best effort to wake up and be sociable, sharpening his wit on three cups of black coffee. He had perhaps overshot the mark ever so slightly in that regard, and he jittered in place after knocking. His hands had a fine tremble to them that he would get under control by the time the door opened. He didn't need to look respectable, per se, but he did need to look sane and sober, and vibrating in place would not achieve that.

He knew the figure he cut. His suit was a stylish, navy-blue three-piece number borrowed from Adam's wardrobe, as his own suits were regrettably outdated, through no fault of his own. However, Adam was ever so slightly broader across the shoulders than he, and about an inch shorter, making the fit less than perfect, albeit perhaps only to a tailor's eye. His hair, so brown it looked black, was neatly parted and slicked back. But no amount of personal grooming could disguise the way he was paler than he should be, or the dark rings under his eyes that spoke of too many sleepless nights. He had a lean and hungry look about him that was impossible to hide.

Respectability wasn't his concern. He didn't need Morgan Hollyhock to mistake him for a classy young gentleman. He just needed Morgan Hollyhock to be intrigued enough to invite him inside.

He knocked again.

"I have it," Morgan called from within, and the door pulled open to reveal the man himself. He blinked once before recognition settled over his features, though still not the recognition Sebastian was hoping for. His gaze grew cold and shuttered.

Sebastian smiled and raised his hands, gloved palms facing outward. In his right, tucked between his thumb and forefinger, was Morgan's watch.

"I seem to have something that belongs to you."

"You stole that," Morgan said flatly.

Sebastian held out his hand, offering the watch back, and Morgan snatched it from his palm.

"Tell me why I shouldn't take you down to the police this instant," Morgan growled. It was a good tone coming from him, and Sebastian wanted to hear more of it.

"Because you want to know why I'm returning it?"

Morgan examined the watch. It was in exactly the same condition as it had been when taken, from the initials engraved inside to the dent at five o' clock.

"Very well," Morgan said shortly, in a tone that brooked no nonsense. "What do you want?"

Sebastian stepped neatly over the threshold, his hands clasped in front of him. He generally found that once he was through the door, it was much easier to convince people to allow him to remain.

"First and foremost, to apologise." Sebastian had never offered a heartfelt apology to anyone in his life, but the words came easily enough. "I only took your watch to get your attention. It's a terrible habit, I know."

"Why do you want my attention?"

Sebastian had never been accused of bravery, and had to steel himself before saying, "My name's not Tom, and yesterday wasn't the first time we met."

Morgan hesitated, looking him over as he had done the previous day, but this time, to far greater depths. "Sebastian?" he ventured, as carefully as if handling some rare and delicate thing, as full of thorns as any rose.

Sebastian's name had never sounded so good to him, like a rush of relief straight through his core, waterfalling into some hole of which he'd hardly been aware.

"I thought I knew you. There was this sense of familiarity, but then, when you introduced yourself...I thought I must be imagining your likeness. Why didn't you say something?"

Sense and decency suggested that Sebastian admit to having panicked and lied in order to avoid having any sort of reunion in front of unwanted spectators. But his pride had been wounded when Morgan had failed to recognise him, and demanded that wound be repaid in kind.

Unfortunately, Sebastian was on much better terms with matters of pride than those of sense or decency.

"I didn't want to get into it in front of my friend. You see, I've given considerable effort to leaving my past behind me."

The hurt Sebastian had been looking for flickered over Morgan's face. Hurt, and confusion.

"Oh," Morgan said faintly.

Sebastian immediately felt rotten.

"Well, it was good of you to come and try again, however belatedly." Gathering himself, Morgan attempted a smile. "Even if you did have to steal my watch to do it. I suppose that's not out of character. Have you been well? It's been…" He paused, as if considering whether to continue. "It's been over twenty years. You've changed."

"Not where it counts."

"Why don't you come through," Morgan offered. "Let's sit down and…"

Morgan's flat was fashionable and well-kept, and gave the impression of belonging to a quiet, studious man. Sebastian followed Morgan to the living room, where books lined the shelves, and notebooks and leather-bound journals could be found on most available flat surfaces. There were sounds from the kitchen, as of someone cooking; presumably whomever Morgan had been speaking to as he answered the door.

"My man, Sterling," Morgan said, correctly guessing Sebastian's curiosity.

"No wonder you're bored, if you haven't even got the responsibility of keeping your own flat."

"You're not wrong."

Sebastian took a seat on the sofa as directed. He stretched out, spreading his arms along the back of it and crossing one knee over the other, making himself at home as Morgan took the armchair opposite, the coffee table acting as a barrier between them.

Sebastian cut straight to the chase.

"Do you remember when we were boys, the kinds of games we used to play? Daring each other to do the most ridiculous things without our parents catching on?"

"Raiding the kitchen and catching frogs in the back garden," Morgan said slowly. "Rifling through my mother's makeup collection."

"Well, it seems I never outgrew the habit of saying yes to every single challenge that came my way."

"What does that have to do with me, after all this time?"

This was the delicate bit.

Sebastian teetered at the edge of a great chasm, at the bottom of which it was all thorns, no roses. The safest thing to do would be to back away from the edge, ask for a cup of tea, and invite Morgan to reminisce about old times. It might hurt a little, but it was unlikely to cause any lasting damage. If Sebastian continued his balancing act right along the edge, every step ran the risk of losing that careful balance and falling into the pit. There would be no coming back from that; he would be dashed to bits by the fall, and those golden childhood memories would be tarnished, and their friendship unsalvageable.

On the other hand, if he kept his balance, he had the chance to forge their relationship anew.

And also win twenty pounds.

The risk hardly seemed worth it when he looked at it like that.

But he'd always been terrible at risk assessment.

Turn back, he told himself, but it was like watching a car crash from afar. He couldn't stop the next words from tumbling out of his mouth any more than he could stop a drunk driver from flooring the gas. In both cases it came down to a damnable lack of impulse control.

"You mentioned a passing familiarity with Eden," Sebastian began. "Forgive my presumption, but it has a reputation in certain circles. Those who frequent it, men and women alike, tend to be a little more adventurous in what company they keep than polite society would dictate."

Morgan's shoulders crept up an inch, pre-emptively defensive. "What are you insinuating?"

"From what I've heard, you don't seem the sort to go for that. Casual hook-ups and the like, I mean. You have a reputation for being quite closed-off—you know that, of course. If you were a woman, they might call you frigid."

"Get to the point, please," Morgan ground out.

"My reputation, on the other hand, is rather the polar opposite. You know my friend, Adam?"

"Adam Cunningham. We've met a few times previously. I really don't have any impression of him."

"Well, his impression of you is that you live as a monk, entirely untouchable. And, given what he knows of me, he thought it would be fun to bet me a tidy sum that I wouldn't be able to seduce you. He doesn't know we were ever acquainted," Sebastian added.

Morgan stared at him like Sebastian had begun speaking in tongues. Sebastian gave him a moment to process.

"So, your approach was to tell me straight up," Morgan finally said, the words coming out somewhat strangled.

"We did used to be friends," Sebastian pointed out.

"Why not shut him down immediately? Why tell me at all? You're not— You can't be entertaining the idea."

With his arms still outstretched along the back of the sofa, Sebastian raised his hands in a shrug. "Why not?"

Shutting his eyes, Morgan pinched the bridge of his nose, his expression pained. "Alright. No. Back up a step. Would you please explain what exactly it is you're proposing here? You're asking me to—to sleep with you? Or pretend to sleep with you? It's unclear, and to be frank, I'm not sure how much clarity I even want."

"Pretending," Sebastian said quickly. The alternative was overwhelming for reasons he didn't want to explore at that time. "You put me up for a few nights, we pretend to be sleeping together, convince Adam to pay up, and kill two birds with one stone."

Morgan bit, looking morbidly curious despite his better instincts. "What birds are those?"

"I win my bet and get somewhere comfortable to stay for the short-term, and in return, I help you alleviate the crushing boredom you complained of in The Stag's Head. You said yourself that your life is an endless procession of vapidity and ennui. I can't offer any philosophical brilliance to make your life more meaningful, but I guarantee I can liven things up a bit."

"I'm not sure I want things livened up to that extent."

"Oh, come on. There's nothing worse than being bored or being boring. You know I was always getting into things that weren't meant for me."

"Are you this upfront with all your victims?"

"I promise, none of them are feeling victimised by the time I'm done," Sebastian assured him. "But no, this is a new technique for me. You don't strike me as the sort of man easily won over by temptation. And, well. Assuming you did eventually recognise me, I didn't really…" His smile dropped to a grimace. "I do have *some* standards. Or one single standard, at least. So, rather than give up on you entirely and lose the bet, I thought I might tempt you in a different way."

Never mind a car crash; this was a train wreck, and Sebastian had strapped himself into the conductor's seat, driving himself full-throttle into a brick wall. At any point he could have taken hold of the controls and tried to stop the disaster, but at every point, he chose to keep ploughing on. Maybe his mother was right, and there was something slightly wrong with him.

"Are you trying to tempt me right now?" Morgan asked doubtfully. "Because I'm not feeling very convinced."

But he still hadn't thrown Sebastian out of the house, which pointed to just the opposite. Or, possibly it pointed to something being slightly wrong with him, too.

"Maybe the rumours are true, and you don't care about sex or companionship. I still think I can offer something you want."

"Enrichment," Morgan said, his tone flat.

"You were so desperate for a spot of interest when you were a boy, cooped up by yourself in that awful house for a year, that you befriended me. I might not know the particulars of your current situation, but I know you're bored, dissatisfied, and perpetually unimpressed with your life and your peers. Let me broaden your horizons and show you some alternative. I know you've never met anyone else like me, and you're curious how I hold up as an adult."

Morgan stared him down for a long, quiet minute, his expression utterly, unreadably closed-off. "No," he finally said. "I think I have the measure of you as an adult, actually." Rising from his chair, he straightened his clothes, and Sebastian rose to mirror him.

"I think you were right the first time. Perhaps we were better off as strangers. If you don't mind, I'm going to show you out now."

Reaching out, he gently ushered Sebastian from the living room back towards the foyer, taking care to keep space between them.

Taken aback by the sudden rejection, Sebastian let himself be shepherded, using the time to scramble together a new plan, cursing himself for not changing tracks when he still had the chance. The fact that Morgan had let him in at all, that he had sat and listened to Sebastian's offer, indicated that the man really was desperate for a change of pace. He must be bored out of his skull. But inviting him to participate in a con, no matter how harmless, had clearly been too great a leap. Sebastian should have started with baby steps and eased him into the idea of excitement. He should have attempted to genuinely rekindle their friendship.

But how on earth was he meant to do that when he'd never expected to see the man again? They had parted ways an entire lifetime ago. They might as well be moving in different universes, their spheres briefly overlapping as children before rocketing off in different directions, far enough that they'd each forgotten the other had ever existed.

They'd been happy back then, though. Sebastian couldn't speak for Morgan, but for himself, age ten might have been the last happy year he'd ever had. Sebastian had less to offer the world now than he did then, and Morgan was clearly harder to impress.

When they reached the door, Sebastian turned to face Morgan, who was forced to halt in order to maintain their distance.

"Let me model for you," Sebastian blurted. "I saw your ad in the paper looking for artist's models. That's perfectly honest work, isn't it? Hire me for that."

"For some reason, I doubt your integrity." Reaching past Sebastian, Morgan pulled the door open and tipped his chin up, indicating in no uncertain terms that Sebastian's welcome had run its course. "I can't say it was nice seeing you again." His mouth twisted, like he'd wished for something different. Like he'd thought about Sebastian at all, over those twenty-one years. "You should have left it at Tom, in The Stag's Head."

Stepping across the threshold, Sebastian only lingered long enough to draw one of Adam's calling cards from within his jacket. "Should you change your mind, give me a call at this number for the immediate future. Do consider it."

And with that, having pressed the card into Morgan's reluctant hand, Sebastian slipped outside and darted down the steps to the street, glancing back just long enough to catch Morgan standing there in his open doorway, staring down at the card like he'd just been handed a venomous snake.

Affecting a show of nonchalance, Sebastian strolled away like he hadn't a care in the world. Always leave them wanting more. He wasn't at all confident that Morgan would be in touch, which was a terrible, slimy feeling, but he'd cracked tougher eggs in his time. The game wasn't over until he gave up.

Still, the rejection stung, and it took him the entire walk back to Adam's to shake it off.

CHAPTER THREE

WHEREIN BRUNCH IS HAD AND
A TENTATIVE OVERTURE MADE

Losing Morgan was a blow, and losing the twenty-pound bet was worse, but Sebastian had greater plans than that. With Kitty's help, he planned to pull off the heist of a lifetime and secure his future in priceless jewels. They were going to rob the National Gallery's exhibit of the 1912 Cheapside Hoard. It wasn't their first jewel robbery, as all the London papers knew—it wasn't even their next jewel robbery—but, if all went according to plan, it might just be their last. Money like that could let them retire not only comfortably but in style.

He and Kitty had a date at noon the next day to visit a little boutique and acquire the disguises that would help them pull the whole thing off, to be tested at a party that evening. By *disguises*, Sebastian actually meant *magically-enhanced beauty products*, which Kitty had pitched as a subtler alternative to wearing balaclavas or stockings over their heads.

Sebastian left Adam's flat a few hours early in order to stalk the streets of London and try to bait someone with too much wealth and too little class into approaching him. It was much easier to meet men by way of mutual introduction, and safer, too, but he was restless and on edge following Morgan's rejection, and more interested in immediate gratification than long-term success.

There was a little stretch of greenery on King's Road, near the place where he was to meet Kitty and Adam: a parkette spotted with oak trees whose leaves were crisp and orange, rustling like paper in the breeze. A few benches stood beneath the canopies, and a path ran down the middle for foot traffic, lightly populated. It wasn't one of the city's known haunts where men liked to meet each other—Sebastian knew all of them by heart—but it was as good a place as any to sniff around for someone bored and gullible.

It was foolish, he was well aware, and likely to earn him nothing more than a wasted morning. But it felt good to walk with purpose, and catching strange men's attention in the park gave him a thrilling sense of power and delicious danger. It wasn't impossible that a quick, impulsive shag could lead to something more lucrative. At any rate, it was a chance he was willing to take. If nothing else, he could relieve a passer-by or two of their wallets and prevent the morning from being a total wash.

He strolled from one end of the parkette to the other before settling himself against the trunk of the largest oak, his back to its bark as he lazily fished a cigarette from the pack in his pocket. He was less interested in the act than in the aesthetic of smoking; it gave him an excuse to lounge around outside with a careless attitude, and it lent him an effortless attraction. In certain places, a man only had to stand and smoke for five minutes before someone would come along expressing jealousy of his cigarette. This parkette wasn't one such place, but Sebastian was confident that, if the timing was right, he could make anyone jealous of anything.

He hadn't counted on Morgan being the first person to walk by.

They stared at each other for a beat, Morgan coming to a dead halt in the middle of the path like he'd stumbled upon a ghost. Sebastian broke the stillness by exhaling a plume of smoke, and Morgan blinked as if shaking himself from a spell. Tipping his chin up with a crooked smile, Sebastian offered a wordless invitation or a challenge for Morgan to approach. In response, Morgan shook his head and dropped his gaze, a much more dour smile on his own lips, before stepping off the path and onto the grass.

"Fancy meeting you here," Sebastian said, expertly covering his own surprise at seeing the man again so soon.

"I had an errand," Morgan replied, giving him nothing.

"I thought you would have pretended not to know me if we ever met each other in the street."

"And I half expected you to be waiting on my doorstep when I came out this morning."

"You were thinking about me?"

"Not at all."

Laughing, Sebastian took a final drag from his cigarette before flicking it away. "Alright. Why are you talking to me, then? I have no other borrowed items to return, and I thought you were very clear in wanting nothing to do with me."

"I'm not going to start seeing you everywhere I go, am I?" Morgan asked.

"Do you think I'm stalking you? This isn't even your neighbourhood. I'm meeting friends for a day out, if that reassures you at all."

"It doesn't."

"I hope you're not thinking of me as some curse that's attached itself to you. This is really a complete coincidence."

Morgan looked unconvinced. "Two chance meetings back to back after such a long time with no sign of you at all? You'll forgive my suspicion."

"Maybe it's fate pushing us into each other's paths after so long," Sebastian offered carelessly. He hardly believed it himself, but he wanted to.

"You didn't spend the night out here, did you?"

"Worried about me?"

"Excuse me for asking," Morgan huffed.

"If you're really concerned about my wellbeing, you can take me to lunch."

"It's too early for lunch."

Sebastian had expected a flat rejection, but that wasn't a no. He tried again, with more hope this time. "Brunch, then?"

"Why would I do that?"

"You tell me."

Morgan narrowed his eyes. "Fine. Brunch."

He took Sebastian to a stylish, though not pretentious, little restaurant, and ordered for them both, perhaps mistrusting Sebastian's choice in drinks. Sebastian wasn't an idiot; he wouldn't have ordered the most expensive of anything on the menu, or at least, not on their first time out together. Still, he was accustomed to partners who were controlling in their generosity, so he didn't make a fuss about it.

Brunch proved to be a simple affair of sandwiches, but there were many of them, and the bread was thickly-sliced and grilled, and they were stuffed with generous helpings of ham, melted cheese, and roasted apples. An additional bowl of fresh-picked apples sat in the middle of the table, red skin waxy and inviting, in contrast to the warm, savoury smell of the main course. Sebastian had to pace himself to avoid devouring his entire serving at once.

Morgan settled back in his chair and looked at Sebastian from across the table. They were seated by the window, overlooking the little garden boxes, whose flowers were dry but still clinging to life, and beyond that, the street, bustling with pedestrians. The restaurant was crowded enough, with conversations chattering away in every corner, that it provided a paradoxical kind of privacy with little risk of being overheard.

"So," said Sebastian. "Are you reconsidering my offer to model? I'd ask if you were reconsidering my other offer, but maybe I shouldn't push my luck."

"Let's not talk business while we're eating. Tell me about yourself, instead. Something other than your criminal habits, I mean. What have you done with your life since we last spoke?"

"Since yesterday?" Sebastian teased.

Morgan made a disgruntled sound. "Try harder."

"Very well." Sebastian worked through his first sandwich for a moment, considering where to begin, or rather, the least of himself he could reveal without shutting Morgan out entirely. "I play the piano and the violin, and I have a deft hand for spellwork," he offered.

"I believe that," Morgan admitted begrudgingly, nodding to the elegant shape of Sebastian's hands. "You pursued an education, then."

"I'm largely self-taught, in fact."

"You were always clever enough for it. And despite that, you turned to…"

"To crime?"

"You fell on hard times and did what you had to in order to survive," Morgan guessed.

Only so far as most everyone in London had fallen on hard times at one point or another, especially once the ugly war had erupted. Sebastian was nothing special in that regard, and he certainly didn't want to talk about it. "Generous, but no. Try again."

Morgan studied him, and Sebastian watched him intently in return.

"You've never been bored?" Sebastian prompted. "You seem terribly bored, all the time."

"Not enough to start stealing people's pocket watches. Are you sure you're not just a deviant?"

"Oh, I am," Sebastian promised with a smile. "But one that you can relate to."

Morgan chose not to touch on that, at least not yet. "So, your music and your magic. Where did you learn that?"

"I picked it up here and there, along the way," Sebastian said airily, as if those weren't crafts requiring years of dedication and practice. "Did you ever get formal training for your art?"

"Like you, I'm self-taught, but I only dabble, really. It's a personal hobby, not anything close to a calling."

"Ah, and I'd had hopes of seeing my likeness in all the finest galleries," Sebastian joked. "Do you keep all your art in your personal collection, then?"

"To call it a collection is generous, but most of it, yes. Some I give away. Some I discard. It's the act of drawing itself that I enjoy, less so the end results. So, if it's fame and notoriety you're after, you'd be better off looking for an artist like Jules Coxley or some such. You won't find any of that with me, I'm afraid."

Jules Coxley—now, there was a contemporary artist with work worth fencing, if not forging. Nudes were commonplace in the art world, but Coxley had raised his portraiture of the human figure to something altogether divine.

"I know some people were placing wagers on whether the authorities would get Coxley for indecency charges or something similar." Sebastian polished off a second sandwich. The grease from the cheese and the butter from the grill was delectable. "Do you like his work?"

"He's talented, no question about it, and popular too, which is a hard thing to achieve."

"I expect he's somewhat too risqué for your tastes," Sebastian said, watching him closely.

"On the contrary, I find his disregard for social decency to be quite liberating," Morgan said quietly.

Sebastian was equal parts astonished and delighted. "Do you draw like him?"

Morgan shook his head. "No, no."

"But would you?" Sebastian pressed. "If you had a model willing to do it, or you weren't too shy to ask for it. If you could, would you?"

"I've never considered it."

That was a lie. Sebastian bet that when Morgan closed his eyes, he could picture those silhouettes sketched in bold charcoal, bodies so intimately entwined that he would blush to ever see such a pose before him—

"That's a shame," said Sebastian. "If you ever change your mind, do call me up. I'd consider it a privilege to be drawn like that."

"Are you so ravenous for attention?"

"Of the right kind, yes."

"And most of it is the right kind," Morgan surmised, pushing the bowl of fruit towards him.

"Your words, not mine," Sebastian said lightly, selecting an apple. It had a perfect autumnal crunch when he bit into it.

They ate in silence for a minute, the last of the sandwiches gone and the apples fast diminishing.

"Have you done it before?" Morgan finally asked. "Taken similar bets from your friend, I mean."

"I thought we weren't talking business while we're eating."

"The meal is over."

"I'm still chewing." Sebastian lifted his apple pointedly.

Morgan's mouth twitched, but he resisted crossing his arms like a petulant child.

"I haven't taken bets like that, no," Sebastian said, enjoying Morgan's impatience. "But I've seduced men in order to get some short-term security, a roof over my head and the like, certainly. It's just always been my own idea."

"You're comfortable whoring yourself out to make ends meet."

"People have done worse things to get by. Why? Do you find it distasteful?"

"Not distasteful so much as alien. It doesn't bother you? Wearing a mask and playing a part in order to tumble into so many different strangers' beds?"

"What bothers me is going cold or hungry or without a place to stay."

"Not enough to get a proper job?"

Sebastian held himself back from bristling. "I asked you to hire me. You refused."

"Hm," said Morgan.

"Look." Sebastian devoured the end of his apple and set the core aside on his now-empty plate. "Am I right in thinking you have an open schedule today? You must not have plans, or you wouldn't have agreed to brunch with me at the drop of a hat. Come with me while I meet my friends for an afternoon of shopping. Whatever alien or criminal notions you have of me, let me dissuade you of them."

"Am I supposed to believe you have no ulterior motive but to raise my opinion of you?" Morgan's expression was perfectly closed off.

"Of course I have an ulterior motive. Say hello to my friend Adam and let him believe we're shagging and you've fallen for me. A single afternoon of minimal effort on your part will win me twenty pounds. If you're charitable enough to buy brunch for a perfect stranger—and after twenty years, we really are no more than strangers—then you're charitable enough for this, surely."

"I said no to your little scheme yesterday. Why should I say yes now?"

"Because I'm not asking to stay in your house or even your company for more than a few hours. You need never see me again, coincidental meetings notwithstanding. If we happen upon each other in another public park, you're free to pretend you've never met me before in your life." Leaning in, Sebastian tapped the table in front of Morgan's plate with one sharp finger. "But you're the one who approached me today. Whatever higher ground you held is lost. So. What do you want?"

A muscle jumped in Morgan's jaw as he worked soundlessly for a second before admitting, begrudgingly, "I couldn't stop thinking about you after you left."

Sebastian grinned, triumphant, ignoring the fact that he'd hardly been able to stop thinking about Morgan, either. "Now what?"

"I'll accompany you today." Every word sounded like a tooth pulled. "I'll cooperate and help you convince your friend that you've won the bet. But if he's sceptical by the end of the afternoon, that's on you. I'm not interested in any prolonged games. And this is pretend only," Morgan stressed. "If you give any indication that you're actually trying to seduce me—"

"Not a problem," Sebastian said immediately. "It's all pretend, and there won't be a hint of genuine seduction happening."

"One afternoon to assuage my curiosity." Morgan's mouth twisted to one side. "As you said, you're the most interesting thing to happen to me in a long while."

Sebastian reached across the table to give Morgan's hand a quick squeeze. Morgan's hand was warm, broad and squared-off, and he didn't shy away from the touch, despite Sebastian's expectations.

"You won't regret this," Sebastian promised.

"I already am," Morgan returned with a sigh, withdrawing his hand to pull his wallet out and pay the bill. "When do we meet your friends?"

"About half an hour. Just enough time for you to get comfortable acting friendly towards me." With a wink, Sebastian rose from the table, eager to steer Morgan back outside and get to work.

It was perfect. He'd charmed Morgan well enough the previous day that the man had come back for him. Unwittingly, to be sure, but it was the end result that mattered, not the road taken. Though they still had both feet firmly planted within Morgan's comfort zone, surrounded by nice restaurants and well-to-do shops, Sebastian's world lingered in the peripheries, stealing glances at them from every dark alleyway and blind corner that they passed.

Sebastian would ease Morgan into things. If the afternoon went well then Sebastian would invite him along to his evening plans, but first, the man needed warming up.

It was as they strolled along King's Road, warily acclimatising to each other's company, that a display in a jewellery shop window stopped Sebastian dead in his tracks.

A diamond necklace winked coquettishly at him through the glass. But not just any diamond necklace. *The* diamond necklace: the largest, most expensive, and most famous piece of contemporary jewellery in all of twentieth-century London.

Sebastian had seen the Rose Diamond's likeness in paintings and magazines before, of course. He knew the exact shades of pink that comprised it, from the massive rock in the centre to the paler, smaller diamonds that made up the thick collar, just as he knew the number of individual diamonds, and the cut of every one. But such knowledge was a far cry from seeing it in person. Displayed with a care and pride befitting the Crown Jewels themselves, it sat front and centre in the jeweller's window on a mannequin bust of black velvet. The diamonds glimmered in the sunlight, throwing tiny rainbows around the display case. Sebastian stopped stock-still in front of it, momentarily breathless and wanting nothing more than to slip inside, lift it from that mannequin as one might lift a lover in a gentle embrace, and bask in its beauty.

He was in love.

Nothing he'd ever stolen—not all his steals combined—came close to the majesty and worth of the Rose Diamond necklace. In that moment, the Cheapside Hoard was nothing more than a hazy daydream, insubstantial and unimpressive.

"Look at that," he breathed. "You don't see that out and about every day."

"It's fit for royalty," Morgan said. "I can't imagine anyone wearing it casually. What's the price on that thing?"

Sebastian, who knew exactly what the necklace was worth and what they were asking for it—two slightly different numbers—merely shook his head. "A king's ransom, I'm sure."

"What on earth are they doing, leaving it out in plain sight like this? They're tempting fate."

"That jewel thief, you mean? He's been making headlines for months now. They must have some impressive security measures in place if they feel confident to leave it out."

"My cousin Alphonse finds the thief captivating. Originally, I was following the stories to keep him up-to-date, but now, I have to say, I'm following along out of my own interest. It's like something out of one of those pulp novels, the way this thief keeps getting away with it, and stealing a bigger prize every time. It makes for good entertainment."

"Who are you rooting for?" Sebastian asked, pressing close to Morgan's side. "The thief, or the detectives on the hunt?"

Morgan snorted. "The private investigator, Mr. Johnson? Didn't you hear he's off the case?"

"Is he?" Sebastian asked with great interest. He hadn't heard that, in fact, though he might have guessed it if he'd spared the man more than a passing thought. "What happened?"

"He suffered a very public fall from grace in August. It turned out he'd been blackmailing a woman. He was convinced she was secretly this famous author, and he was demanding money in exchange for his silence on the matter. I was there, actually, when it all came out. We were at a dinner party together and he was discredited in front of a great many people—we saw the very blackmail letters he'd written her—and then his wife denounced him and left him in front of everyone. It was a disaster. He fled town that very night rather than try to clear his name, which I suspect is proof enough that the accusations were true."

"My," Sebastian said, delighted by the news as much as the fact that that was the most Morgan had spoken since their reunion. "I noticed that his column in the paper had gone strangely silent of late, but I didn't think much of it. Do you think Scotland Yard as any hope of catching the jewel thief without him?"

"Not much. They've been largely useless so far, haven't they?"

"Largely," Sebastian agreed, returning his attention to the diamonds. "Can you imagine the lifestyle one must lead to enable such a purchase?"

"I'm sure it's loaned out more often than it's sold. Extravagant pieces like this usually are."

"That's a shame. Something like that deserves a proper home rather than being passed around like a common whore."

Morgan glanced at him, amused. "I'm afraid it's beyond my means. If you're looking for someone to buy you a piece like that, you need to aim higher than the likes of me."

"Aiming higher comes with its own unique problems," Sebastian informed him as they resumed their stroll.

Pastel shopfronts in sky blue, baby pink, butter yellow, and pale mint lined either side of the street, with stately red brick towering above. Motorcars grumbled past, and shoppers laden with bags of purchases or optimistic wallets thronged the sidewalks in fashionable coats and scarves. Morgan looked like he belonged among them; Sebastian looked like someone's shadow.

"Tell me, though: what would you do if you had that kind of money?"

"I don't know," Morgan said. "Probably nothing so drastically different than what I'm doing now."

"You're either very boring or incredibly content."

"Probably the former. I have enough money to live comfortably, and I don't have any great aspirations that leave me striving for more than that. I don't really know what I'd do with significantly more money than I already have. But that's rather an obnoxious answer."

"It rather is."

"I'm sure you have very specific and very detailed plans, if you were to come into a sudden windfall."

"Yes, and all of them absolutely dripping with hedonism."

"Good food, fine clothes, and a party every night of the week?" Morgan guessed.

"An expensive home in every country so I can go wherever I please, whenever I please."

"Where would you go first?"

"America," Sebastian said immediately. "I want to see New York. Have you ever been?"

"I haven't. I toured the continent fresh out of university, but I've never been west."

"You'll have to come with me once I'm filthy rich. It'll be my turn to treat you."

"So far I've treated you to a single meal. But alright. I'll consider joining you in New York, should you ever find yourself with more money than you know how to handle."

"I don't think there's any amount too great for me to handle," Sebastian said confidently.

"Building your fortune one twenty-pound bet at a time?"

"Something like that." Sebastian dropped his voice and stepped close enough to nudge Morgan, elbow to rib. "Really, though? There's no dream hanging just out of reach that money would make achievable?"

"Not really." Morgan's tone was light, his gaze wandering the shop signs. "You know they say money can't buy happiness."

Sebastian rolled his eyes, disgusted. "Something only ever said by those with more money than the general populace can imagine. Of course it can buy happiness. You're just not trying hard enough."

Morgan shrugged, seeming disinclined to argue. "Maybe so."

"Not money, then. What if you had no responsibilities holding you back? No one else's expectations? Is there nothing different you'd do then?"

"If I were in an entirely different situation, you mean."

"Something to think on. Speaking of building my fortune one bet a time, we should head back towards Sloane Square to meet Kitty and Adam. Are you ready to convince them we're shagging?"

"Who's Kitty?"

"Adam's girl. She's cagier than he is, so she'll be the one most suspicious of us. Although, considering I stayed with them last night, he'll have his own suspicions. They'll both take some convincing to pay up, so I hope you're ready to put on a good show."

"And then what happens?"

"You don't have to play along after that if you don't want to. Once I have my cash in hand, you're free to drop the charade if it's not doing anything for you."

Morgan didn't look uncomfortable so much as grimly resigned to the experience, which Sebastian was beginning to suspect had less to do with the particular scenario and more to do with who Morgan was as an adult: dour and put-upon on even the happiest of days. Sebastian chose not to take it personally.

"I'll be sure to make it worth your while," Sebastian said.

"Don't exert yourself on my account."

"Not at all. To the contrary, I find the prospect of broadening your horizons to be invigorating."

Morgan shot him a suspicious sideways glance, but didn't break his stride. "Not too invigorating, I hope. I'm open to a little excitement, but I don't want to get involved in anything that could land us in real trouble."

"Define 'real trouble.'"

"Anything involving the law."

"Not to be crass, but I didn't think you really had to worry about that sort of thing," Sebastian said. "Families like yours rarely do."

"I might be able to buy my way out of trouble, but it's still an inconvenience I have no desire to experience."

That might throw a wrench in Sebastian's hope of getting Morgan to accompany him out that evening.

"Say there's a sliding scale of activities open to you, with murder and treason at the far end, and something relatively harmless at the other. Like attending a certain kind of party, for example. Are you adamant on avoiding the scale altogether, or are you open to dipping a toe in the shallow end, if no one gets hurt?"

"A certain kind of party," Morgan repeated suspiciously.

"The kind where people might partake in certain substances or engage in certain relationships that might be discouraged in the wider world."

"The kind that tabloids like to write about, and that gets raided by the authorities on a regular basis."

"A slight exaggeration. You said you've been to Eden multiple times before."

"Until I decided the risks involved weren't worth whatever meagre entertainment it offered." A beat. "You've already made plans, I take it?"

"Only if you're amenable."

They walked in silence for a moment as Morgan seemed to weigh the pros and cons of returning to Eden.

"I suppose I'd be a hypocrite after a certain point," he finally said. "I've already committed a number of arrestable offenses in my life, and I'll likely commit them again."

"As far as Adam knows, you're in the process of committing one right now," Sebastian agreed. "Come to Eden with me tonight. Have a little fun. I promise it won't be raided."

"You can't promise that."

"Then I promise that if it is, I'll make sure you escape unscathed."

"You have practice in that regard, do you?"

"Absolutely. Look, here's Kitty and Adam. Say hello and remember, pretend you're fucking me."

Looping his arm through Morgan's, Sebastian raised his other hand in greeting to his friends as he dragged Morgan along to meet them.

CHAPTER FOUR

ON THE USE AND ENCHANTMENT
OF MAKEUP PRODUCTS

"Darling!" Kitty purred, swooping in to peck a kiss to either side of Sebastian's face like they'd been apart a week instead of a few hours. "Introduce me to your new friend," she requested, stepping back to look Morgan up and down with a glittering black gaze. "He looks to be a fine young gentleman."

"Morgan Hollyhock." Morgan offered his hand to Kitty first, and then to Adam, which was slightly awkward, as they were already acquainted. Adam gamely gave him a shake anyway. "Sebastian's told me about you."

"Charmed, delighted," Kitty said. "Did he invite you to tonight's party? Have you already had lunch? I thought we might get to shopping straight away."

"Let's do that," Sebastian agreed, leaning lightly into Morgan's side as if the man was going to object. He might need some convincing, but he seemed far too polite to dig his heels in now that they were in company.

Adam caught Morgan's eye with a smile. "Shopping," he said in that tone men often used when discussing the subject, although his was laced with fondness. "A necessary evil, isn't it? But what good is money if not for spoiling our friends?"

"And he does spoil me," Kitty confided, as if it were some great secret. "Tell me, Morgan, do you have a girl to spoil?"

"Not at the moment," Morgan said neutrally. "But Sebastian seems happy to help me keep it from burning a hole in my pocket."

Kitty laughed. "I think we're going to get along very well."

She caught him by the arm to sandwich herself between him and Adam, setting off on their expedition with a jaunty step. Sebastian stayed close to Morgan's other side with his hands in his pockets, walking close enough to bump their shoulders occasionally, but otherwise not touching.

"Where to first?" Adam asked. "Do you need a new dress for tonight?"

"No, I'll spare you that experience," Kitty replied. "Besides, it's so much more fun shopping for clothes with my girlfriends. What I want for tonight is some fresh makeup."

"Have you ever gone makeup shopping before?" Sebastian asked Morgan.

"I can truly say that I have not. My first horizon to be broadened, I suppose."

"The first of many."

"Here?" Morgan asked, nodding to a glossy department store as they walked past, only for Kitty to dismiss it out of hand.

"Too mainstream. I'm looking for more specialty items than what that place offers."

She led them off the main thoroughfare to a side street housing more boutique shops: independent sellers and artisans who sold to specific niches rather than trying to appeal to the broadest possible spectrum of customers. Her preferred merchant operated out of a little hole-in-the-wall shop with a dark brick face and a door of cerulean blue, squeezed in between a hat shop and a tailor's. The door had a silver bell on the other side that chimed whenever the door opened or shut, and it announced their presence with a cheerful tinkle as they filed inside one at a time, with Adam gallantly holding the door for each of them before entering last.

Sebastian knew the shop, though not as well as Kitty. The lighting was surprisingly dark considering the place sold beauty products. Lanterns hung from the ceiling, but they were dim and cast the room in an orange glow rather than lighting it up bright white as in a department store. The walls were lined with dark wood shelves, with mirrors hung in between at regular intervals. Smaller mirrors stood in round frames on the countertops, offering enhanced magnification for those who wished to scrutinise their face in greater detail, admiring themselves or picking out flaws, real or imagined. Glimpses of their little troupe flashed by at different angles as they moved into the centre of the room.

The smell of magic hung in the air like incense.

It was intoxicating without overpowering. Someone less finely attuned to magic might not notice it at all. If a single makeup product was separated from the rest, a pot of eyeshadow or a tube of lipstick, it would hardly give off any aura at all. But with so many items crowded together, the effect was staggering to someone like Sebastian, who was more sensitive to magic than most.

Rows of eyeshadow and blush stood atop the tables in their little pots. Shiny tubes of lipstick lined the shelves like bullet casings. Mascara, eyeliner, kohl, nail polish, lotions and soaps and oils—there was a product for every body part, each carefully crafted like potions in an alchemist's shop of old, infused with spells to grant the wearer special glamorous effects or health benefits.

Such special effects were Kitty's bread and butter, and they were about to become relevant to Sebastian as well. He'd dabbled in makeup before, but never to such an extent, nor as seriously as his partner. Kitty believed a disguise would come in useful for their job at the National Gallery, and if Sebastian could talk his latest squeeze into paying instead of shelling out himself, all the better. It was only a matter of convincing Morgan that he wanted to see Sebastian in makeup.

Sebastian doubted it would prove much of a challenge.

A glance at Morgan indicated that the other man lacked even a passing familiarity with the stuff. Unlike Adam, who showed polite interest in the subject without having any strong opinions, Morgan looked overwhelmed, if not intimidated by the shop's wares.

"See anything you like?" Sebastian asked.

"I didn't realise there were so many different versions of the same things."

"You would think that, until you're trying to find a very particular shade of something, and nothing is exactly right," Kitty said, nodding hello to the shopkeeper. "And of course, the cheaper products never have enough pigment to show up nicely on dark skin."

"You get what you pay for," Adam said. "But you know I'm happy to get you the very best."

"I know you are." She paused in her examination of the eyeshadow pots to give him a quick kiss. "And I have the very best already. But even the cheapest colours will show up on someone as pale as Sebastian."

"I hope you're not suggesting I'll settle for the cheapest," Sebastian said.

"Of course not. I'm just saying, you have a wider range of options."

Morgan did a double take. "This is for Sebastian?" he asked, lowering his voice.

"We're going to a costume party," Sebastian said. "I'll hardly be the only man in makeup tonight."

"I assume you'll be in black?" Kitty asked.

"As always, darling."

"You do look best in the dark and dramatic," she agreed. "I think we can keep it classic: dark red on the lips and black around the eyes. No need to branch into anything too experimental."

"As long as you don't get me that mascara we tried last time," Sebastian said. "It was so stiff, it felt wretched."

Morgan stared, obviously trying to picture him dolled up. Sebastian gave him a smile and a bat of the lashes, and Morgan quickly looked away. He busied himself with examining the contents of the nearest display, and Sebastian caught the moment in which he noticed the magic.

"Is everything in here enchanted?" he asked, sounding startled.

"It's a specialty shop," Kitty replied, blasé.

"Can I help you find anything specific?" the shopkeeper asked, weaving her way towards them between the tables. She was a middle-aged woman with her silvering hair twirled up in a simple knot, her own makeup elegant and unassuming, her style leaning French.

"We're looking for something fun," Kitty said brightly. "We're going to a masquerade party, so we want something that can disguise us well enough to trick our friends. What do you recommend for that?"

"It depends how long you want the trick to last. I have things that can weave an illusion that lasts a few seconds, or as long as they don't look at you directly. Anything stronger—a true glamour—gets more complicated."

"Show us the most complicated ones you've got," Kitty suggested with a dazzling smile.

Sebastian followed Kitty and the shopkeeper around the displays as the woman pointed out the products boasting the most powerful spells meant to alter one's appearance more drastically than any mundane makeup could hope to achieve. Wearing enough of the stuff, he and Kitty could make it so their own mothers couldn't recognise them. It was impressive, but they needed a guarantee that it would last a while, and, in a worst-case scenario, withstand scrutiny from a close distance.

Hence their trial run at the party that evening.

"I hadn't considered that makeup was such a specifically-crafted art," Morgan said. "Do women really go to such lengths to change their appearance?"

"This is mostly for performers of one kind or another," offered the shopkeeper. "Actresses, aging aristocrats desperate to hold onto the beauty of their youth, or plain-faced middle-class women trying to make themselves pretty enough to snare a rich husband. It's generally out of the working class' budget, though some women will save up for months or years in order to invest in something specific."

"I suppose if I were so uncouth as to ask if you were wearing any, you'd deny it," Morgan said to Kitty.

"I'm sure I don't know what you're talking about," Kitty replied airily. "My good looks are all natural."

"Right, of course they are."

She laughed, unoffended and easy. "They are, though. Here, look. What does this one do?"

"This eyeshadow will change the wearer's eye colour to match," the shopkeeper said. "This is the sample pot, if you'd like to try?"

"Let me try it on Sebastian."

Sebastian obediently closed his eyes as Kitty swept the brush over them, coating them in dark copper powder. When he opened them again, Morgan made an involuntary startled noise and took a step back.

"That's very drastic," Morgan said.

Sebastian turned to catch himself in the mirror. His irises were the colour of old pennies, vivid and ever-so-slightly unnatural. He rather liked the colour, actually—they lent him a predatory air he thought was quite alluring—but they were no good for blending into a crowd.

"If you met anyone with eyes like that outside of a costume party, you'd immediately suspect them of altering their looks," Kitty said. "There's nothing subtle about it."

"No," Morgan agreed, still staring at Sebastian, seemingly captivated. "No, the effect is glaringly obvious."

"Too memorable," Sebastian reluctantly agreed.

"There are other, more realistic colours," the shopkeeper said, "if you want to use them in everyday life as opposed to a party trick. And there's no shortage of other tools to play with. Kohl that alters the shape of one's eyes, lipstick that makes every spoken word sound terribly fascinating, no matter how trite, and blush that makes one's skin irresistible to the touch."

It was tools and tricks like those that Kitty and Sebastian intended to use to make good their getaway after their big heist. Not so much making themselves irresistible, but rather, the opposite: unrecognisable or unseen.

"Isn't it dishonest, though?" Morgan asked. "Love spells were outlawed for good reason, after all."

"It's a grey area," the shopkeeper said delicately. "Regulations have been suggested, but so far they've all been shot down in their infancy."

"I don't think adding a little glamour to your makeup is on quite the same level as enchanting someone to fall in love with you," Sebastian said with a laugh. "Being tricked into thinking a girl is prettier than she really is isn't exactly overriding anyone's consent."

"Has it ever been used for more nefarious purposes?" Morgan asked doubtfully. "Trying to trap a richer or handsomer husband is one thing, but what about more illegal acts? Actual disguises, and the like?"

"Oh, certainly!" Kitty said enthusiastically, as if she and Sebastian weren't conspiring to use it for exactly that. "There are countless stories of spies using such glamours to alter their looks—as recently as the Great War, but all through history, really. It's fascinating stuff. But these days, it's in much more demand for actresses than espionage."

The shopkeeper nodded along.

"Do you never wonder if she's pulling one over on you?" Morgan asked Adam.

Adam gave an easy shrug. "I like how she looks, but I don't love her for her face alone."

Kitty rolled her eyes, but she was smiling. "Easy for you to say that now, with me looking like this. What if I washed my face one night and came to bed looking like an old hag?"

"This is a test," Adam informed Morgan. To Kitty, he said seriously, "I would cherish you regardless of haggishness, and perhaps offer you some moisturising creams. Or a pumice stone."

"In any case," Sebastian said. "I'm not looking for makeup to transform me into a beautiful young trophy wife. I like these ones." He collected a handful of what he deemed the most useful products, ignoring the price. "Thoughts?" he asked Kitty.

"Those should do nicely."

"How do you know so much about makeup?" Morgan asked as the shopkeeper rang them up, his tone somewhere between judgement and honest curiosity.

"Kitty has been enormously influential, of course, but mostly I know about makeup the same way anyone else does. Observation only gets you so far. Trial and error and hands-on experience gets you the rest of the way."

"You do this recreationally," Morgan ventured.

"Certainly, on rare occasion. Am I the first man you've met who's dabbled in it?"

"The first that I know of, anyway. We move in different circles. I might know of Eden—who doesn't?—but it doesn't mean I'm part of that culture."

"That's a shame," said Sebastian. "I think you'd look fetching with a light gold shimmer over your eyes."

"No, thank you. I'll leave such looks to braver men than I."

Morgan raised an eyebrow when the shopkeeper read him his total, but didn't otherwise hesitate before paying. As he handed over his bill fold and the shopkeeper nestled the items into a discreet paper bag, Adam drew Sebastian away a pace and murmured, "I thought he threw you out when you went to see him yesterday?"

"You know I don't give up a challenge that easily," Sebastian returned.

"You said you weren't even all that interested in him."

"That was before you dared me to seduce him. Besides, he's clearly interested in me, and that's more important."

"Clearly."

As Morgan collected his scant change, Kitty gave Sebastian a pleased little nudge in the ribs with her elbow, and Sebastian preened for Adam, who shook his head with a smile, ruefully conceding that Sebastian had indeed won the bet. The money would change hands as soon as Morgan was out of sight.

Sebastian wasn't easily given to trust, but Adam was easy with his money, and wouldn't go back on a wager over something so paltry to him as twenty measly pounds, never mind that such an amount could be life-changing to someone like Sebastian.

Not that Sebastian was in any great hurry to get rid of Morgan and wrap things up. Just the opposite, in fact. He was increasingly confident that Morgan could be talked around to offering food and board, and paying his way was even better, but more than that, Sebastian enjoyed teasing the man and needling reactions out of him. Given enough time, he could chip away at Morgan's armour until finally the whole shell fell away to reveal the man's vulnerabilities beneath. He didn't remember Morgan being so boarded up as a boy, but then, twenty-one years was a long time. God knows Sebastian had changed, too.

And until Sebastian wore him down, Morgan was very attractive when he was annoyed.

Exiting the shop's dim mood lighting to return to daylight was jarring, and Sebastian blinked as his eyes adjusted. Daylight had consistently seemed too bright to him since his release from Blackwood. He ought to invest in a pair of sunglasses. They were stylish, and would add to his air of mystery. Perhaps Morgan could be convinced to buy him some.

As the group returned to King's Road to continue their stroll, window-shopping and admiring the venues, a young man called out to Adam from a café patio. When Adam and Kitty pulled away to say hello, Sebastian took Morgan by the arm and drew him in the other direction.

"They'll be tied up for a good quarter hour at least," Sebastian told him. "Adam's a talker, and Kitty's even worse. Let's kill the time elsewhere."

"He's not part of your plan to broaden my horizons?"

"Most of Adam's friends already move in your social group. You know perfectly well there's nothing interesting about them. Let's have a look in here." He pointed to a quaint little bookshop up ahead. "You're a reader, aren't you? Your place is full of books."

"I didn't think a bookshop would be your idea of an exciting time."

"It depends what sorts of books they're selling."

The bookshop was more generously lit than the makeup shop, with the sun slanting in through yellowed windows, dust motes drifting in the beams. It was a cosy place, filled to the brim with books, which lined every inch of shelf space and lay stacked high on tables. Sebastian wasn't much interested in books, but he knew the value of a rare tome or first edition. Such things weren't his usual fare, but he liked to consider himself a well-rounded criminal, and he knew a thing or two about a thing or two, including the rare book trade. It was unlikely he would chance upon something worth any real money, but he couldn't resist taking a look just in case. Wherever he went, it was second nature to keep an eye peeled for anything of value, no matter how unlikely the circumstance.

It only took a moment of browsing to realise that what the shop might lack in monetary value, it made up for in rare books of another kind. Tucked away at the back around a corner was a carefully curated selection of erotica and pornography, graphic enough to make one stop and stare.

He resisted the urge to beeline straight to it. Instead, he casually made for the bookshelf blocking that section from the rest of the shop, which housed row after row of pulp novels. Morgan followed after him, dutifully looking over Sebastian's shoulder to read the titles.

"I see you've found the romances," Morgan said. "I must say, you don't strike me as much of a romantic."

"Nor do you, but you clearly recognise the books. Have you read them?"

"No, but apparently, I've met the author."

"You know the mysterious M. Hayes?" Sebastian pulled a novel from its shelf, thumbing through the flimsy pages.

"Met," Morgan corrected, "not know. The woman I mentioned who was being blackmailed by that private investigator, Mr. Johnson—he insisted she was behind M. Hayes' secret identity. This all came out at my aunt's dinner party in August, as I said. The woman denied everything, of course, which doesn't mean much on its own, except that Jules Coxley—that local artist, the erotic painter, you know— He stood up and claimed to be the actual writer behind the name."

"That sounds like a very eventful dinner party."

"More so than usual. In any case, I haven't read the books, but I've seen Coxley's art, and if his writing is half as sexual, I should hesitate to even open the first page."

"Colour me intrigued. I've seen his art too, though I haven't had the chance to study it. But M. Hayes' books aren't erotica. There's no shortage of sexually-charged scenes, but they're pulpy adventure romances, at heart." Returning the book to its shelf, Sebastian moved around the corner. "The proper erotica is over here."

"You don't need to show me—"

He paused in the process of tipping one book forward off its shelf. "No?"

"I'm neither a curious schoolboy nor a blushing virgin waiting to be impressed."

"You don't think erotica has any audience outside those two categories?"

"I'm sure it does, but I'm equally sure that I am not its target."

"That depends on the specific subject matter, doesn't it? I'm of the belief that there's the perfect work of erotica for everyone, somewhere in the world."

"The chances of finding mine in this particular shop are rather slim."

"Are your tastes so exotic? That might explain a thing or two. Such as why you didn't take me up when I offered—"

Morgan pointedly cleared his throat, one eyebrow raised as he tipped his head to the front of the shop where the bookseller bustled about the tables.

"Apologies," Sebastian said smoothly. "Of course, I forgot you're an artist. Do you prefer the visual to the written word? Because they have those, as well."

"I prefer to keep my fantasies within the confines of my own head, thank you."

Sebastian had never had a single fantasy he hadn't wanted to enact. Most of them involved the theft of priceless jewellery, but sex came a close second.

He shook his head. "What a waste."

"Let's see if Adam and Kitty are done by now," Morgan suggested pointedly.

As Morgan returned to the front of the shop, Sebastian gave the shelf a quick scan, hunting out the dirtiest title. Before Morgan could miss him, he slipped a thin book from the shelf and tucked it inside his coat, then followed him out with a self-satisfied grin at the promise of future mischief.

CHAPTER FIVE

IN WHICH A PARTY IS ATTENDED AND MAGIC IS TESTED

Most makeup was designed to attract attention and transfix its audience. Kitty and Sebastian were going to considerable effort to do just the opposite. They had a blush that would convince the viewer's gaze to slide right over one's face. Kohl that made it difficult to look one in the eye. Eyeshadow to lend a nebulous appearance, where the eye's shape and colour shifted between one blink and the next. Lipstick that made it easy to forget the words those lips spoke, like dialogue in a dream.

Some such makeup, they bought from specialty sellers, like the boutique they'd visited earlier that afternoon. Most, however, had required more work on their part, twisting the products from their original purpose of attracting attention, until they could be convinced to do just the opposite.

They intended to wear the makeup to disguise themselves during their robbery of the National Gallery's Cheapside Hoard exhibit, which was their highest-profile heist to date. But first, Kitty insisted those disguises be tested in the most stressful environment available: a party at Eden.

"Eden puts *too* much stress on the illusions," Sebastian argued.

The four of them were back at Adam's. Kitty and Sebastian were sequestered in the powder room where they stashed their rarest and most powerfully-enchanted makeup away from prying eyes, examining each and every element as they decided what most needed testing.

"You can't resist being the centre of attention," he continued. "You'll be wearing all this fancy makeup and fighting it every inch of the way in order to flirt and dance with everyone who so much as glances in your direction. We can't get a good read on the stuff like that. It's a waste of supply and effort."

"As if you're any less an attention whore." Kitty rolled her eyes. "We need to know the limits we're working with. Or do you not want to wear any makeup tonight at all?"

"Morgan expects me to, and I'd hate to disappoint him."

Kitty leaned against the counter, looking at Sebastian with bright eyes. "Do you think he's into that?"

"I think he's into a lot more than he realises. He just needs a little nudge in the right direction."

"I have to say, I never expected you to win Adam's bet so easily."

"You of so little faith."

"I never doubted your abilities, darling. But you hadn't heard of Morgan's reputation! Truly, he seemed one of the least scandalous, most serious men in all of London. As far as anyone's been able to tell, he's lived an entirely sexless existence. Some theorised that he wasn't interested in anyone at all—not just disinterested in dating or marriage, mind you, but in sex altogether. Others thought that perhaps he'd taken a vow of celibacy to live as a monk. I really can't exaggerate how incredibly boring he seemed before you walked in and glued yourself to his side."

"I don't know what to tell you," Sebastian said with an easy shrug. "He seems a perfectly normal man to me. A little repressed, certainly, but no more so than his peers."

"Don't beat around the bush." She pressed close, digging an insistent finger into his ribs. "You *have* worked your way into his bed, haven't you? What's he like?"

"It's been less than thirty hours since I met him!"

"I've seen what you can accomplish in a fraction of that time."

"A gentleman doesn't kiss and tell."

"You're not a gentleman. You're a thief, a con artist, and a convict, and you've always told me everything before. Has he been living a secret double life this whole time, hiding his appetites from society, or is he a blushing virgin you had to deflower?"

"Neither," Sebastian said with a laugh, definitely not thinking about deflowering anyone. "He just likes his privacy, and, seeing as he's my meal ticket these days, I'm going to respect that."

Kitty pouted and socked him lightly on the shoulder. "Spoilsport. You will tell me everything about him once the game is up, though, won't you?"

"Of course I will, darling," he promised, pressing a quick kiss to her temple, over her slicked-down curls. "I always do. Now, shall we go out and give him a little show?"

In the living room, Sebastian took a seat in the big wingback, a handheld mirror in his grasp, and Kitty settled herself on his lap, straddling him with her brush in one hand, the other balancing her makeup tray against his shoulder.

"Do you want to learn how to do it?" she asked Morgan.

"I'm not sure it would come in especially useful," Morgan replied, though he watched with great interest. "Is there a reason you're doing Sebastian's makeup instead of Adam's? Sebastian implied he knows how to do it perfectly well himself."

"Would you rather be the one doing it?" Sebastian asked, tipping his head back to glance teasingly at Morgan.

Morgan huffed in reply.

"I can do my own," Sebastian agreed, facing Kitty once more, "but Kitty has so much more practice at it, and I want to look my best tonight."

"I thought it was a masquerade party. How much of your face are people actually going to see?"

"You never know when the mask might come off. I like to be prepared for any situation."

Kitty had an excellent eye for makeup, and, equally important, she knew Sebastian's style. She brushed his eyelids with powder so dark it looked like charcoal that glittered when the light hit it, like he was wearing gunpowder. She traced his waterlines with kohl so vivid and black it resembled the greasepaint worn by stage actors, and his lashes, she coated with mascara that would make him envy of any silent film star. The faintest touch of blush adorned his cheeks, lifting him out of that vampiric pallor to something with a little more life; though, combined with his striking eye makeup, it lent him an aura of feverish danger rather than rosy-cheeked health. His lips, she painted in glossy crimson so dark it was plummy, as predatory as it was inviting. He watched his reflection transform in the little mirror he held over Kitty's shoulder, catching glimpses of himself every moment or two, whenever he was allowed to open his eyes.

He loved how he looked in makeup. Besides the simple aesthetic, he enjoyed the transgression of it, and how it transformed him into something neither this nor that. The point wasn't to disguise himself as a woman, nor to mock those individuals who wore their sex in opposition to that prescribed by society. Sebastian's makeup served to highlight the cut of his cheekbones and the angle of his jaw, highlighting his masculinity at the same time it introduced a new-found femininity to his looks. It didn't make him look delicate or laughable. Instead, it served the same role as a poisonous butterfly's brightly-painted wings: warning of something deadly, but whose warning was lost to those who didn't know how to read it.

"How's that?" Kitty asked, leaning back with her wrists crossed behind Sebastian's neck. "Does it suit?"

Sebastian gave himself a final look-over in the mirror. "Perfectly serviceable," he decided.

"This doesn't attract the wrong sort of attention?" Morgan asked.

"It's attracting *your* attention, so I think it's doing just what I want."

"As long as your priorities are in order," Morgan said dryly.

Kitty twirled her makeup brush between her fingers. "Last chance to wear some yourself." They would never waste their enchanted makeup on him, but they had no shortage of the mundane stuff, and Sebastian was devilishly curious to see Morgan in it. "Sebastian would be more than happy to do it for you."

"Maybe another time." It was an obvious brush-off, albeit a polite one.

Sebastian didn't push him, though in that moment, there was nothing he'd rather do than find out what colours suited Morgan, up close and personal. He had to firmly push that thought out of reach, startled by its suddenness and intensity. It was enough that Morgan had agreed to accompany him to Eden.

The only reason Eden wasn't Sebastian's favourite club was because he knew too many of the people frequenting it. In another life, one in which he didn't occupy himself by taking advantage of people, he might have enjoyed it on a more regular basis. Everything about it seemed designed to appeal to him: glitz, glamour, and that certain kind of debauchery that made its home in the youths of the upper class who had more time and money than sense, and who had never experienced a single consequence for their actions, and thus lived fearlessly.

The party that night had everyone dolled up in glitter and makeup and flimsy little masks that did nothing to hide their identities from the handful of press that liked to mill around outside sniffing for a scandal. Sebastian, Kitty, Morgan, and Adam waltzed in arm in arm with papier-mâché masks perched on their noses and makeup ringing their eyes like they were walking onto the set of some glamorous film shoot.

Kitty looked luxurious on Adam's arm, as always, with an enormous feather wrap flouncing in time with her steps, her heels clicking smartly over the floor and commanding the attention of everyone in the club. Feathers to match the ones on her shoulders sprang from her headband, a little crown of jewels dangling to the middle of her forehead, flashing every time they caught the light. Adam was dressed beautifully in a smart tuxedo, though he'd foregone any of the flashier statement pieces favoured by his better half.

Sebastian, on the other hand, had raided Kitty's room for accessories, and was draped in strings of pearls over his own borrowed tux. Dressed all in black, with his dark hair slicked back and his eyes glittering from behind his mask, he knew he looked like the kind of bad idea that was irresistible to a certain kind of person.

Morgan was in a cream-coloured suit, the only one of their entourage not in black, though he had allowed Sebastian to wrap a string of glass beads around his collar in place of a tie in order to give his look a little added glimmer. His ashy hair was parted smartly, though it was only visible from the back, as he wore a great silvery mask in the shape of butterfly wings to obscure his face. It caught the light like a mirror and Sebastian was hard-pressed to look away.

"You look marvellous, darling," Kitty murmured as she and Sebastian removed their own masks, she pinning hers to the back of her head, and Sebastian letting his hang down his back between his shoulders.

"Imagine how much better I'd look in diamonds instead of pearls."

"You should convince your new beau to buy you some."

"Since when do we have to *buy* what we want?"

"Let's just see how our makeup holds up tonight, shall we?" she said with a wink.

Eden's architecture was strikingly modern: an enormous, wide open room supported by sharp pillars decorated with lines of gold, a sweeping bar with an entire wall of glittering bottles behind it, and a great set of white stairs at either end of the room leading up to a second-floor balcony overlooking the first. Hanging plants and trailing vines gave the place its name, though Sebastian doubted the original garden of Eden had quite as much alcohol or live music. What they did have in common was an abundance of temptation and sinners eager to revel in it.

Morgan, surprisingly, didn't seem particularly uncomfortable in the club. He still held himself separate from the other patrons, his manner still aloof, but Sebastian suspected he was putting on a front. Eden was all about the hedonism and debauchery of the post-war twentieth century, and Morgan was altogether too repressed to fit in with such a crowd. Still, it pleased Sebastian to see him try. There was great entertainment in watching him like a fish out of water. Not that Sebastian was given to cruelty, but he'd take a laugh where he could find one.

Youthful bodies swirled across the floor in spangled costumes of black and gold, glasses of champagne and bright cocktails in their hands, and little tins of pills or powders being passed around to snort or swallow. It was decadent; it was dangerous. Finding a mark to con or rob in a place like Eden was like catching fish in a barrel. Half the fish were literally begging him to hook them. It felt like home.

"The masks don't do much to disguise anyone, do they?" Morgan observed, his hands in his pockets as he looked around the dance floor.

Some people hadn't bothered with masks at all, or, like Kitty and Sebastian, had discarded them as soon as they were inside. Morgan kept his own perched securely on his face like its silvery wings could protect him from the world.

"They're more about providing plausible deniability," Sebastian replied.

"You're not afraid of showing your face in a place like this?"

"Why should I be?"

"Are you afraid of anything?" Morgan only sounded like he was half joking.

"You should buy me a drink," Sebastian said, changing the subject, because he certainly wasn't going to answer *that* honestly.

Morgan accepted his demand like he'd been expecting it, and followed Sebastian amiably to the bar. Sebastian had never had trouble getting served before, so it was a new experience when the bartender's eyes repeatedly slid over him like he was no more than a shadow. When Sebastian leaned in and raised a hand, the bartender's gaze landed on him, brow furrowed, but his attention quickly slipped sideways the instant Morgan stepped up.

Interesting, and promising.

He let Morgan order for both of them—whiskey on ice, nice and simple, nothing like the extravagant cocktails Kitty would be coaxing out of Adam. The bartender seemed relieved to move on and let Sebastian's presence slip from his mind entirely.

"Is it doing what it's supposed to do?" Morgan asked as they turned to face the dance floor, sipping their drinks. "I have no problem noticing you, though."

"I can tell," Sebastian purred.

Morgan grumbled something unintelligible into his drink, and Sebastian elbowed him lightly.

"You don't have to hide it. We're supposed to be showing off for Adam and Kitty anyway, and no one will look twice at two men making eyes at each other in here. You've got your mask, and I've got my makeup. No one can recognise us."

"Your friends already seem convinced that you've won your bet fair and square. There's no need for us to play it up any more than we already have."

"I promised to make your life more interesting. That's going to be difficult if you insist on staying so rigid."

"I'm here, aren't I?" Morgan retorted. "Maybe this is enough interest for me today."

Kitty had flitted off the instant they set foot inside, pulling Adam along in her wake as she made her rounds. She and Sebastian had agreed to each take a different role that evening. She would be pushing her makeup's enchantment to its limits, seeing just how much direct attention it could deflect, while Sebastian waited on the sidelines to test how invisible he could make himself. He was curious to see how it would go. Normally, the purpose of such a party was to draw as much attention to oneself as possible, and normally, he lapped it up, becoming whomever his companions most wanted him to be. To make himself a wallflower in a place like Eden felt counterintuitive.

Luckily, Morgan showed no inclination to stray from Sebastian's side, so he'd have at least a little company, though it was a fraction of what he was used to.

Morgan seemed immune to the effects of Sebastian's makeup. Whether that was because he'd witnessed its application, because he'd been told beforehand what it was meant to achieve, or because he was so focused on Sebastian and suspicious of his motives to begin with, Sebastian couldn't be sure. In any case, as long as Morgan wasn't present to witness any future heists, his immunity shouldn't prove an issue.

"That's Jules Coxley," Morgan said, nodding to a figure across the room. "The artist we talked about earlier."

"Do you want to go see him?"

"Aren't we supposed to be pretending we don't know anyone?"

"Not at all. Parties are for socialising. No one inside needs to hide from each other; it's the press and the authorities sticking their noses in where they don't belong that we want to avoid."

"The press and authorities never infiltrate the place?"

"Sometimes," Sebastian allowed. "But unless you think Jules Coxley is an undercover agent, we don't have much to worry about."

Taking Morgan by the arm, Sebastian led him to the artist, who was a short, dark-clad man with wild brown hair curling around his goblin mask. He was mid-conversation, gesturing animatedly with a drink in hand to his companion, who was a tall, brown-skinned woman in a mask of rhinestones and an aggressively shiny silver dress. The two paused their conversation at Sebastian and Morgan's approach.

"Coxley? Morgan Hollyhock," Morgan introduced himself. "We met at my aunt's garden party in August."

"I'll take your word for it," Coxley said, giving him a good looking-over and apparently coming up blank. He offered Morgan a friendly, impersonal handshake. "There was a lot going on that night."

"There was indeed. It kept me from telling you how much I admired your art."

"Thank you." Coxley was visibly pleased by the compliment, though in a way that suggested he had no shortage of vocal admirers.

"My friend Sebastian here is an art enthusiast," Morgan went on. "He wanted to meet you."

"My pleasure," Coxley said, extending his hand.

As Sebastian accepted it, Coxley's gaze skimmed Sebastian's face, wandering over his features before drifting back to Morgan like Sebastian was no more than a shimmering mirage. Sebastian kept a polite smile fixed in place, though he didn't say a word, curious as to how quickly the man might forget his existence if he didn't do anything to make himself memorable.

"Let me introduce my friend," Coxley said to Morgan. "You might remember Deepa from the garden party as well."

The rhinestone-clad woman shook Morgan's hand, flashing a smile before turning to Sebastian. Surprised by her attention when he'd done nothing to warrant it, he recovered quickly and brushed a kiss over her proffered knuckles, her fingers flashing with rings. When they caught each other's gaze, the spark of direct eye contact was as electric as it was unsettling after being so thoroughly ignored thus far.

"Deepa was one of my models, though she's since found remarkable success as a socialite independent from her modelling career. I only wish I could take credit for it."

"He flatters me," Deepa said, her voice low and amused and musical, an Indian accent curling around her words. "I'm sure I would never have made it so far without him."

Sebastian studied her, staring more openly than he would ever get away with in polite daytime society. A sense of recognition itched in the back of his mind. He was sure they'd never met before—he was too good with people to forget a face—but he felt a kinship with her, and from the way she kept stealing glances at him, she felt the same. Carefully, he sent a little tendril of magic whispering towards her, keeping it light so as not to attract attention. As soon as it reached her, he whipped it back as her gaze snapped to his, dark and interested.

She was cloaked in magic even more heavily than he was. Her makeup was laced with as many enchantments as his own, but designed to attract and seduce instead of deflect. Even more impressively, similar magic was woven through every seam of her dress, pulling men and women into orbit like she was the sun itself.

He gave her a charming smile, letting a little sharpness show through. It was hardly a surprise that he was only one of several con artists frequenting Eden. Like Morgan, she was on high alert, attuned to her surroundings and, having ulterior motives herself, was naturally suspicious of everyone around her. She returned his smile with a little dip of her head, one predator recognising another.

"Morgan here spoke so highly of your work, I had to go to the trouble of tracking you down," Sebastian said to Coxley, easing into the conversation.

Coxley blinked at him, visibly struggling to shift his attention. It was as if Sebastian was speaking to him through a dreamlike veil, while the others stood firmly rooted in the waking world. Sebastian was impressed.

"My tastes run more to the Old Masters, personally," Sebastian continued, "but you certainly have an eye for the finer things in life, don't you?"

"I'm sure I can't compare to Rembrandt and the like, but I do strive to entertain. Have you seen my show at the National Gallery? I'm being overshadowed by the Cheapside jewels now, but so it goes."

"We'll have to stop in and take a look." Sebastian had in fact glimpsed Coxley's show on his most recent trip to the museum, but he'd been there on illicit business and hadn't lingered. "Morgan is an artist," he added.

Morgan elbowed him, subtle but hard.

"Are you?" Coxley asked, clear-eyed once more as he rounded on Morgan.

"It's a hobby," Morgan said, smiling through gritted teeth. "Really, nothing very good or very serious."

"He's far too modest," Sebastian said, giving Morgan a little push towards Coxley. "I'm no artist myself, so I can hardly hold a decent conversation with him about it. You two should talk shop."

"What kind of art do you do?" Coxley asked.

As soon as he was assured they were locked in mutual conversation, Sebastian beamed to Deepa's side. "You're wearing a very impressive collection of spells," he murmured, his hands clasped before him as he leaned in to whisper in her ear.

"Thank you. You should see me when I'm being serious about them."

"Oh, this is a casual look for you?"

"I could ask you the same thing. Most people don't come to Eden to be overlooked."

"This is just a bit of fun."

She hummed, sounding amused but unconvinced. "Your friend seems out of his depth," she observed.

"With me, or at the club?"

"Both. He really doesn't know what he's getting into, does he?"

"I'm sure I don't know what you mean," he said lightly. "Perhaps you're confusing me with someone else."

"I think you and I have quite a bit in common."

"I'm flattered," he said with a smile, "but I really don't know what you mean."

"No?" She turned the full strength of her smile on him; it was like looking into the jaws of a hungry lioness. He got the impression that she was sizing him up. "Come, let's talk somewhere private. I have a question for you."

CHAPTER SIX

A DRINK, A DANCE,
AND A CRIMINAL PROPOSITION
(NOT IN THAT ORDER)

Taking him by the arm, Deepa led Sebastian to the toilets, where a cluster of glittering youths crowded around the sinks, doing lines of what Sebastian assumed was cocaine. He didn't care for the stuff, personally; it made him jittery, and Kitty said his personality was intolerable on it. He believed her. He sometimes found himself intolerable even when he was perfectly sober.

Backing Sebastian into one of the stalls, each one of which had its own personal chandelier hanging above it, Deepa shut the door behind them both.

"It must be a terribly important question to justify this level of secrecy," Sebastian commented, tucking his elbows close to his body to avoid knocking against the walls.

"Forgive my impudence," Deepa said, "but you look like a man who knows a thing or two about thievery."

"Whatever do you mean?" Sebastian asked, laying it on thick.

Deepa looked like she wanted to roll her eyes, but had long since trained herself to suppress the urge. "Call it intuition. My dress has an extraordinary number of good-luck charms sewn into the beading, and ever since I started wearing it, my guesses tend to be accurate. And I think that out of everyone present tonight, you might be the one best suited to help me with a little problem I have."

"And what's that?" Sebastian asked, feigning disinterest. "Not that I'm saying you're right," he added. "This isn't an admission of anything. Just out of curiosity, you know."

"I'm looking for a rare plant."

He laughed and relaxed. "Then I'm afraid you've misread me after all. I have a respectable range of skills, but botany is not my forte."

"A rare magical plant," she continued, watching him closely, "kept under lock and key as if it were made of the rarest gemstones, for all the effort its keepers put into preventing anyone from laying a hand on it."

His curiosity piqued despite his best intentions.

"Between your skill at thievery and your handle on magic, I should think you up for the task."

"What plant, and why is it so closely guarded?"

"*Osculum purpurea*. Commonly known as Oberon's Kiss."

Sebastian let out a long whistle, his eyebrows raised. Oberon's Kiss was one plant he did in fact know: a magical specimen once used in love potions, now deeply illegal, and the plant's trafficking highly regulated.

"That's one way to catch yourself an endlessly loyal patron."

"I don't need a love potion to bewitch a man body and soul. I mean to sell the plant to a collector whom I know for a fact would give her right arm for such a specimen."

"To what end? I hate to bring ethics into it, but most people who talk about wanting an Oberon's Kiss want it for nefarious purposes."

"She doesn't. Plant-keeping is a personal hobby of hers."

"Oh, in that case," Sebastian said sarcastically.

"I'll pay you two hundred pounds to retrieve it for me."

Two hundred pounds was mouth-wateringly enticing.

"I want a cut of the sale on top of your initial offer," he returned immediately. "Ten percent."

"Five."

"Too low."

"Five, and I'll give you something even better than money."

He scoffed. "There's no such thing."

Leaning close in the little toilet stall, her voice dark and full of promise, Deepa said, "Five percent, and I'll tell you how to get your hands on the Rose Diamond necklace."

Sebastian's heart skipped a beat, his mouth going desert-dry between one breath and the next. "How would you know anything about that?"

"I'm attached to the arms of a great many rich and important men. I have access to places of which you can only dream. And I know what security they're using to guard that necklace. It's very impressive. What is that information worth to you?"

"It's research I can do myself," Sebastian countered, but his whole body was strung tight with wanting.

"It's research you wouldn't have to do. I can save you all that time and effort in exchange for this favour."

"Plus the two hundred pounds," Sebastian said. "Plus the five percent."

Deepa extended one hand, the stones in her rings glinting in the light of the chandeliers. "Is that a deal?"

"You'll get your plant," Sebastian promised, taking her hand to press another kiss to her knuckles. She smelled like honey and vanilla.

"Then you'll get the secrets of the Rose Diamond. It was a pleasure to meet you, Sebastian. Meet me at the Victoria Gate entrance to Kew Gardens on Monday at three in the afternoon, and let's discuss this in greater detail, yes?"

"It's at Kew?"

"Talk later," she advised.

"In that case, I'll retrieve my friend and leave you to your evening." Swinging the stall door open, he held it for her as she glittered out, acting every inch the gentleman he wasn't. "Until next time."

Morgan had returned to his place by the bar, where he was making a sport of rebuffing as many people as possible through the iciness of his gaze alone. Sebastian slunk up to him from the side, avoiding his direct line of sight to test whether Morgan's immunity to his makeup had worn off at all after a few minutes apart.

Morgan didn't look all that different compared to Sebastian's impression of him at The Stag's Head. He was dressed up fancier, to be sure, with glitter on his mask and draped around his collar, but he still held himself aloft from his surroundings, refusing to mingle with the crowds or even acknowledge the possibility that enjoyment could be found in such a place.

Sebastian knew better now than to write him off as a lost cause. Morgan might be made of ice, but Sebastian had already made progress in chipping away at him. There was something delicious about teasing someone who wanted things, yet had so much bitter self-control. It provided satisfaction Sebastian had never found when tempting commonplace marks.

He inched closer until he was but an arm's length away from Morgan. Leaning one hip against the bar, he made his pose effortlessly inviting and his gaze dark and heavy, promising all sorts of wicked things, plum-red lips curved in a knowing, self-satisfied smile. But the gunpowder-coloured eyeshadow kept people from meeting his gaze, and the blush dusting his cheekbones made his face strangely unmemorable to anyone who looked at him. He was simultaneously the most striking figure in the club, and the most forgettable. He could do anything, and no one would have the wherewithal to point the finger at him after. The sense of power was incredible.

Morgan shifted, turning in Sebastian's direction to survey that half of the club. They stood face to face, and at first, Morgan looked through him without recognition, even blanker than their first meeting at The Stag's Head. A stab of disappointment caught Sebastian in the chest like a knife before Morgan blinked, as if waking from a daydream, and his gaze sharpened as he met Sebastian's eye.

Sebastian's heart leapt, thrilled. Morgan was still largely immune, then. It was of vital importance that they understood the enchantments' limits. But in that second, as a sardonic smile lurked in the corner of Morgan's mouth below his mask, Sebastian wasn't thinking about makeup or enchantments or heists at all.

"I was wondering where you had disappeared to," Morgan said. "I thought it would have been easier to pick you out of the crowd, but you blended right in."

Interesting. "Did you miss me?"

"I took the opportunity for a moment's peace and quiet, both of which I suspect will be in short supply now that you're back."

"You're not wrong. Dance with me?"

"I'm not much of a dancer," Morgan demurred.

"It doesn't have to be complicated. Just put your hands on me and follow my lead."

"Let me get you another drink, instead," Morgan bargained.

"No one's going to be judging you," Sebastian said with a laugh, taking Morgan by the wrist and insinuating himself right up against Morgan's front. Chest to chest, Morgan was solid and warm, and Sebastian wanted to lean into him and find out how much of his weight Morgan could take. "It'll give you the chance to get a better look at me close-up," he murmured, gently bullying Morgan onto the dance floor. "I know you want that."

Morgan slotted himself against Sebastian and took up the dance with less reluctance than anticipated, his hands resting easy on Sebastian's waist.

"It's a vast improvement over the last time I saw you with makeup," he agreed.

Sebastian almost missed a step, catching himself just in time. "What? When was that?"

"You were ten. You got into my mother's makeup just to prove you could. Do you not remember?"

He only remembered glimpses of that summer before it had all been washed away by the wretchedness that followed. He remembered Morgan: the brightness of his smile, rare as it was, the fun of luring him away from his endless studies, his quietly steadfast generosity. But he remembered precious few of their actual adventures together.

"You painted your face like a clown," Morgan informed him. "This looks better."

"I believe it. Your mother didn't catch me, did she?" Sebastian was sure he would have remembered that, if nothing else.

"She knew someone had been going through her things. She questioned me about it the next morning. I told her it was all me."

It was October and Sebastian was surrounded by sweat, perfume, and alcohol, but for a second, he swore he could smell summertime oranges, sweet and fat with juice. "You covered for me?"

"I didn't want to risk you being sent away." Morgan looked askance. "I missed you when you were gone, you know."

"Well!" Sebastian's voice was too loud, too obvious in his avoidance of the subject. The orange smell burst like a flimsy soap bubble. "I hope you're enjoying having me all to yourself now."

"It doesn't bother you? Being overlooked by everyone else?"

"It's a new experience," Sebastian admitted, looping his arms around Morgan's neck like they were slow-dancing. "You're welcome to stare all the more to make up for it."

"My models expect me to stare at them. My art has left me with a few impolite habits."

"I don't mind. Tonight's enchantments aside, obviously, I wouldn't wear any makeup at all if I didn't enjoy being the centre of attention."

"Vain."

"Exceptionally so. But you're too modest. You could do with a little more vanity yourself. Now: dance with me."

He drew Morgan deeper into the throng of dancers as the music changed to invite a quick two-step. Morgan was a competent dancer, easily able to keep up with Sebastian, though clearly not accustomed to following another's lead. Sebastian relinquished control and let Morgan take over, though he didn't let him drop the pace. Morgan was so focused on matching Sebastian's steps that he didn't seem to notice how the other dancers were less concerned with their own two-steps, and more occupied with feeling each other up through their clothes. Their dances had a lot more groping and tongue than Sebastian and Morgan's, which was a pity, but the night was young.

Morgan looked good in motion, with a pink flush to his face, barely visible behind his mask, and a light sheen of sweat against his hairline, tempting his hair to escape its product and give in to boyish curls. He kept up with Sebastian until he was out of breath, at which point Sebastian graciously allowed him to come to a standstill. Morgan had a real smile on his face for the first time since Sebastian had found him, and though his gaze was downcast like he was embarrassed by his own exuberance, his smile lit him up beautifully.

"You can get me that second drink now," Sebastian said. "I think we've earned it."

Unfortunately, as Morgan caught his breath, he began to take notice of his surroundings. As the party crept past midnight, the drugs and the drinks reached a crescendo, flowing freely from cups and between one person and the next. The dancing had turned to heavy petting, and the conversation to kissing, and then more than kissing. Sebastian had seen it all before, to say nothing of his own participation in such acts, but it seemed a terribly new and unexpected experience for poor Morgan.

"This is—" Morgan broke off, clearing his throat and tugging at his collar.

"More than you expected?"

"Rather."

"Too much?"

"I don't know where I'm supposed to look. Aren't there any alcoves or coat rooms for them to sneak off to?"

Sebastian laughed. "Certainly, and I'm sure they're making good use of such places. It's not a lack of options driving people to make out in plain view. They like the attention, and they know it's safe to do that here."

"It's indecent." Morgan sounded mortified, shifting his weight with his arms crossed high over his chest, radiating insecurity and looking like he wanted the floor to open up and swallow him whole.

"Relax a little." Sebastian slipped an arm around Morgan's shoulders, rocking him lightly back and forth. "Just ignore them. It's not like they're going to grab you and demand you participate."

"Are you sure?" Morgan didn't sound entirely like he was joking.

"Darling, I promise: you're oozing unavailability. No one's going to proposition you as long as you keep standing there looking like you've got a stick up your arse."

"Is this normal?" he asked stiffly. "Do people make a habit of getting off without regards to privacy in all the parties you frequent?"

"Some of them, sure."

"Have you ever?"

Grinning, Sebastian pulled Morgan closer against his side. "What would you most like my answer to be? It's not hard to imagine me like that, is it? Easy. Inviting voyeurism. Enjoying the spectacle."

"I'm not imagining you like that," Morgan said, too quickly. "I'm just trying to understand the appeal, because at face value, it's entirely lost on me."

Bringing his other hand to rest in the centre of Morgan's chest, Sebastian asked, "Would you like me to show you?"

Morgan wet his lips, a gesture born of nervousness rather than temptation. "I don't think that's a good idea."

"No?"

"We're not actually an item, and I don't like an audience."

"Adam and Kitty already think we're fucking," Sebastian pointed out. "They expect something of us in a place like this, where all manner of couples are free to act as they please."

"Even if we were involved like that, I wouldn't do it here."

"Not even a kiss?"

Morgan hesitated, and Sebastian held his breath, his stomach suddenly full of silver butterflies to match Morgan's mask.

But Morgan stepped back, removing Sebastian's hands from his person. "I agreed to play along with your bet because you weren't actually trying to seduce me. Don't change the rules of the game now." He looked away. "I should go."

"Oh, don't be like that. Let's go back to the bar; I won't make you dance anymore if everyone else is making you uncomfortable."

Morgan took a careful step back, shaking his head. "It's well past midnight, and I'm too old to enjoy staying up through all hours of the morning."

"You're not that old," Sebastian protested. "You're, what, thirty-three? Hardly an octogenarian."

"I'm old enough to value a good night's sleep over another hour of partying. Go back to your friends; enjoy the rest of your party. I had a good time, but I'd like to go before something spoils it for me."

That didn't make any sense to Sebastian, but arguing would only encourage Morgan to distance himself again. Reaching out, he caught Morgan lightly by his jacket cuff. "Let me walk you out, then."

Morgan allowed it, perhaps only because he thought resistance wouldn't be worth the effort. Sebastian would take what he could yet.

"I'm glad you had a good time," Sebastian said, looping their arms together to hold Morgan captive as they wound their way to the club's exit. "To be honest,

I'm surprised you stayed as long as you did. Was my company not as bad as you anticipated?"

"You've never been bad company," Morgan said, determinedly not looking at him. "Just the opposite, in fact. That's the problem."

Startled by the admission, Sebastian nearly tripped over his own feet. "This is the drink talking, isn't it?" he asked gleefully. "I wish I had time to get you properly drunk so you'd relax and open up a little."

"That's another reason I'm going home now."

As they came to the doors, Sebastian drew Morgan to a halt and, pressing close, he quickly said, "Reconsider my offer to model for you," giving him an easy excuse to keep in touch. "You still have Adam's card I gave you; you know where to find me. I know: you're going to say it's a bad idea. But you had a good time today, didn't you?"

"It's not a bad idea," Morgan said slowly. "Sebastian…"

Resting one hand on Morgan's chest over his loop of glass beads, Sebastian leaned in to press a kiss to the side of Morgan's mask. "Sleep on it," he suggested, stepping back to a respectable distance.

Morgan looked pink again under the silver shimmer of his mask. He stood unmoving as Sebastian melted back into the crowd before shaking himself from whatever reverie and turning firmly on his heel to exit Eden.

CHAPTER SEVEN

IN WHICH SEBASTIAN MODELS
BUT DOESN'T UNDRESS
AS MUCH AS HE WANTS

The phone rang early the next morning, jarring Sebastian from sleep. He glared at the weak sunlight filtering through the curtains, his face pressed to the pillow. He disliked acknowledging the morning time, and he disliked it even more following a party from which he went home alone.

In the hallway by the kitchen, the ringing cut off as Adam picked up.

"Hello, this is Adam Cunningham." A pause. "Sebastian? Yes. Is this Morgan Hollyhock?"

Sebastian perked up, raising his head and listening intently, though his ears weren't so sharp as to pick up the other speaker's voice.

"I'll fetch him. Wait one moment."

By the time Adam tapped on Sebastian's door, Sebastian was out of bed, a robe flung on and one hand running through his hair to make himself presentable as if Morgan were there in person instead of on the line.

"How did he sound?" Sebastian demanded the instant Adam opened the door.

"Neutral," Adam replied unhelpfully. "He does keep his cards close to his chest, doesn't he?"

"Not that close. You saw him yesterday."

"I saw him leave you at Eden to come home with us again."

"Are you saying you don't believe I've successfully seduced him yet?"

"I'm saying any man properly infatuated with you should be keeping you close. Seeing you out shopping together, I was convinced. Seeing you at Eden? Suddenly I'm sceptical."

"He's calling, isn't he?"

Adam shrugged. "I think it's fair to say you've won five pounds for getting him to Eden." He drew the appropriate note from his wallet, offering it between two fingers. "The rest you'll win when he invites you round to his and gives you a place to stay."

Sebastian narrowed his eyes even as he plucked the note from Adam's hand. "Changing the rules of the wager is cheating."

"I think *you're* cheating," Adam countered easily. "Anyway, you should be proud of me for not taking everything you say at face value."

"Fine. If I sleep over at his, you'll pay up?"

"Move in with him and I'll pay up."

"Consider it done." Slipping past Adam into the hallway, Sebastian headed straight for the phone, lifting the receiver as he leaned one shoulder against the wall. "To what do I owe the pleasure?" he purred, playing into his morning rasp.

"Are you still interested in modelling?" Morgan asked.

Adam was right. His tone was perfectly neutral.

"Or should I assume you've already moved on to your next scheme?"

Sebastian hid his smile against the receiver. "That depends. Is it only my modelling skills you're after?"

"Modelling only," Morgan stressed. "And is that something you really want to discuss so openly over the phone?"

"You're right. I'll be over shortly."

"Wait—"

Sebastian dropped the receiver back in its cradle, inordinately pleased. "I haven't lost your bet yet," he told Adam, who had lingered in the kitchen doorway to eavesdrop the whole time. "By this time tomorrow, I'll be collecting my remaining fifteen pounds."

"I wish you all the luck in the world," Adam replied, turning back to the kitchen to put the coffee on. "I take it you'll be having breakfast before heading out?"

"I'll take something to eat en route."

"Looking a bit overeager there, aren't you?" Kitty asked from her place at the breakfast table. "He must be something special after all."

"Adam's cash certainly is," Sebastian retorted, slotting two slices of bread into the toaster before heading back to his room to get dressed.

Kitty was right, of course; there was a rarely any benefit to giving a mark the upper hand and letting them believe that Sebastian wanted them more than they wanted him. He didn't mind playing the hungry or fawning lover, but he never leaned into that angle until the other party was already good and hooked.

If Morgan Hollyhock were just a regular mark, Sebastian might consider him a challenge, and he'd never backed down from one of those before. But Morgan was more than that. He had the potential to actually mean something to Sebastian. That summer they'd spent together when Sebastian was ten years old felt like an old bruise, swollen and tender to the touch. Everything had fallen apart so quickly after that summer had ended. A tiny, superstitious part of Sebastian thought that maybe, if he could get things back to how they'd been before everything had gone so pear-shaped, he could undo the damage done to his life. Maybe, instead of that bruise getting steadily darker and sorer, it might actually start to heal.

It was nonsense, of course. There was no going back, and there was no undoing all the myriad ways Sebastian's life had fallen apart after saying goodbye to Morgan for what neither of them had realised would be the last time.

A challenge was like a bet: something to be won, no matter how impossible. He would rekindle his friendship with Morgan, he would convince himself that everything was actually fine—that *he* was fine—and he'd win that bet, all in one fell swoop.

Dressed as sharply as he was capable in Adam's borrowed suit, he slathered his toast with butter and jam before pressing it into a sandwich to keep his fingers clean and headed out into the autumn morning air.

Morgan was waiting for him; he opened the door much faster than he had on Friday, though as before, he kept Sebastian standing on the step for a moment longer than he would ever do with a proper guest.

"Generally, my models and I arrange something in advance," Morgan said. "I didn't mean for you to immediately come over and show up on my step."

"You called me and asked. I took it as an invitation."

"You take most things as an invitation, don't you?"

"It's worked out for me so far. May I come in?"

Morgan allowed him into the foyer before stalling him again. "Did you win your bet?"

"No, thanks for asking. I'm afraid going home without me made for an unconvincing finale to the night."

At least Morgan had the grace to look embarrassed about that. "Say I play along with your game a little longer. What exactly would that entail?"

"You get the pleasure of my company with none of the deceit," Sebastian said immediately, which was of course itself a lie. It had been years since Sebastian had been entirely honest with anyone. Possibly twenty-one years, though he shrank from calculating the exact timeline. "As far as my friends are concerned, they'll believe I'm conning you as I've done all be others, but between you and I, you're in on the whole thing. And in private..." He spread his hands. "We can be whatever you like. A return to the olden days, or something entirely new."

"But at no point are you actually pushing to get into my bed."

"I certainly wouldn't say no if you invited me, but no, I'm not pushing if you're not interested. My priorities are Adam's twenty quid, a few square meals a day, and a roof over my head. Anything else is an added bonus."

Morgan nodded. "So, to be absolutely clear, you're moving in with me and I'm buying you whatever your heart desires exactly as if you were my mistress—but without us actually sleeping together."

"That's entirely your call. Sex is very much on the table if you want it. Or in the bed. Or up against the wall—"

Waving one hand, Morgan cut him off. He looked pink again, and also annoyed. "Yes, alright. I get the idea, thank you." Stepping aside, he finally invited Sebastian into his flat proper. "Let's go through to my study."

"Just modelling?"

"Just modelling."

"As you like," Sebastian said cheerfully, coming up to walk alongside him, his stride long and easy with his hands in his pockets.

Morgan kept one eye on him as they made their way upstairs and down the corridor to the study. It was a decently sized room with a large, north-facing window, a desk, a scattering of plush chairs, and another well-stocked bookshelf. Judging by the drawings pinned to the walls and the stacks of sketchbooks on the desk, it was in this room where Morgan liked to work.

Once they were both inside with the door shut behind them, Morgan said, "I pay my models ten shillings an hour. It's under the table, but it's honest work. Not that you seem much concerned with honesty."

"Honesty is well and good, but I'm more interested in the fact that it's easy work."

"You say that now, having never tried it."

"How hard can it be? It just comes down to standing around and looking pretty, doesn't it? What more experience do you need?"

Spreading his arms, Sebastian dared Morgan to tell him he wasn't pretty enough to make a good model. Even with his borrowed suit, even with his pallor, the dark circles under his eyes, and the remnants of the previous night's mascara smudging his lashes, Sebastian knew the appeal he held. It was only a question of whether that appeal would be acknowledged.

It was difficult, navigating the world with an attraction to men and an intent to attract like-minded men to him. There was a risk inherent to every interaction—the impossibility of knowing for sure whether his targets wanted him the way he wanted them to want him.

In his experience, even the most straight-laced could be tempted if he looked at them just the right way or offered them just the right thing. In Eden, Morgan had danced with him, only to shy away from the more intimate goings-on around them. But now, in private? They were free to trade looks and speak plainly without self-consciousness rearing its awkward head.

Arms outstretched, Sebastian turned in a slow circle, playfully keeping his gaze on Morgan as he moved. He was tall and lean, with an elegant sharpness to him that made him seem predatory, even indoors, and he moved with a dancer's grace, self-assured and confident. His clothes were fitted decently, though not perfectly, and hinted at the body underneath. Everything about his appearance, from his style to his movements, was cultivated to say *look at me, pay attention to me*. To suggest just enough danger, just enough transgression to make a certain type of man sit up and lean in a little closer, wanting a taste.

"I was made to model, surely. It's only been a lack of opportunity preventing me so far." He preened and batted his eyes, playing it up. "Wouldn't you like to be my first time?"

Morgan shut his eyes for a second, visibly gathering strength. Sebastian allowed it, and was rewarded when Morgan opened his eyes again and asked, his voice remarkably calm in a way that had to be forced, "Are you comfortable losing a layer or two?"

"Undressing? Absolutely. I'm so glad you asked."

"Just the tie and jacket," Morgan stressed.

"Just that? It hardly seems worth mentioning."

"Is a two-hour period manageable for you? With breaks, but that's my preferred length per session."

"I'm agreeable."

"And for that, compensation is one pound."

Sebastian nodded. "As advertised, yes. Lovely." He glanced around the study, toying with his shirt collar just enough to give the idea of unbuttoning it. "Shall we jump straight in, or do you need time to get your things in order?"

"Stop," Morgan said firmly.

"Relax. I'm not trying to seduce you other than convincing you to agree to this modelling arrangement. Having told you about the bet, I can't seduce you, or at least, not properly. I can proposition you, and make overtures, and flirt, certainly, but none of that is a seduction because I've already showed my hand. That said…" Sebastian abandoned his last dregs of innocence as he sidled closer. "Sex is still on offer, if you change your mind about that, too. I should be delighted to get you into bed. But seduction is the wrong word for it."

Morgan made a noise of polite disagreement before moving on. "In any case, I won't have you model this very minute. It's almost noon, and I need lunch before undertaking a two-hour commitment. You should have come by this afternoon. Which I would have told you on the phone, if you hadn't hung up on me in order to leave immediately."

"I can come back another time," Sebastian said, affecting carelessness. "It's not as if I have any pressing engagements one way or another."

"Stay for lunch, and we can get to it afterwards. If you're not busy."

"As it happens, my schedule is wide open. I'd be delighted to stay."

◆ ◆ ◆

The afternoon returned them to the upstairs study, well fed and content as the sun rolled west, hidden behind a blanket of dark autumn clouds, threatening a storm.

"A pound for two hours," Morgan repeated. "I don't generally do this more than once a week, but if it goes well, I could ask you to return. That's not an invitation to turn up unannounced," he added. "It's only a possibility that I might ask you back. Conditional on your good behaviour."

"I understand."

Sebastian looked around the room with open curiosity, poking through the scattering of art supplies on the desktop before turning to peruse the bookshelf. He wasn't trying to make Morgan twitchy or goad him into snapping at Sebastian to keep his hands in plain sight, but it was a fun by-product of his genuine interest in the place. There was nothing worth stealing in the study, especially not when Morgan was offering him easy money, but he couldn't resist having a look around.

Still, it was no good aggravating his generous new benefactor, no matter how temporary that generosity may prove. Sebastian slung his hands in his pockets, affecting an effortlessly casual stance. "How would you like to do this, then? Shall I just…?" He mimed taking off his jacket, one brow raised in inquiry.

The thought of Sebastian undressing entirely was perhaps too much for Morgan. "Lose the jacket, but let's remain mostly clothed, please" he suggested, busying himself at his desk to avoid meeting Sebastian's eye. By the time he retrieved his drawing pad and a charcoal pencil, Sebastian had stripped down to his undershirt, his shirt, jacket, and tie neatly draped over the back of the nearest armchair.

"Is this alright?" he asked innocently. "You said to stay mostly clothed, but really, where's the fun in that?"

"Right," Morgan said faintly.

Sebastian flexed as subtly as he could, showing off his arms. They were lean but toned, and when he shifted, the shadows accentuated the curve of his bicep.

Morgan cleared his throat. "If you'd take a seat?"

Sebastian dropped into the armchair and crossed his legs, one knee over the other, and folded his hands on top. "I haven't actually seen any of your art yet," he said conversationally as Morgan took the chair opposite him. "How dreadfully awkward would it be if you finished my portrait and when you showed me, it was something scribbled together like a child would do, and I had to pretend to be impressed?"

"You were impressed enough when we were actual children," Morgan said. "Unless you were pretending then, too."

"Oh, I was genuinely impressed at the time," Sebastian assured him. "Your skills were excellent for a twelve-year-old. It's only a question of whether they've improved alongside your age."

"You're not making any effort to charm me into inviting you back after this, are you?"

"Am I not?" Sebastian hummed and drummed his fingers against the carved wooden arms of the chair. "I think you will, though."

Morgan should have shut the door on him the moment he turned up on the step with his pocket watch. He should have turned Sebastian out the instant he propositioned him—for the indecency of the suggestion, if not the dubious morality of it. Instead, he'd sat there and listened to Sebastian's offer, and then gone out with him the very next day. He'd called him up the day after that. Of course he was going to ask Sebastian to come back again.

"If you would turn your head fractionally to your right? Chin tilted up? And now lean back and relax. Yes, thank you."

Sebastian basked in the weight of Morgan's attention. The lamplight coupled with the darkening sky threw shadows over Sebastian's form, making the pose more dramatic than it would have been in full sun. His cheekbones stood out beautifully against the rest of his face; his throat vanished in a sea of blackness, only to re-emerge where his collarbones cut up, elegant and swooping, above the neckline of his undershirt.

This was likely the only time Morgan allowed himself to admire other men, when he was locked away in the privacy of his study and safe behind the wall of his sketchbook. In public, he'd perfected the art of keeping his gaze cool and clinical, wearing a mask whether he was in Eden or on the street. Most men found it freeing, having the chance to express themselves in private alongside like-minded individuals. Morgan still seemed buttoned-up. There was a lack of trust between them still, or a lack of familiarity, anyway.

"Can you hold that for ten minutes? We'll start with shorter poses, until we get used to each other."

"As you like." Sebastian shifted imperceptibly, then dropped his chin in an almost invisible nod. "I'm ready."

Morgan set his pocket watch on the desk beside him. "I'll tell you when the time is up."

"You know, this is actually—"

"No speaking, please."

Sebastian huffed in quiet amusement but obediently fell silent, and Morgan bent his head to his work, charcoal flying over the page.

The two hours passed quickly, all told. Sebastian was a willing model, exuding patience even when Morgan asked him to hold his position for twenty or thirty minutes at a time, and he didn't try to force the conversation after Morgan made it clear he wanted silence. Unfortunately for Morgan, conversation was far from the only weapon in Sebastian's arsenal. Though the act of drawing should have been enough to occupy Morgan's attention, Sebastian turned himself into a long line of sprawling distraction.

He wanted to tempt Morgan into coming closer, into touching him. To make a study of his long fingers with their immaculate nails, his fine-boned wrists, and how the muscles of his forearms twitched and tensed as he shifted positions. To trace the lines of his collarbones with more than just charcoal, to touch his cheekbones and the sharp cut of his jaw—

Sebastian honestly wasn't there to seduce the man. He wasn't even there to *pretend* to seduce him, as he had been at Eden. It was only force of habit making him lounge so, and turning his gaze darkly amused and inviting. Seduction and pickpocketing: two compulsions he just couldn't shake. Not that he particularly wanted to shake either. They made for good entertainment, and, as much as he wanted to impress Morgan and be the perfect model, it was incredibly boring to sit there on his best behaviour without a word of conversation between them. So, he teased, and Morgan studiously ignored it.

Finally, the last second ticked over and the session came to an end. At Sebastian's inquisitive look, Morgan nodded.

"That's all for today."

Sebastian broke his position slowly, returning both feet to the floor and stretching his arms up over his head like a flower unfurling after a long night. He stretched so deeply that his back audibly cracked, and he groaned appreciatively before dropping his hands to his lap and smiling over at Morgan.

"Did you get anything good out of it?"

"I think so." Morgan cleared his throat. "Would you like to see?"

Sebastian rose and padded over to him, coming to peer over his shoulder at the work. Morgan offered the drawings up wordlessly, turning to study Sebastian's face for a reaction.

"You've made me look dashing!" Sebastian exclaimed, delighted. "Is this how you see me? I'm so handsome."

Morgan rolled his eyes but didn't try to take the drawings back. "I'm sure you've realised that before."

"I do enjoy being reminded." Sebastian studied the drawings a moment longer, not even having to feign his admiring noises, before returning them to Morgan's waiting hands. "They're beautiful. You have quite the skill with a pencil."

"Thank you."

"Why didn't you ever draw me when we were boys? You were always doing those landscapes and still-lifes. I would have thought I'd be more interesting than that."

"I didn't think you'd be willing to sit still for it," Morgan said with a shrug.

"Well, I'm willing now. So? Do I pass the test?"

Morgan fished in his pocket for a pound coin and dropped it into Sebastian's upturned palm. "You've certainly earned your pay. I confess you were a better model than I expected, and yes, you've passed the test.

I'd be pleased to invite you back for future sessions, provided you continue to behave."

Sebastian pocketed the money with a smile, dipping his head in a short nod of gratitude. "Delightful. Shall we say this time next week, or…?"

He willed Morgan to say *no, come back sooner*, or, *actually, I've reconsidered my position and I would quite like to be seduced after all.* The fact that Morgan had taken him up on his modelling offer made either outcome more likely than they had seemed back on Friday, when Sebastian had first sought him out at home.

The safe thing to do would be for Morgan to bid Sebastian good afternoon and send him on his way. Put him from his mind and move on, back to safer waters where there were no handsome, sharp-tongued con men swimming like sharks eager to sink their teeth into Morgan's tender flesh and take advantage of him.

Sebastian wanted Morgan to admit that he was tired of being safe.

"You're still staying with Adam?" Morgan asked.

Sebastian shrugged, feigning nonchalance to hide his thrill at the question. "Until he gets sick of me butting into his time with Kitty, but that's not much of a problem." He patted the pocket that housed his newfound money. "Not now that I have this, anyway."

"That won't last you a week." Morgan paused. A muscle ticked in his jaw as he fought against what must surely be his own sense of self-preservation. His interest in Sebastian won out. "Your friend still needs convincing before he'll pay you?"

"Unfortunately."

"Stay the night." Morgan immediately shut his eyes like he was disappointed in himself.

Sebastian, who had a much stronger sense of self-preservation, merely lifted one brow, awaiting elaboration.

"I mean in the guest room."

"You're not worried I'll make off with the silverware in the small hours of the morning?"

"As long as you leave me a fork and a knife I expect I'll manage well enough."

"No spoons?"

"I don't care that much for soup."

"Alright," Sebastian said slowly, doling out his glee in careful little morsels. "Then yes, I'll stay the night."

CHAPTER EIGHT

A MIDNIGHT VISIT
AND AN OFFER ACCEPTED

Morgan set up the guest room with little fuss, though Sebastian was sure his man would do it if it weren't the weekend, and offered Sebastian a spare robe for the night. It was a heavy forest-green thing with gold details, the sort of luxury Sebastian stole to get his hands on, yet Morgan wore it so rarely that it served no purpose other than to lend to guests.

They retired by nine-thirty. It was impossibly early by Sebastian's standards, and after Morgan shut him in there, he sat on the edge of the bed, wondering what to do with himself. There were a few books stacked on the bed's headboard and a radio sitting on the little desk by the window, but Sebastian was too restless for either.

He undressed and changed into the robe just to have something to do, and because he didn't really intend to sneak away in the middle of the night, silverware or no. The robe was silk-lined, deliciously cool against his bare back.

What he wanted to do was interrogate Morgan as to the meaning of this invitation. Was this an offer good for a single night so Sebastian could win his bet, a place to sleep born o

f pity? Or did Morgan want something more from him? Sebastian knew which option he preferred, but neither one really explained why Morgan had shut him in the spare bedroom and left him all alone.

Sebastian generally favoured a subtler approach to find out what people wanted from him. He then took pride in becoming whatever they wanted, chameleon-like. But he'd already shown Morgan too much of his hand for that to work, and besides, the man seemed to respond well to the mostly-honest approach he'd taken so far. Very possibly, Sebastian was the only person in Morgan's life who'd ever been so upfront with him. Maybe it was a refreshing change of pace. It was a change for Sebastian, certainly.

Before Sebastian confronted Morgan to ask what he wanted, he took the opportunity to investigate Morgan's home under cover of darkness. He started with his guest room, which was obviously the most accessible, though he doubted Morgan would be so careless as to leave anything incriminating lying around. The books were dull philosophical works; the radio was tuned to mediocre jazz. The desk had no drawers, with only a pad of blank notepaper and a pen sitting atop it, for the convenience of whomever was staying over. The closet hosted a row of summer jackets, put aside now that the days were getting colder, but there was nothing in any of the pockets.

Sebastian went as far as checking the back of the closet for a hidden door: not because he expected to find anything in such a modern flat, but rather because he needed to kill time until he was certain Morgan was asleep so he could sneak out to explore the rest of the place. When probing the closet didn't take very long, he proceeded to check every other wall of the room, followed by the floorboards. To his disappointment, there were no secret compartments whatsoever, but his efforts took him past ten, which he considered late enough to safely emerge into the hall.

At the end of the hallway was Morgan's bedroom, but between that and the guest room was the toilet and then the study. Sebastian crept to the toilet first, rifling through the medicine cabinet but again, finding nothing of interest. There were no recreational pills or powders of note, only aspirin, cough syrup, iron supplements, and a few salves for topical cuts or irritations, backing up Morgan's claims that he was an entirely boring man.

The study was next. Unlike the toilet, which Sebastian had a valid excuse to visit if he was interrupted, the study was very much off limits, and if he was caught red-handed he'd have to be quick in order to talk himself out of trouble. He was passingly familiar with the layout from his modelling session, but, under Morgan's watchful eye, he hadn't had the chance to go digging through the desk. If the man kept any secrets at all—and Sebastian had never met a soul who didn't have at least one—they would be locked away in his private study. Sebastian left the door open a crack, and, avoiding the electric lights, whispered a little illumination spell to light his way.

Morgan's afternoon drawings were spread across the desktop where they'd been left, dark and bold. Vainglorious though he was, Sebastian resisted the temptation to look through them again. Instead, he knelt behind the desk in order to search the drawers one at a time, relishing the opportunity to learn more about his reserved host and erstwhile friend. He'd built his career on his ability to dig into the nooks and crannies of other people's lives, sniffing out secrets he could use to his own advantage. Never for anything so crude as blackmail, but rather, a more psychological advantage that allowed Sebastian to gently manipulate them in one direction or the other. There was nothing sinister or even particularly complicated about it.

In this case, he wanted to know whether Morgan had left a past string of lovers, and if so, how many of them were men. Morgan was discreet, and the dullness of his public life made him look perfectly respectable. But he hadn't flinched when Sebastian propositioned him, and his discomfort in Eden hadn't seemed directed at the queer couples any more than the heteros. The concept of sodomy didn't seem shocking or even particularly interesting to him. Otherwise, he would have vehemently denied Sebastian's suggestion that they pretend to hook up. He would have been offended by the mere hint of it.

If anything, he seemed blasé. He'd danced with Sebastian at Eden. Yes, he'd been put off by the blatant sexuality on display at the club, but that didn't seem related to people's choice of partner so much as their insistence on coupling right in front of him like rabbits at a petting zoo.

One of the bottom drawers held a bottle of good scotch; the other had nothing noteworthy. The middle drawers had paperwork and official documents that Sebastian wasn't terribly interested in at the moment. The top drawers housed empty sketchbooks and art supplies: pencils and charcoal and pastels, and a little tin of watercolours that looked unopened. Then there was only the top centre drawer left: wider than the others, but not as deep. Holding his breath, Sebastian eased it out, and was rewarded with a stack of filled sketchbooks. They were perhaps less personal than love letters or a diary, but just barely.

Withdrawing the sketchbooks one at a time, his stomach flipped, all butterflies at their contents. Though Morgan's drawings were a far cry from the erotic fantasies of Jules Coxley's art, he was no stranger to the human body. Nude figures filled the pages, some anatomical studies of fat and muscle, others more portrait-like; some subtle and demure, others brazen in their nakedness.

Morgan wasn't shy, then, or put off by the naked form. But he had repeatedly rebuffed Sebastian's offers to strip.

Sebastian entertained the possibility that it was something personal.

Well, that was a question easily answered. He'd had enough snooping for one night; he was ready for something more scintillating.

Tucking the thickest sketchbook under one arm, he tidied the desk back into its original state and exited the study, heading for Morgan's bedroom, his bare feet silent against the carpet.

Tapping lightly on the bedroom door, he eased it open without waiting for an answer. When Morgan made no sign of stirring, Sebastian lingered in the doorway, watching him with dark-eyed intent. The man was no more than a shape in the blue darkness, a curve of blankets against the pillow. Carefully, Sebastian sent his illumination spell bobbing further into the room like a little faerie light to cast its glow over Morgan's face.

"What?" Morgan croaked, fumbling to sit up and turn on the bedside lamp. He looked foggy with sleep, his thoughts moving slower than was their habit, and all he could do was stare.

Sebastian's robe reached just past his knees, like a girl's party dress, tied around his middle with a sash. His calves and the deep V of his chest showed tantalising glimpses of bare skin, though nothing indecent. Enough, though, to catch Morgan's eye.

"Did I wake you?" Sebastian asked, his voice pitched low to match the night.

"It doesn't matter," Morgan said hoarsely. "What is it?"

Sebastian smiled and slunk inside, shutting the door behind him with his heel. "I wanted to ask you more about your art."

"It's almost midnight."

"Do you want me to go?"

Morgan wet his lips. "No. What do you want to ask?"

From under his arm, Sebastian withdrew the sketchbook, dropping it gently against the covers where it fell open to a spread of male nudes, their forms rendered in careful detail.

"Why didn't you take your opportunity to have me undress?"

Morgan's face reddened attractively and he clenched his fingers in the duvet. "You'd never modelled before. It didn't seem right."

"You've been looking," Sebastian pressed, his mouth curved in a wicked smile. "I told you I was willing. What if I refuse to come back for a second round, and that was your only chance?"

"You have a very high opinion of yourself. There's no shortage of bodies to draw."

Sebastian tsk'd and waved his hand. "Yes, yes. There are countless other fish in the sea. But tell me you only want to draw me in all these tedious clothes and make me believe it. Can you?"

Still so near sleep, Morgan's voice came out impossibly soft. "What do you want, Sebastian?"

Sebastian wanted a hundred million different things, only some of them from Morgan specifically. But Morgan's gaze, as sleep-soft as his voice, seemed to be searching for an answer more intimate than the list of luxuries Sebastian would have rattled off. Shying away from the prospect of emotional intimacy, Sebastian steered them towards the much safer waters of physical intimacy, instead.

He set the sketchbook on the bedside table, atop another of Morgan's dry old books. When he extended his arm, the robe shifted just so, revealing a sliver of bare chest all the way down to his navel. Traipsing nearer, he came to sit beside Morgan on the bed, crossing his legs to let his robe ride up his bare thigh. He really did like the garment; he'd have to take it with him when he left.

Before he could say a word, Morgan sighed. He was still under the blankets in his pyjamas, the plush duvet piled around his waist and his pillows at his back, his eyes bleary.

"This is absurd," he said, dragging one hand over his tired face. "Do I look like I'm open to being seduced right now? Whatever you're doing, it's the middle of the night, I'm hardly awake, and I don't find anything about this situation particularly alluring."

That was a lie. In the robe, Sebastian was more alluring than he'd ever been.

But he let that go.

"Let's talk art, then. I'm genuinely interested, you know. Do you draw anything besides nudes these days? Or semi-nudes, as the case may be?"

"Yes, I draw things other than nudes, which you would know if you went rifling through the rest of my belongings. You searched the desk in the study, I take it?"

Sebastian nodded.

Morgan sighed yet again. "I also draw portraits. Landscapes. Still-lifes. All the usual suspects. I find the process rewarding. I enjoy the feeling of creating something with my own hands."

"Do you ever use magic to draw?" Sebastian asked curiously. "To coax the lines this way or that, add a dash of colour or bring the sketches to life for a moment?"

"That defeats the whole purpose. You might as well not draw at all."

"I can understand that." Sebastian tilted his head contemplatively. "When I was learning to pick pockets, I refused to use any magic, just to make sure I could do it properly in any circumstance." He briefly remembered the sensation of having his magic blocked in prison and his skin crawled before he shook the memory off again. "But I use magic to do it now, of course. It makes everything so much easier."

"Sometimes ease isn't the point."

Sebastian made a non-committal sound. "The real question is, when you *are* drawing people, all else being equal, do you prefer your models clothed, or naked?"

"I'm more interested in drawing bodies than clothing, yes. There's nothing inherently sexual about it."

"No, I can see that," Sebastian agreed, nodding to the sketchbook. "All those drawings, and not a hint of eroticism. I must admit to being disappointed."

"It takes an enormous amount of trust to come into someone's home and undress for them. To betray that trust by putting them in a sexual situation is unprofessional and disrespectful. I'm not Jules Coxley; I have no notoriety or success to my name that makes people flock to me asking to be painted like that. I'm a nobody with a hobby for figure drawing, the same as anyone might find in any second-rate fine arts course at university."

Sebastian raised his hands in surrender. "You're a gentleman, through and through. Most commendable." He dropped his hand, the one closest to Morgan, to the bedsheets between them. "But I think we can both agree that I'm not some innocent model who stumbled upon your ad and is in danger of being taken advantage of by some wealthy predator. Which you're not, by the way. I know you're not, even if I haven't seen you in two decades. And even if you were, I'm more than capable of looking after myself, and I know what I'm doing when I try to instigate something with someone. It is exceedingly difficult to disrespect me."

"Say that like you're proud of it," Morgan muttered.

"Let's circle back around to the matter of that bet. We can approach it in a way your professionalism will appreciate."

"Will your friend pay up now that you've stayed over?"

"Not quite."

Morgan just looked at him, tired and expectant, until Sebastian crumbled.

"He says he'll believe it when I move in with you." It rankled him to admit that their performance hadn't fooled anyone, and the words came out surly and under his breath.

Morgan was silent for a long minute, staring at him owlishly from under his rumpled bedhead. The urge to reach over and run his fingers through those mislaid curls came out of nowhere, and Sebastian had to firmly slide his hands under his own thighs to resist the temptation.

"Do you want to move in with me?" Morgan finally asked.

"Is that an invitation?" Sebastian returned with the utmost care.

"It's just a question."

Morgan was back to that unreadable neutrality again.

"I want to win that bet."

"I assume you have a plan. If I hear you out, will you be satisfied and let me go back to sleep?"

"Yes."

"Then by all means, cater to my professionalism."

Taking a breath, Sebastian nodded to himself before laying it out as rationally as he could. "Let it be a business arrangement. Yes, we're running a little con on my friend, but our relationship with each other can be entirely honest. We can discuss our terms ahead of time, detail our boundaries and what lines we can or cannot cross. We'll be in it together, so you can feel secure in the knowledge that I won't be trying to seduce or rob you, or anything else you're worried about. I don't double cross my partners, and I don't jeopardise my chances of winning whatever I have my eye on. Does that allay any of your concerns?"

Morgan looked neither concerned nor reassured. He looked entirely stone-faced. Clearly, Sebastian had misstepped. Again.

"I have nothing but your word for any of this."

Sebastian walked his fingers closer to Morgan. "That's not a rejection."

"You win twenty pounds, food, and shelter. I win the dubious pleasure of your company. For how long? Your friend didn't mention anything about a deadline in his bet. Should I expect you for a week? A month? Longer? Or are you going to disappear like a ghost the moment you get what you want from me?"

Those sounded like some abandonment issues they needed to unpack, but for now, Sebastian said, "One week." The Cheapside Hoard would be his in mere days, and he would hardly need to rely on friends when he had irreplaceable jewels, instead. "It's Sunday night—"

"Call it Monday morning."

"Monday, then. After that, if turns out we can't stand each other, you needn't worry about me entrenching myself in your guest room. I take no pleasure in hanging around longer than I'm wanted."

"That's not my concern," Morgan said.

"What isn't?"

Morgan didn't clarify. "There need to be boundaries. Honesty. Trust. We'll show enough intimacy to convince your friend that you've met his terms, but absolutely no more. If I ever get the sense that you're trying to get something out of me when we're in private, the game is up. If you want something from me, you need to be straightforward and ask for it. I won't be manipulated."

"Do you trust me not to play you when we're alone together?"

"No," Morgan said flatly. "This is a terrible idea."

"But you want to do it."

His mouth twisted to one side in reluctant admission. "I want your company. I just don't trust it."

There was exactly one person in the world Sebastian needed to trust and be trusted by in return, and that was Kitty, because their safety and freedom quite literally depended on their combined competence. He'd built his entire identity around being a thief and a con artist for so long that his inherent untrustworthiness felt comfortable, like a well-worn shirt. He had no idea what to do with the idea of wanting someone other than Kitty to trust him, and wanting to actually earn that trust. He didn't even know where to start with it.

"I'll agree to your terms," he said. "Whatever boundaries you like. Draw up an official contract, if it makes you feel better, and I'll sign it if that's more trustworthy than my word. Just say yes."

Morgan studied Sebastian like they'd never left that modelling session. Maybe he saw a devil, or a misguided soul that had strayed from the path of decency when he looked at him. If Morgan couldn't trust him enough to consider him a friend, then Sebastian hoped he saw him as something tempting and otherworldly. Better a devil than some poor ex-convict to be pitied.

"Say yes," he coaxed.

Morgan blinked slowly, as if under a spell, though there was no magic in the room but the faint orb of illumination.

"Yes," he whispered.

Relief and delight flooded Sebastian. A man like Morgan would abide by his word as surely as if he'd signed a contract in blood. Sebastian would have a place to sleep and three square meals a day for at least the next week. And, unless he really tripped things up in a spectacular way, Morgan would keep him longer than that. Sebastian had far too much practice playing the perfect, malleable companion to be cast aside.

Whistler had been an exception. That had never happened before, and it would never happen again.

Leaning forward, his hand light on Morgan's knee through the bed covers, he pressed a quick kiss to Morgan's cheek. "You won't regret it." Before Morgan could react, Sebastian stood, letting his robe fall back in place. "As promised, I'll let you go to sleep now. Good night, and sweet dreams."

He slipped from the room as much like a shadow as he'd entered, pulling the door shut behind him with a soft but definite click. On the other side, he heard Morgan groan and sink back against the pillows.

Sebastian smiled to himself as he headed back to his own bed. Morgan might be regretting allowing Sebastian into his home, much less taking that bet, but that feeling wouldn't last. Sebastian would make sure of it.

CHAPTER NINE

WHEREIN A GREENHOUSE SERVES
AS A MEETING POINT,
AND A GIFT IS RECEIVED

Morgan did not write up a literal contract. It wouldn't have had any legal binding, and of course there was no paperwork in the world that could cow Sebastian into honesty, but he would have signed it if Morgan asked. Truthfully, he had no intention of biting the hand that fed him, but he could hardly expand Morgan's horizons without nipping him a little.

Despite Sebastian's keenness to get Morgan out in the world and spend time together, the man unfortunately had prior engagements: meetings with his bank, and other such tedious business. Sebastian was thus left at loose ends on Monday morning, and took himself out to keep that pound from Morgan and the five from Adam from burning a hole in his pocket. His first order of business was to lift a few wallets. The second was to buy himself a new suit—a new one of everything for his wardrobe, in fact—so he could stop wearing Adam's hand-me-downs.

He'd been released from Blackwood in mid-May, and the only suit that had survived his incarceration had been somewhat old and shabby even before his conviction. Whistler had bought him a handful of new suits when Sebastian had moved in, but the bastard had reclaimed them and every other gift Sebastian had earned from him immediately following their fight. Relying on other people to get by was to exist in a capricious state, in constant uncertainty and flux. There was nothing Sebastian loved better than having material goods he could unequivocally call his own.

Once he was dressed tip to toe in sleek black, he felt more like himself than he had in months. Whistler hadn't liked him in black; he said it looked funereal. Sebastian thought it was mysterious and romantic. It was only one of a dozen reasons why they hadn't worked out.

When Sebastian checked in with Sterling at lunchtime, he found that Morgan was still out, his afternoon booked up. So, Sebastian whiled away another hour practicing his pickpocketing skills, and then his shoplifting, entertaining himself by seeing how many trinkets he could hide in his new suit without being noticed.

The benefit of a good suit was that people were less likely to suspect him of wrongdoing. After all, most crimes committed by well-dressed men ran more along the lines of fraud or embezzlement than petty theft. He may have started as a petty thief and he might yet dabble in it to stay sharp, but he was quickly moving up the tiers of criminality. A jewel thief was held in much higher regard than a pickpocket or street urchin. Soon, his exploits would be making headlines not only in England but across the continent over. The thought of such notoriety was delicious, sweet as dessert.

Kitty and Deepa would be the ones to help him achieve that notoriety. As the afternoon ticked closer to three, Sebastian made his way to Kew Gardens, lingering by Victoria Gate until he saw Deepa approach. She was dressed less flashily in the daytime, but she cut just as striking an image in the sun as she had in Eden, and passers-by turned in their tracks to look at her. Her dress was in marigold colours, saffron and burgundy and orange-gold, with her lips, nails, and heels all in glossy crimson, and her long hair hanging heavy over one shoulder in a rope-like braid. Though she clearly enjoyed the attention, she allowed no distractions, and made her way in a straight and purposeful line right to him.

"Hello again," she said. "I'm glad you decided to come."

"I was too intrigued not to. What's the plan? I don't suppose it's as easy as you pointing me straight to the flower."

"If only." With a smile, she set off onto the garden path, drawing Sebastian with her. "Oberon's Kiss is classified as a dangerous magical plant, and they don't keep those anywhere open to the public. But I know where they house it, even if I can't get inside. That's where we're going."

"The Tropical Fern House?" he guessed as they passed a directory mounted on a signpost.

"They don't keep the Kiss in there, but they have some of its brethren on display, and the real thing is close by. I'll show you."

Sebastian lacked an appreciation for plants or flowers. Like art, they could be pretty enough, but, also like art, he only cared for the monetary value of any given thing, less so the aesthetic. So, though he paid close attention to the path they took from Victoria Gate heading north into the gardens, and close attention to the temples, greenhouses, and buildings that they passed, it was with the intent to plan a heist rather than out of appreciation for its beauty.

The Tropical Fern House was a little glass building that, from the outside, looked like nothing so much as an ornamental bauble, a glass paperweight whose artisan had trapped an infinite number of live plants inside the glass before it cooled. Lush fern fronds and fiddleheads pressed up against the windows, giving the impression that the entire building was a living, breathing thing.

Deepa held the door open for him and the instant he stepped inside, he was enveloped by a breathtaking crush of humidity. It was sweltering; moisture hung heavily in the air, like mist, and droplets clung to the tip of every leaf. The billowy heat was a welcome change from the crisp autumn air outside, and Sebastian breathed deeply, soaking it in. He hadn't used to mind the cold so much, but recently, he found it set his teeth on edge.

"If the Kiss was accessible to the public, this is where it would be. It's a tropical flower, so you must be careful to keep it hot and wet during transport. The cold would shock it."

"And obviously, no one's interested in paying for a dead plant."

"Definitely not dead," she agreed. "And any damaged leaves or petals will result in you being paid only half of what I'm offering for a full, healthy plant."

"Understood. It won't be an issue."

Already, Sebastian was calculating the amount and type of magic needed to keep the plant in its own climate-controlled bubble for the time it would take him to steal it from the garden and get it back to Deepa. A challenge, but not a concern.

"Will it be labelled, in whatever secret place they have it stashed?"

"Best to be confident in its appearance, in case it's not." From her purse, Deepa drew a page cut from a botanist's fieldbook, unfolded it, and handed it to him. A watercolour of a pretty purple flower, painted in meticulous detail, looked up at him. "It has a distinctive look, and obviously, the effect of its pollen on anyone who breathes or tastes it is unmistakable. But I wouldn't recommend that approach. I want nothing left to chance."

"And the security?"

"Nothing compared to that of the Rose Diamond," she said, flashing a smile. "There is the Kew Gardens constabulary to watch out for; they'll have someone patrolling the area, but they aren't used to seeing much action. You'll want to avoid catching the attention of any workers who might be inside tending to the plants. Whatever happens, I don't want anyone hurt."

"Of course not," Sebastian said, offended. "I'm a thief, not a thug."

"Then I'll show you where to access the room where they keep their dangerous tropical specimens."

Glancing around to ensure they were alone—which of course they were; otherwise Deepa would be swarmed by fawning admirers—she took Sebastian to the greenhouse's back wall, where she stopped, her expression expectant. That wall was as covered in greenery as the other three, the glass completely obscured by so much vegetation.

"There's a secret room back here?" Sebastian asked. "How do you get in?"

"That's what I'm hiring you to figure out."

"But you're certain it's here."

"Absolutely. One of the gardeners confided in me after I made his acquaintance."

"I would think finding your flower's location would be the tricky part. You got this far on your own. What's stopping you from making the actual steal yourself?"

"An unfortunate lack of experience. The stakes are too high to make this my first attempt at a robbery, and frankly, I have no interest in it as either a career or a hobby. I thought it best to play to my strengths and outsource everything else to a professional."

"And what are your strengths, exactly? Or, rather, let me guess. Seduction, manipulation, and playing into your looks, whether they're real or glamoured. I don't mean that as an insult," he added. "As you said, we have a lot in common."

"Sebastian," she chided. "You know better than to suggest a lady's looks are anything but real."

"Are you a lady?"

"As much as you are a gentleman. But to answer your question: My real strength is that I'm cleverer than people take me for. They see a pretty face and assume there's no brain behind it, because you can have one or the other, but never both."

"You said you wanted to sell the Oberon's Kiss to a collector. This seems like a lot of trouble to go to, hiring me and financing a heist, just for a simple pay-out. What's so important about this collector that you can't find a simpler, less risky way to make your fortune?"

"Maybe I like the risk," Deepa said, leaning in with a wicked smile.

"If you liked it that much, you wouldn't be outsourcing anything."

"True enough. But you'll do it?"

Exhaling, Sebastian shut his eyes and sent his magic out to feel for that hidden door. Sure enough, a glimmer of magic met him from behind the wall of shivering ferns.

Frowning, he opened his eyes to glare through the fronds. "I can't tell whether the magic's coming from a protective spell to hide the door, or from whatever plants are on the other side of it."

"But you will be able to figure it out?"

"Certainly. I've never met a door I couldn't open."

"Is one week enough time for you to get in and out?"

"I should think so, barring any unforeseen circumstances. Is it time sensitive, getting it to your collector?"

"It would be preferable, yes. Getting it by Friday would be ideal. That's reflected in your payment."

"And the secret to the Rose Diamond's security?" Sebastian asked, stepping closer.

"I'll tell you everything the moment you put that flower in my hands," she promised. "But not a second sooner."

"And why should I trust you to keep your word?"

"Despite my appearance, I'm not actually running a great criminal enterprise. I have no interest in getting my hands on the Rose Diamond for the same reason that I have no interest in breaking in to steal the Oberon's Kiss myself. It's too much danger for my taste. I'm happy to facilitate the flower changing hands, because I know the collector personally, and I trust her not to go around dropping the pollen in people's drinks or trying to enchant half of London with the stuff. And this matter is simple enough to set up. But the Rose

Diamond? Never mind actually stealing it—I have no network in place to fence it or transport it out of the country. The wider public might not care too much about some obscure flower, but they have an avid interest in that necklace, and I don't want to spend the rest of my life looking over my shoulder waiting to get caught. I would much rather sell that information and then wash my hands of the knowledge entirely. I like my parties, Sebastian, and my fancy dinners and my nice dresses. I have enough men lined up willing to buy me diamonds and priceless jewels that I don't need to risk my neck stealing them."

"A convincing speech. But how do I know you really have that information about the Rose Diamond in the first place?"

"I went out a few times with the insurance agent who owns the jeweller's where it's currently displayed."

"And?"

"He let me try the necklace on. He didn't let me watch him disarm the security, but I was there when he did it. I felt it happen." She shrugged. "I can't prove it to you. If you don't believe me, I can find someone else to steal the flower for me. Someone who will be happy to be paid in cash alone."

He might not necessarily believe her, but it was easy to imagine her wearing that pink collar of diamonds, and he'd never wanted anything for himself as badly as he wanted that. He resolved to return to Kew Gardens and steal the flower as soon as possible. He would have returned that very night, in fact, would he not have been double booking himself. As tempting as the Rose

Diamond's secrets were, he and Kitty had already made arrangements for a different burglary that night. Kew Gardens would have to wait.

"By the end of the week," he promised.

"You're staying with Morgan Hollyhock?"

"For now," he said evasively.

"Then we'll be in touch."

With a smile, she took her leave, retracing her steps out of the Tropical Fern House, leaving him with his magic swirling around the fiddleheads, looking for the seams of that hidden door. He followed her out some minutes later, with enough time between their exits that they wouldn't be thought of as a couple, but not lingering so long as to allow some stranger to enter the greenhouse and find him there.

He returned to Morgan's in time for tea, hiding the day's pickpocketing prizes in the pockets of Morgan's closeted summer suits before traipsing back downstairs to join his host for tea.

"Sorry for being absent today," Morgan said over their meal. "I had some unavoidable meetings. Obviously, if I'd known I'd be hosting, I would have scheduled them further apart to leave time for you. But I prefer to get my appointments done all at once, whenever possible."

"Oh, good. I'd hate to think you were purposefully avoiding me. Maybe we'll see more of each other tomorrow."

"We will," Morgan confirmed.

Supper was poached salmon and potatoes with lemon and mint, with fresh greens on the side.

Sebastian hadn't thought it possible to miss green vegetables until Blackwood taught him what it felt like to crave a food all the way down in one's bones. Now he appreciated every bite. They ate uninterrupted for a minute, Morgan enjoying the quiet company and Sebastian enjoying the generous serving sizes.

Partway through his salad, Morgan broke the silence to venture, "You bought a new suit?"

"I did! Do you like it? The black isn't too depressing for you?"

"It's very handsome. Though, if you'd waited another day, I would have bought it for you."

Sebastian paused with his fork halfway to his mouth. "Really? Now you tell me."

"Another time," Morgan said mildly. "Though, not this evening. I'm afraid I must insist on an early night. After a full day of appointments, I'm really not up for any excitement until tomorrow at the earliest."

"Not to worry," Sebastian said lightly. "I was actually planning on an early night myself. So many mornings in a row really did me in."

Morgan looked sceptical, but he nodded along without accusing Sebastian of any subterfuge. "I got you something while I was out," he said as they reached the end of their meal.

From his pocket, he drew a carefully-folded handkerchief, which he handed to Sebastian. Inside was a silver ring set with a fat pearl, the design simple but modern.

"I saw it in a shop window and it reminded me of the pearls you wore to Eden," Morgan said. "It's alright if it's not your style. I just thought…"

"I love it," Sebastian said quickly. He tried it on both hands, testing the fit, before settling it snugly on his left ring finger.

Morgan seemed pleased that his gift had been well received. "It looks good on you."

Rubbing his thumb against it to turn the ring around on his finger, admiring the way the pearl shone dully in the light, Sebastian was inclined to agree.

CHAPTER TEN

ON THE NATURE OF WILD MAGIC,
AS EMBODIED BY A BUMBLEBEE

At midnight, hours after Morgan had gone to bed and the house had been quiet for long enough that Sebastian was confident he wouldn't stir before dawn, Sebastian left his own bed. Donning an all-black outfit that lent itself to athleticism, he cracked open the bedroom window. The night air was brisk, and he pulled a cap over his head to keep the wind off his ears and to shadow his face under the brim. The drop from the window was steep, but there were plenty of hand- and footholds in the building's exterior, and with a little care and effort, he was able to climb down rather than being forced to jump.

Once on solid ground, he straightened his clothes and stole to the gate, slipping through as smoothly and silently as a cat, before striding down the street like he was going about his business in broad daylight. With the streets so deserted, it took him barely fifteen minutes to walk from Morgan's Portman Square home to his destination on Regent Street, a neat skip west.

Kitty was waiting for him in a skinny little alley between a fruit market and a bakery, three doors down from their target of the night: Felton's Pawnshop & Antiquities. Sebastian slid into the alley beside her, giving her a nod of greeting. Like him, she was dressed all in black, wearing a slim-fitting men's suit and a pair of sensible riding boots.

"In and out," she confirmed. "You take the front, I'll go through the back."

"I still think this amounts to little more than a smash and grab," Sebastian said.

"I heard a rumour that old man Felton has his jewellery case protected by magic. He set it up once we started hitting the papers. If it turns out to be no more than hot air, then it's an easy job. And if it's true, then it's another feather in our cap, isn't it? A good warmup for tomorrow night."

"After we get hold of the Cheapside Hoard, I think we should aim even higher," Sebastian said. "Something that makes pawnshop jobs like this look like child's play."

"You clearly have something specific in mind."

"What would you say," he began, dropping his voice and crowding in close like the walls had ears, "if I told you I know someone who can give us information on the Rose Diamond necklace?"

Kitty drew a sharp breath. "What kind of information?"

"I have to do a job for her first."

"Whoever this person is, how do you know she's not taking you for a ride?"

"Instinct."

She scoffed. "I'm not putting any eggs in that basket until she gives you something concrete and verifiable. Now, come on, let's go."

"Even if her information's no good, we should be aiming higher than pawnshops," Sebastian grumbled. "This feels like a waste of our skill."

"Say that after the job's done and we've got another pocketful of jewels. You want to steal the Rose Diamond? Fine. Get that info and we'll see how useful it is. But right now? It's always smarter to stash as much as you can before you try the biggest job of your life. The more we steal now, the less pressure there is for the National Gallery heist to go perfectly. If we fuck that one up, we won't be left high and dry, and the same goes for the Rose Diamond—*if* we do that one at all. I'm not agreeing to anything just yet. So, this might feel like a waste of time to you, but I'm trying to invest in our futures, and I'd appreciate a little more cooperation."

"I'm cooperating." Sebastian raised his palms. "I'm just saying, I think we're better than this."

"Then prove it." She pointed him towards the mouth of the alley, one hand between his shoulder blades. "In through the front, disarm that jewellery case, then come out the back once I've cleared a path for you. Two minutes, and not a second longer."

Kitty and Sebastian had been breaking and entering for years, not counting his time inside, and Sebastian was confident that by this point in the game, they'd perfected their method to an art. They worked together like a well-oiled machine, and though the unexpected did still occasionally pop up, there was very little that could throw them off course or slow them down.

And it was hardly as if either of them was new to burglary. Even before throwing his lot in with Kitty, as a whippet-lean teenager Sebastian had known his way around a lockpick set. He'd set his sights on smaller targets back then—nothing nearly so glamorous as irreplaceable diamonds, but rather, cash and rings, silk scarves, and the like. That sort of common thievery had been a step up from the pickpocketing of his youth, just as the more recent jewel jobs were a step up from common thievery, in turn.

The Rose Diamond job, theoretical though it was, would be the biggest and most impressive of all. If they could pull that off, that was the sort of take that meant a life of luxury followed by a comfortable retirement. Neither of them would ever have to steal again. Neither of them would have to so much as look at the other side of the law.

But Sebastian wasn't an idiot. He knew himself, and he knew the temptation to slip his fingers into places they didn't belong would never leave him, no matter how well-off he might be. Whether Kitty kept her bad habits would be her own business.

Felton's pawnshop was nothing special. Sebastian could have managed it without Kitty, with one hand tied behind his back. Blindfolded, even. Still, he was a professional, so he set aside all thoughts of the Rose Diamond, of the future and the past, and focused his full attention on the task at hand.

Kneeling in the shadows by the front door, lockpicking kit in hand, Sebastian jimmied the first tool into the lock, its companion poised at the ready, and then he slipped a little tendril of exploratory magic in alongside it. His magic curled through the keyhole, an extension of his senses, albeit muted, to take a look around the shop's interior. There were no wards in place to prevent this exploration, which made the going significantly smoother.

Even the smallest and weakest of wards raised Sebastian's hackles. The walls of Blackwood were made of the things, heavy stone bearing down from all sides, designed to smother the magic in one's veins. Sebastian had spent nine months in that hellhole. The claustrophobic sensation of having his magic constrained just out of reach, a once brightly-burning fire reduced to pathetic embers—he'd never forget that feeling. Blackwood, for all that it claimed to be a bastion of twentieth-century advancement and civility, was as good as a medieval torture chamber.

Assured that Felton wasn't employing any wards that would prevent his use of magic, Sebastian withdrew his exploration and finished coaxing the lock open. He pushed through the door so slowly and so gently that the little bell on the ceiling didn't have a chance to ring, and he shut and relocked the door with equal care behind himself. Casting an illumination spell, Sebastian used its pale glow to guide him straight to the counter.

There, on the shelf underneath the cash register, sat a glass display case holding Felton's most valuable jewellery. Withdrawing it, Sebastian set it down atop the counter and leaned in close to study it. When he ran one finger along its face, a little tingle of foreign magic sparked up to greet him like the tiniest electric shock.

A step as soft as a cat's tread sounded from the shop's back room, and Sebastian paused, turning without alarm as Kitty join him.

"A hundred and ten seconds," she said. "Can you open it, or are we taking it with us?"

"I can open it. I just need the right spell to break the seal."

"Can you force your way in?"

"As a last resort. I assume if he's gone to this much trouble, an alarm will go off if I break it. Maybe even if we remove it from the premises."

"Work quickly," Kitty advised.

Sebastian was good with magic. It liked him; it always had. Though it had been cut off from him in Blackwood, he'd learned some very interesting theories as to the nature of magic during his time there. His neighbour, who'd been sentenced on much more serious crimes than he, had introduced him to all manner of new ideas, and since his release, Sebastian had worked tirelessly to find out how he might use that new information in his favour.

According to his neighbour, magic was a wild entity that could be tapped into and used to far greater effect than most people realised. Most people were only taught a smattering of spells and party tricks, and were discouraged from ever reaching their full potential. The kind of magic that Sebastian's neighbour talked about was ancient and untamed, and thus mistrusted by the well-to-do British, repressed and uptight as they were. But there was so much more to it than charms and spells and incantations, his neighbour claimed. In the right hands, with the right attitude, magic was capable of absolutely anything.

So, freed from Blackwood's shackles and the shackles of his own upbringing and expectations, Sebastian learned to do other, less conventional things with magic. Now, after months of practice, he found he had a knack for convincing other people's magic to talk to him. Because if magic was its own entity, a source of power springing from the world itself rather than something born inside an individual, why shouldn't it speak to him if he invited it?

Sebastian placed one hand palm-down on top of the case, shut his eyes, and began a conversation. Not verbally, and not entirely mentally, either. Rather, he extended a little of his magic sensibilities towards the case with an invitation for its magic to come to him halfway, the way two cats might stretch towards each other to sniff noses when meeting for the first time. Magic, he found, was accustomed to being used as a tool and nothing more, shoved this way and that to perform whatever rigid uses polite society demanded of it. It was never acknowledged as its own entity, and it was very rarely allowed to play.

Thus, when Sebastian reached out to it with a greeting and a request rather than a rude demand, it often reacted positively. Not all the time, of course; some magic was as serious-minded as whatever person first cast the spell. But Felton's magic seemed bored and a little neglected, and so it shimmered up to Sebastian with cautious enthusiasm.

All Sebastian needed was for it to communicate which spells it had most recently performed. Unless Felton changed the metaphorical key to the safe on a regular basis, one of those spells would likely serve to disarm the case. Knowing nothing about the pawnshop owner, Sebastian could hardly guess the most likely spell he'd used to lock it; he'd have better luck blindly guessing a five-digit combination on the first try. There were simply too many spells one might employ, and that was only taking into account the most commonplace. If Felton's tastes ran to the more obscure or overly complicated, Sebastian wouldn't have a hope in hell of guessing which one he'd used.

Luckily, Felton's magic was cooperative. When Sebastian asked, it told him. Or rather, it told his magic. The smell of flowers filled the shop like honeyed perfume, and when Sebastian raised his other hand, the shape of a little creature formed in the air, cobbled together from specks of dust and pollen.

"Is that a bee?" Kitty asked doubtfully from over Sebastian's shoulder.

The bumblebee, which had materialised out of next to nothing, sat on Sebastian's fingertip for a second before bobbing down to the jewellery case, where it situated itself against the clasped lock, and inserted its stinger into the keyhole.

"I've never seen that before," Sebastian said, bemused.

But he didn't have time to linger. Not only was their time up, but the instant the spell had been cracked and the case opened, Felton's magic had cartwheeled up towards the ceiling, delighted at having been freed from its duty, and, in a shower of sparks like an exploding lightbulb, gleefully returned to its master.

There was a startled sound as of someone being woken from a deep sleep, followed by a thump from the room above the shop, where presumably Felton made his home.

"Hell," said Kitty. "Come on, grab that and run."

Flipping open the jewellery case, Sebastian grabbed its contents, shoved them inside his coat, and followed Kitty in hightailing it out of there. They darted into the back alley as footsteps came pounding down the stairs. There was no time to linger and properly lock the door behind them, so, turning to their established backup plan, Kitty and Sebastian went tearing off in opposite directions to reconvene and split their spoils at a later and safer date.

Sebastian skipped back to Morgan's, high on the adrenaline of a narrow escape and a job well done.

Climbing the building's exterior, he retraced the route he'd taken at midnight, and returned to his bedroom through the open window by which he had departed. The stolen jewellery, he tucked away in a hidden pocket in the bottom of his bag, which he kept in the closet. His clothes, he stripped off, folded neatly, and placed under the mattress. Changing into his nightclothes, he slid under the covers, twisted his fingers in the sheets, and stared up at the ceiling, willing his heart to calm down enough to catch a few hours of sleep before daybreak.

But, no matter how he tried, he couldn't stop thinking about that stash of jewellery in the closet, and how the stones might look in the light, and feel against his skin, and what price they might fetch. By the time dawn's first rays stole into his room from around the curtains, he was lost in the tenth iteration of a fantasy in which he stole the Rose Diamond with equal ease, and he hadn't slept a wink.

CHAPTER ELEVEN

IN WHICH CERTAIN IMPULSES
ARE ACTED ON IN A PUBLIC PARK

"Let's go out today," Sebastian announced over breakfast. "Anywhere; it doesn't matter, as long as I can stretch my legs and breathe some fresh air. Let's make a day of it."

"You're especially boisterous this morning," Morgan observed, glancing at Sebastian over the top of his paper. "I take it you slept well?"

"Decently," Sebastian lied, in good cheer. "It's nice not having to overhear Kitty and Adam going at it in the next room." That part was true.

"We can go out. Lunch and a museum, perhaps, or are you angling for a shopping trip?"

"A museum will do beautifully." Perfectly, in fact. "It's no fun shopping if my companion isn't half as tempted by the things in front of him as I am."

"No, I'm afraid I'm not the best company for that. But a museum, certainly. Do you prefer art or natural history?"

"Art, of course. Sciences and the natural world are well and good, but you know I'm more interested in people."

"As a con artist, I suppose you have to be."

"You needn't make it sound so mercenary. My vocation sprang up as a result of my fascination with people, not the other way around." And his fascination with the concept of having money.

"If you say so."

"We should see Coxley's exhibit at the National Gallery. You're friends now, so you have to see it."

"I wouldn't call us friends based off a single conversation."

"Well, I want to see it, anyway." He didn't actually care much one way or the other about Coxley's show, but those paintings weren't the only thing on display at the gallery. "We should go."

Morgan folded his paper down in favour of his coffee. "I take it from your attitude that you want an early start? Early for you, I mean. For most people, this is well past mid-morning."

Sebastian rolled his eyes, waving Morgan aside. "Mid-morning is a perfectly acceptable time to start the day. And yes, I'd love an early start. Let's get out of here and find some entertainment."

"I did warn you that I make for very boring company."

"I don't regret your company whatsoever. I just think it would do you some good to get out of the house more frequently. For recreational purposes, I mean, not just tedious business commitments."

"You're not wrong. Let me get dressed, and we'll be off."

True to his word, Morgan had them out the door within a quarter hour. He hailed them a cab to Trafalgar Square, which hardly seemed worth the fare when the weather was decent and they both had capable legs, but, as it wasn't his money, Sebastian didn't protest. There, they joined the casual crowd of people filtering in and out of the National Gallery. Jules Coxley's exhibition garnered enough gossip that even a week in, people were flocking to see his work in droves, and Morgan and Sebastian blended in without notice.

Coxley's paintings filled an enormous room, hanging stately and distinguished on the walls. As with all fine art, Sebastian was tempted to cut the canvas free, roll it up, and smuggle a few pieces to freedom, but in broad daylight with so many witnesses, he resisted the urge. It was a silly temptation, anyway. Coxley was popular, but his paintings' worth couldn't compare to more classical pieces, and the money Sebastian could make fencing his work wasn't entirely worth the risk. So, he did his best to appreciate the art on its own merit. He was moderately successful.

"Which one is your favourite?" he asked Morgan.

The exhibit showed off the full range of Croxley's abilities, from his vivid, impressionistic flowers to his dreamy, Pre-Raphaelite fantasies of the human form. Across all his work, floral and human alike, his colours were bright and saturated, his brush strokes bold, the paint thick and swirling in stiff peaks off the canvas. He had painted erotic daydreams from Greek mythology—Leda and the swan, Artemis and her nymphs—as well as less recognisable scenes from his own imagination, all brought to life and embodied by his models.

"His Lady Godiva is striking," Morgan said, nodding to the life-size painting of a dark-haired beauty on a huge chestnut horse. "You met the girl who modelled for it. Deepa, at Eden?"

"I recognise her. Is that your favourite, though?"

The painting was beautiful, Deepa's likeness even more so, but Sebastian would bet that the female figure, no matter how lovely, didn't do as much for Morgan as the masculine sex.

"What about this one?"

Sebastian nudged Morgan a few steps to the right until they were standing in front of a smaller painting depicting two men, one winged, locked in what Sebastian suspected was a passionate embrace. Though it was titled "Jacob and the Angel," Sebastian was sceptical as to whether they were fighting so much as cradling one another in a lush riverbed.

"What about it?" Morgan asked.

Sebastian laughed. "You're so coy. You don't need to pretend to be anyone you're not."

"We're in public," Morgan reminded him.

"No one's paying attention to us. Everyone here is looking at the same paintings with the same interest. They want to be scandalised."

"By Coxley, not by me, thank you."

"Fine, fine. But you can be sure that I'll be getting detailed opinions from you on every single one of these paintings the moment we're alone."

"That won't bore you? My opinions on art can go on rather long."

Sebastian was confident in his ability to steer any such conversation away from the technicalities of Coxley's craft and towards the eroticism. And he found that the longer he spent in Morgan's company, the more of his opinions he wanted to hear, like they were boys again, soaking up each other's words like the sun.

"You said you wouldn't use magic in your art. Do you think Coxley does?"

"There are rumours that he enchants his paintings for attention, but I don't believe them. He would want his paintings to attract attention on their own merits, I think."

Sebastian nodded. He couldn't sense any magic clinging to the canvases, and though he knew little of the artist personally, Morgan's assessment rang true.

"Tell me what you think of this one," he said as they turned a corner of the gallery to a fresh wall. "What do you think about that kind of magic?"

A tall painting showed a fey figure seducing a woman in a bed of ferns, streams of magic erupting from her body in obvious pleasure, a physical manifestation of her climax.

Morgan wrinkled his nose in polite distaste. "He's drawing on some very Romantic notions of self-expression, clearly."

"You don't approve?"

"It's a fantasy. My approval is irrelevant."

"You've never done anything like that?" Sebastian teased. "I suppose you're wound much too tight to ever let go with a partner—if you've had partners at all, which is yet undetermined—but not even alone? All by yourself, when there's no one around to judge your unforgivable lapse in rigid self-control?"

"I see Coxley isn't the only fantasist present," Morgan said dryly.

Suddenly, Sebastian wanted nothing more than to see Morgan let go like that. The wanting hit him like a brick to the chest with such force, he nearly staggered. For all of his teasing, Sebastian had never given serious thought to Morgan, sexually-speaking. They'd been childhood friends, then strangers, and then cautious allies, none of which lent themselves to sexual fantasies. Sebastian had offered to take him to bed, of course—such offers came as easily to him as picking locks or pockets. Just because he'd propositioned Morgan didn't mean he'd actually *thought* about it before now.

Glancing around to ensure that everyone else in the room was busy studying the art, Sebastian let slip a little flash of his own magic, mimicking the streams of light pouring from the woman.

Morgan made a shocked sound of strangled outrage and swatted Sebastian's hand down, looking for all the world like Sebastian had turned around and exposed himself to the gallery of visitors rather than merely show off a little magic.

"Put that away!"

"What's the matter? It's not illegal."

"No, but it's not polite," Morgan whispered in heated response.

"Polite?"

"Proper," Morgan corrected himself. His fluster was delectable. "It's uncivilised and it draws attention."

"It's not hurting anyone. No one is even looking in our direction. Have you honestly never done this yourself?"

"As a boy, before I knew better. Certainly never as an adult."

"You're missing out. Go on, give it a try. The feeling is incomparable."

"Letting your magic out in the privacy of your own home is one thing. In public—"

"You'd be shocked at the number of people who let their magic out in public. I might be flashier than most, but I'm hardly unique in this respect. It's so freeing. I promise, you've never felt the full scope of your power until you let it go without any spells to hold it back."

"I don't need freeing, thank you. I'm perfectly fine as I am."

Sebastian snapped his magic back into himself and leaned his weight into Morgan's shoulder, lightly knocking him off balance. "What a killjoy. Coxley must be looking down in such disappointment."

"Looking down on me from where? He's alive, and I'm sure he's already forgotten I exist."

"Your repression is an insult to the spirit of his work. Shall we move on?"

"I think we should. You're a menace, and you ought to be removed from polite society."

"Fresh air and a walk would do us both good," Sebastian agreed. With any luck, the brisk outdoors would clear his head of those distracting wants. "But there's another exhibit I want to see before we go."

In fact, it was this other exhibit that had lured Sebastian to the National Gallery in the first place. A museum was a perfectly innocent location for a date, as Morgan only knew him as an instigator of minor mischief rather than a proper thief. But, as much as Sebastian was enjoying his morning out with Morgan, he'd actually suggested the National Gallery for business, not pleasure. Though, the pleasure was a very nice bonus.

His business was to scope out the Cheapside Hoard jewellery exhibit one last time. He led Morgan through the art-lined hallways at a casual, meandering pace, frequently stopping to point out one painting or another along the way, being careful not to betray his interest in their destination.

He and Kitty had already cased the joint, together and individually, and they were both confident in their ability to steal the jewels that made up the museum's prime attraction. They wouldn't have time to break into every individual case and steal the entire show, more's the pity, but they had discussed at great length which display would yield the prize of greatest value. They were to do the job that very night, and Sebastian wanted one final look beforehand to make sure the gallery hadn't made any last-minute changes to their security.

Upon reaching the Cheapside exhibit, Sebastian had to physically restrain himself from flitting off between the glass cases like a meadow-drunk butterfly, instead attaching himself firmly to Morgan's side.

"Marvellous," Morgan commented mildly, peering down at the exhibit cases. "I take it this sort of thing is more to your interest than the paintings?"

"They both have their place. I wouldn't hang jewellery like this on my wall, and I wouldn't wear one of Coxley's canvases around my neck."

"I don't think these are meant for wearing."

The jewels blinked up at them, dimly luminous: treasure plucked from a bygone age and looking out of place beneath the museum's electric lights. Softer illumination spells would have flattered them better, but the displays were guarded by magic to prevent sticky-fingered thieves, and any ornamental magic would have interfered with that. In their cases, laid out on velvet sheets like stars in the night sky, shone rubies and diamonds and pearls set in silver and gold; rings, buttons, and drop earrings; glittering insect-shaped brooches, a timepiece set in solid emerald—which was a particular favourite of Sebastian's—and enamel perfume bottles.

"They haven't been worn in a terribly long time," Morgan said.

"No, they're all from kings and queens who died a thousand years ago, aren't they?" Sebastian agreed airily, feigning ignorance.

"You're a few centuries off the mark." Morgan tapped the little plaque below the display, which explained that the jewels were on generous loan from the London and Guildhall Museums, which had placed the collection as being from between the sixteenth and seventeenth centuries.

That was something of an oversimplification. The collection as a whole might have been put together around the late sixteenth century, but some of the older jewels had been in circulation for hundreds of years before that. The very oldest could be considered truly ancient, tracing back to Byzantine and Greco-Roman times. If Sebastian were more susceptible to a sense of wonder, he might have been awestruck by their age, like a worshipper in a church of holy relics.

But Sebastian wasn't that way inclined. There was no treasure too old or too impressive to have a price assigned to it, and no jewel he didn't want to wear. Locking such beauties away behind glass like a fairytale princess in a tower should be considered a worse crime than stealing them, in his opinion.

He pretended to have no interest in their provenance. "It's all the same thing after a certain point, isn't it? A few decades, a few centuries—anything from before the nineteenth century might as well be from the Dark Ages, as far as I'm concerned."

Morgan narrowed his eyes. "You're having me on."

"A little bit, yes. But only a little. I wouldn't know the difference between old English treasure and ancient Egyptian treasure, you know?" He absolutely would. "I'm not here for the history of it. I only wanted to see it because I like the glow of the gold and the glimmer of the gemstones."

That part was true enough, though he was also there for the whisper of magic in and around the display cases. Rapping his knuckles against the glass of the largest display, a spark of touch-sensitive magic surged up to meet him, as expected. The guard in the corner of the room sharpened, locking in on him; Sebastian pretended not to notice, already drawing away as if some other display had caught his attention.

To his relief, the case's magic felt the same as it had on his last visit. The time before that, when he'd snuck in one night after the museum was closed, he'd determined that the slightest touch to the glass would raise an awful commotion. But during visiting hours, the same spell was toned down, as the magic was frequently set off by careless or overenthusiastic viewers. The guards and curators checked in on it often, but they weren't so paranoid as to change or remake the spell on a regular basis. That was good news.

"Are you finding the glow and glimmer satisfactory?"

"Very much so, though I must say, I prefer jewellery I'm actually allowed to wear."

"Are you very concerned with what you're allowed to do?"

"Not at all, but this stuff isn't really my style anyway. It's all a bit gaudy, isn't it? I like my accessories a little sleeker, if not subtler."

"That's just as well. I wouldn't know how to get my hands on this kind of thing, if you told me you had your heart set on a Colombian emerald the size of your fist."

"Would you try to get it for me, if I asked?"

"No," Morgan replied, but he was smiling.

Sebastian nudged him with an elbow. "What if I asked for something easier? Like a gold ring, or a diamond-set watch?"

"I already bought you a ring. You're wearing it right now."

"I am. How about a new suit? You did say you would have bought me that, if I'd waited."

"I did say that."

They exited the National Gallery at a leisurely pace, with Morgan allowing Sebastian to stop and point out any art that caught his eye. Still, he discouraged him from lingering too long, likely concerned that Sebastian would burst out some fresh show of magic to publicly embarrass him. It was a fear Sebastian encouraged, talking with his hands so Morgan was worried that any gesture might be the one to erupt in flashy spellwork.

It wasn't illegal to work spells in public; they probably wouldn't have even been asked to leave the museum. But Morgan was right: most people were far too buttoned-up to go for it. Doing it out in the open was marginally more acceptable, so Sebastian steered them away from the gallery to Horse Guards Road, heading for Saint James's Park.

"This was one of my favourite places in the city, growing up," Sebastian said conversationally as they strolled towards the open stretch of green.

"Did you stay in the area after we lost touch?"

"Ah, no, not really. But before we met, I was all over London. A century earlier, I'd have made an excellent street urchin."

"I heard about your father," Morgan began awkwardly. "Your mother…"

Sebastian quickly shook his head, truncating that line of questioning. "I wasn't a ragged orphan child, if that's what you're imagining. I had my mother until I was fifteen. She used to take me here to watch the ducks when I was small."

"Do you still come to do that?"

"Not so much anymore, though I must say, this place is good for finding sitting ducks of another kind."

"Do I want to know?"

"Probably not." Turning off the street and into the park, Sebastian continued, "She would show me 10 Downing Street and Buckingham Palace and tell me that one day, if I was very lucky, I could make my home in either of them."

"Did you believe her?"

"Of course not! I was no lost prince, and even as a little boy, I had no illusions that I would ever become Prime Minister. As I got older, I realised how little I'd enjoy either life—either as a royal or a politician. I'm not cut out for it, in case you hadn't noticed."

"You'd enjoy living in the lap of luxury, though, wouldn't you?"

"Who wouldn't? But none of the responsibility that comes with it."

"A consort to royalty or the Prime Minister, then," Morgan offered.

"As a means to an end, certainly, but that would never be the end goal itself. I have no interest in being tied down to someone wealthier and more powerful than myself for the rest of my life. Everything I do, I'm working towards self-sufficiency."

"And how is that going for you?"

"Better than you might think," Sebastian said with a wink. "But don't worry. It's still far enough in the future that you'll have me by your side for a while yet."

"Thank god for that," Morgan said, with utter dryness.

They strolled along the park path, clouds meandering overhead as the trees rustled orange and yellow in the breeze. Distantly, the ducks conversed, arguing over breadcrumbs. The day felt idyllic, and, in the spacious park, it was easy to tune out the bustle of London traffic and pretend the two of them were somewhere else, somewhere private, with neither past nor future breathing down their necks. Sebastian wanted to put the rest of the world on pause and keep Morgan all to himself for a while. He felt buoyant as he hadn't in years, like his sharpest edges had been smoothed down by childhood memories resurfacing after decades of dormancy.

The clouds parted just enough to let the sun glance through, and for a blink, the lighting made the park look like late summer instead of autumn. Sebastian was ten years old again, his hand around Morgan's wrist, dragging him out to the garden to look for frogs. Sebastian could taste the flowers' perfume, the roses Morgan's mother grew, and the smell of the warm pondwater where little shadows flitted under the surface.

Then and now, Morgan was warm and solid beside him, and when they walked close enough for their shoulders to touch, Sebastian's heart kicked against the backs of his ribs. It was very possible that this sudden desire to kiss his friend didn't come entirely out of thin air. Maybe if they'd spent more than a single summer together, if they had grown up together, Sebastian would have wanted to kiss him years ago.

He couldn't remember the last time he'd wanted to kiss someone specific. Kissing in general was well and good, an enjoyable pastime, especially as a prelude to other activities, whether those activities leaned more towards sex or robbery. He liked both. But to want to kiss *someone*, rather than just anyone—he hardly knew what to do with that, but found, unexpectedly, that he rather liked the feeling.

Nothing had to be complicated. Faced with wanting to kiss his friend, Sebastian determined to act on it the same way he acted on every other want: by reaching out and taking hold of it with both hands and refusing to let go.

Leaning into Morgan just to feel him press against Sebastian's shoulder in return, Sebastian said, "Now that we're out in nature, tucked away from respectable society and prying eyes, tell me: have you really never played around with magic, in the bedroom or out of it?"

"My magic is very functional."

"Well, yes. If function is all you've ever used it for, then it would be. May I?"

"May you what?"

Carefully, so as not to spook the man, Sebastian sent an exploratory tendril of magic towards him as he had approached countless other people and enchanted objects in his life. Sebastian's magic whispered up to Morgan, curling around his hand as if to shake it in greeting, and Morgan's own magic stirred in response, waking up.

"What are you doing?" Morgan asked, more curious than offended.

"I'm just saying hello," Sebastian replied innocently.

Morgan's control over his own magic was too great for Sebastian to coax it out as he had coaxed Felton's magic out of that jewellery case. Talking to magic that had been left to enchant some object was almost always easier than talking to magic inside a person. People were generally bonded to their magic so strongly that the two were inseparable. It had been a long-held belief that magic originated inside people, after all; it was still the belief held by the majority. External magic—wild magic, as it was called—had been all but eradicated in Britain centuries ago.

But what people didn't realise—what the governing body of magic users didn't know or wouldn't admit—was that all magic was wild. It had never been domesticated and bred into a distinct species, but rather tamed enough to give a wolf the demeanour of a lapdog. But a wolf was always a wolf, even if it had forgotten how to act like one.

Sebastian let a burst of sparks tap out from his fingertips, bright gold and red against the grey autumn day, and Morgan jerked his hand back like he'd been burned. Not out of fear of Sebastian's magic, but rather, out of fear that he might give into temptation and let his own sparks out in solidarity.

"I wish you wouldn't do that," Morgan muttered. "You're much too old to be playing with magic in the streets. It makes you look like a vagabond."

"If this is your reaction to a little magic show, I shudder to think what you'd say if I offered to take you behind that hedge over there."

Morgan missed a step. "I'm sorry?"

At the first hard refusal, Sebastian would back off and call it a joke, but until then, his smile grew wider. "The path doesn't get much traffic over there. I could give you a hand, burn off some of that tension you're carrying."

"Thank you," Morgan managed, "but absolutely not. I'm going to pretend you didn't say that."

That was nowhere near hard. "Still too risky for you? That's alright. The park gets quite secluded up ahead, once you get into that wooded area. There, I guarantee we'll have a good five minutes of privacy. That's more than enough time to take care of you if I'm on my knees."

"Are you mad?" Morgan hissed. "You can't talk about things like that!"

"Is it only the talking that's a problem? Because I can do it without talking about it."

"Do you have no sense of self-preservation whatsoever?" Morgan asked incredulously.

"You're overly cautious. Come on."

Taking Morgan by the hand, Sebastian set off for the trees, dragging his companion in his wake. Morgan lagged behind, but made no attempt to actually break free of Sebastian's grasp. With every step, Sebastian felt lighter and less inhibited, which he'd hardly been in the first place. Morgan's heartbeat pounded against Sebastian's palm, as rapid with excitement as Sebastian's own.

When they reached the trees, dappled gold shadows obscuring them from the rest of the park, Sebastian turned on him and asked, "How many people can see us right now?"

"What if someone's walking in the woods?"

"They're not; you'd hear them. How many people can see us?"

"None," Morgan admitted.

Stepping forward, Sebastian backed Morgan against a trunk. "Then, if I say I want to kiss you, you can't refuse out of fear or propriety. You can only refuse if you really, honestly don't want me to."

Morgan's gaze dropped to Sebastian's lips before stuttering up again. "Someone might come by."

Sebastian smiled and drew on his power, whispering the same spell he and Kitty had used on their makeup before: to disarm passers-by and encourage their attention to slide right over them.

"They won't notice. I promise." He crowded close, left hand on Morgan's chest, toying with the knot of his tie. The pearl ring was the same silvery grey as the silk tie; just the right shade to flatter Morgan's eyes.

"We had an agreement," Morgan said.

"No seductions," Sebastian agreed. "This is just a kiss. No ulterior motives. Just because I want to."

"Nothing is ever *just* anything with you."

"Say you don't want me to."

When Morgan didn't answer, Sebastian kissed him.

It was quick, a fraction of what Sebastian wanted from him, but even when Morgan's mouth parted in surprise under his, even with the heat of his body soaking through their clothes where Sebastian pressed against him, he didn't push for more. It was only a test, and then he drew back, searching Morgan's face for a reaction. Morgan blinked, his eyes wide and pupils large and dark in their seas of grey, but he didn't move.

Disappointed, Sebastian gathered himself and made to withdraw. Before he could, Morgan caught again him by the hand, his thumb brushing the top of the ring.

They both stood frozen for a second, waiting for the other to move first.

Just when Sebastian was about to apologise, Morgan tugged him close and instigated a kiss of his own. Caught off balance, Sebastian stumbled into him and they met mouth to mouth with bruising force and far more hunger than Sebastian had initially dared. It was as if Morgan was trying to make up for every minute of the past few days they'd spent together without touching. He wrapped his arms around Sebastian like he would have him then and there, his earlier reservations be damned. When Sebastian licked against his lips, Morgan let him in without hesitation, and Sebastian moaned appreciatively into his open mouth as Morgan's hands dropped lower to squeeze Sebastian's arse.

As if Sebastian's moan had broken some spell he was under, Morgan suddenly cut off their kiss and pulled back to hold Sebastian at arm's length.

But he didn't push Sebastian away, and he didn't try to escape the scene.

"Well," said Sebastian eventually. "That answers one question about your reputation. No blushing virgin has ever kissed like that."

"Who's been saying I'm a virgin?"

"People," Sebastian said dismissively. "Don't be offended," he added. "It's a perfectly neutral descriptor."

"Not the way they're saying it, I suspect." Morgan took a deep breath, then asked, "What was that?"

"It doesn't have to be anything."

"A real answer, please. Because we talked about this, and I know I made myself clear that I didn't want any attempts on your part—"

Sebastian raised his hands. "I didn't mean anything by it. I was simply having a nice day, and you've proved yourself unexpectedly wonderful company. I just wanted us both to enjoy ourselves for a minute. Genuinely, that's all there was to it. I wanted to kiss you, so I did."

"You're sure that's all it was?"

"My hand on my heart," Sebastian swore, doing just that.

Exhaling in a gust, Morgan nodded. Was he reassured? Disappointed? Sebastian had no idea. One hand in his pocket, Morgan offered Sebastian his other arm. "Alright then. Shall we head on?"

Unaccountably relieved that Morgan was taking the kiss in stride, even if his greater reaction to it remained unreadable, Sebastian accepted the offer and glued himself to Morgan's side once more.

He dropped the cloaking spell as they left the park and re-joined the pedestrians on the street, every class of person bustling along in the lunchtime rush. He made no effort to keep his hands to himself as he might have done otherwise. When he was out with company, he generally tried to be better behaved, keeping his pickpocketing limited to the busiest of streets when there was no one with him to slow him down if he needed to make a run for it. But his mood was too bright from that kiss, not to mention his anticipation of the National Gallery heist that night, and he couldn't help himself from dipping into other people's coat pockets and open purses as they walked by.

Sebastian didn't use magic when it came to recreational pickpocketing. On serious jobs, yes, but he liked to keep his skills sharp and his fingers clever. Overly relying on magic for such things would eventually lead to carelessness, and carelessness was a death knell in that line of work. He kept Morgan engaged in lively conversation the entire time, such that the other man didn't notice Sebastian's activities at all until he had the bad luck of reaching for the pocket of a man who must have been a guard dog in another life.

"Hey now, watch yourself," the man snapped, drawing his coat close and throwing an arm out to distance himself from Sebastian.

"Apologies," Sebastian said without breaking stride. "I stumbled." To Morgan, he directed a light eyeroll and a shake of his head at the man's rudeness.

"Come at me again and I'll break your fingers," the man warned.

"Leave off, it was an accident."

"Was it? Or were you trying to lift my wallet?"

At Sebastian's side, Morgan went stiff, shooting Sebastian a sharp, questioning look. Sebastian minutely shook his head, denying everything.

"I bet if I shook you down, the coppers would be right interested in what fell out," the man said, following them down the street.

"Time to go," Sebastian suggested to Morgan, and, flashing him a cheeky smile, broke into a run.

Swearing, Morgan followed suit, and together they bolted through a gap in traffic to the other side of the road, leaving their antagonist cut off behind a line of motorcars and unable to pursue them further. Though Sebastian slowed to a jog after that, he didn't stop running until they turned the corner and were entirely out of sight.

"What the hell was that?" Morgan demanded, coming to a halt with his hands on his knees, red-faced and panting for breath, clearly angry. Unfortunately, it was a good look on him.

"I didn't take anything from him, I swear," Sebastian said, still grinning and still high from the thrill of the chase, even though he'd been the one being hunted.

"From *him*," Morgan repeated. "What about the hundred other people we've walked past today?"

"Oh, come on; it's a harmless game. No one got hurt, and I didn't get caught. Everything's fine."

Morgan straightened, running one hand through his sweaty curls as his jaw worked furiously on unspoken words. "Let's take this conversation inside," he said shortly.

CHAPTER TWELVE

WHEREIN SEBASTIAN GETS DRUNK AND SULKS IN THE BATH

It took Sebastian the entire walk back to Portman Square to understand that Morgan was genuinely angry—Morgan, who spent the walk three paces ahead of Sebastian like he couldn't bear to look at him.

They got two steps inside Morgan's front door before rounding on each other.

"You knew I was a petty thief," Sebastian said. "The very first thing you knew about me was that I'd stolen your watch."

"I thought that was done to provoke me."

"You can't expect a leopard to change its spots so easily. Why are you so upset? I haven't taken anything else from you."

"I thought the whole point of this exchange was for me to provide you with every amenity. What am I missing, that you have to go out and do this? You're only asking to get caught."

"But I didn't get caught," Sebastian countered. "A stranger hurling insults without proof carries no weight. There were no cops on the scene; there was no one around to threaten me."

"And what about next time?" A muscle ticked in Morgan's jaw. His agitation was palpable, fists clenched by his sides. Sebastian really didn't think the situation called for it.

"Is this a test?" Morgan pressed, desperate for some explanation that made sense to him. "Are you just trying to see whether I have enough emotionally invested in you to bail you out of jail?'

He paused and Sebastian held his breath. It hadn't been a test, but now he very much wanted to know the answer. Morgan himself didn't seem to know. The moment stretched, becoming unbearable. Something in Sebastian's face must have betrayed him, indicating that he wasn't taking the situation as seriously as Morgan would have liked.

Morgan pulled back, crossed his arms, and said, "I won't. Not for something so petty."

His words struck Sebastian like a slap to the face. They stared each other down for a second, both of them bristling like alley cats from the indignity of the argument.

It was Sebastian who broke first, his lip curling in a sneer. "You'd leave me to rot over a wallet and a few rings? Fine. I'll save you the trouble."

As he hadn't yet removed his coat or scarf, he had the satisfaction of turning around and walking straight back out the door, ignoring Morgan's frustrated protest. Of course, it wasn't entirely satisfactory. Such things rarely were. His bag of meagre belongings remained upstairs in the guest bedroom, and, more importantly, so did his stash from Felton's pawnshop. One way or another, he would have to return to retrieve it. Sneaking in through the window again was always an option if all else failed.

Alternatively, though he certainly didn't feel it in the moment, in a day or two his pride might be recovered enough for him to return and have a civil conversation with Morgan. Or at least, he might be up for pretending to be civil. He would undoubtedly be feeling more generous once the Cheapside Hoard jewels were in his possession. Come dawn, he could afford to be magnanimous and forgiving, if he so chose. He could afford to be anything he wanted.

Quarrels were inevitable in any relationship. Business partners, friends, and lovers were all susceptible to them. Kitty and Sebastian fell into the categories of both friends and partners, and god knows they'd had their fair share of arguments, and likely would have again.

Sebastian just wasn't sure what kind of relationship he and Morgan were in. What he did know was that

Morgan's house with comfortable and his food was good.

And also, that Sebastian had really enjoyed kissing him, and would have liked to do it again, at least several more times.

Sebastian could replace him with another man within the week, but he'd be an idiot to let Morgan slip through his fingers because they'd both lost their tempers. What other man in London had Sebastian once considered a friend? What other man made Sebastian want to push him up against a tree, wrap them both in magic, and kiss him insensate? Sebastian had no intention of apologising for his pickpocketing or for anything else, but he would try to salvage what they had. It was worth an attempt, if nothing else.

But first, he would let Morgan stew in it and realise just what he was missing out on.

Sebastian walked all the way to Adam's townhouse. He had enough money on him to hail a cab, but it seemed a waste when he had two perfectly functional legs, and the weather hadn't turned so bad as that. He kept his hands in his pocket and his head down, walking briskly and with purpose, avoiding the temptations of any passers-by until Morgan's neighbourhood was at his back. After that, anyone was fair game, and by the time he reached Adam's place, he had a nice pocketful of coins and baubles to keep him company and soothe the raging frustration of the earlier argument.

When no one answered his knock at the door, he let himself in and grouchily made himself at home. When evening rolled around and Kitty returned, it was to find Sebastian lounging in a tepid bath with a bottle of wine at his side. He was feeling marginally better by then, though no less inclined to apologise. If anything, over the course of his bath he had grown increasingly disinclined.

This was what came of approaching people honestly, he decided. He had introduced himself to Morgan as a pickpocket, and still the man thought he could mould Sebastian into whatever shape best pleased him. It was the same as every common mark who thought Sebastian as malleable as a soft wax doll, to be bent and sculpted whichever way they liked. Sebastian had hoped that by going to Morgan as a friend and a partner in crime, Morgan might see him as his own person, already shaped. How unforgivably naïve of him.

Sebastian knew better than that. He should have kept things simple with no room for complications, but instead, he'd allowed his boredom and dissatisfaction with the Whistler situation to push him to try something new. (He deliberately ignored the nostalgia tugging at his hand, trying to coax him back to that golden summer.)

A sloppy, amateur mistake. He'd be better off stealing his things back from Morgan's room under cover of darkness and relocating to a different part of the city. The take from the pawnshop and Deepa's Kew Gardens job would finance his wildest lifestyle for at least a year; the Cheapside Hoard, for decades, if not longer. And once he got his hands on the Rose Diamond necklace, he'd never have to run a con on another man ever again. He skimmed his fingers over the water's surface, turning their plan for that night's heist over and over in his mind's eye. He was tight with anticipation, his frustration making him as edgy as the drink made him blurred, cancelling each other out. Which wasn't the best way to go into a job, but it was far from the worst.

The bathwater ran over his ring like it was trying to reclaim the pearl for the ocean. He hadn't taken it off. It wasn't worth much; it certainly wouldn't go far towards funding his future dreams the way his other jewels would. But it was a gift, and it was pretty, so there was no reason not to keep it.

Sebastian was distantly aware of Kitty's return, and then more keenly aware of her presence when she found him soaking. As he explained his decision to walk away from Morgan, somewhat tipsier than his norm, she gave him the most judgemental glare ever directed from woman to man.

"Tell me again why that's easier than going back to him and making nice?"

"He doesn't deserve me," Sebastian said with a haughty sniff, raising the bottle to take another swig. He was only halfway through; he'd never been a heavy drinker, and, considering he had no real sorrows to drink away, he wasn't going to start in Kitty's bath.

"I don't think I deserve you in this state, either. Adam certainly doesn't, so get out of there and pull yourself together before he has the misfortune of dealing with you."

Sebastian looked speculatively at the bottle, debating whether he should continue until he met the bottom.

"Self-pity doesn't suit you," Kitty said.

"That's not what this is. I'm just taking a moment to appreciate what I have."

"You haven't got anything," she said shortly. "You're in the flat of your best friend's beau, drinking his wine and running up his water bill. Now stand up and let me get a look at you. Are you too drunk for tonight's job?"

"Not at all. Fetch me a towel?"

"Give me the wine."

They traded, and he wrapped the towel around his waist as he stood up, demonstrating that he was indeed steady enough to proceed as planned. He held out his hands, which, despite the half-bottle of red flowing in his veins, didn't so much as tremble.

"I've never let personal matters jeopardise the work. I've known Morgan Hollyhock less than a week, and you think I'd let him twist me up to that extent? Please."

Though her mouth was still pursed, Kitty nodded, and stepped back far enough to let him out of the bath. "Good. In that case, come to tea. You need some solid food to soak up that drink before we head out."

Sebastian towelled off and began getting dressed as Kitty handed him his clothes one item at a time.

"He was upset by my pickpocketing." Sebastian tried to sound careless, but his words came out sulky.

"But he *knows* you're a pickpocket," Kitty said blankly.

"Hence my frustration."

"Was he upset by the thievery itself, or was he upset at the prospect of you getting caught?"

"Probably both. He's so terribly risk-averse in every aspect of his life—I don't understand how anyone can live as safely and dully as he does!" He buttoned his shirt with minimal clumsiness.

"He took you into his home and his bed," Kitty pointed out reasonably, lobbing his socks at him. "Even if he was hoping his charity would cure you of your criminal ways, you're both still men. If he was truly as dull and risk-averse as you claim, he'd be settled in a miserable marriage to some poor unsuspecting woman by now."

Straightening up after pulling on his socks, Sebastian fixed her with an incredulous look. "Do you think I'm judging him unfairly?"

"A little bit. For heaven's sake, we can't all be ex-convicts and notorious jewel thieves! He might be a bit boring, and certainly no one I'd want to take out for a night on the town, but I don't think he's nearly as bad as you're pretending he is."

"Fine," Sebastian said peevishly. "I'll allow that his penchant for sodomy carries with it a certain degree of risk. But I'm not giving him any more than that. You're supposed to be on my side."

"I am on your side, you idiot. That's why I'm trying to convince you Morgan's a good thing that you should hang onto a little longer."

"You just want me out of your hair so I'll stop intruding on you and Adam."

"Yes," she said emphatically. "Anyway, you can drop Morgan once the Cheapside take is fenced. After that, you'll be set up to live as independently as your heart desires. Getting those jewels is one thing, but until we can sell them on, you need someone to provide for you, and Morgan seems as good as any, if not better than most. So, swallow your pride, pull your head out of your arse, and go back to him. And be sure to keep your hands clean when he can see you."

At the dinner table, Adam took one look at Sebastian and said, "Bad day at the office, dear?"

"Fuck off," Sebastian replied, sinking into his chair to poke sullenly at his food.

It was a chicken and vegetable dish on rice that smelled delicious, and he knew he'd eat all of it, but he wished he were the kind of person who could refrain from eating in order to make a point about his emotional state.

Which was frustration and dissatisfaction, absolutely nothing more.

"Any plans for the night?" Adam asked delicately, glancing at Kitty.

"You know our plans," Sebastian said.

"I was asking to be polite. They could have changed since the last time I saw you."

"They haven't."

Adam and Kitty communicated something silently with their eyes, and Sebastian rolled his. That was one of the things he hated most about couples: the way they had their own secret language, speaking in minute shifts of expression. He and Kitty had their own, of course, as a result of being such close friends and partners for so many years, but it was obnoxious observing it in anyone else.

"I'm fine," he said, for the hundredth time that evening. "Thanks for your concern. I'll cop that the wine may not have been my most mature decision, but I'm clearly not drunk, and the rice will sober me up the rest of the way."

"Right," said Adam, and stood up to swap out Sebastian's glass of white for a cup of water.

Sebastian begrudgingly allowed it.

"Darling, look," Kitty said. "At the risk of engaging in emotional honesty, which we both despise, I don't think your head's in the right place to do this tonight. God knows why, but I think you're more bent out of shape over your little spat with Morgan Hollyhock than you want to admit."

"Don't be ridiculous. I'm perfectly fine. There's no reason for the job not to go ahead as planned."

"You do seem a little out of sorts," Adam said.

"We can reschedule," Kitty offered.

"I'm fine," Sebastian insisted. "I got frustrated, I had a few more drinks than I should have, but I'm already sobering up. Morgan Hollyhock is irrelevant to the job we do tonight, and irrelevant in general. He's not important, and I don't need him."

"Spoken like someone with zero emotional attachment."

"I'm sure whatever you were arguing about will blow over quickly once you go back to him," Adam said. "It's not as if he actually kicked you out. Maybe he'll even be the one to apologise first."

"He'd have to be, because I'm not apologising at all. In any case, that's a scene for another day. Tonight's job is more important and more interesting, and it's just what I need to get my head back in the game."

"Are you sure?" Kitty asked seriously. "There's no shame in pushing it back another night or two."

That was a bald-faced lie and they both knew it. There would be incredible shame in admitting that his fight with Morgan had rattled him to the extent that he couldn't do his job. If he were anyone but her closest friend, Kitty would have smacked him upside the head and replaced him with someone more reliable for so much as hinting that he might be unable to perform his role as expected.

"I'm fine," he said, and forced himself to believe it. "Let's do this."

CHAPTER THIRTEEN

IN WHICH CRIMINAL PURSUITS
DO NOT GO ACCORDING TO PLAN

Kitty and Sebastian stole up to the National Gallery at two in the morning, slinking around the perimeter like a couple of foxes until they reached a little service exit around the back. The night was still and quiet, the air crisp and the sky indigo-black behind rolling cloud cover. Every so often the moon pierced the clouds to turn their path silvery, but they were confident in the darkness and needed no assistance.

Inside, there were two guards per floor, making their rounds with no sense of urgency, and none outside. The main entrances and exits were locked for the night, but the service exit was open, allowing the guards to step outside for periodic smoke breaks. Kitty and

Sebastian had mapped out the whole building, and knew precisely how to get from the service door to their target. The Cheapside Hoard waited for them at the other end of their mental map, glimmering in the moonlight and beckoning for them to hurry.

It was Sebastian's job to disarm the exhibit's security, divert the guards' attention, and keep them distracted until Kitty had made the lift and got away clean. There was really nothing to the plan at all, and as long as they were both focused and competent, very little could go wrong. It was a step up from robbing old Felton's pawnshop, but only just. Sebastian could have done it in his sleep.

They crept through the gallery, soft-shoed steps mouse-like against the tiled floors, hugging close to the walls and staying in the shadows. They both wore their enchanted makeup, but only as a last resort. If the guards caught sight of them, there would be no disguising the fact that they were intruders of ill intent. The best they could hope for was that their faces would be unmemorable, and any descriptions offered up to Scotland Yard after the fact would be contradictory and incomprehensible.

Which wasn't to say that their makeup and inherent stealth were their only lines of defence. Sebastian cloaked them both in a blanket of living shadows. The glamour wasn't impenetrable, and it was strongest when they stuck to the real darkness, but it should buy them a few precious seconds to escape if the guards came upon them.

Sebastian was feeling for magic as he went along, but the National Gallery as a whole was not enchanted with security measures. That would take far too much energy to maintain. Instead, only the jewellery exhibit itself was protected, with each glass case shimmering with a guarded aura. He and Kitty could safely approach the displays, but as soon as they attempted to touch the glass, all hell would break loose. They wouldn't be physically harmed—using that kind of dangerous magic carried too many liabilities, and the museum didn't want to inadvertently harm a clumsy guard rather than a potential thief—but the magic would be very bright and terribly loud, calling every guard in the vicinity to come down on them like a pack of hounds at the hunt.

Sebastian's job was to prevent that.

He only needed to disarm a single case: naturally, it was the largest and most heavily protected. Crosses made of rosy-violet sapphires, fiery opal brooches, diamond rings, carbuncles and emeralds inlaid with enamel and gold filigree and set in the shape of beetles or salamanders: small pieces, but numerous, gathered together in a glass box like Snow White in her tomb.

Unfortunately, the pocket watch Sebastian coveted wasn't among them. It had been crafted by a seventeenth-century artist of unsurpassed skill: a delicate gold timepiece set in a Colombian emerald, the stone as rich a green as had ever existed. The watch was housed in its own separate case, and they simply didn't have enough time to break into more than one. Having studied the exhibit from every angle beforehand, they'd determined which case would yield the greatest pay off, and they couldn't afford to get distracted by personal fancies along the way. Sebastian consoled himself with the fact that, once the pieces were sold, he could afford to commission a watch set in whatever precious stone his heart desired, if he found himself yearning for such a thing down the line.

Their target stood in the middle of the room, a great octagonal case with a two-foot diameter, the magic shimmering aggressively over the glass like an oil spill. Sebastian crept up to it as if approaching a wild animal, with Kitty hovering at his side like a shadow.

"Sixty seconds to disarm it, sixty to grab the stuff, and another sixty to get out unseen," she murmured.

"Not a problem."

But this wasn't friendly magic like that at Felton's. He could tell just from approaching it that it wouldn't be convinced to abandon its post so easily. He was wary of even sending his own magic out to greet it, uncertain of just how reactive it would be.

A different approach was needed, as he'd assumed it would be. It was naïve to think that any and all magic could be coerced with little more than an amicable gesture, and Sebastian did not trade in naïveté. This spell had been set by a professional for the sole purpose of guarding priceless treasures. Sebastian had come prepared to disarm the exhibit by any means necessary, and he'd expected that would require some degree of force.

Bending his knees, he put himself at eye level with the case. Kitty slipped away to position herself by the doorway, watching for any sign of activity in the rooms beyond. Sebastian trusted her enough to tune her out entirely and focus everything on the spell.

The magic was highly sensitive, aware of his presence even without him touching it. As he studied it, his face an inch from the glass, it crackled and snapped like a dog at the end of its leash.

It was strong stuff.

Sebastian was stronger.

Priming his own magic for a fight, he sent it out in a rush, overpowering the security magic like throwing a heavy blanket to smother a fire. There was no convincing the enemy magic to make friends, no gentle coaxing for it to forget the purpose of its spell. He came down on it hard and fast, not attempting to undo the spellwork, but rather, aiming only to subdue it long enough for Kitty to get in there and out again before triggering anything.

The alarms could sound once they were both outside the building. They could scream at the top of their lungs and flash their lights so brightly they could be seen from the continent, for all Sebastian cared. The security magic thrashed in his grip, snarling ferociously, but he only needed to hold its jaws closed for sixty seconds so Kitty could grab the stuff, and another sixty for them both to escape.

With sweat beading along his hairline from the exertion of holding that enemy magic down, he careful raised one hand and pressed a single gloved fingertip to the glass.

No reaction.

"Ready," he said, inching away from the display.

But his success came at the cost of his shadow glamour. He didn't have the strength to maintain it and subdue the security magic at the same time. Kitty gave him a sharp look as it dissipated like morning mist, but he could only shake his head, annoyed with himself for the lapse as he traded places with her, she going to the case as he went to the doorway.

He had to wrench his gaze away from the case in order to effectively stand watch, and he trembled with the effort of keeping that magic subdued from several yards away. Grinding his teeth, he glared through the darkness, daring any guard to materialise. Kitty was right, though he would never in a million years admit it to her. He wasn't in top form. They'd both known the National Gallery would employ strong magic to guard the Cheapside Hoard; he'd staked it out ahead of time in order to know exactly how strong it might be. He'd been prepared.

But then, instead of resting up and taking care of himself like a boxer before stepping into the ring for a prize fight, he'd moped around drinking with no concern as to how that might impair his performance.

Amateur, lovesick behaviour. His lip curled in a sneer as he berated himself, his breath coming harder and heartbeat kicking against his ribs as he struggled to keep control. Simultaneously focusing on the magic and on his lookout duty was near impossible, taxing him to the breaking point. He clenched his hands in fists, leather gloves creaking as he tried to ground himself, but his attention kept slipping. Keeping that magic quiet was the priority.

Behind him, he could hear Kitty breaking into the display, deftly unscrewing the top of the glass case from its sides, working quickly as she flitted from one corner to the next. He could picture her movements perfectly, each step matching up to the slightest of sounds. She eased the lid off the display before placing it on the floor, the sound like setting an empty drinking glass against a tile. Then, a harsh tinkle of gemstones clashing against each other, seeming louder than it really was as Kitty swiped the jewellery into her bag.

She was thirty seconds into her allotted sixty; Sebastian had to hold the magic for ninety more. He sucked in a breath. He was overheating, his face and palms clammy against the museum's cool night air. The magic kicked against his grip and he squeezed his eyes shut, brow furrowed in concentration as he wrestled it back under control.

A warning prickled between his eyes like a sixth sense and he refocused, gaze sharpening, as a figure stepped into the far doorway of the next gallery room down from theirs.

Sebastian went so still he could hear his own blood rushing through his veins. Behind him, Kitty fastened the bag securely and strapped it to her back, the jewellery inside bundled so tightly, it didn't make a sound.

"Plan B," Sebastian said tersely, not taking his eyes from the figure.

She only faltered for a single step before abruptly turning away from him and the direction they'd come to make her exit another way.

"Hey there," the guard called. Sebastian could hear the puzzled frown in his voice. "Is that you, Will?"

Sebastian didn't know what the other guard, this Will, sounded like. He couldn't imitate him. "Shit," Sebastian breathed.

The guard broke into a jog, gathering speed as he approached. Sebastian couldn't defend himself and keep the magic under control at the same time. It would take him sixty seconds to get out of the building— eighty, if he took the Plan B route—but if he had a guard breathing down his neck chasing him out, that took him all the way down to Plan F.

He needed to hold it together. Once Kitty was out of the building, the greatest risk would be over. Getting her and the jewellery clear was the most important thing. If he came face to face with a guard, the glamours woven into his makeup should keep him safe. If they searched him, they would come up empty-handed, and if they tried to identify him, their efforts should slide right off him like water off a duck. If they tried to apprehend him, he only needed to give Kitty those eighty seconds to clear the perimeter before he was free to drop that enemy magic, alarms be damned, and defend himself until he was able to escape. It was far from ideal, but he'd be fine.

Except that as soon as the guard came up to him, grabbing him roughly by the arms and giving him a shake like a terrier with a rat, Sebastian panicked. In that instant, he was back in Blackwood, with a guard shoving him into his cell for the first time. His cold, dark little cell where he couldn't see sunlight and that he wouldn't leave for another nine months.

He dropped his hold on the museum's security magic and it shattered like brittle glass. The alarms wailed out like a pack of hounds, bell-like, and the lights flashed like fireworks, momentarily blinding.

Sebastian flinched hard, one arm thrown across his face to shield his eyes. His only saving grace was that the guard reacted in kind, and Sebastian recovered first. Disoriented as he was by the lights and the noise, Sebastian bolted, shoving past the guard to take the Plan F route out of the building.

Shouts from the other guards ran out. The original guard's partner, presumably Will, joined him first in the Cheapside exhibit—

"Did you get a look at him?"

"No, he's done something to his face, he's all a blur—"

And then a set of footsteps pounded after Sebastian from one room to the next, following his trail.

Cursing, Sebastian slammed into the door that would let him out, fiddling desperately with the lock as the guard bore down on him.

"Shit, shit, shit," he whispered furiously.

His hands were shaking so badly he could barely grasp the lock to turn it, sweaty fingers slipping off the metal as he yanked the handle. He made it through the door as the guard grabbed hold of his collar like catching a cat by the ruff.

"Got you! Turn around, let me see what's going on there—"

Sebastian snarled, feral with panic, and wrenched free, nearly choking himself in the process. Throwing himself through the door, he slammed it against the guard before taking off at a run. He couldn't manually lock the door from that side, and he didn't have the strength or the time to slither his magic into the lock to do it that way, either. A shut door couldn't hold the guard for long.

The night air was a relief against his sweaty skin, sharpening his senses just enough to keep his legs under him. His knees were watery, buckling as he ran, but he didn't fall. He felt top-heavy, in constant danger of tripping and falling on his face, only catching himself at the last second with every step.

He'd never gone up against magic as strong as that, and never been so exhausted by it. He needed to shake off that guard before re-joining Kitty, but he was out in plain sight with the guard hot on his heels. The slammed door had only bought him a second's lead, and the guard was in fighting form compared to Sebastian. He couldn't outrun his opponent, and his glamoured makeup might make his features indistinct, but it clearly wasn't deterring the guards from giving chase. They hadn't tested *that* in Eden. He needed to disappear.

Pulling in a breath like a drowning man, Sebastian pulled his exhausted magic around him like a cloak, willing it to hide him. Like a mirror, his magic reflected the night around him, and the guard's footsteps slowed, confused. Sebastian couldn't turn himself invisible, but if he blended into his surroundings well enough, he might be able to sneak away before the guard recognised the illusion.

Slowly, hanging onto his magic tightly, afraid of it falling away like a child afraid of losing his protective blanket in the night, Sebastian shuffled away from the guard. They were only a few yards away from each other, the guard flashing his torch around the museum's lot, glaring at every suspicious shape and shadow.

The waving beam of light actually helped Sebastian's illusion. Though his mirrored cloak couldn't withstand close scrutiny, a single light moving around like that served to make the glamour more disorienting. One step at a time, Sebastian zigzagged away from the building until he reached the row of trees by the perimeter. Pressing his back to the broadest trunk, he let his knees finally give out, sinking to the haunches as his spell dissolved.

A rustle from the branches above his head warned him of Kitty's presence a split second before she dropped to the ground, landing lightly on her feet.

"What the fuck was that?" she hissed.

"Their security was stronger than anticipated," Sebastian wheezed, which was true, and also the closest thing to an apology he was willing to give.

"Was it? Or were you just not up to it?"

Sebastian bristled, his already wounded pride smarting under the blow. "The alarm didn't go off until you were out of the building, and we both got away clean. What do you have to be angry about?"

"You only got away by dumb luck."

"I wasn't the one with the jewels on me. The guard got a look at me, but he can't describe my face. Even if I'd been caught, I never would have ratted you out. You were never at risk."

"I know you wouldn't rat me out," she snapped.

"Then why are you yelling at me!"

She stared at him for a beat, her dark eyes black with fury, before snarling and punching him in the shoulder. "We got the job done, but this was a fuck-up," she declared, turning on her heel to march away from the museum towards Orange Street, her hands in fists around the straps of her rucksack. "I never should have agreed to do this tonight. You weren't in your right head for it."

"What are you talking about?" He ran to catch up to her, furious and mortified at the way he immediately stumbled and lost his breath. "I didn't realise the security would be so strong, and that's on me, admittedly, but—"

She spun to face him again, so abruptly he nearly tripped over her, and jabbed one finger accusingly into his chest.

"You're emotionally compromised. God knows what Morgan Hollyhock has done to get you twisted into knots over him, but it's something. I don't care how you fix it, but you need to get your shit together if you want to do the Rose Diamond job. Either go on a bender and get laid, drink till you forget about him, break into his house to steal his valuables, go back and shag him one last time—I don't care. Do you whatever you need to resolve this mess. Because right now, if

216

you're upset and distracted, I can't trust you to do your job. And if I can't trust you, then we can't work together. Do you understand?"

Sebastian bit back every mean, knee-jerk retort until a drop of blood welled up from his tongue where his canine punctured it. When he was sure he wouldn't say anything irreparable, he managed a short, "I understand."

"Good. Don't come back to Adam's till it's sorted."

And with that, she left him standing in the street in the dead of night with nowhere to go but back to Morgan.

CHAPTER FOURTEEN

A MOST UNPLEASANT BARING OF THE SOUL

Daybreak found Sebastian on Morgan's front step yet again. He hadn't decided whether he wanted to go through with actually knocking. It felt like admitting a terrible weakness, but then, the previous night had proven that he was terribly weak.

Sebastian had been a different man, before prison. Not drastically; not in any way a casual acquaintance could pinpoint. But there were subtle little things different about him now, and they frustrated him to no end. Blackwood had shaken him to his very foundation. Though he'd pretended to brush it off like it was nothing, even managing to keep Kitty in the dark as to the extent of its effects on his psyche, he wasn't the same man he'd been before entering its gates.

He was constantly hungry, no matter how full his plate, and he disliked the cold, the dark, and tight spaces, though none of those had ever bothered him before. He checked in with his magic constantly, compulsively, afraid every time he reached for it that he would find it gone.

Those were minor aggravations. Given enough time and hard-headedness, he was sure he could work through them.

More distressing was the fact that he was *sensitive* now. More prone to impatience and frustration, both qualities sounding a death knell for a con artist. And, horribly embarrassing: he was lonelier. He longed to be around people. To be surrounded by a crowd, or to watch pedestrians coming and going in the park, to hear their casual chatter and watch their freedom of movement. And, even more than that, he craved connection. Conversation, and physical touch, something genuine and skin to skin.

He'd never craved anything genuine before in his life, and he didn't know what to do with the feeling. He shied away, mistrusting the sentiment even as the loneliness and the yearning grew deeper and wider inside him like a chasm. It was as if Blackwood had reached into him and scooped out everything on which he'd built his career and his identity as a confidence man, leaving him shivering, uncertain and lonely in its wake. Rendering him useless, and with a sense of self that felt like looking into a shattered mirror.

And then, as if in answer to that loneliness, there was Morgan. A call back to a simpler, happier time before Sebastian had known what loneliness was. He'd barely thought about Morgan by the time he'd reached his teenage years; barely remembered him at all by the time he was an adult. But it had only taken a chance encounter for those memories to come flooding back, and though they were hazy, unfinished around the edges and missing gaps here and there, they left Sebastian aching.

He didn't know how to get his life back to the way it had been before. After Blackwood, he'd tried to return to his old habits like nothing had changed. But his failure with Whistler and his disastrous handling of the National Gallery job, to say nothing of the way he'd fumbled the whole Morgan situation, was proof enough that some things, once cracked, couldn't be put back together.

In the end, he spent so long standing on Morgan's step in indecision that his choice was removed entirely. The door pulled open and Sebastian whirled to face Morgan's man Sterling, who regarded him with a clinical, if sceptical, air.

"Good morning, sir," said Sterling, giving Sebastian a cool look over the tops of his wire-rim spectacles. "Can I help you?"

Sterling was a heron-like man nearing retirement, with neat grey hair that was balding on top, and dressed in an immaculate suit that looked like it had never known a wrinkle, never mind going through the indignity of being laundered.

"Is Morgan in?" Sebastian could hardly pretend he was there for any other reason. "Or have you been told to turn me away?" he added, when Sterling didn't immediately reply.

"May I inquire as to the nature of your visit?"

"You know I was a guest here for a few nights. I left some of my belongings upstairs."

"Would you like me to collect them for you, sir?"

Sebastian was torn. It was the perfect way out: he could get his things back without having to sneak in through the window, and he could avoid seeing Morgan again. But that would lose him his chance to make up with what could be a friend, as well as lose a very comfortable living arrangement. Loneliness urged him to make amends. His selfishness urged him to do the same, for the sake of a warm bed and a safe place to stay. Only his pride resisted.

But none of those were the deciding factor.

Sebastian couldn't risk Sterling discovering the secret pocket in his bag housing those jewels stolen from Felton's pawnshop, and Sebastian could hardly direct him to the clothes hidden under the mattress without inviting questions he didn't want to answer.

"I'd prefer to collect them myself," he said, as much as it pained him. "If Morgan doesn't want to see me, I suppose I could come back another time."

"I think it would be best for you to come through now. Mr. Hollyhock doesn't appreciate a drawn-out drama."

Sebastian raised his brows. "Is that what he called this, or do you enjoy creating drama of your own?"

"I do not, sir. I hardly think Mr. Hollyhock would employ me if I did."

"Have you worked for him long?" Sterling was a window into Morgan's personal life Sebastian hadn't yet had the opportunity to exploit.

"Yes, sir," Sterling replied, offering no details.

"You must know him well. A good valet is hard to come by, or so I've heard. You must be very good at keeping secrets."

"Mr. Hollyhock is a man who values his privacy."

"Meaning, you won't talk to me," Sebastian guessed. "You're protective of him? You're old enough to be his father, certainly. Do you think of yourself as fatherly?"

"He's a grown man who can manage his own business, sir. But yes, I would like what's best for him."

"And I'm not it."

"You know, he has spoken of you, sir," Sterling said, his tone perfectly neutral. "I had hoped when you turned up last week that you might be good for him. But it was only a small hope. The past rarely does anyone in the present any good."

Sebastian floundered into a double take. "Wait. He talked about me prior to last week?"

Sterling dipped his head, expressionless.

"That can't be right. He didn't even recognise me when we met."

"He might not have recognised you immediately, but he certainly remembered you, sir."

Sebastian needed to get in there and get his things. How hard could it be to convince one man to let him through the door? He really had lost his touch. And it wasn't just the wine from the previous evening, or his frustration from fighting with Morgan. It was something deeper, more fundamental.

"What if I said I came to apologise?"

"Did you, sir?"

He ground his teeth. "Please just tell me whether he's in or not."

He didn't know what he hoped Sterling's answer would be. He didn't want to apologise to Morgan, but he wanted back in his life. He wanted things as they'd been in St. James's Park when he'd kissed Morgan against that tree and Morgan had kissed him back. He didn't want to do the work to mend their relationship; he wanted to magically undo the damage done to it. It would almost be preferable to grab his belongings from the guest bedroom without seeing Morgan at all, hawking those stolen jewels, and getting himself a room in a flophouse where he could be alone.

Almost.

Living alone seemed terrifying. Offering Morgan a convincing apology felt demeaning.

Sebastian was a mess.

"Wait here a moment, sir," Sterling finally said, and shut the door in Sebastian's face.

Sebastian spent the next two minutes in agony, physically fighting the urge to run away. It wasn't that he was conflict-avoidant; at least, not normally. But what his pre-Blackwood normal had been was drastically different than what it was now, and locked out on the street, standing on his not-quite-friend's, not-quite-mark's step wasn't where he wanted to come to terms with that. He was on the verge of an epiphany, or perhaps a breakdown, and he wanted nothing to do with it. He certainly didn't want any witnesses.

The door opened when Sebastian was halfway down the steps, and he turned, caught in the act of fleeing, to meet Morgan's eye.

They stared at each other for a second.

Morgan had evidently been roused from bed, the heavy green and gold robe Sebastian had so liked wrapped tightly around his broad shoulders. For the first time in his life, Sebastian didn't know what to say.

It was Morgan who broke the silence. "Well." He cleared his throat, arms crossed, blocking the doorway. "What do you want?"

"I don't know," Sebastian admitted.

"Is that a new angle, or is that actually the first honest thing you've said to me?"

When Sebastian didn't answer, Morgan sighed and stepped back, holding the door open. "Come inside. You look cold."

"I wasn't sure you'd come back," Morgan said, once they were both seated at the breakfast table, the kettle whistling from the counter in the corner.

"Did you really talk about me before meeting me again at The Stag's Head?"

That wasn't how Sebastian had intended to open the conversation, but it was the only thing he could think about, running through his head on a loop.

Morgan raised his brows. "To Sterling? I may have mentioned you once or twice when the topic arose."

"What topic was that?"

"My childhood. That summer, specifically."

"I never thought you would have remembered me."

"I'd just survived pneumonia that winter, hardly left my bed through the spring, and fully expected to spend the summer locked in my house with no one but a tutor and a mountain of missed schoolwork to catch up on to keep me company. Instead, I met you. That's not something easily forgotten."

Morgan's gaze dropped to the table top, lacing his fingers together. "And then you disappeared."

Sebastian winced, guilt burning through him even though it hadn't been his fault and there was little he could have done. Maybe it was guilt for not remembering Morgan as readily as Morgan had remembered him all those years.

"One day, your mother stopped coming to teach me. No note, no explanation for me or my parents. They found me a new tutor within a week, and as far as they were concerned, that was the end of it. People drop in and out of each other's lives all the time."

"I didn't know she just disappeared on you like that," Sebastian mumbled. "I never thought about it, but I would have assumed that she'd have made her excuses to your parents. Professional pride, or something."

Morgan shook his head. "I tried to find you when I was a bit older. I looked for your parents in the public records, but there was nothing. Not even an obituary. It was like your whole family had disappeared off the face of the earth. I kept digging until finally my father told me the rumour that your father had been wanted over some bad debt, and that I shouldn't expect any of you to resurface. He said it with such finality, and I hardly had any other leads." He gave a stiff shrug. "I was fifteen, at that point. I didn't have access to my own money yet, so it's not like I could hire anyone to track you down. I thought about it, though. But my parents weren't interested in humouring me to that extent. After that I went to university, and once I did have access to my money, it had been so long that I assumed that if you wanted and were able to get in touch with me, you would have done. So, I let it go."

Sebastian cleared his throat. "If it makes you feel better about the fruitlessness of your search, I never had any idea where my father went, either."

"I'm sorry."

Sebastian shrugged. What else was there to say about it?

"In any case: that's why I didn't think it was really you when I saw you at the club, even though you looked familiar. I was so used to you being this ghost in the back of my mind that I couldn't believe it when I finally saw you in person again."

"You make it sound like you were actively keeping an eye out for me for twenty-one years," Sebastian said, trying to laugh.

Morgan just looked at him impassively.

"You weren't," Sebastian said uncertainly. "We've both moved on and lived entire lives since then."

"Hm," said Morgan.

The kettle shrilled, and he rose to pour two mugs of tea, adding milk and sugar to Sebastian's without having to ask before returning to the table and setting them both down.

Sebastian had no idea where to go from there. The wind was very much taken out of his sails, and he could hardly demand an apology from Morgan on top of the man having given him *that*. Sebastian was all wrong-footed and off-balance. The only thing he could think to do was backtrack to the last place he'd felt reasonably secure, and try to find a better path forward from there.

"I think," said Sebastian delicately, "that we ought to reiterate a few basic points of our situation. For clarity's sake."

Morgan's expression was an impenetrable mask as he gestured for Sebastian to continue.

"When I first came to you, the relationship I proposed was wholly transactional. I provide entertainment, and you provide the bare necessities needed for me to get by. At least, that was my understanding. Were you on the same page at that time?"

"I was," Morgan confirmed.

"Of course, entertainment is a nebulous thing. I offered to liven things up a little and broaden your horizons—intentionally vague promises, but you agreed."

"I did."

"You knew I was a thief and a con artist when you first let me into your home, just as I knew you were a reserved, upper-class gentleman with a stick up your arse so big you could barely move for it."

"Thank you," Morgan said flatly. "We also agreed that, play-acting aside, there wasn't to be any real intimacy between us."

"Are you really pretending you didn't kiss me back? I'll take half the blame, but no more than that."

Morgan scowled.

"What I mean is, we both knew who we were getting involved with. Problems cropped up when we expected the other to act against his nature. Is that a fair assessment?"

"You're saying I was a fool to expect you to stop stealing just because I offered you food and board."

"Just as I was an idiot to think you'd react favourably, or even neutrally, to my pickpocketing." Sebastian spread his hands. "We are who we are. We knew going into this that we'd make strange bedfellows. The question now is whether you want to give it another shot."

Morgan sipped his tea in silence for a moment, deliberating on the matter. "Not like that," he finally said.

Sebastian's heart sunk.

"We tried it your way, granted, only for a few days, but I don't think I can do it. I don't want to. I'd rather have you as a friend."

"A friend?"

"Something genuine. Not this charade."

"Something genuine?" Sebastian had to stop mindlessly repeating everything Morgan said. He shook himself. "What would that entail, compared to our original arrangement?"

"It wouldn't have to be so very different. You can still stay here. I still want to give you whatever you want. But I don't like that transactional feeling, as you described it. Maybe that's impossible to avoid. I don't know."

"It's not impossible. I'm just not sure how to do it," Sebastian admitted. "It's been a long time since I tried to have anything genuine with anyone."

"God forbid you let yourself experience emotional vulnerability," Morgan said dryly. "Is that it?"

Sebastian shuddered. "Is there any way we can do this without that part, please?"

Rising from the table a second time, Morgan loaded the toaster with thick slices of rye before setting the table with a tray of butter, a jar of apricot jam, and another jar of strawberry jelly. As he waited for the toaster, Morgan leaned one hip against the counter, like he needed distance from Sebastian in order to continue.

"I wouldn't really have let you rot in jail," he said, like they'd never strayed from the topic in the first place. "It was a cruel thing to say, and untrue. I only wish you'd give me some sign that you realise the risks involved. Pickpocketing might be a petty crime, but the consequences can be serious. Your dismissal of the situation upset me."

"It's true that pickpocketing doesn't really rank on my list of risk-taking behaviour."

Morgan gave a sharp sigh, turning away.

"No," Sebastian said quickly, "I mean, I've done worse things than that. So I forget that pickpocketing even counts, if that makes sense."

"Worse than trying to cheat your friends out of small change, I presume."

"I don't con my friends. That's the problem; I don't know what to do with you. When I'm talking about you to Kitty or Adam, you're just a pigeon, but when we're alone—"

"You're not conning me," Morgan said. "Everything you've got from me, I've given willingly."

"I haven't been entirely honest with you," Sebastian bit out.

"About what?"

"Things. Situations."

"Do you want to tell me the truth?"

"Yes? No. I don't know. It's complicated."

"Right," Morgan said slowly. "I can wait, if you need more time. You can tell me when you're ready."

"How are you so—" Sebastian gestured to encompass all of Morgan's being, body and soul. "Why are you so nice to me?" he finally demanded. "Opening your home to me, buying me things, keeping me fed— No one does all that without expecting something in return."

"I'm doing it because I enjoy it. I like having you around."

"No one enjoys my company for its own sake," Sebastian countered. "I'm impulsive and I lie and I cheat and I steal and I can't sit still. People only keep me around because I can do things for them. Kitty keeps me because we make a good team, and Adam keeps me because I make Kitty happy. But you haven't asked me for anything, and I have no idea what to do with that."

Morgan looked mournful, like Sebastian had just carved himself open with the butter knife. Sebastian wanted to strike that pity right off his face, and immediately hated himself for even thinking it when the man had only ever been good to him.

"Tell me something, then," Morgan said. "Some secret you've been keeping. If I have to ask for something from you, let it be that."

Sebastian scraped together what little courage he had. If nothing else, he had to explain himself in order to avoid repeating past mistakes, even if it left a bad taste in his mouth. Morgan deserved at least that much effort. Maybe if he tried hard enough, if he got through this initial baring of the soul, that bitter taste would dissipate and being with Morgan would taste like sweet summer oranges again.

"Before I met you," Sebastian said slowly, "for a few months I lived with a man named James Whistler."

"I know him," Morgan allowed, folding his arms. He looked casual rather than defensive.

"We had nothing in common and our temperaments weren't well matched, but he gave me everything I wanted. Fine food, drinks, a place to stay, and a bed. Not that he was particularly good in it, but." Sebastian waved one hand dismissively. "It is what it is. I've had worse."

"Did you go out together? I feel I would have met you sooner if he'd introduced you to any of his friends."

"No, the whole thing was very secret. He kept me as a pet, of sorts, tucked out of sight for his entertainment alone, like a bird in a cage. Or a cat," Sebastian added, mouth twisting to one side at the reminder of Whistler's story.

"You didn't find that chafing?" Morgan asked with a frown.

"Of course I did, but it was only ever meant to be a short-term arrangement. We both knew I was using him, though perhaps he wasn't aware exactly how mercenary I really was." Sebastian lifted one shoulder in a disaffected shrug. "As long as he kept buying me nice things, I was perfectly alright with letting him treat me like that. He was a safe, if boring, harbour until I felt secure enough to move on to better prospects."

"On to me."

"Technically, yes. But I didn't actually leave Whistler of my own volition. Like you, he had certain opinions about my criminal activity, though he was less concerned about me meeting a bad end and more concerned about the optics of the thing."

"I'm hard-pressed to judge a man for not wanting to associate with criminals."

"He had no idea I was actively engaged in any criminal activities. Other than in bed with him, anyway. Rather, he found out that I'd been to Blackwood."

The toaster popped, jarring them both.

Morgan seemed at a loss for words. It made sense; Blackwood was something of a bogeyman to polite society, after all. Sebastian took a draught of his tea, bitterly enjoying Morgan's discomfort.

"When?" Morgan finally asked.

"Get the toast," Sebastian said quietly. Only after Morgan turned away to fetch the plates and pluck the rye from the toaster did Sebastian continue. "I got out in mid-May."

Returning to the table, Morgan slid one plate towards Sebastian before sinking heavily into his chair. "God. That's so recent."

"For me to have so quickly fallen back on my wicked ways?"

"I didn't say that."

"You meant it."

Sebastian desperately wanted the conversation over with. He sat still, his expression one of perfectly bored contempt, but inside, he was squirming. Whatever Morgan's reaction was to be, whether he was about to retract his desire for genuine friendship, Sebastian couldn't stand waiting for it. He was drowning in uncertainty.

"Just ask whatever you want to ask," he snapped.

"What did you do?"

"Theft," Sebastian replied, before Morgan had even finished his sentence.

"What on earth did you steal to merit Blackwood?"

"Nothing special, but I robbed a magistrate, so they threw the book at me to make an example of my case."

"Blackwood, though. That's for criminals with dangerous magic. You're not dangerous."

"See my previous point."

"And that wasn't enough for you to choose a more honest career path? Something that can offer your life any stability?"

"So I can break my back working for pennies in the factories?" Sebastian scoffed. "No, thank you."

"It's more reliable than picking pockets, surely."

"Have you ever been inside a prison?" Sebastian asked in a forcedly pleasant tone. "I imagine not. I was in Blackwood for nine months, and they were uniformly wretched."

"That is rather the point."

"Yes, of course it's the point! But it's one thing to sit out here and say, yes, that's a fitting punishment for the crime, and another to waste away in there with the wards pressing in from all sides so you can't conjure so much as a single spark." He dropped his gaze to his hands, flicking his fingers to strike up a glimpse of fire before smothering it against his palm. "You start believing you've lost your touch, or that you could never do magic in the first place. It drives you mad after a while."

"I'm sorry."

Sebastian brushed him away. "It was my own fault, wasn't it? But the company was decent. That's more than most can say."

"Oh?"

"My neighbour and I talked back and forth through the wall. No idea who they were—I don't even know whether they were a man or woman—but they were awaiting execution when I got out. Treason. Murder.

They'll be dead in the new year, barring a miracle." He shrugged. "A pleasant conversationalist, nonetheless."

Neither of them had touched their toast. Morgan buttered both portions before they got cold, then nudged Sebastian's back towards him. Sebastian opened both jars of preserves, electing not to choose between them at such a stressful time, and dolloped them onto his rye.

"I won't pretend to understand your life," Morgan said, "but how are you not afraid? You don't seem to care whether I'll throw you out, and you continue to steal even after serving time. How do you do it?"

By lying through my teeth, Sebastian wanted to tell him. How could Morgan not see that he was afraid? He was afraid of having to live on the street, of going hungry, of ending up back inside a prison cell. Of meeting the same end as his mother. Of losing his magic for real. He just used that fear as a driving force, like coal on the fire, to keep moving forward. He'd been afraid for so long that it hardly registered as fear anymore. It was spite and hunger and motivation to improve his lot in life.

In Morgan's defence, Sebastian had got very good at hiding it, even from himself.

"I'll explain this simply, since I know you've led a sheltered life. I don't mean that as a jab; it's a fact. You have." Sebastian put his jam knife down to hide the tremor in his hands. "Work is hell. The only thing you can rely on is that it will kill you—either the machines will get you on the factory floor, or your body will break down over years of service until you can't work anymore and you'll die a cripple. After my father vanished, my mother moved us north and worked herself to death to keep us afloat; I've seen the effects of hard labour on a body first-hand. I grew up being told it was my lot to experience the same.

"The factory managers don't care; you're far more easily replaced than a single cog in one of their infernal machines, because everyone has to work. Even if they know it'll kill them. Because the alternative is too terrifying for them to contemplate. I spent my teenage years in the factories, and at other 'honest jobs' besides, and I can tell you without any hesitation or second-guessing that I'd rather take my chances on the streets and risk prison—again—than ever go back to that."

His piece done, Sebastian finally drew a breath, reaching for his tea with finely-trembling fingers.

"God." Morgan's voice cracked on the word. "I'm sorry."

Sebastian shook his head, not trusting himself to speak.

"I can't fault you for trying to make a better life for yourself. But you're tempting fate if you want to avoid prison a second time."

"I'm tempting fate no matter what."

Morgan lapsed into silence again and Sebastian looked at his mug of tea, pretending to find it more interesting than it really was. They both turned to their neglected toast at the same time, though Sebastian doubted Morgan had much more of an appetite than he did, just then.

"Whistler cut you off after learning of your past?" Morgan eventually asked, a frown furrowing his brows.

Sebastian nodded.

"And by telling me upfront, you're daring me to treat you the same."

"Your man Sterling says you don't like drama. You'll never find more drama than with me. It's the only brand of excitement I can offer. If you don't want that, say so, and we'll put an end to this...whatever it is we've got going on."

It was Morgan's turn to examine the contents of his mug. "I don't want to turn you out. And I don't want you to go back to prison."

"What do you want?"

Morgan glanced up to meet Sebastian's gaze, simultaneously intent and shy. Sebastian held his breath, waiting for whatever Morgan was working up the nerve to admit. Did he want anything beyond friendship? Because that, Sebastian would try to give him. If he wanted another kiss, that would be easier. Sebastian had far more confidence in his worth as a lover than a friend.

"The way you're so unafraid of everything," Morgan murmured. "That's what I want."

Sebastian barely held back a laugh. It might come out hysterical if he let it. "You mean, how can you be less afraid, too?" Sebastian sipped his tea, desperate for something to do. "I don't recommend getting arrested, though it would probably do the trick."

"Ah, perhaps not."

"It's not really something to be taught. But I'm certainly willing to try. Our little arrangement—our charade, as you called it—would have been good for that."

Morgan ate his toast in serious contemplation for a few minutes, mulling it over, before finally giving a decisive nod and meeting Sebastian's eye.

"Stay with me, eat my food, and let me buy you things. I want that for you. And for me. I want us to make up for all those years when we didn't know each other. I'd only ask you to stop stealing while you're with me. I know you're going to protest about the leopard changing its spots; I know I can't change you to that extent. This isn't a demand or an ultimatum. But as long as you're literally in my presence, I'd appreciate your honesty. What you do during our hours apart is none of my business, as long as I can turn a blind eye to it, and as long as you're safe."

"That's a reasonable request," Sebastian allowed, hope tentatively unfurling in his chest like a new butterfly carefully unfurling its wings.

"Good." Morgan exhaled. "Now, putting aside plausible deniability for just a moment; have you done anything since moving in with me that I should be concerned about? Whatever your answer, I'm not going to turn you in," he added. "I just want to know whether I should have a lawyer on call."

Felton's jewels were burning a hole in Sebastian's bag upstairs. Kitty had taken the Cheapside haul from the National Gallery; he could deny involvement in that one, at least.

It wouldn't do to admit that he was planning to sneak out again that night to steal a rare magical plant from Kew Gardens. It might be a lower-risk theft, but Morgan would surely have some objection.

"You have absolutely nothing to worry about," Sebastian said with a smile.

Morgan didn't look like he entirely trusted him, but he looked like he wanted to.

CHAPTER FIFTEEN

ON SECRET GREENHOUSES,
DANGEROUS FLOWERS, AND LOVE SPELLS

For a plant that was supposed to be as dangerous to society as the Oberon's Kiss, it proved exceptionally easy to steal. Kew Gardens was designed to welcome visitors, and apparently, that extended to its secret greenhouses no one was supposed to know about. Though Sebastian enjoyed a challenge, he even more enjoyed getting paid for doing relatively little work.

There was indeed a hidden door in the Tropical Fern House, just as Deepa had indicated. That night, when the gardens were closed to the public and there was no one around, Sebastian slipped through the wall of greenery to trace the outline of that hidden door with his fingertips, inviting any magic present to speak to him.

The magic that raised its head to greet him was little warier than Felton's had been, as if the spellcaster had emphasised how important it was to keep this door safe. But it was boring, doing nothing but hiding a door day after day, and the magic was eager to stretch towards Sebastian to say hello, hungry for a little enrichment. Presumably, no one had ever tried to break into the room of dangerous magical plants before, or at least, not since this most recent spell had been cast to hide it. The magic had no experience in turning away unwanted intruders, and indeed, didn't seem to know that it was supposed to, especially if the intruder met it with a friendly face. It was far more golden retriever than guard dog.

"I don't suppose you'd let me through if I just asked nicely?" Sebastian murmured, prodding gently at the spell to see how it would react. It was malleable against his magic, easily giving way under the pressure as if it were no more than a dandelion fluff dispersed by the breeze.

Splaying five fingers against the door, Sebastian pushed it open without any resistance at all.

"Thanks very much," he said to the magic as he stepped through. "And I don't mean this as any reflection on you, but this is embarrassingly shoddy security."

The magic came to perch on his shoulder like a little creeping vine, watching with great interest as he entered the forbidden room.

Maybe the problem with the security was that gardeners tended to be nurturers, Sebastian mused as he slunk inside. Proper security needed more aggression than tender loving care. Clearly, whomever had cast the spell had been thinking lovingly of their plants rather than thinking mistrustfully of anyone who might want to get to them. They should have been thinking of things like slugs and invasive weeds. Not that Sebastian meant any harm to the plants within, but he certainly meant to steal them. Or one of them, at least.

The secret room wasn't particularly large, but it was densely packed with a great variety of plants, and it took him several minutes to comb through them to find the one he wanted. There was a ridiculously phallic pitcher plant that curled its leaves towards him as he went by, looking hungry. A Venus-flytrap that Sebastian could only assume had been enchanted watched him as he passed, rows of little eyes staring at him from around the rim of each pink trap, like the eyes of a scallop. It was unsettling, and Sebastian didn't dare turn his back on it. The largest plant in the room was a blue-leafed tree taller than he was, whose branches swayed to track his movements, presumably with the intent to devour him if he strayed too near.

In the far corner stood a sign warning that the plants sequestered there were venomous, and only to be handled with gloves and eye protection. Sebastian steered clear of that whole area, turning his attention instead to the table in the middle of the room, which was covered in more moderately-sized and friendly-looking species. Flowers and cacti and succulents looked up at him, all of them lush and verdant.

In the centre, like a king in court, sat the Oberon's Kiss.

It was a little purple flower with layers of flared, pointed petals like tissue paper, rich violet on the outside and growing lighter and pinker towards the centre, where bright gold pollen clustered, looking enticingly edible. The leaves were dark and tapered, the young ones curled up like fiddleheads before they unfurled.

The plant looked innocent enough. The flower was pretty without being ostentatious; the kind of potted plant one might keep in the corner of a desk, or on a bookshelf. Sebastian had done his research prior to breaking into the garden, and he was certain he'd found the right flower. But its magical aura was faint and unassuming, a mere shimmer in the air like mist. He would have guessed that a flower as legendary as the Oberon's Kiss would feel more impressive, somehow.

It was funny, Sebastian thought as he circled the flower, looking for the best angle to pick it up without jostling any of its leaves. Oberon's Kiss was, by every measure, more dangerous than any diamond or jewel, but people poured much more effort and energy into protecting the latter than the thing capable of making illegal love potions. If only rare plants had the same monetary value, Sebastian would consider shifting his career sideways to focus on their theft and trafficking, instead.

Of course, if rare plants were more valuable, the security surrounding them would skyrocket, rendering the entire thought exercise a moot point. Anyway, decorating himself with plants, no matter how rare or magical, couldn't compare to decking himself in diamonds and pearls.

Curling both hands around the pot, Sebastian gently lifted the plant from the table, holding it up to examine it at eye level.

"Whoever Deepa's mysterious collector is, I hope she's a responsible sort of criminal," Sebastian told the plant. "The last thing we need is a load of legitimate love potions flooding the city."

Warily, he brought it closer to his face, peering into the soft, smudgy pollen in its centre. Love spells and love potions had long been outlawed in the United Kingdom, which was one of very few magic regulations with which he actually agreed. He might make his living by tricking people, but he never forced anyone to do anything against their will. Half the fun of conning a mark was in knowing he'd manipulated them. Stealing their ability to say no would spoil the game—not to mention, the thought of removing anyone's free will made him queasy. Being physically imprisoned was bad enough; being imprisoned in one's own mind had to be worse. It was too violent for his tastes, and he was too sophisticated a criminal to act like a thug.

So, no, he didn't want to be responsible for putting the Oberon's Kiss in the hands of someone who might trade in love spells, but he wasn't going to let his personal ethics stand in the way of a pay day, either.

Deepa said this mystery collector didn't want to use the plant for any nefarious purpose. Sebastian was sceptical, but it was good enough to clear his conscience.

He gave the plant a surreptitious sniff. He might be against the making of love spells, but he was still curious about the effect the pollen had on a person. He'd never been in love, as far as he was aware, and there was some masochistic little part of him that wanted to know what it was like. It smelled delicious, neither mulchy nor overly perfumed. It smelled like a fruity, sugary dessert, and his mouth watered like a switch had been flipped.

He wondered, for one wildly self-indulgent second, what it would be like if Morgan were present. If Sebastian had a little taste of the pollen, and Morgan was the next person he saw, how would he feel…?

"What was that?" he asked himself, infinitely annoyed.

There was no place for daydreaming in the middle of a job. And daydreaming about love, no less. An unforgivable lapse in professionalism regarding his work both as a thief and as a con man.

Transferring the flower firmly to his left arm, he tucked it against his ribs, balancing the bottom edge of the pot against his hip as he clamped down on the side with his elbow, holding it in place at a slight forward angle so the leaves and petals wouldn't get crushed under his arm. With his right hand free, he gently shuffled the other plants on the table into the space the Oberon's Kiss had left, hoping to buy a few extra minutes in the morning before anyone noticed it was missing. Pleased with the display, he retraced his steps to the hidden door and made his exit, weaving the magic back in place behind him as he went.

"It was nice meeting you," he said to the magic before making his escape. "Better luck keeping the next round of intruders out."

The magic sighed and settled back into its post. Of course, it wouldn't do any better next time, because Sebastian had never been very good at telling magic to keep people out of anything, and it wasn't as if he could weave an entirely new, stronger spell to hide the door without rousing suspicion. That was as good as leaving a calling card, and Sebastian had no desire for the general public to connect this little theft with his grander jewellery heists.

Although it might be funny if they did, he supposed. A pity that Mr. Johnson wasn't still around writing his useless newspaper columns to invent some conspiracy theory about why London's notorious jewel thief might suddenly turn his attention to a rare magical plant. The people would have to get their entertainment elsewhere.

Sebastian guessed there was but a slim chance that Morgan would recognise the plant, but still, he didn't want to risk it. Instead of returning to Portman Square, he trekked the thing back to Adam and Kitty's, protecting it from the chill night air by building a tiny tropical bubble of humidity, like its own portable greenhouse. From there, he called Deepa, who came straight over, neither of them willing to meet out in the open with such contraband, even if it was the middle of the night.

"It looks good," she said, studying it where it sat on Adam's kitchen table.

"You're no more a botanist than I am. How can you tell I haven't screwed you over?"

"I can tell it's not dead, it's got all its petals, and it hasn't had any chunks bit out from the leaves." Leaning in to look straight down on the flower from above, she studied the little cluster of pollen, just as he had done. "Did you try it?" she asked, glancing up at him through her kohl-lined lashes.

He shook his head. "Didn't want to risk damaging the thing. Anyway, there was no one around for me to try it on."

"It smells delicious. Warm, and spicy." Straightening, she drew a bundle of crisp notes from her handbag. "Two hundred pounds, as agreed for a safe delivery. Your five percent will follow once the plant has successfully changed hands."

"Thanks very much." Sebastian was tempted to inhale the notes as if they were a sprig of flowers themselves, but he clung to his dignity and resisted. "Do you know what she plans to do with it, your collector? You said she wasn't interested in love spells, but this is a lot of money and effort to go to for a decorative houseplant."

"It's to be a gift for a plant enthusiast in her close circle. No drug rings, no black-market potions, no criminal enterprise. Just a personal matter between friends."

"A bouquet from the florist wouldn't cut it?"

"The enthusiast in question is a florist herself. Presumably, my contact needs to go to more impressive lengths to get her a gift this time. It's for a special occasion, she says."

"I see. Well, it's none of my business anyway. I'm much more interested in your information on the Rose Diamond."

"Yes, of course. As promised." Taking one of the chairs, she laced her fingers together on top of the table, bracing herself on her elbows like she was in a business meeting. The gold bracelets ringing her forearms knocked pleasantly against the wood.

"After hours, the shop has a magical alarm system in place that operates on three levels, each activated by touch. The first protects the shop's outer walls. It's like a forcefield, deflecting casual passers-by. Simple enough. The second is more aggressive. A single touch to the bricks will set it off, alerting the shop's security guards. I'm told they can arrive on the scene within three minutes, though I suspect that is an exaggeration." Raising one hand, she made a so-so gesture, bracelets jangling. "I would put their response time closer to seven. Either way, not something you want to gamble with."

"How sensitive is that, exactly?"

"If a fly so much as lands on the wall, the alarms will activate. Not that a fly could land on it," she added. "The forcefield encompassing the shop is thick enough that any insect or small animal will bounce off it. My host wanted to show off for me, so he encouraged me to break through it and set off the alarm. It took a firm shove to get my hand through the field, but the second layer, almost nothing. I walked my fingers over the bricks so lightly I could barely feel them, yet my first touch was enough to bring it all down. There are flashing lights and wailing sirens to attract attention, as well as stationary lights that illuminate the whole building, shooting straight up into the sky like a beacon, bright enough to bathe the entire city block in light. If you're caught in that, there will be nowhere to hide that the guards and the police can't see you."

Sebastian drummed his fingers across the table, calculating the risks. "And the third level?"

"The doors and windows are set up to trigger the same alarm system with the same sensitivity, but will also administer a shock to whomever touches them. That part, I was not interested in experiencing first hand. But my host assured me that any intruder on the receiving end of such a shock would be immediately rendered unconscious."

"That seems a liability. What if some careless drunk were to stumble and try to catch himself against the door? The shop would have to take responsibility for any ensuing injury."

"I suppose so, if the drunk stumbled hard enough to break through the forcefield." She shrugged. "The owners evidently decided their diamonds are worth more than the life of any clumsy Londoner."

"What about the necklace itself? Where do they keep that after hours?"

"In a combination safe in the back office, under the desk," she replied promptly. "I'm told the safe is made with state-of-the-art technology, whatever that's worth."

"That all sounds like a terrible amount of work. What's stopping me from stealing this thing while the shop is open and none of those alarms are up?"

"While the shop is open, the necklace's display case has a similar, if not identical spell guarding it, not to mention the on-site security guards and numerous witnesses you'll be dealing with. It will be difficult either way, but if you're hoping to grab it in broad daylight without anyone noticing, you are, and I mean this respectfully, out of your mind."

"Fair enough." Sebastian rotated the plant in its pot, admiring his last steal as he plotted his next. "I think there's no safe that can't be broken into, and there's no spell I can't dismantle."

"Then I look forward to the morning when I will read of the Rose Diamond's theft, front and centre," Deepa said with a dark smile. "It was a pleasure doing business with you, Sebastian."

CHAPTER SIXTEEN

IN WHICH EMBARRASSING EROTICA IS READ AND FAILS TO IMPRESS ANYONE

Sebastian had broken into Kew Gardens, outwitted its magic, stolen the Oberon's Kiss, and got hold of the secrets concerning the Rose Diamond necklace. That, combined with Morgan having forgiven him for his pickpocketing escapades, meant that Sebastian was back in his element. The stress of confessing to his past in Blackwood and the fear of Morgan rejecting him melted away entirely in the face of Morgan's concern and the reopening of his offer to let Sebastian stay in his home. Things were still going his way after all.

So, Sebastian buried his shame and anxiety six feet deep like a body in the garden. What's done was done, and there was no sense in dredging all that unpleasantness back up to parade it around. Nothing good or constructive could come from that kind of introspection.

"You remember how yesterday, you asked if I'd engaged in any questionable behaviour since moving in with you?" he asked over a late breakfast.

It was late by Morgan's standards, at any rate. It was perfectly respectable by Sebastian's. Less respectable was the way he was obviously baiting his poor companion, his tone lilting with innocence in a way that couldn't fail to put the other man on high alert.

"Yes," Morgan said slowly, his eyes narrowed in suspicion and his coffee paused halfway to his mouth.

"It's nothing bad!" Sebastian assured him, enjoying the man's subtle panic. "Nothing illegal or risky whatsoever."

As he'd been thinking over his latest ill-gotten goods, he'd remembered that he had another stolen item in the guest room, one that might prove relevant to the broadening of Morgan's horizons: the little volume of erotica he'd lifted from that bookshop on their first day out together.

"You're beginning to worry me."

"Everything worries you. But it's fine; you just reminded me that I have something upstairs that might interest you. Do you have plans for the rest of your morning?"

Morgan's suspicion deepened exponentially. "If I say no, am I going to regret it?"

"Not at all," Sebastian promised with a smile.

Traipsing upstairs like he owned the place, Sebastian led Morgan to the guest bedroom where his stolen book of smut lay on the nightstand. *Pepperika*, it was called: ninety-seven pages of assorted short stories printed on cheap newsprint. A pretty redhead in a minuscule black dress with one finger pressed to her lips winked at the reader from the soft, battered cover. She had a tiny waist and enormous everything else, gorgeous in an anatomically improbable, pinup kind of way.

He handed it to Morgan with a flourish.

Morgan glanced at the cover, flipped through the pages, and blanched. "This is pornography."

"Erotica."

"Semantics. How exactly is this supposed to interest me?"

It was less a matter of semantics and more one of legality, but Sebastian let that go.

"Partially I just wanted to see your expression when you read it, but also, have you never read erotica before? Not as a joke or a vague curiosity, but to actually get off."

"No." Morgan skimmed the pages more intently. "I have to point out that any work describing women in this much detail probably isn't going to do it for me."

Sebastian rolled his eyes and gestured for the book to be returned. "No, obviously not. There were queer books that I considered, but I thought it might induce too much panic. Keeping one in your house, I mean, not the content itself. Clearly, you're familiar with the lifestyle. Anyway, it's not about the literal words: it's about giving yourself permission to enjoy yourself. Because that's what you're really scared of, isn't it? Giving up that rigid sense of control you've built."

"And you think reading erotica is going to solve that," Morgan said doubtfully.

"I think that even if it doesn't, it'll be a fun exercise." Sebastian slipped the book inside his jacket and smiled when Morgan's gaze tracked the movement. "Let's go back to your study and see what happens, yes?"

What happened was Morgan standing in the corner with his hands over his face, burning red, as Sebastian paced the floor with one hand behind his back, holding the book aloft with his other. The story he'd chosen was titled "Pepperika and the Master of the House," and was written in a baffling pastiche of early nineteenth-century works, as if the author had grown bored of the contemporary voice dominating the rest of the collection. It was twenty pages long, and wasted no time on exposition before diving into the good stuff. Sebastian's voice was clear as he read aloud and ringing with amusement, both at the words themselves and at Morgan's absolute mortification.

"Her breath shuddered as he drew her into his strong arms and crushed their lips together, his roving tongue plundering her gentle mouth as surely as a hunter plundered his prey—"

"Please stop."

"And her goddess-nectar dripped wetly down her thigh as, quivering, she collapsed into his embrace. She could feel his prick pressing against her stomach, hot and hard like velvet-gloved steel, and her breath quickened, pulse fluttering, as she realised she could touch it. Oh! The feel of him in her hand made her mouth water and her insides tremble with fear and anticipation. The prospect of him entering her flowery folds in that most intimate way—"

"This isn't sexy," Morgan interrupted.

"Would it help if I changed the pronouns?" Sebastian asked, pausing. "Are all the lady-bits upsetting you?"

"No, I assure you, I'll be equally horrified regardless of pronoun. It's less the subject matter and more the prose, I'm afraid."

"It has illustrations," Sebastian offered, holding the book out. Morgan edged away. "Look, they're much nicer than the writing. Not that that's a hard bar to clear, but."

"The drawings are fine, but I don't want this."

"I can see that. Let me skip the foreplay to the sex itself—something I would never suggest in real life, by the way. But a hole is a hole; maybe you'll find that easier to relate to."

"God," Morgan said, beet red as he turned away entirely to face the window. "I shudder to ever hear your bedroom talk. 'A hole is a hole'—bloody hell."

"You don't like purple prose, you don't like bare vulgarity; that leaves a lot of middle ground for me to explore. Do you really not want to give me a single hint?"

"When I agreed to have my horizons broadened, I meant my general lifestyle, not my sex life. It was actually serving me perfectly well, though you seem determined to disbelieve me. I'm not repressed, I'm not inexperienced, and I'm only prudish compared to you. There's nothing you can read that's going to shock me. Shock and distaste are two entirely different things. The only thing you're going to accomplish by reading me more of that book or any of its ilk is your own entertainment."

"Which is a valuable end in itself, in my opinion."

Morgan half-turned so Sebastian could see his profile, though he seemed reluctant to leave the safety of his self-imposed exile by the window. "It's not a bad end," he confessed. "I missed your energy about the house on Tuesday night. And I do like the sound of your voice. Almost as much as you do."

If that last bit was meant to take Sebastian down a peg, it didn't work in the slightest.

"You missed me. Is my return all you imagined?"

"I hadn't imagined Pepperika."

"Did she ruin our reunion?" Sebastian teased. "What would you like to do instead?"

He could think of a million things they could do instead. He wanted to run his hands through the perfect ashen waves of Morgan's hair. He wanted to push him up against the wall and kiss him until they tasted like each other. He wanted to take him by the hand and run through the hallways of a too-big house, hunt for frogs in the garden, and peel oranges together, that fine mist bursting from the rinds until their noses burned and their fingers were sticky.

He wanted to turn back time and try to pick up his childhood where it had left off and forget everything that had happened after that summer. He wanted a best friend to grow up with, and he wanted to take Morgan down the hall and into the bedroom and do things with him that Morgan wouldn't even be able to say out loud without blushing.

How much of that did Morgan want, too?

"I'd appreciate something that causes me less embarrassment, please, sorry as I am to remove that source of amusement from you."

"No more erotica?"

"If you don't mind."

Sebastian flipped the book shut and sidled closer. "But you liked when I kissed you in the park."

Morgan swallowed. "Yes."

"You'd like if I did that again."

He nodded wordlessly.

"Do you still think I'm such a bad idea?" Sebastian purred, resting one hand lightly against the knot of Morgan's tie.

"Maybe not *such* a bad idea."

"The kind of bad where I might stir things up a little, but I won't ruin your life."

"Something like that."

"And you're into that," Sebastian clarified.

"Apparently." Morgan sounded disappointed in himself, and Sebastian laughed.

"You don't have much experience with bad ideas, do you?"

"I've always been very careful to play it safe. It's worked out for me perfectly well, but I can't say it's been especially interesting."

"You're no Pepperika, clearly." Sebastian lifted the book again to tap the spine against Morgan's chest. "Tarting it up, seducing men left and right."

"I wish you'd stop making me out to be some blushing virgin. I'm really not."

"Not at all. I think you know exactly what you want; you've just had a hard time acting on it. Obviously, out of the two of us, I'm Pepperika."

"I like you better than her."

"I know: you're not interested in women like that. But you're not opposed to a little femininity, are you? You liked me in makeup, after all. Would you like to see me in it again?"

"The enchanted stuff?"

"Not necessarily. Whatever you like. I can do more besides just makeup, too. What about what she's wearing?"

Morgan's gaze dropped to Pepperika's little black dress, straps slipping off her shoulders and her stockings rolled down, kitten heels shining and flirty.

"Would you like to draw me in something like that?"

"How can you just say these things?" Morgan asked desperately. "We're not even together."

"Imagine how I speak to the men I'm actually fucking."

"How do you have so little sense of shame?"

"Practice, darling."

With a shuddering breath, Morgan shut his eyes. "I do like the look of you in makeup, and I do want to draw you like that," he admitted, like he was only brave enough to say it if he didn't have to look Sebastian in the face. "And I do want to know how you talk to the men you fuck."

"That's a far cry from your original, 'no intimacy when we're alone together,' rule," Sebastian noted. "I'm not sure how it aligns with us wanting to be friends, either. So. Where do we stand now?"

Morgan opened his eyes, but he still couldn't look at Sebastian. "I made that rule for a reason. And I do want us to be friends."

Sebastian slunk closer, twining both hands around the back of Morgan's neck, still holding onto the book, though neither of them paid it any attention.

"Fucking me might still be a step too far," he agreed, letting his gaze drop lazily to Morgan's mouth. Morgan's gaze stuttered to his mouth, in turn. "But we've already kissed once before. It should be safe enough to do that again."

"Just a kiss." It wasn't clear whether Morgan meant it as a firm statement or a question.

"For now." Sebastian tipped forward until there was nothing but a whisper of breath between them.

There, he held his place, balancing delicately as if on a high wire, waiting for Morgan to close the gap. It was a risky gambit; he might be waiting a long time, if Morgan needed to have a moral crisis about it.

But Morgan rewarded Sebastian's patience and kissed him after a single second of hesitation, wrapping his arms around Sebastian's back to pull their bodies flush. Sebastian melted into him like honey, running his fingers through the short hair at the back of Morgan's head with one hand as he pressed the book flat between Morgan's shoulder blades with the other. When he opened his mouth, Morgan parted his lips in turn like he was starving for it, and their tongues met in the middle—tentatively at first, then with hunger. It was everything Sebastian wanted in a kiss, passionate and demanding, though there were far too many clothes between them.

And the clothes would stay, unfortunately. He had no intention of taking Morgan to bed just then. He had a good enough grasp of Morgan's character to know that would be too fast a move, and the man would panic, rebuilding his walls in record time to put distance between them once more.

That Morgan wanted him, Sebastian had no doubt, but he needed to be guided towards the idea rather than thrown in the deep end. After quarrelling once already, the last thing Sebastian wanted was to spook the man.

Also, there was something slightly absurd at the thought of bedding a man before noon. Intimacy was for the evening time, when the light was low and golden, the shadows making everything sultry and more flattering than it could ever hope to look in the bold light of day. Night time was even better for it, when inhibitions were at their lowest and people were more willing to slip into that dream state of love and lust. Mid-morning was for brunch, errands, and social engagements, none of which lent themselves to the illusion of romance and forbidden sexuality on which Sebastian relied.

He pulled back, projecting reluctance at breaking the kiss even as he studied Morgan's reaction.

"You're a very hard man to say no to," Morgan murmured.

He hadn't let go of Sebastian's waist; his lips were close enough that Sebastian could feel the breath from his words, and the temptation to lean in and catch him in another kiss was unbelievably strong.

Sebastian resisted. He wasn't supposed to be the one getting tempted.

"You don't have to say no at all," he returned.

Apparently, those were not the magic words, because Morgan gave a rueful smile and stepped away, breaking contact entirely. "I really do." He cleared his throat. "This wasn't how I planned to spend my morning."

"What *did* you have planned?"

"I don't know. I hadn't assumed I'd see you at all. As far as concrete plans go, they're not until this evening. If I can trust you to behave, would you like to come to dinner with a few of my friends? It's a casual get-together, and nowhere near as exciting as your own friend group, I'm sure—"

"I'd love to," Sebastian interrupted. "What friends? I didn't think you had many."

"'Friends' might be too strong a word. Acquaintances, anyway. You know my cousin Alphonse?"

"I met him once, briefly, the same day I met you at The Stag's Head. 'Acquaintance' is even too strong a word for what we are."

"Well, it's him and his wife and a handful of her friends. Alphonse has been worried about me, I think, and he's taking it upon himself to keep me company and cheer me up. I considered cancelling, but it seems rude to throw his good intentions back in his face. And he's right; it would probably do me good to get out of the house and see some people."

"He seems like good company. I'd be delighted to join you, if you really want me there."

"I do. When you walked out after our argument on Tuesday, I wasn't sure whether you'd come back. And I couldn't stand the thought of losing you again so soon after finding you. If I can't be honest with you, I'm afraid there's no hope of ever being honest with anyone. So." Morgan shrugged. "I like you. I miss you when you're not here. And you might be a bad idea, and I might yet regret doing away with the rules of our arrangement, but I don't regret bending them as much as I have."

"I think you'll find I'm very flexible. I can bend a long way before I break."

Morgan snorted. "I believe you. But we're moving at two very different speeds. You need to slow down if you want to keep me moving forward at all."

"I can slow down. Dinner with your cousin sounds like a nice, slow, perfectly civilised way to spend an evening."

"It won't bore you?"

"There are only so many hours a dinner can go on." Sebastian closed the minuscule space between them, and Morgan let him. "I'll go slow," he murmured. "Like honey. But I bet you're going to be ready to speed things up sooner than you think."

With both hands on Morgan's chest, Sebastian pressed in close, sliding one knee in between Morgan's thighs. Morgan stiffened and went perfectly still at the sudden pressure, pulling in a sharp breath and holding it. Sebastian smiled, pleased and cat-like.

"Don't worry. If dinner bores me, I'll have the rest of the night to look forward to, after we get back home."

CHAPTER SEVENTEEN

WHEREIN THEORIES ARE SHARED REGARDING LONDON'S FAVOURITE JEWEL THIEF

Six p.m. found Sebastian by Morgan's side as they exited their cab and ran up the steps to the front of Alphonse's cottage-style house outside the city, trying to dodge the rain. It was cold and dark, as was typical for an October evening, and especially typical for a Thursday. Though he didn't anticipate the company to be particularly scintillating, Sebastian looked forward to a warm meal and a stiff drink.

Alphonse greeted them at the door a second later, with his wife by his side. She was a stunning young Algerian woman, dark-haired and dark-eyed, with a bright, sharp smile.

"Hullo, Morgan, old thing! Everyone else is already here." Alphonse bustled them inside, plucking their hats off as they crossed the threshold. "You know Elizabeth and Arthur, don't you? And Jules Coxley, I think you've met too, what? And Jacobi you know, of course—everyone knows Jacobi—"

"I don't believe we've met," his wife cut in smoothly, looking Sebastian up and down before offering her hand, her shake firm and business-like. "Aaliyah Kaddour."

"Sebastian. A pleasure to meet you," Sebastian said with his most charming smile.

"Sebastian?" Alphonse echoed, visibly puzzled.

Sebastian smiled peaceably in response, and Alphonse shook himself out of it.

"Righto, come in, come in, let me take your things. Go straight through to the dining room, we're all set up at the table. The food should be ready in ten, but we've got appetizers if you're starved."

Shedding his outerwear into Alphonse's waiting arms, Sebastian followed Aaliyah to where the rest of the company was seated around the dining room table. Jules Coxley, he recognised, looking just as artfully dishevelled at his friends' house as he had at Eden, but everyone else was a new face. Sebastian could hardly partake in his favourite pastime of reinventing himself for a fresh crowd when he was glued to Morgan side, but the thought of being unknown to them was a thrill all the same. The sheer potential was unmatched.

"Everyone, this is Sebastian," Aaliyah announced to the room with a sweeping wave. "Sebastian, this is

Jasmine; Alphonse's man Jacobi; Elizabeth and Arthur Leicester; and Jules Coxley. When Morgan said he was bringing a friend, we had to cram in an extra seat, but Elizabeth generously offered to take the hit."

The dining room table was a solid, square thing that could comfortably sit two people per side, but Elizabeth, Arthur, and Coxley had squeezed in together to make room, with Arthur in the middle. It looked to be a tight fit, prone to rubbing elbows and knocking knees, but none of the three seemed in the least perturbed by the arrangement. Opposite them stood two empty chairs waiting for Sebastian and Morgan. As Alphonse came trotting back into the room, beaming at his guests, Sebastian and Morgan took their seats, and Aaliyah reached over to pour them each a dash of red.

"Help yourself," Aaliyah added, nodding to the basket of soft brown rolls in the middle of the table. "Jasmine baked them fresh this afternoon, and there's molasses butter."

The bread smelled heavenly, but it looked like everyone else had already finished eating their share. Sebastian could easily demolish all the remaining rolls, but it rather went against the image he wanted to cultivate. Morgan glanced at him, immediately clocked his hesitation, and took two rolls for each of them, pulling the dish of molasses butter to sit between their plates.

As he slathered his rolls in butter, Sebastian studied his companions for the evening. Alphonse, he already had a read on, which held up on their second meeting: the kind of airheaded, affable character who would make the perfect mark, undoubtedly prettier than he was smart. Sebastian had to remind himself that everyone present was off-limits.

On Alphonse's right was Jacobi, who had the stately, dignified bearing of a long-serving valet, confident in his control of the house. However, he was seated at the table like a peer, and seemed entirely immune to the way Alphonse was in constant physical contact with him: touching his hand, bumping their shoulders together, and generally behaving in a manner Sebastian couldn't imagine a valet such as Sterling ever allowing from his employer.

They were sleeping together, Sebastian decided. And Alphonse, at least, wasn't subtle about it. Jacobi, on the other hand, wore a mask of smooth serenity, giving nothing away.

Opposite Alphonse and Jacobi, on Sebastian's other side, sat Aaliyah and Jasmine. Jasmine was a dark-skinned black woman whose fashion was as bright as Aaliyah's was jewel-toned, and when she spoke, a rich Caribbean accent flowed through her words. If Sebastian could guess that Alphonse and Jacobi were sleeping together, there was no chance that Aaliyah was in the dark. Yet, she seemed entirely at ease.

Because, Sebastian quickly determined, she and Jasmine were likewise entangled.

Fascinating. He wondered how much Morgan knew, or guessed, about his cousin's household.

Which left the last side of the table. Elizabeth, Arthur, and Coxley sat facing Sebastian and Morgan, entirely comfortable with being crammed on top of each other. Elizabeth was a classic blonde beauty, exuding an enviable air of self-confidence. Her husband, Arthur, whose waxed auburn moustache might be the most interesting thing about him, seemed a quiet, steady sort. And then, on Arthur's other side, was Coxley, the known eccentric. He and Arthur had a habit of finishing each other sentences, and both seemed equally comfortable in close proximity to Elizabeth.

Sebastian drank in their dynamic as he finished his second roll. What were the chances the three of them were also sleeping together? Morgan clearly didn't know the whole of it, if any, or he wouldn't have been worried that Sebastian might get bored.

After a moment, Jacobi went to the kitchen to check on the state of things, solidifying Sebastian's suspicion that he was, or had been, a valet. Though everyone got up to fill their plates in the kitchen, Jacobi was the one who dished everything out, and who carried a fresh bottle of wine to the table as they all returned to their seats. The meal was a tender lamb roast with parmesan asparagus, honey-glazed carrots, and Yorkshire puddings baked to a golden crisp. Sebastian fervently hoped there was enough for seconds.

As they dug in, Sebastian was aware of Coxley's gaze on him, but he was content to ignore it and make pleasant small talk with the others until the man made his move.

"Jasmine," said Elizabeth, "are you finally going to tell us what Aaliyah got for your birthday?"

"Is it your birthday?" Sebastian asked. "I didn't know; I would have brought something." He might be a bit of a selfish, self-serving prick, but he knew the value of a good gift, if only to encourage the recipient to gift him in turn further down the line. "Many happy returns."

"It's not until Saturday," Jasmine said, bobbing her head, "but Aaliyah said her gift came through early and wouldn't keep. She gave it to me this morning."

"Did she get you something extravagant?" Alphonse asked. "She must have."

"She got me a new flower for my collection," Jasmine said, smiling at her companion.

The dinner guests all visibly deflated at the anti-climax. Sebastian, however, perked up.

"How classic," he offered.

"Not just any flower," Aaliyah bragged.

Sebastian suspected he knew exactly how unique it was. The plant-trafficking world was, as it turned out, incredibly small.

"Oh, no, it's much more impressive than that," Jasmine agreed. "So impressive, in fact, that I'm in disbelief as to how she could have found such a specimen in London. But she won't tell me how she did it."

"It was a gift! Just enjoy having it."

Elizabeth leaned in. "Is it very rare, this specimen?"

"Extremely," Jasmine confirmed, looking extraordinarily pleased with herself.

"And regulated," Aaliyah added smugly, taking a sip of her drink. "But I'd settle for nothing less than the best for your birthday, no matter the difficulty put into getting it."

"Was it very difficult?" Sebastian asked. "Getting your hands on this thing?"

Aaliyah shrugged. "Not really, to be honest. If you're willing to throw around enough money, you can get your hands on just about anything."

Jasmine knocked her shoulder into Aaliyah's. "Don't spoil it," she chided. "And *don't* tell me how much money you spent."

"What are you going to do with this plant, whatever it is?" Sebastian asked. Jasmine didn't seem the type to traffic in illegal magic components, but one could never be sure.

"I don't have any plans for it," she admitted. "I never thought I'd lay eyes on the thing, never mind own one myself. Probably I'll just keep it somewhere I can admire it, and otherwise leave it alone. I don't want to draw attention to myself, having it in my collection."

Aaliyah cleared her throat.

"Oh," said Jasmine. "Well, there is one thing I might do with it. But that's just for my personal use." Picking up her drink, she took a dainty sip.

"Ah," said Alphonse wisely, "it's one of *those* plants. I know better than to fool around with that sort of thing. You'll probably want to keep it tucked away somewhere safe, what? Definitely nowhere the cat can get to it. Remember what she did to our poor Christmas tree?"

"I remember that being at least fifty percent your fault," Aaliyah said.

"Right, well, somewhere tucked away from me and the cat both, then, what?"

"If it's as rare and sought after as you say, it may be worth investing in a little extra security," Sebastian suggested. "A cloaking spell, at the very least, to keep any unwanted attention from landing on it."

Elizabeth laughed. "That sounds like very serious business. Surely you don't need to go to such great lengths for a little flower, do you?"

"No, he's right," said Aaliyah, looking at Sebastian keenly.

Elizabeth's expression fell from amusement to dismay. "Oh, Aaliyah, tell me you didn't do anything questionable, procuring this thing."

With a careless scoff, Aaliyah brushed her concerns aside. "Don't worry about it. I'll be sure to whip something up to keep us out of trouble."

"Something with a bit more integrity than whatever the last owner was using to guard it," Sebastian said innocently, into his drink.

"Sorry," Coxley finally said, "but have we met before? I'm normally very good with faces, and you're familiar, but I can't quite place you."

Morgan glanced back and forth between the two of them before offering, "You met at Eden the other night. We had a brief chat about art."

Coxley frowned. "Were you both wearing masks?"

"Yes," Sebastian said, before Morgan could answer truthfully. "And we didn't stay all that long."

"I remember *you*," Coxley said to Morgan. "Your mask was silver, shaped like a butterfly." Turning back to Sebastian with his brow furrowed in concentration, his gaze flickered over Sebastian's face, cataloguing every feature. "But you, I can't pin down at all. Which is most unusual for me."

"Maybe you'd just had a few too many drinks by that point," Arthur suggested, not taking his friend at all seriously.

"Hm." Coxley sounded unconvinced, but he didn't pursue the mystery.

Sebastian was well pleased by the impromptu interrogation. If a man such as Coxley, who made his living by paying attention to people's details, couldn't remember his face, Sebastian was confident his makeup would provide adequate protection in any scenario. If he and Coxley had met again in passing, he doubted Coxley would have spared him so much as a second glance. It was only the fact that they were seated together at the same table for an extended period that had him puzzling over that niggling sense of familiarity. Those guards from the National Gallery, if they'd got a look at his face at all, wouldn't prove a problem. He'd hardly realised he'd been worrying about that until the worry abruptly fell away.

"Never mind Eden, though," Sebastian said. "Morgan told me you were all present at that dinner party in August that yielded such exciting gossip. I'd love to hear more about that. Something about blackmail?"

"Oh, yes, that was me," said Elizabeth. "That wretched little private investigator was trying to extort money from me. He thought I was some famous novelist." She dismissed that notion as preposterous with a roll of her eyes, stabbing a spear of asparagus on her fork.

"Are you?" Sebastian asked.

"No, of course not. But he was absolutely convinced—so much so, that Coxley here generously volunteered himself as the author to help me escape the limelight."

"But you're not the author either?" Sebastian asked Coxley.

"No," Coxley replied cheerfully. "But I pretended to be for a time. Just until people lost interest in the story. Which didn't take long, all things considered. The gossip mill has a fairly short attention span."

"I must say, I was awfully disappointed," Alphonse added. "I just love those M. Hayes romances. I would have asked Elizabeth to sign my copies, and then I would have asked Coxley, but it turns out, the real author is still a complete unknown. Maybe American. Or maybe a spy?" He shrugged. "No one I can ask for the old signature, anyway, what?"

"Unfortunate," Sebastian agreed.

Privately, he was convinced that the author behind the pen name had in fact been present at that party, and was present now. Whether it was Coxley or Elizabeth, he couldn't be absolutely certain, but he leaned towards the latter. If Coxley had penned those books, they would be more in line with proper erotica like the *Pepperika* stories rather than pulpy romance adventures. He couldn't prove anything, of course, but he could recognise a liar when he saw one, as he was a professional liar himself.

To Alphonse, he said, "That must have been a thrilling evening for you. Morgan tells me you've been following the case of the London jewel thief. Did you get the chance to pick Johnson's brain about it before he got run off?"

"No!" Alphonse exclaimed. "He was monstrously tight-lipped about the whole affair."

"Which I think means he doesn't have the first idea about who's behind it," Aaliyah chimed in.

"Scotland Yard certainly doesn't," said Jasmine, not sounding in the least concerned about it.

"There was talk back in September, when it became clear that Johnson wasn't returning to London," Arthur said, "about how he'd been Scotland Yard's only chance of catching the thief."

"But we think Johnson was all talk," said Elizabeth. "He wasn't making any real progress; he was all hot air."

"We're biased, obviously," Arthur added, laying a hand on Elizabeth's arm. "But the man did seem an absolute waste of space."

"I miss his columns in the paper, though," Alphonse said mournfully. "They were a cracking good read, top notch entertainment, even if they never amounted to much of anything. Can you imagine what he'd have to say about the most recent break-in at the National Gallery? Stealing the Cheapside Hoard! Incredible."

"To be fair, they didn't steal the entire Hoard," Aaliyah interjected.

"All five hundred pieces; can you imagine?" Elizabeth laughed.

If only. Sebastian would have made a literal bed of jewels to sleep in like a dragon if he'd been able to steal the entire collection.

"Have you got any pet theories about who it is?" he asked, not bothering to downplay his curiosity.

"Naturally, there's lots of talk about there being immigrants behind all of it," Elizabeth said, her nose wrinkling lightly in distaste.

Jasmine and Aaliyah gave simultaneous scoffs of contempt.

"I'm partial to the gang theory, myself," Arthur offered. "Some faction of organised crime, you know."

"I rather like the idea of a gentleman robber, myself," said Coxley. "A bored royal or a disinherited aristocrat, like something out of a good book."

"Oh, I do like that," Alphonse piped in admiringly.

"That's marvellously unrealistic," said Elizabeth, though she looked intrigued by the concept, one finger tapping against her fork like she wished she were holding a pen instead.

"I think it's just some common thief with exceptionally good luck," said Aaliyah. "I'm rooting for them, whoever they are, but I'll be surprised if they can keep it up much longer."

"I don't really have my own theory," Jasmine said, mildly embarrassed. "I only skim those sections of the paper. My business is in flowers, not jewels, so it doesn't feel especially relevant to me."

"It's not about relevance; it's about the story," Alphonse protested. "You have to let me fill you in on the highlights, at the very least."

"If you like," Jasmine said, "but I'll only promise to half-listen."

"Half is more than good enough."

"Do you have a pet theory?" Jacobi asked Sebastian, addressing him directly for the first time since Sebastian had sat down.

Sebastian found his attention intense, like the man could cut through lies and nonsense like butter. A man around whom to tread carefully, he determined.

"Not really," Sebastian said, his tone light and giving away nothing of his caution. "I wasn't actually in London when it all started—June, was it?—so I feel like I've missed the first half of the story. I prefer to hear other people's takes on it than come up with my own. What about you?" he asked Morgan, nudging him with his elbow. "Who do you think is behind it?"

"I don't know, but like Aaliyah said, they must be incredibly lucky to have got away with so many robberies so far. Stealing the Cheapside Hoard from the National Gallery was no mean feat."

"Incredibly lucky, or incredibly skilled?"

"Maybe it's a former spy," Alphonse suggested enthusiastically. "Arthur, you were in the military. Do you think one of your people could pull off something like this?"

"I suppose it depends entirely on the person. I'm afraid my personal experience in the army showed me far more buffoonery than genius."

"Do you think it takes a genius to do what our jewel thief is doing?" Sebastian asked.

"Robbing the National Gallery takes a certain combination of luck and skill," Coxley said. "They walked me through their security system when I agreed to show my art. They're not playing around, and our mystery thief was obviously prepared for that."

"Do you think it could have been an inside job?" Aaliyah asked with bright-eyed interest.

"I have no idea. Maybe someone just did a very thorough job of scoping the place out beforehand."

Morgan paused with his wine glass halfway to his mouth, his gaze sliding sideways to Sebastian.

"Are we so sure it's a single thief doing all this?" Jasmine asked. "Do they leave a calling card behind, or are we only assuming it's all one person?"

"Do you mean like a team, or a bunch of copycats?" Aaliyah asked.

"A single thief is a much better story," said Alphonse. "It's so much more dashing, romantic, what?"

"Real life is rarely so satisfying as fiction," Elizabeth said. "I don't think one or two copycats is out of the question."

"I prefer Alphonse's version of events," Sebastian said.

Alphonse beamed.

"I'm not convinced it's realistic," Elizabeth said apologetically.

"The thefts themselves are unrealistic," Sebastian returned. "At this point, the thief must be someone of unusual talents or magnificent skill to have done so much and escaped clean every time."

Morgan gave him a sharp look and Sebastian smiled back, all innocence.

"The guards from the National Gallery say it wasn't a clean escape, though," Coxley countered. "One of them said he actually got his hands on the thief before the man slipped his grasp and got away."

"But he *did* get away." Sebastian swallowed the weak rush of panic at the memory. "That's the important thing."

Aaliyah shook her head. "I think their luck is about to run out, whoever they are."

Alphonse made a distressed little noise.

"I don't want them to get caught," Aaliyah added. "It makes for marvellous entertainment. They can steal all the jewels in England, for all I care. I'd love for them to rob the king himself. I just don't see how they can keep it up forever. It's been fun while it's lasted, but these sorts of things almost always meet a disappointing end."

"Maybe this will be one of the rare ones," Sebastian said.

"That's very optimistic of you," Morgan said carefully.

Sebastian shrugged. "My optimism isn't hurting anyone. You could stand to have a little more of it yourself."

"That's true, Alphonse agreed. "You could learn a few good habits from your friend, old thing."

"I doubt it," said Morgan.

"How did you two meet, again?" Aaliyah asked.

"We knew each other as boys, actually," Morgan said. "We've only recently reconnected."

"I ran into an unfortunate incident with my previous housing situation," Sebastian added, appreciating the change in topic. "Morgan's been terribly generous in letting me stay with him, especially considering we hadn't been in touch for so long."

"What do you do?" Jasmine asked politely.

"I'm mostly a man of leisure these days." Sebastian's tone was airy.

"That's the best occupation," Alphonse said approvingly. "I think more people should give it a go."

Beside him, Jacobi genteelly cleared his throat.

"Oh, right. Er, well, rather, I mean that most people should be afforded the opportunity to try it," Alphonse corrected. "Obviously, it's not so easily done for some."

"I think we can all agree that wealth and leisure is preferable to backbreaking labour," Sebastian said with a smile that felt tighter than it looked.

"I imagine this jewel thief feels the same," Morgan said.

Sebastian glanced at him. "You wouldn't steal a handful of priceless jewels if you were able to?"

"Certainly not."

"I think of everyone present, Aaliyah would be our most likely suspect," Elizabeth posited. "She's fearless."

"I think it would be you," Aaliyah shot back. "You're as goal-oriented as I am, and you've been reading all those mystery novels lately."

"It can't be Aaliyah," Jasmine said. "She would give the jewels to me, and I would be spending my days on a sunny beach somewhere warm instead of running a flower shop as we head into winter."

"I think it would be Coxley," Arthur said. "He knows the National Gallery inside out."

"To what end?" Coxley asked curiously.

"For the thrill of it, and because you'd be confident that you could talk your way out of the ensuing mess."

"Fair enough," Coxley allowed.

Morgan didn't offer his own opinion, which made Sebastian edgier than if Morgan had accused him outright. The man needed distracting. Luckily, Sebastian knew just how to do it.

Under the table, he pressed his knee to Morgan's, slowly and deliberately. Morgan went very still at the touch, and when Sebastian didn't move away, Morgan cast him a surreptitious glance. Sebastian smiled back at him over his wine glass, projecting nothing more than friendly camaraderie. Though clearly suspicious of Sebastian's motives, as he was clearly suspicious of Sebastian's involvement in the jewel robberies, Morgan left his own knee right where it was.

Sebastian's smile broadened as he returned to his meal, and their legs stayed touching right up until everyone's plates were cleared and they returned to the kitchen, trading in their empty dishes for those laden with dessert.

As everyone crowded around the counter, waiting for Jacobi to distribute thick slices of apple-cranberry pie, Sebastian stayed close to Morgan with one hand on the man's lower back. The touch was innocent enough to be dismissed if anyone noticed. Although Sebastian was fairly certain they were in safe company and that no one would so much as blink at the suggestion that he and Morgan were intimately involved, Sebastian kept his touches subtle in concession to Morgan's modesty. As much as he enjoyed aggravating the man, he had no wish to drive Morgan to real embarrassment in front of his friends.

Returning to the table, they dug into the pie, which was sweet and tart and heavy with cinnamon and cloves. Sebastian had deliberately nudged his chair closer to Morgan's when they sat back down, and as they ate, he pressed their legs together from knee to ankle. When Morgan made no strong reaction to that, Sebastian dragged his foot on top of Morgan's, rubbing sock to sock, making the man freeze for a second, mid-bite.

But again, Morgan made no effort to extract himself.

When the man finally relaxed again, sinking into his pie and into the conversation, Sebastian dropped one hand to Morgan's knee. The tablecloth hid them entirely, though there was no hiding Morgan's reaction to the touch. He went stiff, like an affronted cat, and shot Sebastian a warning a look that didn't dissuade Sebastian in the slightest. Morgan could have easily taken Sebastian by the wrist and forcibly removed his hand without anyone else at the table catching on, but he didn't.

Gradually, Sebastian inched his way higher. Morgan's thigh was firm and tense under his palm, and it was all too easy imagining bare skin under his touch rather than woollen trousers. If the way Morgan was holding his breath was any indication, he found it easy to imagine, as well.

After dessert they moved to the sitting room for tea, where the record player crackled warmly in the corner, and a tabby cat emerged to claim Jacobi's lap for dozing. Without the dinner table to offer cover, Sebastian had to get more creative with his touches, but he was nothing if not resourceful. He took any and every excuse to make physical contact: a light tap on the knee when agreeing with whatever conversational point Morgan made; a hand on his shoulder, or trailing down his back; their feet pressed side by side as they shared the loveseat.

The others must have caught on as to the nature of Sebastian and Morgan's relationship; perhaps not Alphonse, but his wife, certainly. But if his hosts or fellow guests caught on, they kept their thoughts to themselves save for a few knowing looks and secret smiles. If he'd correctly guessed their own secrets, it was unlikely they'd go spreading gossip about Morgan's.

And of course, Sebastian wasn't remotely concerned for his own reputation. He only existed in the shadows of polite society. The only reputation he cared about preserving was his talent as a thief, and that was only applicable in very specific, very small circles in the London underworld.

Morgan's composure slipped the longer Sebastian's teasing went on, his complexion turning pinker and his spine stiffer, until finally, he cracked completely.

"Let me take the empty saucers to the kitchen," he said, standing abruptly to collect everyone's cups and dishes. "Sebastian, would you mind lending a hand?"

"Certainly," Sebastian said, rising smoothly.

"You don't have to," Alphonse began, but Aaliyah waved him off.

"Let them make themselves useful if they want," she said, but the look she sent after them as Morgan hightailed it to the kitchen said she saw right through their excuse to speak privately.

"Stop it," Morgan whispered desperately, the instant they were alone. "They're going to see us!"

"So what if they do? They're not going to care. If anything, they'll be happy for you."

"I'll care."

"Do you want me to stop because you don't like it? Or would you be happy to continue if we were alone?"

"We're not alone," Morgan said, which was almost an answer.

"Would you like to be?"

Setting his handful of saucers in the sink, Sebastian slunk right up to Morgan, laying both hands on his chest in order to lean close enough to speak directly in his ear, as intimate as a slow dance.

"Dinner is over; dessert is done. Make your excuses and take me home, if that's what you want. I'm a tease, but I'm not a monster. I can make good on all of tonight's promises if you let me."

Morgan drew a shuddering breath, his hands faintly trembling in fists by his sides as he resisted the urge to touch Sebastian the way Sebastian had been touching him all evening.

"Anyone could walk in on us like this," he said under his breath.

"Let them," Sebastian murmured, his lips grazing Morgan's cheek. "Maybe they're gossiping about us in the other room already. It doesn't matter. I can't imagine a more sympathetic crowd."

One hand came to rest on Sebastian's hip, clenching tightly, more of a spasm than a grope.

"How is it that I can see every play you're making, but they still work so damn well?" Morgan asked helplessly.

"You could say no if you really wanted to," Sebastian pointed out. "I'm not coercing you into anything. I'm just offering."

"It's a bad idea." Morgan's eyes were shut like he was talking to himself.

"It's not *that* bad. While I appreciate your professionalism, I am very explicitly inviting you to abandon it."

Sebastian held his breath, waiting. After a second, Morgan placed his other hand on Sebastian's hip, and pulled him close until their bodies were flush. Sebastian went easily, meeting Morgan's mouth in a quick kiss. Just as quickly, Morgan stepped back to hold him at arm's length, and Sebastian's stomach dropped at the sudden rejection.

But Morgan's gaze was darker and hungrier than Sebastian had ever seen it. "Let's say our goodbyes and go home."

CHAPTER EIGHTEEN

A BROADENING OF HORIZONS

The trick was maintaining that hunger for the whole cab ride home. The cabbie was unknown and therefore couldn't be trusted, so Sebastian and Morgan left the seat between them empty, and kept their hands to themselves. Even speaking was dangerous, because all Sebastian wanted to talk about were all the filthy things they could get up to behind closed doors.

He kept his mouth shut and his hands in his lap and Morgan did the same, sitting so rigidly that no one would ever believe they'd been well wined and dined an hour before. Were it not for the little glances Morgan kept sneaking out of the corner of his eye, they might have passed for business acquaintances, keeping a polite distance from one another on a boring commute.

Beneath his composure, Sebastian was beyond delighted by this turn of events: Morgan's lowering of his defences, allowing Sebastian past his armour and, if things continued as they seemed wont, into his bed. Sebastian wanted a good tumble with Morgan almost as much as he wanted the Rose Diamond. He couldn't think of the last time he'd wanted someone on their own merit, without using the sex as a stepping stone to some greater goal.

And yes, he wanted to sleep with Morgan in order to raise his own value to him—that went without saying. But it came second to the fact that he was genuinely attracted to the man and he wanted to act on that attraction with sheer animal instinct.

When they were back at Morgan's with the door shut behind them, they both stood still, just looking at each other. The wine coursed pleasantly in Sebastian's veins, not enough to make him tipsy, let alone drunk, but it gave him a warm buzz. Every movement was loose and easy, and every thought enticing.

Morgan looked especially delectable: ash-blond hair mussed where he'd run his hand through it in the cab, his pupils large enough to eclipse the grey of his irises, his tie loose and the top button of his collar undone. There was a pink flush high on his cheeks. Like Sebastian, he hadn't drunk enough to account for it, and the knowledge that Sebastian alone had inspired that colour was enough to stoke a little curl of fire in Sebastian's core.

"So," Sebastian began, shrugging out of his coat.

Morgan crossed the distance between them in a single stride, grabbed Sebastian by the shoulders, and crashed into him with a bruising kiss. Sebastian laughed into it, his arms trapped in his sleeves as his back hit the wall. Morgan pinned him there, one knee in between Sebastian's, their bodies pressed together as their tongues met. Morgan made a frustrated noise into Sebastian's mouth, but whether it was directed at Sebastian or at himself, Sebastian couldn't tell.

They kissed like they wanted to eat each other alive, like they'd been waiting years instead of days. It was the kind of hungry passion Sebastian most loved to inspire, where every rational thought and scrap of common sense and self-preservation fell away, powerless in the face of such unbridled want.

Sebastian had never experienced such passion himself. He'd always taken pains to be the cause and the instigator but never the target, and the strength of it blindsided him.

He didn't let his inexperience show.

"Hell," Morgan muttered, breaking the kiss.

He bit at Sebastian's jaw instead, before clasping Sebastian's face and resting their foreheads together, eyes downcast and breathing heavily like he'd been ridden hard and put away wet.

They hadn't even started yet.

"Upstairs?" Sebastian suggested breathlessly.

They fell into bed in a graceless tangle. Morgan hit the mattress first, the backs of his knees giving out against its edge as Sebastian pushed him flat and climbed on top, never breaking their kiss for more than a moment. Morgan skated his hands over Sebastian's ribs, down his flanks and up again, never pausing long enough to actually seek out the skin under his clothes.

"How long has it been?" Sebastian asked, nipping at his mouth.

"Too long. God, it's been—"

Morgan broke off in a gasp as Sebastian fixed his mouth over the pulse point in his throat until Morgan was shaking.

"So impatient," Sebastian chided. "If it's been such a long time already, what difference does a few more minutes make?"

Growling, Morgan grasped Sebastian's shoulders and flipped their positions.

"Stop being coy. You want this as much as I do."

Sebastian laughed as Morgan pinned him to the pillows. "Yes, but unlike you, I can appreciate a little foreplay."

Sebastian lifted his hips and Morgan shut his eyes, biting back a moan. On the next inhale he leant down to capture Sebastian's mouth. In that kiss, Sebastian could feel Morgan's every want and need, and he groaned gratefully at the sensation.

"Get out of your clothes," Morgan whispered, biting at the lobe of Sebastian's ear. "Or is that skipping too much foreplay for you?"

"You're terrible at this." But Sebastian was smiling as he writhed free of Morgan's grasp to shove the shirt off Morgan's shoulders, gleefully popping the buttons as he went.

Morgan seemed about to protest the mistreatment of his clothes before instead sitting up to shrug free of the shirt entirely, shaking it loose and flinging it off into the netherlands of the bedroom floor. With that out of the way he dropped his hands to his trousers, his fingers flitting over the buttons without actually undoing them.

Sebastian folded his arms behind his head. "Go on. I've stripped for you before: I want to see this."

Morgan shifted uncomfortably. "I didn't realise it was meant to be a show."

"Everything's a show, darling. Make it a good one."

He thumbed the top button open. "Right."

Morgan clearly wasn't a performer. While he might not have been self-conscious about kissing, or staring at Sebastian, or getting their shirts off, he was certainly self-conscious about stripping for the sole purpose of entertaining his partner. He didn't seem body-shy, but he did seem awkward. Not because he didn't think he looked good; he just didn't seem to know what to do as the centre of attention. Always the observer and never the observed.

Sitting on the edge of the mattress, he shucked his trousers off one leg at a time. In fairness, it was difficult to remove one's trousers and make the act look sexy. Sebastian could sympathise, but not enough to let Morgan off easy.

"We're supposed to be having fun," he reminded him. "Stop looking so serious."

"That's just my face," Morgan objected.

"Then bring your face over here and kiss me again."

Morgan obliged, turning onto the bed on hands and knees to crawl up the length of Sebastian's body. Sebastian lay back, pretending to be patient as he waited. Inside, he was on fire, every nerve zipping with anticipation. His shirt was splayed open, his undershirt rucked up and his belt removed—still mostly clothed, but in tempting disarray.

Morgan was in nothing but his underpants, his broad shoulders and thick thighs on display for the first time. Sebastian didn't allow his eyes to wander. There would be time for that later. For now, he kept his eyes fixed on Morgan's face and a lazy smile on his lips, wordlessly daring Morgan to make the first move.

Slowly, Morgan lowered himself to his elbows so their lips were almost brushing.

"Are you going to tell me again that I'm a bad idea?" Sebastian murmured.

Morgan kissed him before the last word was out.

He moved like a dam had broken and he'd left all restraint on the other side of the bedroom door. He sank into the waiting cradle of Sebastian's hips, chest to chest and ribs to ribs, a full-body embrace as Sebastian arched to rub up against him like a cat.

As good as it felt, Sebastian was planning ten steps ahead. It was second nature to him; he didn't even have to stop and think about it. As he made all the right noises, one hand in Morgan's hair, he calculated how best to lead Morgan through the steps of this particular dance. What acts would bring him the most pleasure, which ones would give him the best impression of Sebastian, but without moving too quickly and scaring him off. It was a delicate line to walk, and not always obvious.

For example: most of the men Sebastian conned wanted to fuck him, and they wanted to be on top. But if he let them do that the first time they fell into bed together, he ran the risk of them getting bored and discarding him too quickly. On the other hand, if he teased them too long without letting them stick it in, they would inevitably get frustrated and again, cast him aside before he'd got all he wanted from them.

With Morgan, it wasn't a risk of boredom or frustration so much as a risk of overwhelming the man. Morgan seemed to take sex more seriously than Sebastian's average partner. Not that it was some sacred thing; just not entirely casual. Semi-formal, maybe, was the best term for it.

So: for their first night, maybe they wouldn't even finish removing their clothes. Unless Morgan suggested some alternative, Sebastian assumed the safest route would be getting off as they were currently doing, with full-body friction, and probably a hand at the end. Low-enough stakes that Morgan was unlikely to get all up in his head about it.

But Morgan didn't seem interested in playing along with Sebastian's careful calculations. Instead, he was extremely interested in bringing Sebastian to the edge with embarrassing speed. Working one hand down the front of Sebastian's trousers without actually removing them, Morgan dropped flat, one leg thrown over Sebastian's to keep him in place. He latched onto

Sebastian's throat in a wet, biting kiss as he worked him with single-minded efficiency like it was a race.

Caught entirely off guard, Sebastian gave in before he even knew what was happening. Too late, he realised that Morgan intended to finish him without getting off himself, something Sebastian had never before allowed a partner to do, not wanting them to get the upper hand. He would have protested, or found some way to swap positions, but then Morgan did something clever with his wrist, and all of Sebastian's higher brain functions flew out the window.

He came with a breathless, laughing curse, and Morgan smiled against the side of his neck where he'd left Sebastian a truly impressive hickey.

"Fuck," Sebastian said, grinning up at the ceiling. "That wasn't as coordinated as I'd intended."

"Do I get points for spontaneity?" Morgan asked, teeth grazing Sebastian's skin as he put the finishing touches on his work.

"I'm certainly not complaining. How do you want yours?"

"The same. Anything." Rolling his hips against Sebastian's thigh, he moved his kisses from his neck to his shoulder and then his collarbone, laying himself out on top of Sebastian to mark a line down the centre of his chest. "I should have asked you what you liked beforehand, but I had a feeling you would have given me some vague, non-committal answer."

"I like a lot of things."

Morgan's laugh was a huff of hot air against Sebastian's solar plexus. "Exactly."

"Tell me what *you* like," Sebastian said, poking Morgan's shoulder. "I owe you one."

"I like a lot of things, too." Pausing in his ministrations, Morgan propped himself up on his elbows to look Sebastian in the face. "Do whatever you like best. So I'll know for next time."

"You're very confident we'll be doing this again," Sebastian noted, his grin creeping wider.

Morgan rolled his eyes and rolled off Sebastian to the side, dropping onto his back. "My mistake," he said, his tone withering. "You'd better give me your best right now then, if I won't have another chance at this."

"I like this version of you," Sebastian informed him gleefully, sitting up to face him. "Do you have this whole facet of your personality that only comes out in bed?"

"No surprise that you act exactly the same in bed and out of it, considering you've spent every waking moment trying to get me here."

"And it paid off."

"Sebastian."

"Don't fret, darling. I'm not going to leave you hanging."

He reached over to trail his fingers over Morgan's hand where he was playing restlessly with his waistband. Under Sebastian's touch, Morgan stilled, glancing at him expectantly.

"Don't be upset with me," Sebastian said, mostly just to see the flash of worry in Morgan's eyes. "If you don't like it, tell me to stop."

"If I don't like what?" Morgan asked suspiciously.

Sebastian smiled like a cat.

His magic surged out in a wave, dark coils of smoke bursting from his chest to swim through the air like serpents, coursing their way to collide with Morgan with the force of a juggernaught. The magic knocked him flat and breathless, pinning him on his back as it covered his body like a living creature.

It was wild, unchecked magic, the kind never acknowledged in polite company, the kind Morgan had shied away from in the museum and the park. It was dangerous and taboo and everything Morgan had spent his whole life denying himself.

"Now, with the door shut and no one to see us, tell me this doesn't feel good," Sebastian said, sitting back and crossing his legs under him to watch Morgan come undone.

"Sebastian—" His voice was rough with yearning, and he bucked against the magic in an effort to reach him.

Sebastian took pity and relented, coming forward to bracket Morgan's hips with his knees, his hands settling by Morgan's shoulders.

"Is this what you wanted?" he asked, his voice a mere breath.

Morgan nodded frantically. Gone were his manners, his poise, his dignity—it felt so good to see him so dishevelled. "Sebastian, god—give me anything."

Sebastian kissed him, licking deep into his mouth like he meant to devour him whole. His magic surged up stronger, enveloping them both in a cloud of darkness, warm and billowing in time with their pulses.

"Tell me," Sebastian whispered. "Tell me what you want me to do next."

"Make me feel alive."

The magic engulfed them completely; it was like being in the centre of an electrical storm. The hairs on Morgan's arms stood on end, tingling against Sebastian's skin. Sebastian kissed him like a hurricane, relentless and wild. His magic crackled in the air like lightning and Morgan wound his fingers through Sebastian's hair, torn between tugging him back and urging him on.

"Let go." Sebastian mouthed the words against Morgan's throat. "Come on, let go—I know you want to—"

Morgan shut his eyes and obeyed. His hair was like silk between Sebastian's fingers, his skin slick with sweat, muscles bunching with effort. The magic was hot and heavy, licking at him like fire and just as energetic. It moved in rhythm with Sebastian's kisses and the lazy rolling of his hips, wavelike and crashing against the shore of Morgan's body. As Sebastian's magic curled around him, Morgan finally let go and came crashing over the edge.

His magic burst out in a swarm of sepia and gold, sparking as it crashed into Sebastian, flickering like flame as it met his cloud of dark-coloured magic and exploded in a shower of sparking embers. The combined heat fogged up the windows and ricocheted off the walls—the glass would have shattered if Sebastian hadn't intervened, calling his magic back before any damage could be done. Morgan fell back against the pillows, drained and panting, yet unwilling to part from Sebastian's touch.

"I think you've singed the carpet," Sebastian observed, peering over the edge of the bed before settling back against Morgan's chest.

"I don't care."

"Mm. Was that the first time you've done that?"

"Had sex? No, thank you."

Sebastian nudged him. "Let your magic loose."

"Yes, probably."

"How was it?"

"Electrifying. Taboo. And so terribly freeing."

Sebastian hummed, keenly interested. "That's why it's so frowned upon. It wouldn't do to have people feeling so empowered by something as simple as that."

"Is this how you do your magic all the time? No spells or incantations, just simple, straightforward…"

"I don't have to come every time I want to make a lightshow, but yes." Sebastian propped himself up again to meet Morgan's gaze. "Did you like it?"

"Yes," Morgan admitted.

"Then do it again." Sebastian walked his fingers across Morgan's chest. "Shut your eyes, take a deep breath, and let it go."

Morgan's mouth twisted to one side. Despite his confessed enjoyment, it was still everything he'd been taught to avoid.

"Who will it hurt? Who'll even know?" Sebastian prompted.

Morgan huffed. "Fine."

Sebastian put one hand over Morgan's eyes, holding them closed. "Don't think about anything except what you want to do to me."

Morgan took a deep breath, imagined Sebastian spread out against the sheets, dark and cunning and waiting just for him, and let his magic course out unfettered like something wild.

◆ ◆ ◆

"Do you feel better?" Sebastian asked.

They lay side by side in Morgan's bed, sprawled in easy company, their clothes abandoned in various places about the room. Where Morgan had tugged the rumpled sheets up just high enough to preserve some semblance of modesty, Sebastian stretched out naked in all his glory, his arms folded behind his head.

"I certainly feel more relaxed," Morgan replied, after a moment's thought. "Though I don't know how long it will last."

"I'm up for round two whenever you are."

"I meant—"

"I know." Sebastian turned onto his side, propping his chin up on one fist, the other hand coming to trace patterns over Morgan's chest. "I liked seeing you like that. Unreserved. Not that your more studious persona doesn't have its own charm, of course."

"It felt freeing." Morgan captured Sebastian's hand to hold it over his heart. "Being able to ask for and offer exactly what I wanted with no fear of repercussion. I understand the appeal of living that life outside of the bedroom. But I don't think I can."

"No?"

He ran his lips over the ridge of Sebastian's knuckles and onto the pearl ring. "I like that you're wearing this," he murmured, then sighed. "People know my name and my face and my family. I can't toss all that aside for the sake of indulging every whim and appetite that strikes my fancy."

"It's not about indulging whims and appetites," Sebastian said crossly, retrieving his hand to sit up properly. "That's never been the point. It's about indulging your *self*, and not hiding from the public like some kind of sad, self-conscious hermit. Because you deserve better than that."

"Sebastian…"

"You do," he insisted. "You're a good man, and you know you're wasted hiding away, wings clipped and trimming back your feelings and opinions like you do."

"Well, it's a bit late to start over. If I were twenty, maybe, but I've built a life for myself here."

"You're thirty-three. That's not exactly over the hill."

"I've lived here my whole life. My social circle is exactly the same as it's been since I was a child. My parents' friends all know me…"

"So, go somewhere new."

Morgan scoffed. "Like where?"

"America," Sebastian replied immediately.

"What would I do in America?" Morgan asked carefully.

"God above—whatever you want! That's the whole point!" Sebastian collapsed onto his back, dramatically flinging his hands in the air. "You're impossible. Just leave the country, go somewhere new where no one knows your name or cares how you act. Start over! Do anything! Don't just keep wasting your life here, pacing holes in the floor of the tiny little life you've made. You deserve better."

"America," Morgan repeated, trying the word on his tongue. "Why there?"

"Because that's where I'm going."

"To do what?"

Sebastian rolled his eyes. "The same as I just told you. To start over. To pretend I was never a criminal and I've never seen the inside of a jail. To just…" He raised one hand, turning his wrist in a circle. "You know. Live."

"And you want me to come with you."

"I'd enjoy your company, yes. We could get a nice flat in New York, where no one knows anything about us. You could open an art gallery and be the American Jules Coxley, and see if the colonials are as easily scandalised as the English. It would be great fun. Just the two of us, with your art and my good looks…"

When Morgan didn't chime in, Sebastian trailed off, feeling suddenly exposed. He swallowed that vulnerability, which had come out of nowhere, and changed tracks.

"I'm not suggesting this because I want to drag you along with me." He laid his hand back on Morgan's chest and met his eye, his face earnest. "Don't get me wrong: you were very good in bed."

"Oh, thank you."

"I'm suggesting it because I think it's what you want, even if you haven't realised it yet. Or admitted it." He tucked a stray strand of Morgan's hair behind his ear. "Am I wrong?"

But he already knew Morgan wasn't ready for it. He wasn't even sure he himself was ready for such commitment. Could they do another week of this? A month? And after the allure wore off and became routine, what then?

Well, then it would be time to try something new again.

"I can see you overthinking it," Sebastian murmured, drawing a line down Morgan's forehead, between his eyes, to land at the tip of his nose. "You don't have to say yes. I can't make you."

"You didn't make me say yes to your suggestion of moving in with me," Morgan pointed out. "You didn't *make* me say yes to any of your propositions. But I did."

"And that's worked out wonderfully for you so far, hasn't it?" Sebastian kissed his cheek, his jaw, his throat.

Morgan was silent for a long minute, so long that Sebastian had to check to see whether he'd dropped off.

"Ask me again," Morgan finally said. "In a week or a month from now, after the novelty's faded. Your novelty. Then maybe I'll have an answer."

"That's not a no."

"It's not anything, yet."

Sebastian could work with that. Inviting him to America had been a whim, not fully considered. In a week or a month's time, he might not want to ask again at all.

CHAPTER NINETEEN

A DECEIT DISCOVERED
AND AN ULTIMATUM DENIED

As he climbed into bed that evening beside Morgan, clad only in a loose pair of pyjama bottoms next to Morgan's full silk set, Sebastian considered the possibility that everything was going exactly as it should. He and Morgan were on the best terms they had been since their reunion. Having hashed out their differences and had what seemed likely to be only the first of many rounds of very satisfying sex, Sebastian felt confident that his place in Morgan's home was secure for the near future.

Scotland Yard was still miles out from identifying their jewel thief, and he and Kitty were tackling the Rose Diamond in just two more sleeps. Everything he'd ever wanted was within reach. He could already feel the diamond's cold, sharp bite under his fingers, the weight of the necklace resting against his breast. The thought made him shivery and reckless with anticipation.

Having Morgan was an added bonus. He hadn't expected the man to be such a good lay, and the possibility of doing that again, and doing more, was almost as enticing as the Rose Diamond itself.

Sebastian didn't make friends easily. There were too many hurdles to overcome before he could trust anyone, and few people seemed worth the effort. And he didn't trust Morgan the way he trusted Kitty, or even Adam, but he wanted to. It was tempting to imagine a future together, a similar temptation to imagining a future with the Rose Diamond. One that made his stomach flip, sweetly pleasant.

"This feels like the bedtime routine of an old married couple," Sebastian observed, tucking himself in under the covers.

On the other side of the bed, Morgan was sitting up against the pillow, knees raised to balance an open book against his thighs.

"I'm not sure what I'm supposed to do. Do I just lay here and watch you read?"

Rolling his eyes, Morgan flipped the book shut to reveal it as none other than *Pepperika*. "I thought I might as well give it a shot, seeing as it was already in the house. I'm afraid it's just as awful reading it myself as having you read it aloud to me."

"What a shame. You're not learning anything interesting from it?"

"I think you would have been better off stealing one of those queer books after all, though I shudder to think how those sex acts would have been described. I don't imagine there would be much improvement just because the body parts are different."

"Why don't you demonstrate a few of those sex acts on me?" Sebastian said, lifting his eyebrows suggestively.

Setting the book aside, Morgan turned to face him. "What did you have in mind?"

"Surprise me."

Morgan rolled on top of him, the move made clumsy by the fact that they were both under heavy covers, and Sebastian laughed. Morgan looked like he was trying to hold back his own amusement, folding his arms over Sebastian's chest to stare down at him, slightly cross-eyed from the close distance. He had a smattering of freckles over his nose and cheeks, so light they were nearly invisible. Sebastian had never noticed them before.

"There's almost nothing you can do that I won't like," Sebastian promised.

"You'll tell me if I get especially unlucky and hit on one of those outliers?"

"Of course," he lied.

In perfect truth, he didn't expect Morgan to land on anything unpleasant, and if he did, it would be the sort of mild unpleasantness Sebastian could easily act through. After all, it was much simpler to lie back and think of England than stop a partner in the midst of things to explain that no, he wasn't particularly fond of that position, or no, he wasn't actually that flexible, and doing it like that was going to make his leg cramp, or that he really preferred not looking his partner in the eye like they were communicating something profound while they were inside him, or that he much preferred something fast and rough to slow and gentle. It simply wasn't worth the bother.

If Morgan was one of those sorts who insisted on lovemaking, then Sebastian would grit his teeth and bear it, and make sure Morgan never caught so much as a single whiff as to Sebastian's true feelings on the matter. Sebastian was an actor, in bed and out of it. Especially in bed.

Morgan flattened himself against Sebastian to kiss him deeply, hands roaming under the sheets to find skin. Sebastian mirrored his every movement, slipping his own hands under Morgan's top to hold his waist, his lower back, his ribs. Morgan was warm and solid and the silk felt delicious everywhere it touched.

The lamp light was dim; the rustle of the sheets was loud. Morgan didn't seem concerned about hurrying things along and fucking Sebastian in the traditional sense. Though he was literally on top of Sebastian, there was no domination in his movements, nor any indication of ownership over his partner. Like, even though they were in Morgan's bed, in his home, with his food and his money, Morgan saw Sebastian as his equal.

It was meaningless, really—they hadn't been equals as boys and weren't really equals now—but Sebastian rather liked it, all the same. As Morgan slid their pyjama bottoms down, Sebastian shut his eyes and imagined himself decked in gold and diamonds, in bed with Morgan somewhere hot like they were princes of some decadent, ancient world instead of being trapped in drab, dreary, 1920s London.

With a gasp, his eyes flared open as Morgan slid against him. In all the time he'd spent bedding uninteresting men, they had never once joined him in his fantasies.

"What?" Morgan asked against his throat.

"Keep doing what you're doing," Sebastian said breathlessly. "It's working."

He didn't shut his eyes again, instead, studying Morgan as intently as Morgan had ever studied him. When he came, it was to Morgan's grey gaze locked on his, like falling into a billowing sea.

"That was unforgivably sentimental," Sebastian said afterwards, catching his breath.

"Hm?"

"Eye contact and synchronised orgasms."

"Ah. Should I apologise?"

"No."

Sebastian lunged, shark-like, to catch Morgan in another kiss. The way he wanted Morgan was a revelation. If this was how people were supposed to feel about intimacy, then he actually understood the appeal for the first time.

"We'll just have to be more careful next time to avoid this sappiness."

"Of course," Morgan agreed, straight-faced.

◆ ◆ ◆

Waking up in Morgan's arms was a new experience. It wasn't that Sebastian had never woken in a lover's embrace before, though he generally tried to avoid it. It was the peace and contentment that was unusual. Consciousness returned to him in flits: the feeling of a warm body against him, the faint smell of cologne, sandalwood and wood smoke, Morgan's hair resting against his. Dawn light glanced through the curtains to land in a weak pool on the foot of the bed, pale and unobtrusive. Sebastian stretched his legs out long, pointing his toes without moving his upper body, reluctant to break the cocoon in which he and Morgan existed.

Awake, but only barely, it was easy to give in to idle fantasies, slipping away from the day and back towards the gentle ebb and sway of dreams.

There, Sebastian wasn't afraid of commitment or sentimentality. There, he could imagine taking Morgan with him to New York, and the life they might build together. One of parties and champagne, reckless and decadent in the way only young Americans could be, with diamond cufflinks at Morgan's wrists and ropes of real pearls around Sebastian's neck.

And after the parties, they would have somewhere private where they could escape, somewhere shrouded in magic so no one could ever find them unless they wanted to be found, and they would be utterly free within its walls to be with each other without fear. Somewhere they could fall into bed and stay there for hours or days at a time, where Sebastian need never fear being turned out, because the house was his, and he would never have to rely on anyone's generosity or gullibility ever again.

In this fantasy, Morgan knew about the jewels, and it only made him love Sebastian all the more. He knew who Sebastian was, and what he did, and didn't shy away from it, as he hadn't shied away from the fact that Sebastian had done time in Blackwood. Morgan knew Sebastian in this fantasy as none of Sebastian's partners had ever known him, yet it didn't make Sebastian claustrophobic. He *wanted* to feel seen.

Beside him, Morgan stirred, the rhythm of his breath changing as he left the realm of sleep behind. Breathing him in, Sebastian opened his eyes, and they acknowledged the day together.

"You seem happy," Morgan noted.

"Don't I usually?"

"You usually seem pleased. There's a difference."

"I am happy, as a matter of fact. I was just thinking: how marvellous would it be if I got everything I wanted?"

Morgan snorted. "That's what you fantasise about in bed, is it?"

"Sometimes, yes. Doesn't everyone?"

"What more are you waiting for that you haven't already got?"

"Plenty. Do you want me to list every individual thing? It could take a while."

"Let me guess. A lavish mansion in every country. More money than you could ever spend in your natural life. French food and Italian wine. Bespoke suits. Am I close?"

"Of course you are. Everyone wants those things."

"I'd rather hear about what you already have that makes you happy," Morgan said.

"Are you fishing for compliments?"

He shrugged. "I wouldn't mind feeling appreciated, if you're so inclined."

"Then let me feed your ravenous ego." Settling on his stomach with his hands folded under his chin, which rested high up on Morgan's chest, just below his shoulder, Sebastian said, "You do make me happy. Happier than I ever imagined being in a relationship, if you must know. Not just because you're letting me live in your house and eat your food and sleep in your bed—in which you're very good, by the way. I like your company. I like your face. Is that what you want to hear?"

"Happier than you ever imagined," Morgan repeated doubtfully. "I can't tell whether you're flattering me, or if your standards were so abysmally low to begin with."

"You're a surprisingly good catch. You've slept with men before; you must know that most of them aren't worth holding onto. You might think of yourself as being just as boring as your reputation would make you seem, but you're a good man, and that's a rare thing. I have no use for a moral compass myself, and I'll confess that yours took some getting used to, but, to be perfectly honest, more people could do with such a thing."

Morgan cleared his throat.

"You're blushing," Sebastian informed him.

"That was rather more heartfelt than I expected of you," Morgan mumbled.

It was Sebastian's turn to roll his eyes. "Then let me demonstrate my appreciation in a more expected manner."

Kicking the covers aside, he worked his way down the length of Morgan's body until he found something to occupy his mouth and keep him from spilling any more embarrassing sentiments.

◆ ◆ ◆

Sebastian spent the day in incomparably good cheer. The weather was grey, but his mood was bright; not even Sterling's vague aura of disapproval could bring him down. Morgan took Sebastian's high spirits with good-natured bemusement, allowing them to bolster his own mood to something lighter.

Sebastian mixed drinks for them in the afternoon, impromptu cocktails for their modelling session, of which he spent the duration teasing Morgan beyond his limits. It was exhilarating, be able to finally act on that teasing. Morgan gave into it so much more readily now that they were sleeping together, and every time he succeeded in tipping the man over the edge, Sebastian was thrilled all over again. The novelty simply didn't wear off.

Not that he entirely prevented Morgan from finishing his drawings. Sebastian enjoyed seeing his likeness too much to pull Morgan away from his sketchbook altogether. But the drawings took on an unmistakably erotic bent as the afternoon progressed, until Sebastian had lost almost all his clothes, and Morgan had shed more of his own than was strictly necessary for an artist.

As the afternoon wound down, Sebastian rang Adam up to gloat.

"Are you finally ready to admit I've won, and hand over the last fifteen quid you owe me?"

"You've officially moved in, have you?" Adam asked.

"I haven't stayed at yours since Tuesday night. It's Friday, now. Is that not official enough for you?"

"I suppose it is. Next time you drag yourself out of his bed for long enough to see me, I'll pay up. Fair's fair."

By the time tea rolled around, Sebastian felt invincible.

It only made his inevitable fall from grace all the more painful.

As it was Friday evening, Sterling excused himself from the house after cooking supper, shelving his duties until Monday morning. After tea, Morgan stepped away to do some quick tidying, disappearing upstairs with an armful of fresh linens. Sebastian thought nothing of it until he wandered upstairs a few minutes later, intending to ask Morgan whether he thought brandy or scotch would make a better nightcap. He found Morgan in the guest room, standing by the bed with his back to the door. His shoulders looked stiff, and Sebastian hesitated, leaning against the door frame.

"Sebastian."

Morgan's tone made him wary. As Morgan turned, Sebastian's stomach dropped abruptly, like he'd just missed a step on the stairs. Morgan held Sebastian's rucksack, the pocket unclasped to reveal the glint of jewels within.

"What is this?" Morgan asked quietly.

There was no lie Sebastian could weave that Morgan would fall for.

"You went through my things," he said instead, turning to betrayal as he stalled for time.

"How long has this been here?"

That might be Sebastian's only saving grace. "Since the beginning," he said quickly. "You told me to stop stealing as long as I was with you, and I did."

"These aren't trinkets or stolen wallets from an afternoon of pickpocketing." Morgan gave the bag a shake like he wanted to throttle it. Inside, the gemstones clinked against each other. "Tell me honestly. Are these from that National Gallery exhibit that was robbed? Are you London's jewel thief?"

Sebastian hesitated for a fraction of a second. That morning's dream of being truly known now seemed brittle and unrealistic.

He couldn't do it.

"No," he said; that was one question answered honestly, at least. Kitty had the National Gallery take; this was from Felton's. "They're costume jewellery— cheap crystals done up to look like the real thing. I lifted them from a pawnshop weeks ago, so I could have something flashy to wear to Eden."

Morgan didn't move. "You're lying."

"I'm not! God, do you really think I'd be here begging for food and board if I were the jewel thief? I'm a petty criminal; you know that. You've seen me."

But Morgan shook his head, his expression as closed-off as it had been in the beginning, when Sebastian had returned his stolen pocket watch.

"What's the point of asking me to tell you the truth if you're not going to believe me?" Sebastian snapped.

"I want to believe you. But I can't help feeling that you've been lying to me from the moment we met."

That shouldn't have hurt, considering the truth of it.

"Last night and this morning: that was real," Sebastian said quietly. "Do you believe that much, at least?"

"That was sex. What is there to believe or disbelieve? That you enjoyed it? I believe *that*, certainly. But there was nothing else to it. It wasn't like you said you were in love."

Sebastian went rigid. He hadn't said it, but he'd come dangerously close to thinking it.

"I've been more honest with you than anyone."

But he still couldn't make himself confess to the jewel robberies. His self-preservation was too strong: as strong as Morgan's own sense of ethics, surely.

"The first thing you did on meeting me was give me a false name and steal my watch," said Morgan. "The second was asking me to join you in conning your friend out of cash." He hefted the bag higher. "I know costume jewellery when I see it, and no cheap crystal has ever been made to look as convincing as this."

Sebastian wet his lips, his gaze darting between Morgan's face and the bag. "How am I supposed to convince you otherwise?"

"I don't know." Morgan's mouth twisted to the side, frustrated and disappointed. "I don't think you can."

They both stood still, staring at each other for a second before Sebastian broke free. Stepping forward, he grabbed the bag from Morgan's hands, rough and graceless, and Morgan let it go without a fight.

"If it's costume jewellery, it's worthless," Morgan said. "Leave it. I'll buy you whatever you want to replace it."

"I don't want your money," Sebastian snarled. "I want your trust."

"Then throw those things away."

His lip curled of its own accord. He felt like a rat backed into a trap. He couldn't give up the jewels, as Morgan well knew, but he couldn't convince Morgan of his honesty as long as he kept them. Which was more important? The take, or the man?

There was no competition.

He'd known Morgan all of a week, excluding that blurry, half-forgotten summer. The jewels from the pawnshop and the Cheapside Hoard would set him up for decades, and that was to say nothing of the Rose Diamond necklace. The take had to come first.

But Sebastian had never been able to resist trying to have his cake and eat it, too.

"I meant it when I said you make me happy," he told Morgan, holding the rucksack to his chest. "And I meant it when I asked you to come to New York with me. I understand why you don't trust me; give me more time to earn it. But let me try. I want to know what we're like together. I want that chance."

Morgan held out one hand and Sebastian's heart leapt, hopeful, only to plummet like a lead brick at Morgan's words.

"If that's what you want, then give me the bag and let me get rid of it." Morgan's voice was perfectly even.

He couldn't.

And Morgan knew it.

Twisting the ring off his finger, Sebastian let it drop to the carpet between them, the pearl dull and grey. As he turned and walked out, he hoped with every step that Morgan would stop him.

But Morgan didn't move a muscle or say a word. He didn't follow Sebastian downstairs to the foyer where Sebastian pulled on his coat and boots, knotting his scarf around his throat and drawing his gloves on one at a time. As slowly as Sebastian dressed, Morgan didn't appear on the stairs. Although Sebastian paused after opening the door, giving Morgan one last chance to catch him, to change his mind and ask him to stay, Sebastian remained alone, with only his stolen jewels for company.

Taking a deep breath, he steeled himself and stepped out into the cold dark of the evening. On exhalation, his breath was a plume of silver that wrapped around him like a ghost, effectively disappearing him from Morgan's life for a second time.

CHAPTER TWENTY

THAT ORANGE-SCENTED SUMMER

It had been a hazy summer with blue skies and yellow fields, silver dewdrops in the morning and pink sunsets at night like something out of a picture book. The rain had been warm, plunking off the broad leaves of the geraniums in the back garden, and dropping into the little pond whose water was grey under overcast skies and green in the sunlight.

The Hollyhock house was a beautiful place, stretching in size and magnificence compared to the little flat where Sebastian and his parents lived in the city. The kind of house so large that you could walk from room to room to room without encountering another occupant, because there were too many rooms to be inhabited by a single family, even if that family had servants.

Sebastian's mother wasn't a servant but a tutor, hired to instruct the Hollyhock boy in almost a year's worth of lessons fit into a single summer so he could return to school in the fall without being held back. Sebastian thought it sounded like a miserable use of one's summer, which was supposed to be the only time boys could escape their schooling and live like wild things, as nature intended. Summer was supposed to be sacred, untouchable.

At least Sebastian wasn't being made to attend the lessons himself. He'd been instructed to steer clear of them, in fact, so as to avoid distracting the other boy. But still, his mother's employment meant that for the first time, he wasn't permitted to spend the warmer months running amuck. The Hollyhocks had given Sebastian and his mother a room in which to stay, so that she could make the most of her time in catching their boy up to speed. Sebastian didn't feel like it was particularly generous of them. The house was very large and very quiet, like a museum or a mausoleum. If he had to stay with his mother on the property, he might have preferred sleeping out in the garden under the flowers like a faerie.

If the house was a mausoleum then Morgan Hollyhock was the little ghost of a boy who haunted it. He was two years older than Sebastian and infinitely more sombre, pale and thin like he'd been sick for a long time.

His mum sequestered them both in the sitting room to interrogate the boy about where he had left off in his studies. Morgan answered dutifully in a soft voice, sitting up straight with his hands folded in front of him like he was reciting a piece for the headmaster instead of a temporary tutor.

Sebastian sat off to the side at one end of the empty settee, trying his hardest to behave. A low coffee table sprawled in front of the settee, with a great crystal bowl in its centre holding an assortment of fresh fruit. As much as he tried to pay attention to the academic goings-on, his gaze kept slipping back to the bowl. They could only occasionally afford fresh fruit, though it was easier to come by in the summer, and he didn't relish the prospect of sitting cooped up in this dark little room staring at what he couldn't have.

Morgan noticed him before his own mother did.

"You can take one, if you like," he said.

His voice was weak, probably from whatever illness had plagued him earlier, and it took Sebastian a second to realise the words were directed at him. He glanced at his mother for silent permission, though he'd already started reaching for the bowl.

"No, Sebastian," she cut in gently. "Morgan, that's very generous, but you don't need to play host to us. Sebastian, sweetheart, why don't you go play outside so Morgan can get to work."

The outdoors was more alluring than the fruit, so Sebastian departed with minimal complaint, though Morgan was frowning faintly as he slipped empty-handed from the room.

There was an orange sitting on Sebastian's pillow when he went to bed that night.

He stole Morgan away the next day when the boy was eating lunch, orange in one hand and Morgan's in his other. Sebastian sat them down on the cool garden stones in the shade of the hydrangeas, blooming pink and blue and purple along the side of the house.

"You can have more, if you want," Morgan said, clearly bemused that Sebastian had held onto the orange past breakfast. "We have enough. My parents won't miss them."

Fat bumblebees fumbled their way through the hydrangeas above their heads as Sebastian dug both thumbs into the orange, splitting the rind. He peeled it off in one single, winding strip, checking in on Morgan at the end to see whether the other boy was impressed.

"That's clever," Morgan commented, and Sebastian rewarded him by plonking half the orange into his hand.

"It was a gift," Morgan protested, trying to return it. "I gave you the whole thing."

"You said you had more," Sebastian countered, refusing to accept it back. "We can share."

The orange was perfectly ripe. Maybe it was the summer sun and the flowers' heavy perfume and the butterfly-feeling of making a potential new friend, but it seemed the sweetest, juiciest orange Sebastian had ever tasted.

"What are you studying this afternoon?" he asked, swallowing a mouthful of pulp.

"Maths."

"Ugh. Good luck."

"Thanks."

That night, there were two oranges waiting on Sebastian's pillow.

Sebastian found Morgan in the garden every lunchtime after that, not needing to pull him away from the dark sitting room where his schoolbooks sprawled scattered over every surface. Even grey-skied days of summer showers were brighter outdoors than in that room. And in the evenings, they didn't even have to hide from Sebastian's mother, who came hunting for her truant charge the second Morgan's half-hour lunch break was up.

"Pneumonia," Morgan said, his voice still a rasp.

They sat side by side on the steps leading to the back garden, passing their second orange of the day back and forth as the birds chorused in the trees. As the sun went down, the frogs began to peep from the pond like a tiny, invisible orchestra.

"The doctors said I almost didn't make it. I missed nearly the whole school year."

"Were you stuck in bed that whole time?"

Morgan dipped his head in a short nod.

Sebastian couldn't imagine being bedbound for more than a day. An entire year was unfathomable. "And now you're stuck inside with lessons for the whole summer, too." The injustice of it was striking.

"I'm glad I've got some company for it, at least." Hesitantly, like he wasn't sure whether Sebastian would allow it, Morgan crept one foot to the side until he could tap his shoe against Sebastian's, a single light knock before retreating.

"Do you reckon your parents would be very upset if you knocked off early now and then to come play?"

"Probably."

"Will you do it anyway?"

Morgan glanced at him sideways. After having been confined to a sickbed for so long, the slightest hint of sun gave him freckles, and they stood out starkly over the bridge of his nose before scattering across his cheeks. "I don't want you to get in trouble for distracting me."

"Don't worry about that," Sebastian said confidently. "I can get myself out of trouble. It's not right that you should be stuck inside doing schoolwork the whole summer. You've got to run away with me at least a couple of times."

When Morgan still looked unsure, Sebastian knocked their shoes together with far more force than Morgan had dared. He offered Morgan another orange segment.

"Alright," Morgan conceded.

He was looking down, but there was a tiny smile in the corner of his mouth that made Sebastian feel like he'd won something. Their fingers were stained gold from peeling the orange, and sticky trails of juice ran over the backs of their hands to drip off their wrists and spatter the stone steps.

A painted lady butterfly alighted on Morgan's knuckles, delicate wings stilling for just a second. Morgan froze and they both watched in delighted wonder as the butterfly tip-tapped over the back of his hand, tasting the juice, before taking flight once more.

"That's got to be good luck," Sebastian said.

"We'll have to wait until one lands on you, too."

Sebastian snorted. "I don't need luck. I'm plenty lucky already."

That was true; he'd been lucky enough up to that point. But his luck wouldn't last him past summer's end.

◆ ◆ ◆

It was so late on Saturday night that Sunday morning was about to break. Sebastian stood on King's Road outside the jewellery shop, staring through the darkened window to the display that, in the daytime, held the necklace of his dreams.

The magic encasing the shop was as Deepa had described: a forcefield, invisible but with a rubbery consistency designed to bounce objects back. When Sebastian pushed one finger in, muscling through the resistance, he found the texture like that of incredibly thick jelly. He made sure to pull back before hitting the bricks beneath. Though it was by no means difficult to penetrate the forcefield, it would be nigh impossible to fall through it accidentally. If he were to trip the alarms in the process of undoing the magic, there was no chance he could claim drunken clumsiness had taken him through the barrier.

His mind blank and staticky, he picked the spell apart just to prove he could, mechanically going through the motions until the forcefield fell away.

The next layer of magic had a prickly aura, like a densely-woven thicket. That spell, Sebastian made no attempt to dismantle. Instead, he imagined the Rose Diamond sparkling in the moonlight as it rested on that black velvet bust like a monarch on its throne. There was no moonlight that night; the sky drizzled, clouds blocking the stars, each speck of rain ice-cold and miserable.

Sebastian pictured of himself somewhere warm, somewhere tropical; America or Europe, it didn't matter. Somewhere on a beach, with white sand and turquoise waves, the sun a gold disk in the sky, with the Rose Diamond necklace glittering a perfect, clear pink around his throat and over his chest.

He was alone in that fantasy, save for his stolen diamonds. As rich as a king, with the financial independence he'd always craved, and access to every material good he could ever want. He had everything in the world except for Morgan.

With cold resolve, he gathered himself and rebuilt the forcefield before the wind could pick up and drive the rain against the building and trigger the alarms. He and Kitty would steal the necklace, fence it, and live out their days in wealth beyond imagining. He didn't need anything else.

◆ ◆ ◆

Kitty took one look at Sebastian's face and groaned. "What happened?"

Sebastian barely held back a snarl as he shouldered past her into the townhouse. Dawn had broken grey and gloomy, and though the sun was up, the sky was as dark as his mood. "Morgan suspects I'm the jewel thief and I couldn't talk my way out of it. He and I are done."

"Did he accuse you?" Kitty demanded, following him inside. "Is he going to the police?"

"He asked, and no. He's got no proof apart from instinct, and that might be enough to send the cops sniffing after me, but I'm going to disappear."

"Did he ask about me? If he puts two and two together about those glamours we were wearing—"

"It won't matter," Sebastian interrupted. Pulling her into the powder room, he stashed the pawnshop haul before taking her by the shoulders. "We're getting out of here," he promised, looking her in the eye. "We're stealing the Rose Diamond tonight and then I'm going to New York to reinvent myself entirely. Once we have that necklace, we won't need anyone else ever again. I'll never have to so much as speak to another man if I don't want to. Are you coming with me?"

"I'll convince Adam to take me to France for a while. It wouldn't do you and I any good if we were caught together so soon after the theft."

Sebastian sniffed. "I guess out of the two of us you landed the more reliable man, didn't you?"

"Are you sure this is just a wounded ego over losing a mark?" Kitty asked suspiciously. "I've never seen anyone get you so tied up as this."

"He wasn't a mark," Sebastian admitted begrudgingly.

"What does that mean? You took Adam up on his bet to seduce the man."

"Morgan was in on it."

"What!"

"It's a long story. We knew each other from way back. And then I may have let one or two feelings get involved."

She socked him in the shoulder, which he very much deserved. "The cardinal sin, Seb! I never took you for a sap. How could you be so stupid?"

"I've been asking myself the same thing," he muttered.

"Is this going to fuck you up the way it did for the National Gallery job?"

"No," he said immediately. "I'm better than that."

"That's what you said then, too."

"The Rose Diamond is everything. It's our whole future. The National Gallery job, I was still in knots over him, and you were right. But now I'm done with him for good. He was a distraction and a waste of time and effort. This necklace is the only thing I need, and I'm going to do it right."

She glared at him a second longer before dropping her chin in a short nod, satisfied with whatever determination she read in his face.

"Did I hear I'm taking you to France?" Adam asked, looking up from his book as they left the powder room for the living room.

"Yes, if you don't mind," Kitty said.

"I'm always up for a holiday, but does it have to be France? I was thinking it would be nice to winter in the Mediterranean this year. We could do France in the spring."

Sebastian wasn't exactly jealous of them, but he was undeniably bitter. Kitty had always been lucky. Sebastian believed in making his own luck, and he got by well enough, but he'd always wanted what he couldn't have, and natural luck was one thing he couldn't steal.

Kitty made everything look effortless. Beauty, style, love. The way she'd charmed Adam into wrapping himself around her finger like there was nowhere he'd rather be. Sebastian bet he'd pop her the big question in France or Greece or wherever they ended up. Whether she'd say yes or no, he couldn't say. That she genuinely liked Adam as more than a simple cash cow, he was certain. But whether she valued the ability to lock that down more than she valued her own independence— she could go either way, and Sebastian wouldn't really be surprised no matter what decision she made.

He was happy for them both, really. He just needed to swallow the lump of acid in his throat that he got whenever he thought about his own future.

Kitty came to stand beside him, like she could tell the thoughts running through his head. She probably could; he wasn't trying very hard to hide them. He could feel himself making a lemon-sucking face.

"Don't think about him," she murmured, her hand reassuringly steady on his shoulder. "Don't think about any of that. Just think about that diamond necklace."

Taking a deep breath, he shut his eyes and nodded. She was right. That was his future. With enough riches, he'd never have to worry about anything again. Not food, not shelter, not loneliness, and certainly not heartbreak.

Not that he was heartbroken. Not even close.

"There are fresh sheets in the linen closet, if you want to make up the guest room," Adam offered. "I assume you'll be staying here again?"

"Thanks," Sebastian managed.

Adam looked at him strangely for a second over the top of his glasses. "Don't mention it."

Sebastian belatedly realised that he'd never thanked Adam for anything before, just helped himself to his home like he was entitled to it.

"Listen," Adam said, "about that fifteen pounds—"

"Keep it."

Adam and Kitty both stared at him like he'd been replaced by a doppelganger and begun speaking in tongues.

"You did win the bet," Adam said cautiously. "You slept with him and moved into his house, even if you made a mess of things."

"I never should have taken that bet in the first place. I don't want the money. Let's just forget the whole thing ever happened, shall we?"

Kitty rubbed his back. "Come on now, pull yourself together," she said, not unkindly. "We've got diamonds to steal."

CHAPTER TWENTY-ONE

THE ROSE DIAMOND NECKLACE

The jewellery shop looked perfectly innocuous. That was a trick. Without the threat of magical security, Kitty and Sebastian could have simply broken the front window in broad daylight, reached in, and snagged the necklace without setting foot inside. It could have been over in a few violent seconds, with them walking away several hundred thousand pounds richer and only a few cuts on their knuckles to pay for it, and the cuts would only be if they were careless.

It was fantasies like that that made Sebastian long, however briefly, for simpler times.

Instead of a three-second smash and grab, Kitty and Sebastian approached the shop as if it were an insect with a poisonous sting: small, but deadly. They had too much riding on that necklace for anything to go wrong. If they were caught, their lives were as good as over—that was one thing. Sebastian was confident it wouldn't come to that. They were too well prepared, well disguised, and had too much practice in getting out of tight spots. Of course, that didn't account for bad luck, which could spring on anyone, but no, getting caught wasn't his greatest concern.

His concern was that they would somehow fumble the job and be forced to choose between keeping the necklace and getting away clean. If it came to that, they'd both abandon the necklace to save their own skins. Survival always came first.

But they'd only get one chance at such a monumental pay out. Kitty wasn't comfortable with such a risky, high profile job. Sebastian knew that. If they cocked this up, he'd have a hell of a time convincing her to try something like it again. It had to go perfectly. They needed that necklace.

Standing in the tiny alley at the back of the building, one hand outstretched towards the door, Sebastian concentrated. Brow furrowed, he shut his eyes to every other distraction and turned all his senses to the magic humming protectively around the shop.

"It's as Deepa described," he told Kitty. "The forcefield feels the same as it did last night when I checked it. Once we get past that, one touch to the building, a single finger trailed along the brick, and all hell breaks loose."

"Right," Kitty said slowly. "You said it wouldn't be a problem."

"I can disable it," Sebastian confirmed, though his concern didn't lift.

"If it's what we're expecting, why do you look like that?"

"Because the forcefield and the alarms are the same, but something else is different." Sebastian frowned harder, trying to pinpoint exactly what was bothering him. "It keeps slipping away from me. I can't get a read on it." He weighed their risks with what little information he had. "Let me take the outer layers down and get inside," he finally said. "I need to figure out what's going on."

"If we have to call this off, we might not get another chance." Kitty was tense, bouncing her weight from one side to the other, restless as a cat lashing its tail.

"We're not calling it off," Sebastian said firmly. "I just need to see what I'm working with. Give us a light?"

At his request, she flickered an illumination spell into being, small and faint, to hover over his shoulder as he set himself to his task.

As before, the forcefield was dismissed easily enough, but overall, the jewellery shop's magic was tricky. Trickier than Felton's, and infinitely more complex than that at Kew Gardens. It was on par with the security at the National Gallery, if not even more intense.

But Sebastian was better prepared than he had been at the museum. He hadn't been drinking or wallowing in self-pity. He was focused, determined, and emotionally stable. The only thing on his mind was getting this job done right, and nothing could distract him from that. It would take a fine hand to unravel these alarms, but Sebastian hadn't been pickpocketing all his life to be accused of heavy-handedness this late in the game.

He couldn't sweet talk the magic as he'd done at Felton's pawnshop or in Kew, and he'd known from the moment he first made contact that he had no hope of brute-forcing his way through the thing like he'd done in the museum. This protective spell needed to be unwound delicately, like coaxing a clinging vine off its trellis until the magic no longer had a stranglehold on the shop, and could be safely set aside.

He crept up to the magic quietly and cunningly. It clung to the outside of the building like an oil slick, shimmering faintly in the glow of Kitty's spell, visible only when Sebastian tried his hardest to see it. Even then, it was almost invisible, keeping to itself and focused on its task as diligently as a prison guard.

Sebastian shook off that analogy. Prison was last thing he needed to be thinking about.

He'd never been one for theoretical magic; he'd never had the patience. He could perform simple spells, of course—everyone capable of magic was taught a certain handful in childhood—but he preferred to wield his magic more intuitively, with no need for sophisticated spellcraft.

But as he'd grown older and encountered more and more spells in his professional life that needed unravelling, he was forced to admit, however begrudgingly, that theoretical magic had a purpose.

When he couldn't talk to the magic in front of him and sweetly convince it to let him pass, and if he couldn't overpower it, then the spell had to be unmade.

Unmaking a spell required a precise understanding of how it had been cast in the first place: the exact steps and incantations used to set it. Then, it was a matter of working backwards, gently picking it apart until it had been taken back to the very first step, and then even further back, until there was nothing left.

Sebastian didn't prefer that type of magicwork, but he was competent. He had to be.

Even proceeding as cautiously as he did, the magic put up a fight. It resisted its unmaking, wriggling away from him at every turn. But there was nowhere for it to go: it was caught in two dimensions, flat against the building's surface. Sebastian prevented it from escaping out into the air and raising the alarm that was its purpose, but neither could it escape him by squirming its way through the wall into the shop itself.

That part wasn't Sebastian's doing, and if he could have spared a single second's focus away from his work, it would have made him nervous. The magic should have been able to seep into the building, despite Sebastian's efforts to keep it contained.

Something was inside, blocking it.

"Almost there," he said under his breath, as much to himself as to Kitty.

Her illumination spell bobbed closer as she leaned in to watch his progress. She was on edge, probably even worse than he was, because at least he had something to do. All she could do was stand lookout as he worked.

He was wrist-deep in the enemy spell, plucking at its disparate elements with clever fingers, like playing cat's cradle. It was slippery, and somehow getting slipperier the longer he worked. It felt like trying to catch a bar of soap in the bath, the magic eking out from under his hands with increasing frequency, even though he was so close to being finished.

"Hold still," he muttered to it from between his teeth. "I'm trying to help you. Don't you want to be set free?"

But it was the sort of magic that liked to have a purpose, and it shook his head furiously, resisting its unmaking.

"You can do whatever you want after this," he told it, the greatest temptation he could offer anything. "You don't have to stay here, tied to this boring old shop. You can take to the skies. You can be wild again."

But it didn't want to take to the skies; it didn't want anything Sebastian had to offer. It wanted to be safe, and boring, and dutiful, and it very much wanted to raise the alarm that had been its sole purpose, and get Kitty and Sebastian arrested.

Well—it probably didn't know that raising the alarm would lead to arrest and imprisonment. It probably didn't *know* anything. That didn't matter; the result would be the same. Frustrated by its inflexibility, Sebastian snapped the last thread of the spell rather than taking the time to properly unweave it, getting a nasty little jolt for his trouble, which travelled up his arm to hit him in the back of the teeth.

And then it was done.

The magic dropped like the walls had shed their skin, mistily dissipating against the cobblestones.

"Got it."

His words hung in the air and an unsettling feeling stole over him. Dismantling the spell should have been the hard part, but he sensed something ominous about the shop, vague familiarity dropping into the pit of his stomach like a skipping stone missing its angle and plonking straight down into the lake.

"There's something else going on here," he told Kitty. "I thought with that security spell out of the way, I'd be able to figure out what else was happening, but…" He shook his head. "I don't know. I don't like it."

Kitty examined the shop's back door, drawing her lockpicking set from her pocket. "The magic is definitely disarmed, though?"

Sebastian pressed one hand flat against the bricks. Nothing happened. "Definitely."

"But you can tell something's wrong."

He hesitated. He couldn't tell, was the thing. It was like a sixth sense worrying at him, gut instinct, but nothing he could articulate. If he brushed it aside, he could be walking them straight into disaster. But if he took it too seriously, Kitty would call the whole thing off and they'd lose their shot at the Rose Diamond.

"Worst case scenario?" Kitty asked.

"They have an armed guard inside," Sebastian said immediately. "Or another security spell that's only triggered once we cross the threshold."

"A spell Deepa didn't know about, that you can't sense from out here?" she asked sceptically.

She was right. Sebastian was sensitive enough that he should be able to tell if there were any additional spells inside. He couldn't sense anything.

"We can check the door for booby traps before opening it. But if you think there's something serious waiting for us in there…"

"Whatever it is, it's definitely not magic. If there's a guard, I'll go in with a spell ready to knock him out before he even realises anyone's there."

"And if it's something else? Some secret third option?"

"Then we leave." He tried to sound sure of himself. "No diamond is worth getting hurt or caught over."

"You don't believe that."

"No, but you do, and we're a team, aren't we? If I could steal the damn thing all by myself, I would have already."

She socked him on the shoulder. "Okay. Get in there. I'll keep watch here. You scope the place out for guards or traps, and I'll come in once you signal it's all clear. Ready?"

His mouth was dry, half from the anticipation and half from that lingering unease, but he nodded. "Ready."

Dropping to one knee, Kitty put herself at eye level with the lock, running over it with a fine-toothed comb to check for traps before sliding the first pick into the hole. Sebastian glanced down the length of the narrow alley to the street, which was just barely lit up by some distant streetlamp. When he looked back, Kitty had the door unlocked, sliding her tools back into their case as she turned the handle with her other hand, easing it open.

Inside, the shop was pitch black. For a second, Sebastian was back in Blackwood, staring into the chasm that was to be his cell for the next nine months, waiting for the guard's hand between his shoulder blades to shove him inside.

Still down on one knee, Kitty tapped him on the back of the calf, signalling him forward. Taking a fortifying breath, Sebastian called to mind a simple, reliable sleep spell in case he encountered anyone inside, and crept through the crack in the door.

Everything went mind-killingly quiet. His magic pulsed once, muffled and far away, as if from under a heavy blanket, and then went still. He tugged on it again, more insistently this time, even as the cold fingers of recognition slid down the back of his neck like a trickle of ice water.

His magic didn't answer.

The same wards that had held his magic captive in Blackwood for all those months were hidden inside the walls, smothering him. The instant he recognised them, his throat closed up in panic. He couldn't breathe; he could barely think. Fear flooded him like a switch had been flipped, and his fingers froze, no longer under his control.

His feet had carried him forward even as his mind had stumbled to a halt and he found himself in the administrative office, where the Rose Diamond necklace was supposed to be resting in its private safe, a solid steel monstrosity hidden under the desk. The safe wouldn't be protected by magic, because magic didn't work inside the shop—Sebastian's breath strangled in his throat—but he couldn't proceed. All his hopes and dreams lay separated from him by nothing more been a single steel wall, but he couldn't make himself move forward to grab them.

He didn't know how to break free of the wards. Nine months in Blackwood, and he'd never come close to shaking off their dread grasp. It had felt like being buried under a thick layer of heavy clay, packed so densely that he couldn't move a muscle as it oozed into his mouth and nostrils until he couldn't take a single breath against it. After enough time, the horror dulled, and the days blended together until Blackwood turned into one long monotonous nightmare from which he couldn't wake. But here, now, trapped in the jeweller's shop face to face with those wards once more, the panic was fresh and sharp. His magic thrashed against it, but stayed trapped in his veins.

He wasn't going to have a nervous breakdown in the middle of a job. Certainly not in the middle of the biggest job of his life. But, as he slowly sank to the floor, his back pressed to the wall behind the desk as his breath came in shallow, ineffectual gasps, it became clear that he didn't have much say in the matter. His vision dimmed, going blotchy and undefined around the edges, and his limbs were leaden, too heavy to control.

His thoughts raced, but when he tried to bring them into his mouth to call back to Kitty and tell her what was happening, his tongue was too thick to move, and his voice stayed trapped in his throat. Kitty was going to enter the shop unaware, and Sebastian couldn't do anything to warn her.

Of course, she didn't carry the same baggage from Blackwood, and she didn't rely on her magic as heavily, so maybe she'd be unaffected. Her lockpicks were all she needed to get into that safe; Sebastian had no role to play but lookout, now that the exterior alarm had been neutralised. Except now Kitty was down a partner that she should have been able to rely on, and Sebastian couldn't even tell her why.

The seconds ticked by. Sebastian could practically hear Kitty's expectation from outside, waiting for him to check in and tell her whether she needed to crack the safe or if Sebastian had done it himself.

He hadn't done anything but hyperventilate. Pressing his hands together like he could force them to stop shaking, he sucked in a breath that did nothing to fill his fluttering lungs, and tried to clear his head. All he had to do was stand up and walk back the way he came. This wasn't Blackwood; there were no locks or chains keeping him within reach of the magic-crushing wards. Outside that door, they couldn't touch him. It was so easy. Just get up.

Self-disgust and despair flooded him as he tried and failed to follow those simple instructions. His legs were made of jelly and his mind was watery with fear, even as his conscious thoughts began to whirr back into gear.

He wasn't trapped. The Rose Diamond was literally within reach. He just had to—

"Get up," Kitty growled, yanking on his arm until he clumsily got his feet under him. "I'll leave you here and take the necklace all for myself, I swear to god. *Get up.*"

Breath rushed back into him and he gasped like a dying man granted a reprieve. She gave him a rough shake until he could meet her eyes without staring blankly through her.

"Did you check the rest of the shop?" she demanded. "Are these wards just in the office, or through the whole place?"

"I don't know," he stammered, hating the weakness in his voice.

With a twist of her mouth, she shoved him towards the door where the office met the rest of the shop proper, and he went like he had no control of his own body. He took three steps into the shop, tried to conjure his magic to no avail—he detested that feeling, there was nothing worse—and immediately turned back around to re-join his partner.

"The whole place," he told her.

"Then get out," she said, withdrawing her lockpicking set and nimbly folding herself under the desk, curled up against the safe like a cat by the hearth. "Keep watch from the mouth of the alley. Make sure nobody comes back here."

He didn't ask if she would be alright. She'd already turned her full attention to the safe, and had no more time for him or his dramatics. Throwing himself out of the office and back through the door to the alley, he let the night air hit him like a splash of ice water to the face.

His magic woke up with a rush. Relief struck him with such force that he staggered, one hand braced against the brick wall as he conjured a handful of sparks with his other, just to prove he could.

He was alive, he was free, his magic was alive and free, and in that instant, nothing else mattered. Not the future, not the past, not Morgan Hollyhock; not even the Rose Diamond. Only the breeze against his skin, the rough scratch of bricks catching against his back through his jacket, and the feeling of his magic rushing lively through his veins, unimpeded and uncontrolled by any external force. He'd survived Blackwood, and he would survive anything else.

Quickly smothering the sparks in his hand like snuffing out a candle, Sebastian pulled himself together, drawing a sharp breath and clearing his head. They were still in the middle of a job, vulnerable to witnesses and interruption. But his earlier panic had been replaced by giddy adrenaline, and, though he stood lookout for his partner as instructed, he felt invincible.

Peering around the corner of the alley, he confirmed that there was no one on the street in front of the shop, poking their nose in where it didn't belong. The few people in the neighbourhood who were awake at such a late hour had apparently not noticed anything amiss.

However, there was one figure strolling along the opposite side of the street half a block down, who bore a suspicious resemblance to a beat cop.

Sebastian sneered and melted back into the alley, wrapping the shadows around himself like a cloak as he had done in the National Gallery, though with better results this time. He was vibrating in place, running high on manic energy from what had felt like a near-death experience. Inside, he'd been a liability: worse than useless. Now, he was untouchable.

Fairly skipping back up the length of the alley to the back door, he caught Kitty as she stepped through it, bundling her into his cloak.

"Alright?" he whispered. "There's a copper a few shops down, but he's just patrolling. He hasn't noticed anything." Without pausing for breath, he asked, "Did you get it? Let me see."

"Not out in the open," Kitty snapped, slapping his hand away when he reached for her bag. "Do you want to get caught?"

"Just one look," he wheedled.

"With a cop right around the corner?"

"We're shielded. Just let me peek inside the bag so I know it's real."

Kitty didn't look happy about it, but she relented, unbuckling the bag and opening it just wide enough for Sebastian to catch a glimpse of the pale pink glint within. She only held it open for a second before snapping it shut again, but that second had already told Sebastian that the Rose Diamond necklace was the most staggeringly beautiful thing he'd ever seen in his life. He was breathless. He was exultant.

Kitty cuffed him on the arm. "Hey, concentrate. Can you cloak us all the way home?"

"Yes," he said immediately. "Yes, of course."

"Are you sure? Because if not, we should split up. I can get home on my own unseen if I go over the rooftops."

"No, I'm fine," he said quickly. "I won't slow things down again." He needed to prove that he hadn't been incapacitated just as much as he needed to keep the Rose Diamond within arm's length.

Kitty eyed him before nodding, and Sebastian grinned as relief tsunamied through him. Dropping one arm over her shoulders, he wrapped them both snuggly in his shadow cloak and they edged their way out of the alley just as the beat cop walked past. They froze, waiting to see if he would notice them. Sebastian didn't even dare breathe, his magic singing around him as he concentrated every fibre of his being on keeping the glamour up.

The cop strolled past, one hand on his billy club as he whistled to himself, the tune and his footsteps the only sounds on the quiet street.

Kitty and Sebastian stayed in place with their backs to the wall and their hearts in their mouths until the cop was out of sight. Only then did Sebastian exhale, breaking into a triumphant smile as he pulled Kitty close, toppling her against him.

"We did it!" he crowed, jostling her in celebration. He was careful to keep his voice down and his guard up, but he wanted to shout from the tallest building of Trafalgar Square that they'd just stolen England's most famous diamonds, and they were getting away clean with it.

"Save it for when we're home safe," Kitty hissed at him, but she was smiling, too.

CHAPTER TWENTY-TWO

IN WHICH A PARTY GOES AWRY

They laid the Rose Diamond necklace out on Adam's dining room table, the three of them crowded around it with an air of hushed reverence. Adam looked surprisingly alert, considering it was after two a.m., though waiting to hear whether his girlfriend was going to be imprisoned for the rest of her natural life probably kept him on edge. Kitty looked smugger than Sebastian had ever seen her, and he'd seen her look plenty smug before.

For his part, the adrenaline was wearing off, and he was looking over the edge of a cliff with a very steep drop. He'd never felt closer to crying, and he wasn't sure whether it was entirely out of happiness.

"What now?" Adam wondered.

"Now, we get the hell out of London," Kitty said. "Have you got any loose ends that need tying up before you disappear for a while?"

"I've already mentioned to my friends and family that I'll be going on a little holiday. Escaping the drudgery of yet another English winter, you know. I've booked the two of us passage to the Mediterranean. We leave on Tuesday."

"Sebastian?" Kitty asked. "Loose ends?" Her tone was pointed.

Sebastian wet his lips. He shouldn't have any ties keeping him from leaving immediately. He never had before.

"I've got you on a ship to New York," Adam said, watching Sebastian closely. "You're heading out Monday afternoon at three. Tomorrow. Or rather today, I suppose. Does that give you enough time to do…whatever you might have that needs doing?"

"I don't need to do anything," Sebastian replied automatically.

Kitty and Adam exchanged a glance, one of those silent conversations of which Sebastian was so jealous.

"Well." Adam cleared his throat. "Celebratory champagne?"

"God, yes, please," Kitty said emphatically.

Which was how, half an hour later, Sebastian found himself seated at the table, staring at the necklace, with tears running down his cheeks. The events of the night had caught up to him as he finished his first glass, and an overwhelming exhaustion settled over him like a blanket. He should be happy. He should be ecstatic.

Instead, he was so tired he could barely bring himself to refill his glass, and, though the necklace was more beautiful than ever, his insides were hollowed out and empty. He felt vaguely hungover, though he was barely even tipsy. That was the panic attack from earlier catching up to him, he supposed.

"Alright?" Kitty asked softly, nudging her elbow into his.

"I don't know," Sebastian said helplessly.

They were all quiet for a moment. Then, leaning in, Adam refilled Sebastian's glass and then Kitty's, before pushing what was left of the champagne into the middle of the table, beside the necklace.

"It's been too long since I last pulled an all-nighter," Adam said apologetically. "I'm going to try to catch a few hours of sleep before the sun comes up. Good night, both of you, and congratulations on a job well done."

Standing, he dropped one hand to Kitty's shoulder as he pressed a kiss to her temple. Turning her head, she gave him a quick peck on the lips, both of them smiling against each other, before Adam straightened to give Sebastian a friendly pat on the back.

"I'll join you soon," Kitty promised as Adam headed off.

"Good night," Sebastian echoed belatedly.

The two of them sat alone in the quiet lamplight. Sebastian couldn't take his eyes off the diamonds. He had no idea what he was feeling anymore.

"Do you want to talk about what happened back there?" Kitty asked eventually.

"No."

She nodded, taking another drink.

"It was like Blackwood," he said after a minute. "The way it smothers your magic. It was the exact same thing."

Kitty made a soft noise, her hand on his forearm. He had to resist the urge to snarl and twitch away from her touch. The last thing he wanted was pity, least of all when it wasn't deserved.

"I nearly cost us the job. I nearly cost us everything, just because I couldn't hold it together."

"We did it, though," she pointed out. "You didn't cost us anything."

"It was too close. I wouldn't put up with that kind of unreliability from a partner, and you don't have to pretend that you'd put up with it either."

"You're the one who got us the information on the jewellery shop; you're the one who got us past that magic outside. I couldn't have done any of that by myself. You talk about inexcusable unreliability, but some things can't be planned for. There's always going to be some margin of error when it comes to burglary. I think we did alright for ourselves, all things considered."

"Why are you being so nice to me? I fucked up."

"What am I supposed to do? Take the diamonds all for myself and cut you out of your share as punishment? Swear to never work with you again?" She laughed. "This could very well be our last job together anyway. If we manage to fence this thing as planned, neither of us will ever want for money again."

Sebastian glared at the table top, digging one thumbnail into his palm.

Kitty stopped laughing. "Wait. Is that what you expect of me?"

"You'd be entitled to it," he muttered.

The silence stretched to uncomfortable proportions.

"That's unkind," she finally said. "It's unkind of you to think I'd treat you like that. How long have we been friends?"

He offered a stiff shrug. "It's not about friends. It's about the job."

"Of course it's about friends. How many professional thieves do you think I'm connected to? Any one of them would beg for the chance to work with me, one half of the infamous London jewel thief duo. But I don't want to work with them. I want to work with you, because I know you, and I trust you. And I like you, and I care about you. I'm not going to just throw you aside the second you fuck up a job when it's not even your fault. You're not just some business investment to me. Do you understand? Hey. Look at me."

She caught his chin between her thumb and forefinger, forcibly lifting his face until he met her eyes. "I care about you," she told him fiercely, and the honesty was enough to make the con artist inside him shrivel up in embarrassment.

He sniffed, dropping his gaze again as she swiped his tears away with her thumb.

"Ugh," he said, pretending his voice didn't come out watery. "This is too much sincerity. I need to be drunker."

"You do that." Standing, she patted his hand like he needed more reassurance. Which was true, but he didn't like that he was radiating insecurity. Though she seemed about to end the conversation and leave him to sink, humiliated, into the floorboards, she paused, then said, "Now, listen. About your Hollyhock man."

"Oh, no."

"I know I've been hard on you lately. The pressure was on to do the Cheapside job right, and I wasn't going to let anything ruin that for us. Especially not something as stupid you being preoccupied with some man. But that's done now, and the Rose Diamond job too, and we got away clean on both counts. So, now that I don't have to worry about you getting distracted, if you want to throw yourself headlong into lovesickness, you've got my blessing. Alright? Because you do love him, you dolt. Anyone with eyes can see it."

That accusation hurt worse than any accusation of incompetence or ill-preparedness.

"What if he doesn't love me back the right way?" Sebastian challenged. "I'm not interested in being some rich man's lapdog, not now that I don't have to."

"Who says he wants a lapdog? From what I've seen, he wants you just as you are."

"He hates that I'm a thief."

"I think he hates the idea of you getting caught. Adam can't stand that about my job, either. He's just had longer to come around to do it." She touched his face again, palm to cheek this time, infinitely gentler than the first. "People are allowed to worry about you, Seb. That's not a warning sign."

He swallowed. Something shivery and scared had taken up residence in his heart, like a whipped dog still desperate for a kind touch.

"I don't know what to do with love," he finally admitted in a small voice.

Kitty rolled her eyes and put her arm around his shoulders, holding him close to her side. "You do the same thing as with anything else you want to keep. You hold on with both hands and never let go."

He turned his face into her and resolutely didn't cry.

After a minute, she cleared her throat and straightened. Her dress definitely wasn't saltwater-damp where his face had been.

"Now, I'm going to go see if Adam is still awake for some celebratory sex, and I highly recommend that you get out of here and find some of your own."

"Not sure I'm in the mood," he said wetly.

"You're welcome to stay and listen to our celebrations if that's what you really want, but make sure you get that thing out of sight before you leave the room." She nodded to the necklace, still glinting pinkly on the table. "You should celebrate somehow, whether you stay or go. And you really should get out. I'm going to be loud."

"Fine, fine. I'll leave you to it, harlot that you are."

Pausing in the doorway, she turned to point one finger back at him. "I'm not saying you should go make up with Morgan."

His heart did something complicated, leaping and twisting at the same time. "Don't."

"But you should think about it."

The problem was that he'd barely stopped thinking about Morgan since leaving the man.

♦ ♦ ♦

Eden had never before failed in lifting Sebastian's mood, and he didn't see why it should start now. It was coming up on four a.m., which was a better time to be leaving a party than arriving to one, but he was hardly going to go to bed so late in the game. Dressed in his best suit—which was still his only suit, but that would soon change—with his eyes and lips painted like a film star, he positioned himself with his back to one of the great columns off to the side of the dance floor. There, he crossed his arms, drink held daintily in one hand, and waited to be approached.

He wanted a distraction, and Eden would provide. It always did. He wanted to wash the taste of Morgan from his mouth, chase away the memory of his hands, and feel the victory-thrill of adrenaline for the Rose Diamond job that those blasted wards had stolen from him.

A smaller, more cantankerous part of him wanted to be left alone entirely.

Indulging in a sigh, he took a sip of his drink. He was radiating hostility, every line of his body drawn tense and deflecting company.

The earlier panic had worn off, at least. He was far too irritable, which was a sure sign of his nerves not being as they should, but his hands were steady, and his voice didn't betray him when he spoke.

Not that he was speaking to anyone.

He glared at the dancers flitting around the room, all of them happily coupled off. Most of them would be physically entangled with their partners before dawn, even if they weren't entangled emotionally. Sebastian envied them.

But not so much that he actually wanted to participate when it was offered.

"No, thank you," he said boredly when the first man of the night approached.

The young man, who was some dizzy combination of tipsy and high on god knows what cocktail of drugs and alcohol, pouted in what he clearly thought was an attractive manner. "I was only going to ask if I could top up your drink."

"That's very sweet of you, but I'm fine." He was. He'd only been drinking in sips, his mood too low to make drunkenness a friend.

The second man of the evening approached ten minutes later: an older gent who probably looked distinguished outside of Eden, and, in any other circumstance, would have been close enough to Sebastian's type.

"It seems a crime that someone like you should be left alone with no one to entertain him."

"Normally, I'd agree."

"Is this not your scene?"

"Oh, it's exactly my scene." More's the pity.

"Then let's go find somewhere quieter, just the two of us, to have a chat," the man suggested.

Sebastian was tempted, but not tempted enough. "Not tonight, I don't think."

After several more minutes spent trying and failing to engage Sebastian in conversation, the man finally gave up and left in a huff.

The third time he was approached, it was by a flashy young couple who had to be engaged, if not married, at which point Sebastian removed himself from the floor entirely, climbing the stairs to the second level where things were less densely populated.

"All by yourself tonight, handsome?"

He tucked his glare away in his back pocket at Deepa's approach. She was in a plum sari with gold and teal accents, and more gold on her wrists and fingers, and adorning her neck and ears. She looked like she should be attending a wedding or a coronation rather than dredging through Eden at four in the morning.

"I take it business is going well." She made a show of looking him up and down. "If not for your foul mood, I would have guessed that luck has been on your side lately."

"Business-wise, I'd count myself extraordinarily lucky. But it's complicated."

"Ah," she said knowingly. "I see how it is. Do you want to talk about it? From one professional to another."

"I think we both know that's a bad idea."

"Certainly, but don't you find it ever chafes? Keeping so many secrets, holding your cards so close to your chest at all times?"

"I have a confidant already, thank you."

"You're avoiding the question. Where is your handsome grey-eyed friend tonight?"

"Elsewhere," Sebastian replied shortly.

"And the glamours you were wearing on your face last time? What happened to them?"

"I'm looking for a little more attention this time around."

"You're doing a terrible job of it. These flies want honey, not vinegar. There's no shortage of men and women eyeing you up, but you're scaring them all away with your scowl."

"It didn't scare you away. Why are you alone this evening?"

"A breath of fresh air. Now…" She drew close, her hand on his arm like a conspirator. "Tell me," she said, her voice low with excitement, "is it true the Rose Diamond has vanished from its safe on King's Road?"

"Word travels fast, doesn't it?"

"The alarms failed and private security was dispatched to investigate. It will be in all the papers come daybreak."

"I thought I'd have a few hours more than that," Sebastian muttered.

"Well?" she prodded, poking at him with one plum-painted nail.

"I'm afraid the information you sold me was somewhat outdated. By the time I got there, they'd added to their security."

"How inconvenient. Although, it clearly didn't stop you from getting the job done."

"It was a closer thing than I would have liked."

She shrugged one elegant shoulder. "So it goes. I gave you what information I had; you got your money from me, and your diamonds. I can't apologise because the shopkeepers changed their security after the fact."

"No, I don't expect you to. Nor do I expect us to have any further business with each other."

"For the best," she agreed. "But before we part ways, will you tell me one thing?"

"That depends."

"The necklace. Did you try it on? You must have. What did it feel like?"

They'd all tried it on, he and Kitty and Adam, passing it from one person to the next in a circle, their excitement coming out in hushed whispers like schoolchildren staying up too late. Sebastian had gone first and last, reluctant to let it go now that he finally had it. It was huge and heavy on him, covering him from the throat to the middle of his chest with ice cold, perfectly smooth rocks. Even in the middle-of-the-night lamplight, the diamonds gleamed. The stone in the centre never lost its colour, no matter how dim its surroundings. That one was so much more enormous and more vivid than the others; it was *the* Rose

Diamond, and all the smaller, paler pink stones were mere hangers-on.

Wearing it, Sebastian felt like royalty. More than royalty: he felt untouchable. When Kitty wore it, she looked like a queen, like diamonds were her birthright. Adam— Sebastian felt Adam looked a bit ridiculous in it, to be honest. It really wasn't his style, but he had Kitty in his lap to fasten the clasp around his neck and fawn over him, so it didn't matter whether he looked silly.

Untouchable, though. That was the right word for Sebastian. Because, as perfect as the Rose Diamond necklace was on him, he had no one with whom to celebrate the way Kitty and Adam could celebrate with each other. He kept brushing his thumb over his ring finger, expecting to feel cool silver, but it was bare.

A smile tugged at the corner of his mouth, despite everything. "It felt like all I've ever wanted."

"Was it worth it?" Deepa asked, her dark eyes bright with curiosity.

"Worth what?"

"Losing your friend."

Sebastian scoffed to hide the way his heart lurched like he was going to be sick. "Of course. Friends may come and go, but diamonds are forever."

She arched one impressive brow. "You are a very good liar."

"Thank you."

"I agree, personally. Coxley tells me I'm unforgivably mercantile, but he's never wanted for wealth or status the way you and I have."

Sebastian inclined his head in acquiescence.

"Still," Deepa continued ruthlessly, "you wear the look of heartbreak. I've seen it too many times not to recognise it on a man."

"Absolutely not," Sebastian said immediately. "I must have eaten a bad shrimp or something."

She laughed, her voice intoxicating and far too pleasant to be cruel. "Of course. I will be sure to avoid the seafood. Can I get you another drink, instead? To drown the sorrows I'm sure you do not have?"

Sebastian looked at his glass, mostly empty. "Alright, go on, then. I'll have whatever you're having."

"I'll make sure to order something strong, then."

Returning to the lower-level bar, Deepa lounged attractively as the bartender poured their fresh drinks. "Why don't you let some bright young thing pick you up and take you home to celebrate?"

"I don't feel celebratory," Sebastian admitted, with infinite annoyance. "I should. I should be celebrating the best take of my career. I've built this entire life for myself from scratch, and I'm the highest I've ever been—exactly where I've always wanted to be. I've spent years clawing my way up to this place."

Deepa raised her glass. "I'll drink to that."

Sebastian clinked with her, but his demeanour remained mulish. "It's a funny thing," he said between drinks, "the way such a little disappointment can spoil everything."

"The shrimp?"

"The shrimp," he agreed darkly.

"A more sentimental person might suggest you give the shrimp another chance."

"I despise sentiment."

"Oh, as do I. I have no time for it, myself. But some people seem happy with it. Not everyone is cut out for heartlessness."

"It was sentiment that got me in this state in the first place. Heartlessness served me quite well, until I let my guard down."

"Then it just comes down to what will make you happier. Your riches, or your shrimp."

"Riches won't give me food poisoning," Sebastian pointed out.

"I know which one I would choose," Deepa said agreeably. "I want to be the wealthiest woman in London. But is that enough for you? Or do you want someone to hold you and keep you warm at night?"

"I'm not going to find that in a shrimp. Anyway, I'm not entirely alone. I have a partner."

"You mean Miss Kitty Delaware?"

Back with Adam, Kitty certainly wasn't lonely at all.

A new voice cut in.

"Sebastian?"

He turned automatically at the sound of his name, only to blanche upon facing the speaker. James Whistler stared back at him, holding onto his own drink and looking just as stupid and smarmy as ever.

"Fancy meeting you here," Sebastian said flatly.

"I didn't realise you were still in London."

"Where else should I be?"

Whistler shrugged. "Staying out of trouble, then?"

"As ever. You look well." Of course Whistler looked well. He'd never wanted for anything.

"As do you." Whistler's gaze raked him over, taking in the suit and the makeup with an appreciative gleam.

Resisting the knee-jerk instinct to preen, Sebastian instead fixed a disdainful smile on his face. "I heard you got a cat."

Whistler had the grace to look embarrassed. "Yes, about that. I'm glad I ran into you, actually."

Deepa, who had been watching their interaction like a tennis match, leaned in and said, "Introduce me to your friend?"

"I'd rather not, to be quite honest," said Sebastian.

"James Whistler," Whistler said, reaching past him to offer Deepa his hand.

"I'll leave you to her tender mercies," Sebastian said, pushing off from the bar. To Deepa, he added, "Don't feel obliged to play nice."

"Wait." Whistler caught Sebastian by the arm.

Sebastian glared at him until he removed his hand from his sleeve.

"I'd like a word, since I have you here. Can we have a private chat, just the two of us?"

"No."

"It's about the cat thing," Whistler continued, forging on without regard for privacy. "You see, the thing is, I rather liked having a cat, you know? And taking a cat in off the street like that, I should have assumed the thing had got in scraps before. Street cats are always getting themselves in and out of trouble. It's to be expected. It doesn't mean they make any worse pets after the fact."

Sebastian stared at him incredulously. Whistler offered a hopeful smile.

"You want me back." Sebastian's voice came out flat with anger.

"The cat," Whistler corrected, "and, well, not forever. Three months was—well, it was just too much. It turns out I'm not really a pet person. But…for a single night? Yes, absolutely. You've cleaned up nicely, you know."

"I know," Sebastian snapped. "But it's not for *you*."

Whistler's expression grew colder. "You know I can make it worth your while."

"You don't get to buy me for a single night like you found me soliciting on a street corner!"

"Why not? That's basically what you do, isn't it? You're just less honest about it."

"Even if I were literally selling myself on the street, I wouldn't sleep with you again for any amount of money. You could offer me the Crown Jewels on a silver platter and I'd spit in your face."

Whistler's expression got ugly as if Sebastian really had spit in it.

"You've moved on quickly. I shouldn't be surprised. Found someone better already, have you?"

"I've found someone a damn sight better than you. Better than just about anyone I've ever met, in fact." As Sebastian said the words, he realised they were true, and they hit him in the heart like a physical blow. "You couldn't hold a candle to him," he choked out.

"And he knows what you do, does he?"

"He knows everything about me."

"And he loves you in spite of it," Whistler sneered.

Sebastian swallowed against the sudden lump in his throat.

"Where is he now? This perfect gentleman who loves you just as you are? I would have thought you'd be hanging off his arm tonight, just like you were always trying to hang off mine. He's not here—he's not even real, is he?" Whistler laughed. "How could he be? What real person could ever love a slimy, lying little leech like you?"

Sebastian struck him, a quick backhand that cracked against the side of Whistler's face. Because as Whistler said those words, Sebastian realised they were true, too. He might love Morgan—and that was terrifying in itself—and Morgan might even love him in return, somehow, miraculously, but he wasn't there at Sebastian side, because love wasn't enough.

Deepa, having watched the whole exchange, let out an appreciative whistle.

"You don't know me," Sebastian told the stunned and red-faced Whistler. "You never did."

Without waiting for him to squeeze the last word in, Sebastian turned on his heel and marched back up to the second-level balcony, fuming, with Deepa gliding along at his side.

"That looked very satisfying," Deepa said. "I regret now having handled all my ex-lovers' quarrels with more grace. I would have liked to slap one or two of them." She gave a wistful sigh.

"You're welcome to give Whistler another one if he follows us up here." Sebastian leaned both elbows against the balcony rail, glaring at the dancers below. There was very little actual dancing going on so near dawn, but there was plenty of necking and fondling happening, and Sebastian resented all of it. "I should go."

"Back to your partner in crime? Or back to the gentleman friend who gave you food poisoning?"

Gazing down at the couples, Sebastian weighed his options. Had he really felt so invincible just a few short hours earlier? Now he felt lower than a worm. The night had made him feel worse than he had since entering Blackwood, followed by the most sweeping high of his life. He didn't want to risk seeing Morgan and feeling even worse than a worm. He wasn't sure how much lower he could get.

Morgan would demand an explanation, and an admission. Morgan would offer him a shovel to dig himself deeper. It would be easier to hole up in Adam's flat and wait out the last few hours until he was to board his ship and leave for New York. He didn't need to put himself through all that when he had America waiting for him. Not when he had the Rose Diamond.

"Not everyone has to be ruthless when it comes to love," Deepa said gently, her hand feather-light on his arm.

Before Sebastian could respond, a great commotion erupted from the front of the club, as if someone had let loose a swarm of angry bees. The partygoers all shouted and hooted in raucous, jovial alarm, which was

Eden's equivalent of a guard dog shouting down an intruder. Not that they were being burgled, but Scotland Yard was a buzzkill at the best of times, and Sebastian wasn't interested in getting caught up in any of that nonsense. As the crowd of revellers got pushed further inside by the incoming wave of police, Sebastian mapped out his escape route.

"I think that's our cue to leave," Deepa said. "It was nice seeing you again; best of luck with whatever it is you're doing next."

"Same to you," Sebastian replied, and vaulted neatly over the side of the balcony to avoid getting trapped on the stairs.

CHAPTER TWENTY-THREE

A RECONCILLIATION, A CONFESSION,
AND A HOMECOMING

It wasn't all that difficult, evading the cops and escaping the raid. Sebastian was generally very good at escaping unwanted situations. With his hands in his pockets to ward off the chill of the blue hours, he paced the streets like a restless cat, circling the blocks in aimless patterns. The longer he walked without a destination, the more annoyed with himself he got. It should have been a simple thing, to choose between Adam's house and Morgan's. Either place would be warmer than the outdoors.

At seven, still in the pre-dawn, he entered the nearest bakery just as it was opening, and got himself a cheap coffee and a bag of pastries. Sitting in the corner, he sipped his drink and picked his way through the first croissant, trying not to glare at the other early-morning patrons as they came and went. Now that he was sitting down, his tiredness finally caught up to him. His body couldn't tell whether it was too early in the morning or too late at night, and the bitter coffee turned his stomach and made him nauseous. The pastry was far too rich, all that butter only making his stomach worse. Finally, he gave up and ordered a tea instead, folding up his paper bag to save the remaining pastries for later, when he was in a better state to enjoy them. His half-drunk coffee was easily abandoned, but he couldn't bring himself to leave behind perfectly good food.

Nursing a peppermint tea and willing his stomach to settle, Sebastian returned to the street and found himself in St. James's Park as the sun began filtering its palest beams in between the buildings.

The air was chilly enough for his breath to plume on every exhale, silvery against the backdrop of gently overcast skies and fiery red and gold trees. The grass crunched with frost underfoot. Lifting his cup to his face to breathe deep the smell of peppermint and let the steam warm the cold tip of his nose, Sebastian resolved to let his problems fall away along with the rest of the city. Entering the park was like entering a calmer state of mind. There, nothing and no one could bother him but the ducks.

The ducks and, apparently, Alphonse Hollyhock.

"Hullo there," Alphonse said cheerfully. "Nice morning, isn't it?"

"I hadn't noticed," Sebastian said tiredly.

"I never used to be much of a morning person either. But now, I have to say, having settled into the domesticity of old married life, I've rather come around on the idea of a morning stroll. I prefer it in the summertime, of course, but there's something to it, what? Seeing the frost on the grass and feeling the nip in the air?"

"You get up early just to go for a walk?"

"I know! I can hardly believe it myself. But Jacobi says an early start to the day is the best care for most woes, and then Aaliyah bullied me into it the rest of the way. Not that I've got any particular woes at the moment. They're all around here somewhere," he added. "Jacobi and Aaliyah and Jasmine. Over by the water to feed the birds, I expect. But I saw you walking, and I thought I'd come over to say hello."

"Right," said Sebastian. "Well, hello. I'm afraid I'm not the best company right now."

"Ah, you've got your own woes, have you?" Alphonse said wisely. "Well, you're on the right track to fixing them, according to Jacobi, if you're out for a walk this early."

"I haven't been to bed yet."

"You didn't get caught up in the Eden raid, did you? I heard they cracked down on the place just before dawn. It'll bounce back, of course; it always does. Still, I wouldn't want to be in the middle of it when it happened. Say, you haven't got Morgan with you, by any chance?"

"I haven't seen him," Sebastian returned, somewhat snappier than he intended.

"Just as well. I can't imagine he'd fare well, getting caught up in something like that."

"Actually, I think it would do him good to get in a spot of trouble. Maybe Scotland Yard could help him remove that enormous stick from up his arse."

"Do you think so? I never thought they were all that bright, just between the two of us. I used to pinch their helmets when I was younger, you know. They always made such a terrible fuss about it, but of course they were altogether useless when it came to trying to catch us to get them back. I knew a boy who had a whole collection of them in university." Alphonse shook his head. "Anyway, I've outgrown such games by now, so I should be rather put out to get caught over attending a little party compared to my actual misdeeds, what? And Jacobi would be awfully disappointed in me if I wound up in jail. Still, I know I can count on him to keep my mother from finding out, if worse comes to worst."

"That's what you're most afraid of, is it? Your mother finding out you got nicked?"

Alphonse shuddered. "Yes, absolutely. It would be yours, too, if you knew her."

"I'll take your word for it."

"Shall I point Morgan in your direction if he comes looking for you?"

"Has he been looking for me?" Sebastian asked, not sure what he hoped the answer would be.

Alphonse blinked at him. "Since your party got raided, I thought he'd come looking, wouldn't he? I thought the two of you…"

Sebastian cleared his throat loudly and Alphonse abruptly cut himself off.

"I haven't seen him since Thursday's dinner party," Alphonse offered apologetically. "But if I do run into him, I can tell him the raid didn't give you any trouble, if you like."

"You do that. I'm not sure when I'll see him again." If Sebastian couldn't make a decision soon, he'd be on that ship for America and the choice would be made for him. "Say hello to your cohort for me."

"Will do," Alphonse said, his tone still cheery, though he looked at Sebastian with something approaching concern. "Toodle-pip, then."

Sebastian didn't approach the water to watch the birds or feed them pastry crumbs. He didn't want to risk running into any other early-morning strollers. Instead, he ducked his head and, keeping his gaze trained firmly on the ground, headed for the privacy of the trees.

It wasn't until he was standing under the dappled purple shade of their branches that he remembered kissing Morgan in that exact spot. Their first kiss, and technically their second, too. The thrill when Morgan had grabbed hold of him and kissed him back was on par with that of any jewel heist. Sebastian had felt like he'd won something invaluable that day.

It wasn't worth the jewels, he told himself sharply. A good kiss, a great shag—they were some of life's joys, but they couldn't compare to the kind of future that a wealth of riches could buy. Maybe he'd fallen in love with Morgan a little bit, but it never would have lasted.

Even if Morgan had been more accepting of Sebastian's criminal proclivities, Sebastian yearned for independence too badly. He could never have contented himself long-term living solely off of Morgan's generosity.

It might have been nice to have had his cake and got to eat it too, though. Morgan and the jewels. Love and stability. Not either or.

"I made the right choice," Sebastian told himself.

His chest hurt. He wanted to blame the coffee for giving him heartburn, but he wasn't such a good liar that he could make himself believe it.

"Shit," he whispered to the tree at his back, the same tree he'd pushed Morgan up against. That had only been six days ago. It felt like a blink, and it felt like forever. "Did I fuck up?"

The tree didn't answer, which was probably for the best. Sebastian was feeling too delicate to accept advice from an inanimate object. He might have been willing to accept advice from Kitty, or maybe even Deepa, but then, he already knew what either of them would say.

He hated feeling delicate.

"Sebastian?"

He startled, spilling tea over his fingers as he whirled to face Morgan, frozen with one foot off the beaten path. For a split second, neither moved. Morgan seemed as taken by surprise as Sebastian, though out of the two of them, St. James's Park was Sebastian's haunt, not his.

Sebastian shuffled his tea to the other hand, surreptitiously flicking the spilled drops off his fingers.

"Thank god," Morgan said hoarsely. He stepped off the path, but didn't approach closer. "I've been looking everywhere for you. I heard about the raid at Eden, and then when you weren't with Kitty and Adam, I assumed the worst."

Sebastian's heart was doing something complicated again. "You thought I'd been arrested at St. James's Park?"

"You said this place was special to you. It was the only other place I could think to look. Are you alright?"

He nodded dumbly, his silver tongue at a loss for words.

"Do you want me to go, or can I say something?"

"Go ahead."

"Can you give us that privacy shield you conjured last time?"

Sebastian clearly wasn't the only one remembering their kiss against the tree. With a gesture, he encased them in a bubble through which no one could see or hear.

Morgan looked like a soldier about to march into battle: terrified, yet determined. Perversely, his obvious fear made Sebastian feel a little better.

"I don't want to clip your wings," Morgan said, "or change your spots, or anything else about you. I only ever wanted you safe. But I know I can't keep you safe—I can't keep you at all. I thought I'd been given a second chance when you turned up on my doorstep with that damned pocket watch, only to lose you again. But you were never mine to lose in the first place. No one is made to be kept as a pet. I don't want that for either of us."

"I never got that feeling from you."

"Good," Morgan said strongly. "But what I'm trying to say is—you're like some wild thing. And as much as I liked having you in my house and in my life, as a boy and now, I know you were never really tamed. It would be cruel to try to cage a wild animal in a life like mine. Because I'm just a housecat, really. I'm very comfortable, and very safe, and I know exactly how boring I am."

"Every housecat had to come from something wild at some point," Sebastian offered carefully.

Morgan gave a wry smile. "Generations upon generations ago. We're different species, now."

"Is that it, then? We're different species, there's no reconciling it, so we'd best give up and go our separate ways?"

"I'm not cut out for a life of crime," Morgan said softly. "I'm not a thief, and I don't want to be."

"Actually." Sebastian wet his lips. "I might be cutting down on that aspect of my life. Not entirely, but the time is right to scale back a bit. The pickpocketing will stay, of course, but the grand-scale robberies and heists, I think I'm done with. At least for the immediate future."

"May I ask why?" Morgan ventured.

A confession sat just under Sebastian's tongue, still too heavy to be spoken. He shook his head. "It's time to move on to a new chapter, that's all. I've worked hard. I'd like to live in the lap of luxury for a few years now, enjoying what I've earned." He paused, glancing over at Morgan through his lashes. "That sounds fairly domestic, doesn't it? Maybe still a little wild around the edges, not entirely tame, but…"

"I can't keep talking in metaphors," Morgan said. "Are we alright? That fight we had before you left—can we put that behind us?"

"We're alright." Sebastian bit his tongue, hard enough to sting, before adding, "I'm sorry." He was shocked to find he actually meant it.

"Me, as well." Morgan watched him for a second before nodding, shifting his weight onto his back foot like he meant to leave. "Good. That's all I wanted. Just to know—" He cleared his throat, looking away.

Sebastian broke out of his cocoon to close the distance between them and wrap Morgan in both arms, crushing them chest to chest. Morgan drew a startled breath as Sebastian pressed his face against Morgan's neck.

"I'm glad you found me," Sebastian told him. "I didn't want you to, but I'm glad you did."

Hesitantly, Morgan brought his hands up around Sebastian's back, holding him lightly like he expected Sebastian to break free. In response, Sebastian held him tighter, for once allowing himself to be needy.

"Would you like to come home with me?" Morgan ventured. "It doesn't have to be anything. Just for the night, if that's all you want."

Sebastian shut his eyes, pressing his forehead to Morgan's for a beat. That impossible dream of getting absolutely everything he wanted flickered in his peripheries. He'd never had a dream he couldn't resist reaching for.

Opening his eyes, he straightened up and backed away, holding Morgan at arm's length. "Two things."

Morgan grew serious to match, closing himself off behind that armour that had taken Sebastian so long to get him out of. "What are they?"

"I can't stay the night. I would have liked to, but I'm leaving for America."

"Today?"

"At three."

Morgan floundered. "I see. Were you going to tell me?"

"I hadn't decided yet," Sebastian admitted, ashamed.

"I see," Morgan repeated.

He was impenetrable behind his armour, though not unreadable anymore. Sebastian could tell he was hurt. He wanted to apologise again and kiss it away.

"And the second?"

"The second is something you might not want to hear. Do you want me to tell you anyway?"

"Yes," Morgan said immediately, then just as quickly ate his words. "Wait. Is it about us? Or is it…" He grimaced, then collected himself. "Is it about your…clandestine activities?"

"The latter."

Morgan paled, but set his jaw and gave a firm nod. "Tell me."

Slinking close again, Sebastian draped his arms over Morgan's shoulders and crossed his wrists behind Morgan's neck, hiding his nervousness at the impending confession. If Morgan was brave enough to find him, try to mend their relationship, and ask for the truth regarding Sebastian's criminal activities, then Sebastian had to be brave enough to tell him. And he had to admit to all of it this time, not just the paltry pickpocketing.

"Your plausible deniability will be out the window," he warned.

Morgan swallowed. "I don't care."

Sebastian leaned close to whisper in his ear, a mere breath, because he could still hardly believe it himself: "Last night I stole the Rose Diamond necklace."

Morgan drew a sharp a breath and gave an all-over shudder. But Sebastian couldn't revel in the reaction as he would have done before.

"Was that a good shudder, or a bad shudder?"

"You're fearless," Morgan breathed, pulling back to look Sebastian in the eye, his expression one-part reproach and one-part wonderment as he took Sebastian's hands.

"I'm really not," Sebastian said ruefully.

"Being afraid and doing something anyway is even more incredible. I've never been able to manage it. I take it that's why you're getting out of London?"

"The first ship available. Do you really think I'm the braver one out of the two of us?"

"You don't see me with an illustrious criminal background."

"You don't see me taking in strangers off the street," Sebastian countered.

"You weren't a stranger," Morgan said quietly.

Sebastian had to swallow the funny feeling in his throat before continuing, trying for flippancy. "You can't count *that*. We were children. And you didn't see me hunting you down across the city to try to explain myself or make amends, either. Between that and jewel robbery, I think I took the easier option."

"When we were children, I wanted you to stay and live with me. I still want that."

"I can't." Sebastian's voice cracked on the word. "I can't stay in London. I can't stay anywhere in the United Kingdom. But..."

Morgan's grip tightened on Sebastian's hands.

"You could come and live with me for a bit?" Sebastian offered, his heart in his mouth. "I said I'd put you up in New York when I was rich."

"Yes."

"We'd share a flat and you could have an art gallery. You said to ask again in a few weeks or months, but I can't really wait that long."

"Sebastian."

"Morgan?"

"I said yes."

Sebastian couldn't form a single word, let alone a coherent response. His insides were all aflutter, his mind whited out in shock.

"For all that you're used to taking whatever you want, you're not used to people giving you anything of their own free will, are you?" Morgan asked wryly.

"I don't usually ask." It came out a stutter.

"Because they might say no?" Morgan let go of him, taking a half-step back to hold out one hand between them. "Shall we shake on it? Or— I suppose a handshake doesn't hold much weight for you?"

"It might, coming from you," Sebastian managed.

When Morgan took his hand, a spark of magic darted between their fingers.

"America," Morgan promised.

His magic flooded out in a golden haze, surrounding their hands. Sebastian watched as it dropped like embers to the leaves carpeting the ground, his mind slowly ticking back into gear as it caught up to the situation. Morgan had said yes.

"Three o'clock, you said?"

"I should be at the docks before that," Sebastian said, dry-mouthed.

"Then I suppose I'd best go home to get my things in order. Would you…" Morgan paused, unaccountably shy again, even though he'd just agreed to move overseas with Sebastian. "Would you like to come with me?"

"Yes," Sebastian said immediately, drawing close to wrap his arms around Morgan once more. "Yes, please. Take me home."

CHAPTER TWENTY-FOUR

IN WHICH SEBASTIAN
GETS TO HAVE HIS CAKE AND EAT IT, TOO

They shared a cabin as they sailed across the Atlantic to their new lives. Sebastian had been prepared to smuggle Morgan aboard like one more piece of contraband, but Morgan had cut a deal with whomever was in charge and bought himself a legitimate spot at the last minute. After stowing their luggage—Morgan's a haphazardly-packed trunk, Sebastian's no more than a rucksack—they sat side by side on their little bunk, close enough for Sebastian to feel Morgan's body heat, but not actually touching.

Morgan had packed up his life with surprising speed and willingness, when it came down to it. As if his only ties to London were ephemeral as spider silk, able to be broken without any effort at all. He left Sterling to take care of what few business matters couldn't be handled on such short notice. Sebastian had situated himself just outside the doorway for that conversation, though he had no doubt Sterling was aware of his presence.

"This afternoon, sir," Sterling said, his tone so carefully free from judgment that it somehow sounded all the more judgmental for it.

"I'm aware it's rather abrupt."

"Two-week's notice is considered traditional, sir."

"I think it should take about two weeks to wrap up the last of my affairs. The banks, and selling the place, and whatnot. Of course, if you're not interested in managing these things, I'm sure I can find someone else—"

"You haven't actually terminated my contract yet, sir," Sterling pointed out.

"No, I haven't. I'd rather expected to keep you until you retired." Morgan sounded chagrined.

Sterling was silent for a moment. Sebastian could just imagine his demeanour, standing there stiff-shouldered with his hands clasped behind his back like a great stern bird.

"I'm not particularly interested in finding a new employer for my last two or three years of service," Sterling finally said. "I prefer a long-term engagement, as you're aware, sir. However, I am in a position to consider an early retirement. Something that's been on my mind for the past twelve months or so."

"In that case, let me make it easier for you. For the next two weeks, consider yourself actively employed, continuing to manage my affairs on a daily basis. After that, you may consider yourself retired, if that's what you want, and I'll continue paying your regular wages into the new year, to make that transition smoother for you."

"That's not necessary, sir."

"As far as my conscience is concerned, it rather is."

"In that case, thank you, sir." A pause. "I take it Mr. Sebastian is behind your decision to depart London so abruptly?"

"You don't approve of him," Morgan surmised.

"I'm quite sure it's none of my business, sir. If I may…"

"Go on."

"I've been managing your house for nigh on a decade, sir; your entire adult life. I dare say I know what he meant to you, as a boy. And I've only ever wanted you to be happy. If sailing to New York with him will achieve that, then I wish you both all the joy in the world."

The next words were too low for Sebastian to hear, and he crept closer to the door, blatantly eavesdropping. He hardly had time to scramble back and look innocent when Sterling exited the room a moment later, giving Sebastian a cool, though not accusatory, look as he passed. Morgan came out another moment after that, misty-eyed.

"He took it well?" Sebastian ventured.

"Of course he did. He's too professional to do otherwise."

"We won't be having a valet in America."

"No, but I think we'll manage well enough on our own. It will be good to have a fresh start."

"You were good to him," Sebastian said. "You're good to everyone."

Morgan rolled his eyes even as he drew Sebastian in for a quick kiss. "Don't make me sentimental. I have to finish packing."

And then, mere hours later, they'd left London for the great wide grey of the Atlantic.

"I won't ask you to stop stealing," Morgan said in their little cabin. "I don't expect you'll be able to help yourself, and I don't want you to change on my account. I only want you to be happy. And safe," he added. "Please keep yourself safe. That's the one thing I'll ask of you."

"I always do."

"Patently untrue."

Sebastian laughed, but Morgan cupped the side of his face, bringing him back to stillness.

"I care about you," Morgan said quietly, holding Sebastian's gaze. "I always have."

Wordlessly, Sebastian nodded, his tongue stuck to the roof of his mouth as he accepted that as the truth.

Morgan nodded in turn, seemingly satisfied. "Good."

Unsticking his tongue, Sebastian said, "I won't need to steal anything in New York."

"You didn't need to steal anything in London while you were staying with me."

"I couldn't just assume you were going to provide for me for the rest of my life. No one else ever has."

"I would have. I still will, if you want me too."

Sebastian stared.

"Do you believe me?"

"I might," Sebastian managed, his voice coming out embarrassingly strangled. He cleared his throat before continuing. "I told you though, back in the beginning, that if we made it to New York, it would be my turn to treat you."

"Ah, yes. Of course." Morgan leaned back, bracing his hands on the bunk behind him, his expression caught between curiosity and concern. "You said you stole the—" His voice dropped and he mouthed, "The Rose Diamond necklace," not daring to speak it aloud.

Sebastian couldn't keep his smile from slipping out. "Would you like to see it?"

Leaning in, he treated Morgan to a deep, lazy kiss. At the same time, he began undoing his buttons from the collar down with one hand, slowly popping them open one at a time until his shirt caught his chest in a deep V. Morgan raised a hand to Sebastian's jaw, as he liked to do every time they kissed, before trailing down his throat, as Sebastian knew he would. There, he stopped short, his fingers hesitating over the foreign object before he inhaled sharply against Sebastian's mouth and opened his eyes.

Sebastian grinned, preening. "Do you like it?"

Morgan's mouth worked ineffectually, opening and closing like a goldfish, before he pulled himself together. "You said you were behind the Rose Diamond job, but I didn't expect you to be wearing it!"

"It looks good on me, don't you think?"

"That's not the point! Have you been wearing it under your clothes since you stole it? If you'd been caught—"

"But I wasn't," Sebastian cut in with a laugh and a kiss. "We got away with it."

"But why do you still have it?" Morgan pressed hopelessly. "It's just asking for trouble."

"We have a fence lined up in New York. It's far too hot to try moving within England, and Europe will be keeping an eye peeled for any such diamonds so soon after the theft. I have to get it across the pond somehow, so I thought I might as well enjoy myself in the process." Sebastian touched the necklace, fingers dancing lightly over the cold, pink rainbow of diamonds. "Go on. Tell me it doesn't suit me. You can't."

Morgan groaned into his hands. "I can't," he admitted. "Bloody hell. You look exactly as good as you think you do."

Sitting up, he threw one leg over Sebastian's hips, pinning him by the shoulders as he straddled him. Thrilled, Sebastian lay still under his weight as Morgan folded his arms over Sebastian's chest, leaning in close to study the necklace.

"If it wasn't the most-searched-for valuable in the northern hemisphere, I'd say it was a shame you couldn't keep it. The pink is surprisingly fetching. You look good wearing a few hundred thousand pounds around your neck."

"I really do. Pearls have a certain charm, of course, but they can't hold a candle to diamonds."

"I'll buy you your own diamonds," Morgan said against Sebastian's throat, mouthing at the soft skin under his jaw. He was careful not to touch the necklace itself, as if he might somehow tarnish it, but he kissed Sebastian's exposed skin all around it, mapping the perimeter.

"Nothing quite so monstrous as this," he added, raising his head. "I'm afraid this is beyond my means. But if you could settle for some smaller, lesser diamonds, I'll buy them for you the instant you hand these ones over."

"You could buy them for me before that," Sebastian bargained.

"Get rid of this thing first," Morgan said firmly. "I won't spend a penny on you before that. But," he added, in the face of Sebastian's pout, "as soon as it's out of your hands, I'll give you whatever you want. Say it, and it's yours. But I have to draw this one, single line. I insist on it."

"I suppose that's fair. I can still ask for other things, though, can't I? For the duration of the voyage, I mean. I can't exactly offload the thing before we make land."

"It depends what sorts of things," Morgan said cautiously.

"Sexual favours?"

"I'm not sure I could stop you from asking for those."

"Marvellous. In that case, you should keep undressing me. The necklace might not be the only surprise waiting for you."

"Is that a promise, or threat?"

Sebastian gave an enticing shimmy against the bed. "Take my clothes off and find out."

Obliging, Morgan sat up to work at Sebastian's remaining shirt buttons with far more delicacy than Sebastian had bothered with, peeling the fabric open to reveal his moonlight-pale skin.

"So far, so good," Morgan said, trailing one finger down the centre of Sebastian's abdomen.

Goosebumps rose in Morgan's wake and Sebastian's muscles clenched, shivering at that feather-light touch, his bottom lip caught between his teeth as Morgan reached the waist of his trousers.

"I think I can guess what you're hiding here," Morgan said dryly, tapping Sebastian's belt. "And I'm not sure it's much of a surprise."

"You sound very confident."

Morgan's hand wandered lower to cup Sebastian through the front. "Are you telling me this isn't what I think it is?"

"Oh, it's most assuredly exactly what you think. The question is, what else have I got going on down there?"

With one brow raised, Morgan made short work of Sebastian's belt, opening his trousers as wide as they could go before pausing, as if suddenly second-guessing himself. His knuckles grazed the material within and Sebastian held his breath, grinning in expectation. He watched Morgan's expression change as he realised Sebastian wasn't wearing the expected plain cotton briefs, but something dark and lacy.

In the spirit of cooperation, Sebastian lifted his hips, encouraging Morgan to finish the job. Morgan tugged his trousers past his hips with the kind of cautious reverence men displayed when handling live dynamite. His efforts were rewarded with the sight of Sebastian lounging there wrapped in black lace, a garter belt low around his waist to hold up the sheer black silk stockings that reached the middle of his thighs.

"Do you like it?" Sebastian asked, when Morgan was silent for too long. "Think I wear it better than our friend Pepperika?" He glanced down to Morgan's lap for confirmation. "I think you like it."

"Is this like the makeup?" Morgan managed, once he found his voice.

"I couldn't wear makeup when we were boarding. We're supposed to be blending in as respectable members of society." Sebastian rolled his eyes dismissively at the notion. "But I brought some with me, of course. Shall I put it on?"

"Let me do it?"

Sebastian gestured in silent permission to his bag stowed under the bunk. As Morgan dropped to the floor to retrieve it, Sebastian sat up, peeling his trousers the rest of the way off to discard them over the end of the bed. Returning to the mattress with the makeup kit in hand, Morgan took a moment to sit and simply stare at Sebastian, who sprawled back against the pillow, his open shirt falling off his shoulders.

"Take a picture. It'll last longer."

Morgan shook his head, breaking from his reverie. "I can't get over you," he murmured, kneeling his way up over Sebastian's legs. "Tell me what to do."

"Lipstick."

Morgan dug through the contents before finally landing on a gold tube of Sebastian's favourite midnight-plum colour. When he twisted the end to push the stick out, it looked obscene. He held it to Sebastian's bottom lip with just enough pressure to indent the soft flesh. Sebastian doubted they were going to get past the lipstick to the eyeshadow, but that was quite alright with him.

Morgan dragged the stick over Sebastian's lower lip, applying it much too thick. Sebastian waited, lips barely parted, as Morgan finished the bottom and touched the tube to the top, dabbing a single mark right in the middle like a kiss. His application was crude and heavy-handed, but there was no one else to see. When Sebastian pressed his lips together to spread the colour more evenly, Morgan watched with dark, hungry eyes.

"Come here," Sebastian said, catching Morgan by the back of the neck.

Morgan lunged in, not needing to be coaxed, and their mouths met in a press of slick pigment. When Sebastian pulled back, Morgan's mouth was painted plum to match. His own lipstick was smeared side to side; he could feel it. Things he would never have allowed in the club were not only acceptable but ideal in private.

Poking his tongue forward between his teeth, Sebastian grinned. "You look good like this."

"Not as good as you," Morgan said hoarsely.

"That's because you're not in diamonds and lingerie."

Morgan groaned, crawling forward to get his hands on Sebastian's hips again, broad palms stroking the lace like he couldn't get enough of it. "I don't know if I'm up for that. I might rather just admire you in it."

"Will you draw me like this?"

"Yes. A thousand times. As often as you let me."

"You won't get bored, drawing the same thing over and over?"

Morgan shook his head. "Not like this. Not if it's you."

Sebastian narrowed his eyes. "You won't be embarrassed or overly anxious if I wear things like this out in public? Either under my clothes in the daytime, or on display in certain clubs?"

"You can wear whatever you want. I'll buy you an entire wardrobe of the stuff."

"You won't be constantly worrying about me?"

"I might, but you can take care of yourself."

He narrowed his eyes further. "You won't get tired of me?"

"I don't think that's possible."

"You'll keep spoiling me?"

"I've only ever wanted to spoil you. Even before I knew that's what I was doing."

"You—"

"This line of questioning might have been better done before we left London," Morgan interrupted. "It's a bit late to start interrogating my commitment to you now."

"Commitment." Sebastian scoffed around the little flare of panic he felt at the word. "We can still go our separate ways once we reach New York. It's a long enough journey for you to come to your senses before we make land. We don't have to—"

"Sebastian."

Sebastian shut his mouth.

"I want this," Morgan said quietly, taking Sebastian's hands, which was unforgivably sincere of him. "I'm not going to change my mind. I've already lost you more times than I care to count. I don't intend to walk away of my own volition."

"No, out of the two of us, I guess you were never the one walking away."

"All those questions you just asked me. Those tests. There's one I have to ask you in return."

Swiping his tongue over the mess on his lips, Sebastian nodded.

"I'm going out on a limb here. And I don't regret it, but how do I know you won't get bored of me? My hermit tendencies and the way I worry about you?"

It was a fair question, and Sebastian sat with it a minute to give it the attention it deserved.

"For all my faults—and I know I've got more than most, believe me—if we're friends, then I won't ever screw you over. Not intentionally, at least."

"Is that what we're calling this?" Morgan asked with a quirk of his lipstick-smeared mouth. "Friends?"

"I've never been in love before," Sebastian admitted. "But I think that's what this is. And I don't really know what to do with it, but I want to keep you as much as I've ever wanted to keep anything. Not just because you buy me things, but because you keep giving me second chances. Even when I don't deserve them." He dropped his gaze. "You make me want to deserve them," he muttered.

Morgan made a soft, unidentifiable sound, one hand warm and steady on Sebastian's knee.

Sebastian sniffed before loudly clearing his throat. "That was too much. Did I answer your question? Can we move on?"

Even with Sebastian looking away, the kiss came as no surprise. He smiled into it, the slick paint making their mouths slide against each other.

"Can I give this back to you?" Morgan murmured against his lips.

Sebastian opened his eyes to see Morgan fishing that little pearl ring from his breast pocket. Wordlessly, Sebastian offered Morgan his hand, and Morgan slid the ring up his finger, the silver already warm from being kept over his heart.

"Are we married now?" Sebastian joked.

"I don't want you to feel trapped."

He blinked as the joke abruptly fell away from underneath him. He'd never considered himself marriageable material. The time was, he'd have sooner chewed off his own hand, ring and all, to escape such a fate. He'd abandoned lovers in the dead of night for dropping the vaguest hints about wanting to hold onto him.

And yet, boxed up in this tiny cabin in the middle of the ocean with literally nowhere to run, Sebastian didn't feel trapped at all.

"You'll have to buy me a proper gold band when we make land," he finally said. "I've never heard of anyone making it official with pearls."

The smile that broke over Morgan's face was a thing of beauty. "In the meantime—"

Delving into his trunk, Morgan retrieved the heavy green and gold robe he'd lent Sebastian during his stay. "I know you liked this. I thought you might want to keep it."

Leaning forward, Sebastian allowed Morgan to settle the robe around him, sliding his arms through the sleeves. It was as comfortable and decadent as he remembered. "Thank you. I did like it. And I seem to recall you liking me in it, as well."

"That too," Morgan agreed peaceably. "I also brought these."

Reaching into his trunk again, he withdrew a paper bag of fat, ripe oranges. Digging his thumb into the largest, Morgan split the rind and sent a little spray of mist up from the peel to tickle their noses. Never mind the freezing ocean beyond their cabin, or the grey winter awaiting them in New York. As Sebastian nestled against Morgan's side, hand out to accept the first plump segment of fruit, the air smelled as sweet and citrusy as summertime.

ABOUT THE AUTHOR

Arden Powell is an author and illustrator from the wilds of Canada. A nebulous entity, they live with a small terrier and an exorbitant number of houseplants, and have conversations with both. They write across multiple speculative fiction genres, and everything they write is queer.

Printed in Great Britain
by Amazon

26000189R00223